TORMENT

JACK BRITTON SULLIVAN

Published by
Jack Britton Sullivan
10 N Section Street
Suite 147
Fairhope, AL 36532
brittsullivan0727@gmail.com

Copyright © 2016 by Jack Britton Sullivan

All rights reserved. Published in the United States by Jack Britton Sullivan. This is a work of fiction. Names, charcters, places, and incidents either are the product of the author's imagination or are used fictitiously. Any resemblance to actual persons, living or dead, events, or locales is entirely coincidental.

for AG and Emerson

BILLY

LIMPID GLOW, THAT basin stretched gleaming. It is 1826 and they have not come. No America this far west. From territorial Oregon they travel in twilight through a land that rots to prosper. Territory adjoined by chine. Southeasterly they venture to prospects treacherous and tenfold treachery awaits. Distent, it's omnipresent. Will this world as grasp and you shall.

Billy bounces, watching it pass. Young girl beneath the flap of the canvas. What fortune they seek drains liquid in time, but her face holds ready that moxie. Her jaw and shoulder aclatter. Split flooring of the wagon her bed. You hear its felloes bleating their wear, Billy's mother beseeching the traveler's saint Christopher with prayers for a son and a brother. The mother speaks from the front of their wagon.

"See that Hank is comfortable Billy."

Her response is "talk to your dead."

"Tend to 'em or this wagon will stop!"

"Fuck you and your prayers," grunts Billy, and she's sorry before she says it, though her father does not brake. Resting his hope on the end of his life he rests those hopes on moments. Billy pinches her brother of nine. Gaze at his filthy face. Carious teeth already. A hand through the flap to check on the child, same touch not given to Billy. Vaulting the clapboard, this epicene lass, lands in the salted track. She trots behind the wagon.

"My brother'll die," she says. "A sick kid in the hell of this shit. They've lost their fuckin minds."

She walks the salt lake engarland by cold. Her parents seem unconcerned. Removing her shoes she tastes the salt on the sole of a shoe that is worn. Was ice its prior form? Was some god or another thrown from the welkin to granulate and melt this earth? To ensure that nothing would grow? These are miniscule fears for lucid is Billy and by three in the morning, third day of the year, Billy has found their track, having looped her family by a mile in diameter as they jostled in sleep and dream. Her father scrieving terrain ferocious.

"I could kill 'em to the soul and they wouldn't wake up. They ain't got no business out here."

When the ruddledipped sun mashes eskers stone flat it rises to offend these pilgrims. Billy remains awake. The white lake about is sunned to bleached sugar and the night paranoid flees quickening. It flashes retreat to a landscape prior and she knows what her father will do.

"He'll search for a securer path. But the wagon'll remain in the open."

He angles from the starkness upcountry. Does exactly as Billy says. They still haven't noticed her absence, Billy clamoring and skipping and hopping from night to board them undetected. She pecks at her brother's pale lips, her smile and his own then meet.

"Okay little fella?"

"Some better Billy. I can't whip the coughin."

"Some is better than none I reckon."

Her father halts to dry camp in a cage of datilla. No water. No cover. Llanura. Mountains to hinder and they are blatantly exposed as Billy walays their ignorance.

"This is a terrible choice! We ain't hid from shit! Ain't a goddamn Christian for four hundred miles and what ain't lookin to kill us? You think the Ute ain't seen us travelin? They'll arrow us till we leak!"

"Mind your mouth and see to your brother. Anymore damage to that boy's lungs…" the father's voice emphatically quells.

"Daddy, pull the team in them hills. At least then somethin will hide us. Damn fools and imbeciles get shorter lives for decisions just like this! They's a thousand fuckin things already a watchin and a quarter of 'em dig to shit!"

His strike is through the flap, left to right, twisting her head, dimming the lights and when she lands she is even angrier, spitting blood on the back of his shirt. She eases past Hank, her brother saying "Billy" to press her mouth on the nape of his neck. Their planated seat at the front of the wagon is unsprung and barely enough, but the mother won't ride in the back. Her daughter too unpredictable.

"I'm thirteen daddy, with a mouth for death and sin, but your choices will get us dead. You hit like a fuckin woman."

"Billy," says Hank.

"We're okay brother. I'll leave 'em alone for now."

With the discipline she hardens to bridle within, her father exhaling, relenting. He looks to her, shakes his head. His eyes are on Billy and she stares back, no fear in those coals colored tincture. Her green iris imprisoned by hate. His threats and his strikes, they lack. He should keep his hands on the reins. In this place comeuppance discovers a way and deserts aren't regulated.

2

WHEN THEY EMERGE descending below the vadose tissue of the great salt lake he saw them, the man four nights riding from the northwest region where the Niobrara and White draw close; ahorse a surbate bay with rales in her chest, clackrattling like shellbark hickory, her nostrils hoopflaring with a mixed concoction the color of catamenial youth. Her legs buckled, caught, caracole weak, the man leading the bay through the passes, what passes there were to be led through, tugging on her reins until the crest was achieved, mounting to ride her again.

Dampier Mox is running from capture. Those tailing have reasons for quarter, crisscrossing his track these days and nights after being duly informed, the man pursued wasn't a local, his melancholy air as he walked through the drinkup wholly deplete of rancor, Mox perusing his reflection in a backbar sliver, a coffee order with a whiskey negation, Mox lifting his chin to eye the crapulous mob reflecting and there reflected, his singular fault to fastwatch the face of a scarpainted, white fathered Mission, far from the gathering of seeds. The look was fleeting but the Mission unseated, vomiting invective with a challenge to Mox, his alpenstock pointed with a burin of steel seeking conference with Mox's skull. It wasn't much work for the peaceman. He lofted blows on the drunkard thrown only to stun, but two of the punches broke bone, where the temple and skull were susceptible. Mox's colportage of the relics he vended remained on the floor for the jakes. While liberating the damned he'd become one. Oft the plight of those well intended.

So our missionary sits with five hundred miles on a horse exhausted at three. He has six lynchmen closing on mounts exchanged en route by a foreign militia. They have ample provender and the goal in their midst is to take his life for a wage. No word has Mox spoken except to his horse and no human seen till now. And what pleasure they'll have with his capture, this manciple drunkenly hounded. And he's murdered so early this year. In the past before summons did prostrate this Mox he'd kill in the spring or the summer. Then came that ethereal call: "Dampier Mox, gather your bindle, my message you'll soon profess. To all and sundry sinners, the heinous and barbaric…" though be cautious in bars and slivers of mirrors, that one gaze coming to this, a soul for a soul and we're even. Suicide is Mox's intention. He's had twenty-one years on the planet and twenty-one seems enough. He stares down the throat of his makepiece pistol, blows into the antrum of the arm, flouncing with tension but required to commence he primes and caps the weapon, sliding from the saddle in that gastine waste, conversing to ameliorate guilt, saying "look here horse, I deserve what you'll witness for the pain of your death I've caused." The animal turns, soughing rubato, her physical inanition then lifting. She paws at the marl under hoof. Waits for Mox to act. He thumbs back the hammer, puts the bore to his head and will know in an instant the truth. Mox steadies but the fire is impotent. Double clicks on a single charge. It is then she chooses to speak.

"…you ain't packed your pistol right. I can see that from here."

Billy stands behind Mox holding the bay while smoking from her father's stash. Dampier cannot look. Unquailing voice of a child. He falls to his knees as if assailed by dybbuk to await the coming possession. To pray through the prayers he remembers.

"Stop that shit! They don't get to him! The cold weighs 'em

down and they flop! I tracked them six behind you. They ain't gonna make it here. Otherwise I'd be riflin your pockets. You should be ashamed for ridin this bay till her goddamn hoofs was dust! You got any liquor on ya?"

He casts a singular eye beneath the brim of his hat. Her grosgrain bow is around the bay's neck and the horse is nudging her flank. Mox rises from his knees and in the presence of the girl his stature lessens keenly, though he's taller by a quarter foot. She's not Mox's recollection of what adolescence was when distinctly patterned as youth. She is limbwood corded and stern. A durable cask of lead.

"No. No drink. Who… how old are you and why're you…"

"Billy. Thirteen with family." She points to a declension and makes him look. Their wagon presents like a grave. "Those are my people yonder. Daddy don't cotton to the presence of evil. Not accountin if a devil would look. He likes to travel nights, so when they're asleep, I guard, cause rest ain't important. I was smokin in them rocks yonder. Diddlin, fuckin around."

"You're awfully rough for a child."

"And you're dearth of fuckin sense to put a pistol to your brain when north there's holes that'll hide you, more than holes that won't."

"I ain't habited runnin for a while. Look yonder, he's showin interest. Aw hell, can't be him."

Now their torment will commence in earnest. The man Mox sees doesn't ride with a pack, nor does he know any equal. This mounted rider, minum on plain, approaches the wagon and stops. He's a querist with an interest and what has he here? Boiled eggs drawn from his shirt. The man dismounts and kneels. He borrows salt from his boot, gives a liberal sprinkling, for a taste as common as breath. The shell, albumen, and yellow rose center drop down his gnarled gullet. Without natural teeth the shell is separated and it drops on the ground like a light bulb. Horseshoed bars are slid from his mouth, he tapping with some dunnage to clean them. Surveying the land, the sun as it is, he ponders the wagon's interior. Hank lofts a wheeze and he listens. Weakness is music to him.

*

Threadbare has come. Mox knows him. No other figure supplants. His bounties entertain him but his racket is judgment. As if the pangs of the world re-echo. His handlers abide by his wishes. He selects the bounties he wants. Money holds no sway. Threadbare is Icelandic, outskirts of Reykjavik, a seiner of fish by trade. As a young man he's netted varying fare from grottoes that plash and churn. Brill and turbot. Cod and pilchard. Casting his nets to sustain a small family while American patriots fell. His early years then held constant. He had a family he worshiped and a voice his own, though often such comforts impede us; a thing languishes, spreads, arbitrarily feeding, moulting the logic of man. With all in balance he awoke one day, eschewing the life he knew. He saddled his palfrey then left it ashore to sail his small boat where he chose. Across the Denmark Strait he found his fortieth year on the cusp of an inclement Greenland, Ammassalik to Godthab on foot, while traversing a sheet of ice so thick it was wrest of taiga or tundra, that peneplain ringent with stiletto cold, what depth you'll find in myth. He sees dolmen of ice as he walks the vastness. Radicate tombs for what? He loses teeth like a child and keeps them. While portaging west of the Davis Straits four of his toes turn black. They are gone within a week. He skelps his body to assuage his pain. Then the dousing of life ensues. He enters an Inuit village, south rim of Hudson Bay. Their chieftain is stocky, touchingly smart, wants to know if the Icelander serves as a scout for those hunters enslaving the blacks, for his village of fifty will fight. Threadbare reads his gestures with wile. For solely Icelandic can Threadbare speak though the promptings are more than sufficient. Humiliated he sits and waits in their camp as they jeer and scold and curse him.

A cruet of blood with dulsetwined guts is dumped at his feet to shame him. They surmise his god is the Lutheran deity though they confuse their blasphemous rituals. Threadbare is slightly offended, as he waits for the village to sleep. The man sits by the fire he's built on their verge, where the shells of their homes can be seen. He waits until three before standing. When breaks the dawn irremeable of sun he lights the fires of their penance; forty-nine then burn in their windbroke squats, their squalls fluming like animals trapped, for he's jailed them in their hovels to the door. Threadbare uses the dulsetwined gut. Dried on his spit by the fire. The same gut is then sliced and their chieftain bound, toured by his dewlap skin, around the pyres to hear them suffer. The snow about the houses melts to a greensward as the chieftain is told to strip, to dispossess his skins and wait. With klatching Icelandic he encourages escape as Threadbare counts his steps, fifty then sixty feet, the atlatl zinging its lanceolate head as the shaft strikes the man with a tonking, like syrup being poured in a bucket. Threadbare frees his erection, sprints to the body and like Sybarite, befouls the dying. As Threadbare pumps, he whispers in his ear "my rage I empty in you."

Fourteen months hence he's on Lake Superior, employed by a voyageur. The man's a Yukon born monk with a tonsured skull that swindled his order and ran. He's a pederast of note and a droog replete, defrocked and hiring able-bodied criminals for the larceny of trappers' wares. Take their land and their tools and their deeds. Murder what settlers you find. Threadbare excelled and two dozen are felled by tactics somewhat peculiar, for he enjoys the taking of bone. A function from a guild quite rare. It was even too much for the droog, and though one couldn't say he was encouraged to cease, he collected his coins and walked; into the Dakota's he ventured, an ophiuroid north in that parallax sky, the polestar eclipsing its growth. Threadbare is humbled to see this. The firmament, its quivering flutes. While rubbing his horse with timothy grass he's asked in Siouan his business. The dialect is reasonable, its speaker patient, Threadbare knowing from his hands what he's saying. He returns the question with a terse response by disassembling the question as asked. "Bounty and time," Threadbare repeats, and makes the warrior understand its meaning. After a week they split. The brave has shared in his camp and lived. He versifies thanks with his god over that. Mounts and rides the distance.

*

Dampier Mox is Threadbare's hundredth in the calling of the trade he has mastered. He's acquired Mox's bounty by rumor. A half mile east the couple skylights, perched above the sclerawhite plain. Mox yanks Billy to the ground. From a rockrow cornered by a bush of Gibraltar they crawl to an untenable position, Mox placing a finger to lips, the flesh tatty from the pace he has kept, his skin and tongue flitting irate with a tremor and his blackhearted knowledge, for there is no recourse here.

"Lie still mam. He's seen us. That'un ain't with the six. He's separate from the others I've dealt. Now, you and your bunch are as in it, as in it is diggin down deep. And for that I am truly sorry. I didn't know where my bounty was laid. I wasn't even..."

"Just stop talkin. Your hellin brought him here."

Threadbare nudges his hat and it tumbles mid-back and they are there and they shall watch. His white hair shakes loose and he circles their wagon with a cussed, unpenned lurch. There is tiswin in their packing and he finds it, drinks until the gourd is empty. He smells of tiswin and apples, giving each horse two, and they whinny as he strokes their breasts. Hanks of rope have scarred his limbs. Anfractuous torture of body and mind given by brumal seas. His chest and shoulders are organdy wrapped, wide but violently feminine. He wears the heavy breeks and woolen socks of the seiner or loader of decks, clashing like a jackal and an infant in a cell, before quiescently pointing at their flap, as if what lay inside might surprise him. He wants Billy and Mox to know, to see, to understand that he is grief. As he feints and waits and feints some more they hold the following tether.

"Billy?"

"Goddamn you fella."

Billy snuffs her face in the folds of her arms. Threadbare crawls through the flap. The back of the wagon tends groundward. Weight of an enormous mass. There's no wind but the canvas bloats. What has exhaled within?

"Ain't none of 'em equal to that."

"I just kilt your family."

3

THE SIX TRAILING Mox never realized the flats. Billy and Dampier found them four miles north. Their horses spanceled and joined. The riders frozen in caption. Arranged like slices of fruit. Their fire is of an unknown boscage, for none of the wood is local. Boxwood, catalpa and pine, burned with a curious stench. What cordate leaves or needlespiked fretwork combusted and gyring to dross, went back to a purified ash. Washed here by moraine? Unlikely. The miles of years would have rotted the tinder. Though what riddle in the heart of breathing humans isn't anomalies' duneland? Yet oddities abound, growing odder, for the six around the fire are unharmed. Yes, they are dead, the light bled from their eyes, though neither hair nor skin is awry or creased and they rest like they did at their births.

When Mox released a Morgan from their trailing remuda, Billy ripped the cordage from his hand. She then sprinted the Morgan with furor. Mox yelled twice and cudgeled over leaving, loping in the opposite direction, Billy retracing their trail of approach as if Threadbare didn't exist, Mox searching self-abasement, and if so Threadbare mimics his action will the death of her family be absolved? And then most nimbly else: for is there not in everyman's eye and stress a moment when you see your future in the faraway glance of another, one with soft brown hair and gilderless lips on a sunblackened face disused, she with burgeoning hips of cuspidine matureness and how fast she grows into these. From what womb great sons and daughters. Mox swings his mount to chase.

He finds Billy astraddle the Morgan. She is red in the cold and pondering. An epigone trailer with mortician's task. Greedy to know why this.

"They ain't a shot nor a cut nor a burn on their bodies. No different from them yonderway. I went in, searched for a mark. What coin we toted is there. Hank's between my folks like a portrait. They were joined at the hands by a ribbon. A fuckin tie from a wagon sheet."

Dampier Mox has nothing to say. He rides doddering, northeast of the scene, through her stupor she watches amazed, Mox with his pistol drawn, circling concentric with benign appeasement, the angary and heliotrope bruising of clouds skiey, penumbral and mortal, in this place where death has come. He arcs then makes it wider, no trace of horse or man. This pastureland of salt is untattooed, the buzzards alighting in changeable gryke, deposing themselves as jury. When he returns she is as he left her. Answers his obvious interest.

"Dampier Mox, I'm Billy, but you know that already."

"I brought him here. I done that."

"Such time ain't nigh Mr. Mox. We got holes to dig. This salt'll addle us plenty, and graves of salt won't muster. Let's travel east a piece. How far, I ain't sure."

"I ain't sure of nothin."

"Ain't that what this is?"

They wrap the bodies in cambric finery. A short bolt the mother has purchased. In riffling light they saw the wagon due east for visible hullforked rises. Billy guided the wagon for the next seven days while Dampier Mox drug behind her, the man cutting for sign to weaken the tedium of knowing the pair were alone. Gougecentering the Bear River Range she permitted their Christian burial. Lustrate stones of a wandering sect they find in a cove of snowmelt. The

Ute have caught the pilgrims in transit a dozen years before. Here they choused them to a stand in a stoutened trap a decade prior to Bridger. Billy said, "fuck, this'll do." While she lap raked snow to read their burial stones Mox searched for the smear of a dwelling, no remnant of their being at aught. Uncomfortable, suspicious, he returns to Billy. She seems unconcerned.

"Nothin?"

"Nothin."

"Shit. Hellfire. Let's be about it then."

Through the scent of her family and a mantle of cold they hack and ruthole graves. Billy dug the pit for her brother, a procuress of memories longing, the tip of her pick redding the hole while Mox gathered their firewood. Teeming with life they are, the night fractioned to morning and the hauler transfigured, with the bodies in a row on the ground. Like a campwork entrenchment where this is done daily their labor alleviates fear. When a rookery of predators offensively yammer neither Billy or Mox look to them. They are sound-suasive beasts winged and not, found on mountain and plain. They hear a shaleslide some leagues distant. Unaltered, something goes climbing. They see eyes in the dark though heads become absent. Absent with a move that is satiable. Don't leave your circle of light. Neither in dark or day.

"We need this done. I'm sorry to say it."

"That was my midnight thought Mr. Mox. I ain't had a one since then."

"Take a break. I'll put them in."

She sits back, watches the sameness, no idyll thing to write. Like a mother with sons at war. Are those who live lives sublimely quiet more shocked when nothing works? Who burrows their way into the bosom of a world that would not have them present? Those that have no choice.

"You wanna say somethin Billy?"

The graves are smooth. Emery black. They've churned loose

pitchblende soil. Billy speaks in a voice raped tinny. Her oration strengthened thus. They are words messianic, from an ancient tome. Something the dying might utter.

"This is what happens when expectin ain't tended. When you leave it by itself."

Billy is seated in the angry cold with her head gullied to chest. Loggy brain from the tired she is feeling. Saddened by this rostrum of lunacy. There's the tinkling of ice melting into water and the sun enflames its drip. Creamy silver then not from the limbs where it falls, a quena flute in the valley behind them, and others know they're there. Hoarse voiced, slumped over and seated on the dirt Billy waves her hand. Again the shatter of the quena girt to their ears and Billy urges him on.

"Say what you want. Say it quick. Them sumbitches won't wait."

"Okay," he says. "Okay. We lay these before you what God we know and ask that your arms be opened. As I have caused the death of these people, I pray you'll forgive their misgivins, layin vengeance thrice upon me."

"Fuckin poetry," she says and smirks. "Remember, we're together."

Cumulus clouds with fiery-hulled breasts defeat what sun they had. Their sweat then turns to shiver. A prairie hawk, black backed with eyes of marble, up peak and far from home, serves as nothing special. No sign of where to go. Billy climbs aboard the wagon to get the blanketlined coat, hands it to Mox like a writ.

"It was his," she says.

"I thank you."

They rifle the remainder of the clothing. Enough to keep them miserable. When they are finished they stand face to face and she's put it together and says it. All else is guess and hope.

"Look here Mox, murder is murder and his lone part ain't yours. You done what you did. So has he. The world got plowed and we caught us a tine, but we can't let it cut us in two. His bounty on you ain't met, but that motherfucker ain't here."

"Well said Billy. I hear you."

Billy hefts a pick to hollow three trenches. The cove is filling with snow. She finds a chamfer point with which to scratch, though the weather will take her words. Others here have already been lost:

Daddy	Mother	Hank
Born in 1790	Born in 1803	Born in 1817
Kilt in '26	Kilt in '26	Not no better got

4

"NEVER HAD NO notion of attachin to a man, leastways cause of land or travelin, but this is land to kill you. I don't need another father. That'n we buried last month suited me fine for his time. If you plan on makin me a husband, don't plan on doin it quick, because this winter's wall thick and I intend to be warm, but I ain't gonna be plucked."

They managed the wagon onto the Big Sandy where they camped as the temperature plummeted. The cold hovered like a lecherous man, snow banking in windrows and pushed by blows, tussive wind from Canada's sweep. Its blast to freeze your eyes. Billy and Mox stop pressing their miles when the nightfires of men, undoubtedly savage, debouch on the eastern basin.

Outside their ring of heat and fire the snow has built to waist. Mox constructs four blazes in defiance of the cold while Billy splits their kindling. They're wasted for sleep but alert, the wagon fodderwood pregnant from the journey thusfar as they tramp an arcuate shape, huddling on the river's sloped bank. He decides to bring the animals nearer the circle of horrent blazes roaring, Billy as allusive as cold to wind, saying "bring 'em the fuck on in. More horse. More heart. More warmth. And as far as the camp of those men out yonder… as long as bodies is passin them fires then the selfsame bodies ain't here. All will intrude if that be their way. I'd a granny from Charleston said that. It's to ponder and ponder I do."

The ring of fire is effective against the cold and with the horses affecting broader. She has an opinion on that.

"You copied warmth like a patent discovered Mox. We're alive because of that. And in the loneliest soul of the year. February, here we are. This ain't even clost' to our country of origin and we found the coldest spot. Daftcrazy motherfuckers with no sense a'tall and us in a foreign land."

They feed their fodder to the horses by hand, their spines bedizened with snow, the heat from their backs running in rivulets, drip enough to thaw your fingers. Sklent with intrigue they stare at the wagon asking to hitch and exit. Like chickens decouped they banter and whinny with guttural clucking throats. The vapor from their tongues in wag and bin turn to ice on touch. Billy melts snow for their water, the storm exacting its strength on the fires. Mox must go to the wagon, for what he thinks he can't avoid.

"It's thirty foot away," she says. "But you're likely to land in Sonora."

"Could you… ?"

"It's already done. I can feed and water these horses. She ain't gonna foal in the next ten minutes. Get what you need to get."

He begins his slog to the wagon. While he struggles Billy does not. With guile and an ease of their fetlocks each horse is brought to the tundra. Billy makes a kraal for humans to enter if the cold comes colder still. When Mox returns to bodkin the mare he comes with a foot long blade. No need, Billy has solved it.

"Don't. We'll need her. She'll have it soon. I ain't crawlin in no goddamn horse. It's warmer amongst 'em than in the damn wagon and the sun'll be here directly. We got wood. These fires'll hold."

Mid morning the wind abates. The frieze of the river, its blanketed plain, as immoveable as ferrotype plate. Transversing some snow does coil. They are willowy skinny drifts. Billy awakens with her head on the mare and Mox across her thighs. A cocoon of ice and snow. Panmixia of human steed. All then rise concatenate. Man and horse alike.

"Fires are out. Cold didn't kill us."

"Our second concern," she says.

They survey their lot while standing. No wagon is visible in the blizzard's wake, the horses loath to move, frustrated and boxed by snow; the end of the mare wide with birth, plethoric fluids with a rutilant glow, life again executing as it will. She tries to sit back but the room the mare covets is filled by a shyish Morgan. Dampier takes the initiative, bridling two of the animals, tying all in, before mounting the largest steed. Into the chest high drifts they maneuver, their cloven hooves with torrid power, clearing a path that is wide enough and Mox is proud of their effort. A scissortailed bird peeks in on the happening, but he and those like him leave. There are two too many humans. The peals of horse too loud.

"Is that better? We got room to work."

"Thank you kindly. This foal is gonna drop. Room is at an outright premium."

And drop the mother did, with a clot the size of a medicine ball tailed by the packing of birth, that subsequent life therein; the first quarter as smooth as the steel of Damascus with the shape of a mouth, eyes and teeth, then a snag but the hang is freed. The gaped cavity he pierces with a thin nude arm, the dams' yawing stress increasing, her ampersand eyes confused. He extracted the foal and brought it to chest and it unfolded like a hearthside table.

"Good Mox. You were excellent. Let her kick, stoke the fires?"

"Reckon so. Good idea."

He assisted the foal without offending the mare. She looked at the foal then forward. Tried to rise but failed. Clean that white waste then black dots upon it. They've come from their den by smell. Manifest from fens of ice. Euchre their numbers with vision. Every single beast in that remuda of cold begins rocking in a seesaw motion, Billy's head missed by a hoof. Within a count of one their wagon is rammed and the steed that does the damage mires to his chest in powder. He sees what is coming in the shallower drifts, craving toward man and horse. They tread along the surface of the waistdeep powder like pebbles lakeskipped by a child.

Billy says, "somethin is comin. No, somethin is already here."

Billy twists the dams' neck to her baby, as if in that seeing a world is ordered when order isn't a choice, the ferment growing from a hell be brindled, to walk where men will not, to exhaust in the roll of gray seas, as they shake the cold from limb. The seven here are beset by what they can't see and it waxes in passable drifts. Pulsing to the group like a train. Billy mumbles "wolf" but wolves have come to stead available anguish. The scene is a panic concreted.

The mare bleeds her red, the pair gored slick, and neither can stand in snow to their knees and the mare will not respond. Dampier claws into the higher drifts. The neighing pitched imploring. His foot is then trapped in a frozen stirrup when their attack brings a shout from Billy.

"We're gonna get tore to pieces!"

They've an ignescent yellow austereness, their eyes absorbing the frame of Mox as he preens somewhat unsaddled, the snow falling again and the clouds obscuring their initial assault on Mox, born on his upper leg. He steadies the horse but the animal bolts, dropping Mox directly in the path of a wolf despoiling all civility. "Lord God. Lord God," he says. There's a want, a need for a red meat kill and you can see its hate of hunger. Three others have Billy and the foal embanked on a melting labile drift; the foal, its eyes, rolling expatiate, such fear on its entry to a violable world that it quakes as if birth were a terror-clad chance dependent on consequent horror.

"Get offa me and go on!"

They snap, retreat and parry, Billy kicking and screaming in acerbic yawps as the mare comes to hoof enraged, landing blows to the flank of the smallest wolf though it does not shy or demur. It returns to sidle, to dodge; to take a bright red spile from the dams' front shoulder and she his unguarded ear; Billy wailing with legs like pistons, entwined then apart then redoubling with rage, another shot by her foot to the jaw of a male desirous of Billy's neck. With a quicktwitch bight and flex of his forepaws the assailant goes to ground, dragging himself to Billy, tonguing the bloody snow. When her boot breaks his tooth he stretches his neck. Loge where his gaze is burning. Cinder from a thousand kills. He's decupled with a cunning unmatched.

Dampier can't move and won't. The largest of the pack indecisively positions, its musculature gravid with blood, fur in barbellate spinney, swollen like fetter drawn limbs. "Whoa! Whoa! You bastard! Hold on!" His head and a hand find a felly and spoke as the wolf spars his kicking feet, the wagon behind Mox encased in snow and he can back no farther, the alpha invested in wait. There is mastery and competence in the bloodwort stare. The red in its eyes spalled from the white, there chipped and channeled to flow like lava to and from a heart apace. The wolf, he yawns fatiguingly, his paw the length of Dampier's foot, his nail on his boot to hold him. He divines a death immediate. Mox augers a heel and prays.

"Go on then," says Mox. "I've enough of this world to suit me."

He turns and offers his throat. Expects the sound of bone. Slaver from the beast lands upon his knee, the alpha stifling his pack with a howl of mantic warning in the face of a Mox despondent. The din speeds his heart to burst. Mox looks past the predator's songing, what dead man knows this calm, the corner of his eye catching Billy and the foal and there are three yellow lobos in contrast, this trident on hindlegs howling aface the mother of his children yet born. Billy kicks then kicks no more, listening as the pack ensembles, a tremolo effect enchanting from a distance, but not at the length of an arm. Craning their heads they compete refulgent. Which howl may please their god?

Billy covers her face and the foal and the dam thrash and moan past winded. The mare collapses to the snow spent from the attack and the birth and the living till then. What remains for the travelers is the choice of another who watches, then he fires, the four explosive bursts in catapultic succession, the wolf atop Mox hit directly in the chest, the three around Billy then toppling. They were poised and then they were corpses. No blood on the snow before their spoor she sees and their hearts have been blown from their chests. Fist sized holes erupting. The two wait for the voice of the shooter, but what they receive is a sun, its incommensurable light.

Billy says, "are you bit? I ain't."

"Touched, but the cold'll staunch it. It ain't nearly bleedin."

Billy took the foal to its mother. Perused their frames for hurt. Dampier fingered the wolf in his lap. Themselves before we were us. Knocking his knees he guessed at the weight. Felt the warmth recede.

"What made them shots?"

"Yonder."

Facing north he's a furlong and riding. The wind has slowed the bursts. He calculates while looking for sign. He'd augmented the powder to adjust for the breeze, the blasts catena in echo and his aim was high he thought.

"Hope he's done shootin," she says. "We won't know if not."

Little else but a profile is seen, his hands caressing and stroking the muskets, his eyes sight measuring powder. Four unrifled tubes disobedient at best are rodded for proximal violence. Two muskets he grapes with tiny iron seeds to spread and their pattern is murderous. He goes through his motions with patience, Billy and Dampier breastworking their beasts to receive his downrange volley, his weapons laid in sequence, flat on the snow as if another might come behind him harsher yet. His hands, they reach in the air. The white of a fur drapes the man's shoulders before he ducks to conceal in a windrow. Anamnesis of a dream believed. Yield for such will immingle. He has come because things are inconstant. Hesitate and pause, you're mourned.

"Hope is my current position."

"Hope popped four hearts with four separate shots. I've faith two more will follow. Them currently beatin in our chests."

"That ain't optimistic."

"He shot from six hundred foot with a two foot drift and now he's cut that distance. You better focus on the holes he'll put in you, not the sound comin outta my mouth."

Thirty minutes on their stomachs as they search. The horses shake with the presence of the wolves, the imbroglio red they leak. Dampier initiates the dragging of the lobos due south to a pit where the knotweed peeps and the sun screels snow like current. On the first of his trips there aren't any tracks. On his second he sees and smells them. They've walked east, then west, then mounted, no twang when the arrow releases, its cerulean tip so blue on the white Mox feints as if to deceive it, the four-foot shaft lifting on a draft to whine through the crown of his hat. They've nocked it in parfleche to push the flint forward and that ounce has saved young Mox. His skull is furrowed, some hair is lost, the hat riding to a drift with the arrow.

"I ain't hit! I ain't hit!"

Billy doesn't respond. She hisses for notice with a wary right hand as he crawls through the snow to their fire ring. While he struggles she glasses the plains, her kohl-black eyes denying the glare, badderlock dark and smeared, that face unblenching as it scans the white, he scooting to her side to speak.

"Ain't nothin. Others is here."

"Somethin come skyward outta the snow and went back down doubly quick. I can read a nickel in the bottom of a river, but I ain't seen a trace of the firer."

He said "it makes you wanna move to the city."

"Fuck no, it does not."

A fluvial splash emits from the Sandy before a dog barks a tocsin upriver. The animal sprints between them and the muskets, refusing the lower drifts, crossloping into snow inescapable. When the white eats its body it clambers to the surface, runs another five feet before sinking. They watch the ears and snout, hear the shooter call the dog Sutler, see the jerk of its mouth as it chews. The man then steps clear. Bleached white like calcimine liquid. Sutler heels at his feet to gnaw some more jerky. They're at two hundred feet on snowshoes. His horse nowhere to be seen. Unprovoked but firing he raises his musket. With their ruse complete they attack.

From a drift in their rear they spring. Four warriors, naked to the waist, their cerulean bodies like the tips of their arrows; with hands greased black wielding potstone bludgeons, the hafts chipped in curious ways. One has a hatchet of gneiss, their buskins and loincloths of unmeasured cattalo with Algonkian threats on their lips. Each face is demoniacally skived in layers beneath suet coiffed hair neatly gathered. Thin tedious lines ascend from their necks like a chiromants' stellate dividing. These are fardplaque symbols of internecine idolatry, chthonic tattoos from lore. They wear masks that protect them from us. Fifty years vanward they won't.

The braves land in the circle of Billy and Mox without a knee or a hand touching snow, stalling silent for the pair to refract them, as Billy and Mox take them in. Shifting to their backs they watch the braves flaunt, affluent and refined with gestures. A solitary warrior breaks from their ranks. The man with the hatchet of gneiss. Another scent captivates his interest. He looks to Billy for answers.

"Other," he says.

"What? Ain't no others, just us."

He's not savage enough to ignore her response. He stares and asks for the truth. Veridic and beautiful and terrible the same he inquires "is there another?" She responds "there's just us. Somebody else shot them wolves."

He's quizzically unsure though his perception is valid for the man with the muskets reveals. A hutment of snow is dumped on the brave before the front of his face is erased. The other three warriors are startled, but turn to face his charge. Two of the men are dispatched with shot, the pellets from the musket ripping their flesh; one losing an eye, another his ear, their hands going to their heads for protection, the buck of a pistol shot close, the killer of the wolves atop his horse, encaustic and wheeling to rein, the chest of his mount like an ashlar crushing as the brave less an eye simply snaps. His head is erect and then his chin tilts, the angle sculpted and awkward and plasmic. The fourth stares at the carnage and is sized for his death before he speaks to the horseman in Spanish.

"Mis niños sabrán su furia?"

"Lo dudo mucho," the answer.

The charism of the brave and his prayers begin, the orisons chanted through a velarium of clouds, heard with hands upright. The killer of the wolves allows this. When the brave doesn't stop his pistol is loaded and the move to slay unleashed. He checks the charge and dispenses the shot through his mouth, said oaths renounced in an instant.

When the pair decide to uncoil, the rider is straddling their bodies, the testicles of the drafthorse swinging in their faces as the braves are loaded by years, the man clumping the bodies on the haunch of his horse without lifting his feet from the stirrups. When they are cordwise placed and he knows they have seen he speaks to educate.

"It's an easier scalp when they're warm. Overall, a quicker skinning. There are markets for their teeth and bones down south. But no matter me for your foal has passed and the mother has followed her under. Hitch what you have past the noon melt and drag that wagon to rolling. The dog was cut loose to busy your eyes and I name and feed every one. If they catch you again you will die. Go southwest till you get to the Green and southeast from there to your wishes."

He leaned to glance at Mox where he lay. Neither could discern his face.

"You're Mox? Dampier Mox?"

"That's me. I am him."

"He wants you. Threadbare does. And he likes to carouse with his wanting."

"I am aware of that."

"Aware won't help. Search for something that will. Consider leaving earth."

He tied the bottommost brave to the upmost head and then reshuffled his deck. Yanking loose the smallest he slung him on his shoulder, remounted and lay him to lap, the others fitting perfect as planned. He then spurred the massy draft through the deepest of drifts, four braves and muskets fore and aft, dandling like children entitled.

They all moved on except the dead.

5

THE MOTHER AND foal prove difficult to bury. The mare's pasterns are bound with rope while Billy deals with the foal. On a bed of clean snow she is laid. The mare is drug until the horses cease, but the ground cannot be broken, the ice and the layers beneath the rime a consistent molten carapace run down from boiling heights. Place the dead where the earth has denied you, for no grave will you dig this day.

Billy hefts the first stone from the river. Mox cautiously intervenes.

"We can't rock these horses. We need to move. Them four he kilt have friends."

"I ain't leavin these horses for tatters. Part of me thinks they feel."

"Feel what?"

"Goddamn you Mox! I ain't gotta explain myself!"

Giltedged flames from their crisp dry wood grow weak but the west sends wind. The time it takes to burn the horses isn't an hour lost traveling. A foot of snow tumbles to plain. It has a seasalt smell and both inquire if there was ocean this far inland. They proceed by claiming their gods. Dampier's is the god he senses. Billy's is a deity feared. They discuss what it takes to unify gods into a god drying inland seas. What a mystagogue savior he would be. An oracle of weather that strives to please men by granting their simplest wishes. Or perhaps it would turn from those who require it by denying the speech of humans. For what wouldn't want shut of man at his best and of humans that God themselves. No God that I know comes to mind.

"Billy, we need to move."

Flames dance on the horses and enact their eyes. Hear doom with death as hostage, an ocarina and a drum incessantly streaming, whipping the air in strands. Other warriors have missed the four. They wonder where they've gone and why on the river, though the weather to them is irrelevant. The men in the valley and those that have come can track on puncheoned rock, as well as footed snow. Billy rouses when this becomes clear.

"Snow is thinner on the banks of the river. We go slow and steady and they won't follow. Not in the dark they won't."

He staples a stare. Looks to her. "Why won't they follow at night?"

"Cause we ain't a rumor of interest. Not worth testin the dark. Otherwise, we'd be skewered. Deservedly so I think."

"They're thumpin them drums like they mean it."

"If I'm wrong we can't outrun 'em."

"That wagon won't budge till the snow melts."

"I ain't tied to that fuckin hauler. We can leave it for hardier stock."

*

Night comes to their camp on the Big Sandy River. What supplies they can take from the wagon is loaded on the soundest horses, their heads yerking in hoofclop time; assonant, vitiate and descending whinnies reveal the harshest affected. The beasts least burdened are loaded with gear, the rudimentia of a liveable bivouac, the needmost necessities carried. The saddlebags as packed have a space for a rider but the other must trod on foot. When Dampier returns from the wagon he's hatcheted a dais for burning.

"I'll pack this wood on the endgate nag. It ain't that much to tote. I chopped your bedpiece up. You get in the saddle first."

"What about that sickly?"

"She's stove from fright, but she'll trail us to feed. On what I ain't decided."

Crunching the ice on the banks of the river they make their way downwater. Mox discovers an alternative path. A senda lightly traced. It has the scratchings of a peafowl upon it, a jackrabbit's frilly scrape. They speak and decide to stay close to the river, for the territory about will efface you. Already Mox stumbles where horses do not, for he is a man on foot, trippingly humbled but man nonetheless, vexed by what he's invited; those bogmired shelves of insodal ice where his feet are mercilessly taken. But if they're to eat one must walk, the shanks of his ankles numb from the toes as if they belonged to another.

"Wanna ride for a while Dampier? My boots are oakum pasted. Slush ain't gonna wet 'em. Daddy brung a keg for sealin, with a wagon of nothin to seal."

"Thank you, but no miss Billy. The Green is down yonder somewhere. With dawn this cold'll break."

"You are hell smote positive Mox."

She glances to Mox, he to Billy, her smile enough for then, the pace of the horse between her legs that hip-popping topfuck madness, keeping him pingling forward.

By morning the Sandy-Green merge. An unregenerate weave of waters. No fresh snow and their tracks lay behind them like the surge of a pachyderm dreaming. The imbreachment four span wide. To cover their tracks is like drinking from a river with the hope its depths fall footly. Billy notices the bluing of Dampier's lips, hears the firestone chatter of teeth, his urine staining a path to his knees, because urine is warmer than numbness. The subject of comfort is void. Here is where they are.

"Snow, cold, mountain and plain."

"What?"

"Nothin," says Billy. "Ain't nothin. My whispers come louder than talk. Out yonder is everything to see, without a goddamn thing to want."

Everything to see and without wants and what they see is this: with the cipher of their voices their heads mechanize as if where they are has shrunk. High desert with vale and plain. A serration of sierra glued rereward. The Green and Sandy rivers post splice, enjoin, through flats snowgray, coldshaded. In the distance there are signs of a meridional gorge, southeast looming mountains eventually crossed, rocky peaks where the spires glair whitely; diade tapers quite foreign to here where the continents collided aborning. Billy sees and comprehends and her troubles are lost for the heart of a woman is irrevocable. It positions itself for what man will miss, for a female understandably stirs, when beauty and pain are at stake. She is tissue where man is bone. She is sentience and instinct and he must adapt. No matter, those days are gone. Everyone seems everyone else.

"My mother was good. Tolerant. Never had her place in this world. She wanted salvation. Waited on livin. Lord, how she ate the Bible."

Billy spoke while he listened and guided the animals, his lead to a shelter unknown. She usurped her clothes around her thin body, the heat leaking through her rags as smoke. Her conical breasts atop the partsagged horse projected nipples in lapidary hardness. Billy is whinstone or quartz, displaying tender as needed. When her headwrap slips to her shoulders, she's an outline incomplete. Slit-eyed and smoking handrolled fags, her shadow worrisome fond. Moreso, his need grows daily.

"You want a smoke Dampier? Might warm your blood a bit."

He conceals his erection and answers. "No thank you Billy. I'm fine." Drooping face but he's caught with the question. She knows the man is aware. That she is there all around him and lust can't freeze and that sex is the hand of death, where close some child begets, the life of another begins.

That afternoon it lifts above freezing. They notice the shelter ahead. The diptych fold of the rocky escarpment where it ledges from the slope of the hillock with its subfoot talus in sun. Close to the mergement of the Sandy and Green they clamber in crunching shalebreak, the horses rooting snow in search of stippled grasses and there is peace but it won't hold. With their equipage grounded they decide on their meal, cold beans unsoaked with saltcrumb bread, its portion festooned with onion. As they eat on the ledge they speak of a stand, the drifts manageable here if attacked, from what quadrant or source they're ignorant. Nine miles in the last twenty hours and Dampier is weakened and pale.

"I'm better with the food and I thank you."

"We got coffee, but coffee means fire."

"What'll come knows we're here."

Fifteen warriors from a surrogate trail see the two and crowd the hillock. Their drums are with their elders in that northeast valley and they are painted like their brethren killed. The man with the muskets has circled in the night, miscibling his tracks with theirs, passing the pair without notice, gaining advantage for the briefest of hours and leading the warriors right to them.

"Oh shit," says Billy. "You reckon they think…"

"I reckon they think a great deal."

An underling of the band, a boy of nine, climbs the sparse hillock to speak. He yells in Algonkian that opposing their position is a western slope tinged black. It is warmer with wood and the sun can assault them and there grows forage for beasts. Coarse grass to battle the scours. But don't drink the water downstream. Some fatstock has frozen, tipped in a pool, and the water is rancid though cold. Do they understand? They don't.

"No water! No drink!" he screams in English and it is lost between ear and brain, the warriors cackling as he mimes their options, shoveling fistfuls of snow into his round mouth, rehearsing with dance its melting. He playacts for a stint white men making coffee and the baking of bread by their women. When he lowered his breeches to pretend defecation Billy laughed, nodded and wailed, Mox packing his pistol for the collision to follow before her keenness calmed Mox with a touch. "Holster the weapon," she said. A rigorous silence ensued.

"They's somethin in that pool yonder way. It ain't fit to drink. That, or soon, it's us floatin in it. Stop primin that shooter and we won't."

"Lord, a drink would be nice."

The troop reverses towards the Big Sandy. The young entertainer backs to his horse for he's seen the pistol of Mox. Billy retrieves it, throws it behind them, both showing their palms chin high. The tension decreases enough.

As they defile across the talus they raise their own palms in departure, jerking their heads with their horses. On the bright orange hip of the last horse to vanish bobbles the head of the hunter. His muskets divided amongst them. His clothes are dispersed depending on rank as he floats in a pool upstream. What fatstock did freeze and sink in that pool was the hide of a worthy imagining. Billy's done the best she can. Lifting their palms in widefingered farewell, their hands become pennons, waxwings. Billy spits, refusing to pray. Congratulates, by name, herself. Not being daft has won.

6

SLEEP ACQUIRES BILLY after the encounter as he watches her slump and blink. Her head leans back and the clippings of shale are warm and take her under. When her slumber resounds with a tin rattle snoring Dampier climbs to the crest of the hillock. A glissando of pebbles rain down. The incline opposing seems spring and not winter, the Arapaho's scouting was accurate. Verdant twists with heat-doffed snow, the foliage thriving with the light that is offered, warmer afternoons here protected. The ongoing storms since bleakest December are buffered by walls of stone. Dampier has the space to himself. A rectangular gaol with forty foot breaks. In the clearing below an antelope grazes, to its rear a red bordure, the sun beaming in mundane peach. His foot loosens some shale and as the brittle goes wheeling the antelope perks its ears. With his face to the west he sleeps.

In his dream a friend supposed dead in limbo speaks in an audible tone. The way speech in a dream are your words absurdly, the friend slow and from his hometown, a hamlet near Mayfield, Kentucky. After Lewis and Clark's report on the west the boy longed to follow their passage. Told Mayfield it was he that would go. When he did he went west to a place of the heathen before Christians could tame it entirely, with treaties and guns and disease and death and the marauding of Christianized values. When he parted the people of that tiny hamlet he was told to remain at his washer. Said his mother would die from the work.

"She can't build them fires and tug that kettle! You stay or she'll perish in a week!" The mayor insisted but the boy then countered, "my mouth'll stop chewin directly. Her cost is my food, not me."

This boy is man in the dream of Dampier, thirty years of age and competent, well spoken and furred from the trapping and catchfalls he's learned from his years in the wild. He's had prosperous hunts past the fort of the army, their last Jeff City, Missouri. Northwest from Kentucky he's walked to the fort and the soldiers have begged his return, to wherever, whenever he's come. His retort is prepared, though reckless.

"Yonder country is free till the ocean consumes me and I reckon my luck is good."

A uniformed soldier with attire punky blotted raveled a sheathing of orders. Slapped at his leg with violence. The boy leaped back beneath a stout quoin juxtaposed to the forts wide entrance. Behind the quoin is the land that he seeks.

"The fuckin luck ye desire gets stopped at that river. The goddamn river ye crossed. Why the fuck do ye think this was built? Yon side is the land of the meek. West of here ain't nothin but horribles. Ain't no pussy for that cock you're a growin."

"Your words ain't said with sense."

"Make sense out the bear or the savage that'll fuck ye. Then put that sense to work."

"Thank ye kindly for your welcome my friend."

West of Jefferson City he left the Americans for wilds of an agony parous. With the Osage he bartered nostrums for horses and obtained an unshod outfit. Although they would not permit him to hunt in their herds, he pursued them for days and watched; saw the vultures balanced on ribs, digging the exhaling marrow, the buffalo and antelope and caprine breeds dressed in the field where they lanced them, where they gifted the boy their bones. Weather and starvation sharpened his senses, misery a companion throughout. The pinprick of instinct became his discomfort and then instinct became his breath, his life after failed attempts. Competency came with seasons. Evolved and did not wane.

"I shot an antelope and pared ever' inch. Was no threat to an unneeded creature. As the Osage hunted I was permitted to circle. Close in when their skinners packed up. I took notes on their methods of living. Left when those lessons were learned."

As his dream spoke Mox answered from sleep, unable and not wanting with his quinsy-cough snoring to notice the sun was setting. He reached forward with his hands to touch the dream face, to trace those dream scars, their depths; the territorial night battening with cold, sinking through his homespun shirt, for the coat he'd been given he used as a pillow, awn snowflakes like needles on skin. Dampier asked if the tribes were warring. Was he threatened when he came upon them?

"When caught I wasn't offensive. Without asking I offered a toll. I dismounted and hung my head low. For if dying best die some humble. A lone white the Comanche thought humorous. By three of a brood I was clouted unconscious when their eldest wanted my Bible. The pages alone, not the message within, for he was stuffed with the meat of the grouse. The missions hadn't reached this particular band so clouting, not death was sufficient. When I awoke bemused I was buried to waist and they'd shaved my head for their paper. Dung in piles about. I shimmied my legs and pushed against plain and hastened to ride from that place. They left me a horse and rode. After that was expanse rife with heat, southeast of where you lay dreaming. Where the continent divided my fatigue was immeasurable, the plain I searched of a lye patina. A musk ox I saw in the vastness. Rain and fog, snow and more rain, and I trudged and cursed without answer. The mountains were massaged with dryness, a cold that waffles your skin. The passes never melted, once cloistered and desperate I ate my horse and boiled his bones, in a high mountain baby blue fire. I came to a rift in an oblong valley. Here a spring gurgled and branched. It was rocked but cold with hartshorn scenting, there guelder rose frosted but living. I saw gall wasps, sawflies, ants and bees, though daily the temperature dropped. I found a habergeon jacket worn by the Spanish, some gatherer grafting its mail. My mind was then slow and I thought if I flexed it irreversible harm might occur. I sat in that valley, drank from the spring and decided this was my home. A hovel I dug in a month, its back as deep as the length of my body plus several breadth feet for storage. Lines of ore unmined in the walls. I chipped handfuls and ground it to powder. I dreamed of grim trolls having placed it. Then I dreamed of your dream I am in."

Dampier asks that the dreamant be finished. He's impatient, though sleeping in that deranged deep sleep, where a father, a mother, or a fiend exchange arms, swop heads, steal voices, mutate. A carrefour past then present. Where that horse that you wanted prior to birth becomes the hallux of a reptile, then the breast of an aunt, before you scale to the nipple for flight, winging through a gap of humid convolvulus which is the hair of your mother's square pubis; is a field of corn and a cancerous polyp and a tub of your father's semen, that semen enboiling to birth small you's, while your granny rocks clerics whose promises of Jesus are that HE is actually there; HE then before you with apostles in tow who claim a bit of his flesh, the flesh that returns you to dreaming, and delivers a message from gnomes, littoral creatures that live by the river, the one that you crossed to begin, that river the vein of your god, that god's presentiment bearing. Disfigured dreams have meaning.

Two months went by in the dream of Dampier before the hovel was lined with ice, the bearskin door he'd tacked by peg loosened and torn and flagging. He had no horse to vanish. No cougars had entered but they peeked inside on their way to the spring, where expressing their odors, they cruelly contended his presence.

When the vagrant didn't walk the largest of the males came at dawn past the bearskin door, its militate roar unleashed. The man from Kentucky bunched in a corner for the winter was mordacious and present, with contoured mountains on three of his sides, the hovel a mile above sea. For seven days he sat by day and night abused by the poesy of nature. That truth where the poet resides. There are no more encroachments in the blizzarding snow, but on the eighth dawn clearing, his finish. He is eaten by insomnia, inert with hunger and the hovel has been minced by the blizzard, the smell of his waste about, the male bellying in quietly to toothlock a foot, a blackened frostbit scrog, both feet missing their shoes. The man is pulled from his lair footfirst. His exurb wishes, a hinterland realer, lands him by the spring where he's flipped. Five other cougars are sniffing at the snow where the sledding body has trailed. Blood, urine, feces and clothing engender axon from the hovel like nerve cells. They form a gat where his body was yanked. He's clawed to his stomach so a female can rend him. As she does Dampier is awakened. The bruit of the weapon fired close to his head is up and to the right replicating. Billy fires, kneesits, with an arm rest of musket and her shoes have been left elsewhere.

"Billy?"

"I've killed Dampier."

"Killed what? What have you killed?"

Dampier gets to a knee. Argot of night about them. Locate that sound when there isn't a creak whence it came, wherefore it is going.

"Yonder, look down, that tiredsome copse. Skirr with your eyes that snow to the left and you'll see them moonlit tracks. I stopped its continuance there."

"An animal? What got shot?"

"It was on two legs and murderously janklin. I think it's blooded plenty. But damn if it flanked us alone."

"What is it you see this moment?" Her eyes aren't his. They're perfect.

"Not a thing Mox. It fell in that bunchin, spun into them rocks to wait."

Billy points and blinks, chokes and sobs, fights to hold back tears. Mox climbs to the girl to embrace her. Envelops his coat round her shoulders. Her body is taught but receptive. She says "I heard you talkin loud in your sleep. You were answerin questions."

"Stay close to me for a minute. I'll go down and look."

"No. It's dead. I kilt it. I want you here with me."

Two crashes are issued from the confluence of rivers, from where the brave has performed for the pair. They separate, freeze and shift their attention to the neighing of horses and mayhem. There is yelling, goddamning, gruff violent curses and an emergence of screech ending silence. They draw in, blow forth, and their breath coils to spiral, Billy welding her face to his chest.

"Horses are gone."

"Is that flintlock shootable?"

"Lemme stuff it first."

She breaks from Dampier. Hands through the movements. Suicide throats the shot. Billy rampikes the rod while tamping, says, "fuck" and drops her shoulders. While pouching the assembly Billy adds, "primed. Waitin for you to fire it."

In the moonlight stock is taken of the weapon for a starcast has birthed from the gloam. A chevying cry asserts at their backs. Billy hears it and cups her ears. **1816** is embossed on the stock. **CONVERSION BY ERASTUS-VIN FORGE**. The weapon is carved like stelae, to remind you of purpose and function. He checks the ball. Stud taps the barrel. Moisture beads from the flaking of ice.

"May be snow in that barrel," she says. "It'll blow a lettuce of flame."

"Then the catcher of the ball will know he has seen it prior to his head comin off."

Billy is surprised but convinced of his ardor. She says, "I left my shoes."

"Stand on that rock right there. When it's done I'll fetch your shoes."

He indiscreetly hefts a pistol. Arcane and hidden till now. It bends her wrist aport with the weight of its frame, French and ancient with a bully-fillip stock, an arm of the mounted dragoons. She whispers to Mox a like pistol she's sparked with the accuracy of the man that owned it. He kisses her brow and they smile through their stresses.

"Come back after Dampier."

He descends. Studies the ground. Kneels on a hassock of snow. He looks up to Billy, semaphoring by hand that the tracks drag back to the river. He increases his looping dramatically. She whistles to pull him back in. Billy stands on the rock until he is obscured before climbing to the top of the hillock. She locates her abandoned camp. Reshod she watches and listens. Pushes her pants into boots. Some darknight thing scissors above head and she ducks from the height it betrays. Billy thinks, makes a redoubt of rock. There she constructs a dissembled Billy from what she can find in the talus. Her twin she hides upslope. Shifts it to the right adding touches. It has a rock for a head with a body of coverlets and its musket is a fasces of sticks. With the decoy completed Dampier soon approaches following the tracks of their enemy. Billy lifts her arm, Dampier shrugging his shoulders confusedly. He notices the duplicate Billy. Levels the musket then lowers it. Their deadpanning faces gaze inward.

The spory indentions of crystallized blood cease at the edge of the river. Dampier squats and scratches the divot where the arrow has furrowed his skull. He dips his palms then sucks at the water, laving cold where the skin was broken. The body bobs in an estuarine pool, a sextet of arrows with cerulean tips protruding from chest and stomach. He can smell the buoying parts. A botchworked mule floats near it. The appendages quadruply locked. The head of the mule is intact, the musketman's head on the hip of a horse as his body dances illiquid, the cradling water his tomb.

"Oh," says Mox. "She'll see this."

"Behind you, you fuckin shit."

Shock climbs from his rectum and ladders his spine and it pounds in his temple subduing. He's behind you. His bleeding he's stopped. A poultice of snow has been pressed on his wound till he climbed to the safety of talus. Her ball has lodged in his chest, a fragment in his lung that deflates it. The poultice of snow is rapidly melting and soon the man will bleed dizzy. Rasping, he talks to Dampier.

"I kilt your horses. Them featherstitched fuckers, is what kilt my fuckin mule. That othern in there received the same blue arrows that'll lodge in ye hide like insult. They cut off his goddamned head. Caught 'em with a pile of their own."

"I seen 'em northwest of here."

"Thought ye might. Their remainders was present. You're a mouthy motherfucker now ain't ye?"

Dampier swings his barrel, holds trigger, the man propped on an elbow unarmed. The hole in his chest is oozing and frothing, hemorrhagically winking a purpure red as he looks at his wound then conceals it. He has a long black beard and a nictitate stare with each and every utterance offending. His knife cropped hair stands straight and greasy above a face honed lately by pugilists. His language sprent with abandoner deities. No apologies are requested. None given by either party.

"Your bitch has kilt me afore I kilt you. I kilt your horses to draw us even. Goddamn her for endin my life. What life, that was, was shit, but a shit I's accustomed to livin."

"What was your purpose, if you don't mind me askin?"

Dampier waves at Billy sedately. She hears the two speaking and listens. "Stay there Billy! I'm comin!"

The man offends through a bloodcaked smile. "I's gonna kill you, fuck your missy, then sell her to fuckin Whitey. They's gold on your hide I ain't gonna get cause that cunt can shoot in the dark."

"You always this honest this late?"

"Hell, why not? I ain't never been dead and the fuck if it looks like I'm leavin. Whitey's strow'd money like thousand mile seed all the way over to the states. Threadbare wants your heads. I met 'em two weeks back in the Owl Creek Mountains on the Muddy, a onct' to recall. Not a goddamn word from that gobbledy-gook mouth did I register, but money done talked. A hunerd' for your missy abettin and alive. Five hunerd' for yourself if dead. From the Bighorns south he owns you. You outta be flattered my friend. Threadbare, I call 'em Whitey, tracks solo and he don't miss. Shit! Mama said I'd die thisaway. By the hand of a woman in the dark."

Dampier kneels while he coughs and wheezes. The blood from his chest with the quiet ensuing slows to a trickle then stops, but his eyes won't test the hole. There's a tanglement of dark around him and the damsel who has shot him is moving.

"Reckon you could call her down?"

"You ain't gotta call shit. I heard ever' fuckin word of your drivel."

Billy squats behind a standaway boulder. She stomps the shale underfoot and gathers a piece. Throws it and strikes his head. His knife is then pitched to his high hand side while he rubs at the gash she's inflicted. Touching the blood he licks at his finger, his voice regaining its strength.

"That heapin mound of fuckstroke Jenkins ain't gettin the money for this! I been runnin with the fuck since eighty-eight when Virginia got fuckin stated! I seen Jefferson in a tavern drinkin alone and played 'em a hand of odds! We talked about whippin the Brits! Looky here, still got my beard! Not a gray streak bedded in the black! I's militia afore regular army! In that patrol that killed Forgott's men! At Elberon afore the war! Ten irregulars kilt forty a them bastards, afore regulars were regulars themselves! We cut the cocks off the prisoners, the Mohegan way, and now Jenkins'll get my coin! Ever' damn time he gets it! Drinkin and whores and debt are my plague and imma dyin owin sufferin children! Woe is my perm'nent condition! It aches the droll shit outta me!"

"Ain't a goddamn bit of that true."

"Billy please, this man is dyin."

Her frame, her body entices, and the rant of the man is muted. He slashes downward across his chest, slicing a piece of her boot. Rawhide like a lath peels back. She reverses a step and grins. His artifice the pride in her teeth. Teeth reflecting in the dark from the nether. And though this isn't sufficient for Billy, surety flames Dampier, the man leaping to kick at the handheld knife, its prolonged spin observed by the three until the blade stabbed lunking in the river, wheening droplets like the feeding of fish.

"I was just tryin to get a lil' skin from that good fine nookie you're a totin. You like 'em young, mean and clawey there padre, or do you just like 'em young?"

"I was a man sellin Bibles, no more. He was killed because he attacked me."

"But apparently far from temperance."

"A simple act of defendin myself."

"Stop talkin to this fucker Dampier. They ain't nothin to say ain't said."

"You ain't gotta say shit to me. You're both gonna die walkin downriver and Jenkins'll get nothin but bones. Or your flesh in the scat of a wolf."

"Jenkins won't know you got to us." Billy spoke. Toed at the snow.

"I reckon he'll know indirectly."

"Naw. He won't know that."

"Why, you little bitch," he wheezed.

Billy placed her hands on her knees. Scooted within reach of his arm. Positioned a hip by his head. This lack of respect for a seasoned butcher did exactly what Billy intended. There was a conjurate mumble from the hasp of a lip. A snarl and then his last. Drily evoked as is hate.

"You fairhaired cuntsteak whore!"

"Them is your final I reckon?"

"My final fuckin what you bitch?"

The dragoon's pistol bucked horizontally three inches from the bountyman's head. The pinnule of his nose went first. Then down southeast through the jaw and lower teeth, ricocheting north through his brain. There was a subulate ball-led spew, racking through the shale above them. All and ever and was and will, sprinkled about like colorant. Billy its imbrium succubus. She wore spotted blood measles flaring like infection, wiping at a drop on her brow, clearing others nearer her eyes.

She said "words, motherfucker, words."

Dampier Mox calls forth in the melee, it's deporting sufficed to suspend it, what and when and why he said it, carried away by ghosts, the bountyman's head open to his world, his thoughts both evil and magnanimous, rudely interrupted by death. What proud moments in the hills of Virginia or on the slopes of this interminable declension. His deeds and actions ask your review and the same would ask your judgment, for Billy displays no remorse. Wan hardening you see in eye and gesture as she straddles the tracker to strip at his valuables: a compass, some clacker and a fox squirrel's pelt, jerked kine requisitioned from a settler. There's a morral on his hip containing an ax with branded rebuses from gnosis, its haft a meter in length. He's sewn a buckskin loop in his clothes to secure it so the symbols are touching his body. He could rip it and downcleave his enemy. Those preterit villains not Billy. Though Billy has taken his life. She rummages his packs, therein surgical tools, she removes them and hoists the ax. Reads the unreadable rebus. Looks into a dead fixed eye. It is sunk from the pricket of a quarter ounce fragment and his gaze seems frozen in question. What fane past my physical body? Am I to wait right here?

Billy's anger then bleeds through her search. She'll be known for rages like this.

"This is for the horses you fuck!"

She hits his jaw ligamentous and its connection to the head assembles on his shoulder like a pet. With her foot on his chest she jerks at the haft. The blade of his ax pulls loose. Dampier has seen what she meant to do, recoiling from what she has done. He can't think of an adequate response to the maiming the girl has delivered.

"I think… maybe…"

"Maybe you don't!"

He's stung back with a glance complicated. She has the look of a carline, an odalisque's stare, whoremother, progenitor, to souls in the millions and viability and hate claim her womb. Billy's loins drip from the insult. From not speaking when speaking is tense. Billy rues the able for the able underfoot lay dead in broken pieces. She understands what Mox won't accept. The god that he summons is depiction. It can't see them suffer, won't rescue from pleas, for the crassness of humanity deafens. It can't taste the blood she has shed. Wince if you feel its cold presence. Smell its sweat in the primacy of ice. "Motherfucker, we are alone. Get a goddamn liver, stop mumblin to the sky, cause this is fuckin mean and we're in it! I ain't leavin! That would be dyin! I suggest you assist in oustin his possibles and strippin his weapons and clothes! Get in that pool and toss me that pack, cause I can't swim worth a shit!"

"You need to act your age and let me think before commencin to killin the dead!"

"What the fuckin hell does that mean?"

Her hands go to her side where they fist and ball, before she steps to the tip of his nose, her terseness scathing with the words in her head, but there's a melody she hums instead. He thinks Billy has fled from that pocket of mind where limited space is sanity. Though it's safer to bask in her fury. Slight thump in his corticate sex. The gravel in her voice warming.

"Wish me happy birthday Mr. Dampier Mox. Born at dawn on this day in 1812 and I do not remember a thing."

He works through the figures with his thumb on his shooter in case a bluff means death or injury. She backs away after patting his gun, the man enamored and trembling with fear.

"Happy birthday Billy."

"Don't act like you ain't done figured it. The family in the wagon ain't mine. I come outta other stock."

"I'm sorry…"

"They're fuckin dead. A condition of unrivaled permanence."

"A touch rough… yes, no, don't you think?"

"I'm celebratin not bein them. The sun'll rise while I do it."

7

BILLY SAID HER birth mother whitewashed the firs early spring of '17, but she's unsure of their prior landing. Southeast from Astoria perhaps, the husband employed by Astor's Fur Company, a Columbia Deschutes' representative. Conversant in Sahaptin with a smattering of Penutian he was considered a merchant of fairness. Billy says *that limewater, gluebonded shit didn't kill a goddamn bug*. When the firs were swabbed with the liquid the dead husband's footstool was used. Her cough began with their brooming, same cough that had taken her father. The range of the ailment was a series of hacks, body seisms followed by blooding. Her mother hid the towels her expectorate stained. Billy knew where their soaking took place.

"Mommy, mother, why are they bloody?"

Within twenty-one days the child is alone. Somnifacient amongst menacing trees. The more frightened she becomes the less light the firs filter from a sky she's forgotten is blue, those incarnate trees with lissom arms inweaving and extending to the child of six. Billy must fend for herself. Though their homestead has attracted others. Ten families by number, seventy souls present, having lost their stakes in a flood. When they vote to remain they elect to abandon, not west but east, to cross the Snake River for three in the party are Bannock. Yet another and his wife Kootenay. Another boasts of Paiute blood. As they gather their animals and load whiffletree haulers their spokesman Abijah inquires.

"Has anyone climbed the hill? That honyocker lass with the sickly mother… is there family from the fort in transit?"

No answer from that party of many. Billy listens as her future is discussed. Someone remarks that the flood and its victims are indeed increasing in number. The Columbia cresting its banks. And why should these people who cater to exit know what result she's fashioned, her parents known shielders from exposure to others and no person could say they knew her. After wandering for weeks she has buried her mother as she and the mother her father, wrapping the woman in the sheet from their wagon, having rolled her hemp-roped from their cabin. Billy's mother hadn't eaten for days, the tabes accompanying reducing her weight by a seven count stone in a week. The same number of days since they'd buried the father, since her mother had buried her husband. That Oregon soil lent a suitable start, before the black soil sub-base Billy excavated terminated in porphyry rock. Her mother can't rest at two feet. She'll be bizarrely pieced and spread. Billy then steals a mule from the settlers and the larceny is blamed on the Paiute. She does the very same thing to a Yakima drifter, filching his travois at night. Her mother is carried upriver. Ten miles east of the flooding, she finds a clearing where she can pile scrub. Billy watches the pyre to ash. Expunges the site with prudence. Little Billy then marbleizes. Her innocence sunken and bradded. What heart she locks within. Her face she looks without.

Trusting the tribe in the Willamette Valley isn't an instinctual choice. Billy travels due west to avoid Abijah and she's camped with her mule when she comes. She's a woman from a meatcamp circuitous, eyed by Billy with suspicion. She draws in the sand for clarity. Pictographs of what they are, her group a mile bendfacing on the banks of the river and the men are in the mountains hunting game. The present population contains women and children and a handful of elderly skirmishers. They're building racks, skinning hides and drying caught fish and would Billy join them there?

The woman's tablet of sand and dirt on the beach then brabbles with the river and loses. Upwater, a surveillant demobs from the bank, the water deliquescing from its body, the soddenness it causes wipes at her slate and in Sahaptin the woman says "quickly," gesticulating the camp's direction. Billy nods and clucks and the mule came to her trailing of its own volition, more from a curious bent. What was then in the river makes a stand on the bank to sniff where the woman has drawn. It creaks its jawing like a stoss impinging. They hear water fly from its back. An ichor-like moistness is flung from its spine as it airs itself like weed pollen. They hear its skirl, the wealth of a moan. They are impressed for its coming is thorough. Weir crushing it submerges to waist and chest. Water is pushed from its mouth. Donning blackness, undersurface it glides.

*

In their encampment is an eldress Molalla Tam, christened with the white name Sarah. A perdurable anile in a boater of liana, she'd gone adrift from a band of Comanche, when those people thought the horse was myth. A plainspoken, ferocious, quadroon of ninety-five with languages obtained from their speaking: English and Spanish and her own Shoshonean. Now Penutian and Sahaptin and Salish. French she recalls but abhorred. She spat through her teeth, sang in plain English, laughing as Billy approached her.

"Look how pale. You're too young to roam."

She refrains in Sahaptin so the group comprehends, saying "I never believed the edges of the earth grew others but others alike. The Comanche stole me quite early. And here, right here, another white finds me, a six year old with six year teeth and you think you'll live forever. Look at me, only six teeth left." She yanks at her gums to show Billy. Back to English. "My name is Sarah."

"My daddy know'd a Sarah at the fort. Are you that same Sarah?"

The little girl asks sincerely, but Molalla Tam denies Billy her tongue and continues. Molalla Tam or this quadroon Sarah, speaks and the speech is an amaranth: "child, you listen to me, for both silent and dangerous gods do abound, but they do not exist as you see them. They occupy the face and the heart of this world. They are every square inch of itself. You cannot understand but these people, they do, so we'll incline towards confusion at present. Sit here," she directs and begins. Into the sand she sculpts it. Images stout with belief: Godhouses of water. Repetitive stones. Fulgurite like troches frozen. Adamantine sketches of neolith idols are drawn with expressionless faces. There's a sun that was recent forever. A deserter from womb has a recreant's scream that is soaked in suint and wool. That is born from the pore of its maker. Infundibular drains this world. When the bank is sketched fully Sarah wades in the river, guiding Billy knee-deep in the current. The floor of the river holds the water at bay. Seeps what it wants then releases. There are incalculable stuttering reflections.

"Do you see, can you see, the we are they many? Do you see, can you see, it's churning? The very hair on your arms should bristle. What language we choose shouldn't matter."

"I little understand what you're sayin."

"You ain't got to. Is, is is."

Billy won't sleep in their camp. She's a doddering miniature watching. Days pass and her tasks increase. Packing dried meat. Surmising the weather. When the hunters return she's questioned, Sarah intruding and to avoid her wrath their inanities are expulsed from the camp. She stays apart in her lean-to of thatch. Billy squats in the hut and smiles. When it rains the child remains dry. Though she has no basis for the structure of their language Sarah begs her to stay and she does. Days then months accrue. Billy swears in their tongue and they laugh. Sarah belligerently coaxes the men of the tribe to instruct her in survival. Billy ingests as much as retains, knowing if she stays she will grow in their language and the rarity of permanence as habit. Then the nascent thought develops. She must find some semblance of kind. But who are those that remain to return to? The parents interred precede her in death though Billy has the strangest idea, to intersect roaming whites coming east. Fort Vancouver is her planned destination, but if the honyocker drayworks resettle post flood then best she consider her title, for her parents own registered property. Abijah's aborted hilltop child won't be found in the wreckage of flood. Lies not in the runnels of mire.

Late summer showers and Sarah is begging for Billy to stay on the river. As she collapses her shelter they stand in warm rain, eighty-nine years their difference, homopolar by birth to a world that includes them, though we belong by our right to be separate. Who knows living knows the quiet of pain with its inalienable right to seclude you. Endured suffering has no order. It persists like the whim, then the death of a child, in being, not body, stays with you.

"Billy, please don't go. You're a baby, but me, death calls. Its voice is feminine, confiding. Generous with the thing it requests."

"My folks are people like me."

"I won't choose your words."

'They brush the faces of the other. Fingertips then release. Billy tucks her chin and walks. What has come as child, devises as child, but there are differences sleight has compounded. Magnetized for astounding results. Billy is alert, preoccupied, estranged, but her solitude attends to her senses. She knows that alone is dead. In three days she makes the homestead. There are scars from the flood, crumpled dwellings of Abijah, there deanimate homes of the lost. An abattoir of tureens, scantling and toggery, the bones where a child was slain? Did the brainpan seeing the rising of the water not sprint from diluvial range? Beneath the rootcurled bank were fossils from hulls, where the squats of ancient covesmen have vanished. From millenniums surrendered they speak. See you Billy where their cookfires were lit? On the wall opposing in cudbear and sap drawn totems of postulants rutting. Man on man. Woman on woman. Another with a calumet smoking. There are etchings planetesimal of orbits before us explained by destruction and mirth. Glimworked to nothing but dust. She understands what she can and then looks at the river. She's a child herself and a child she senses once played in the bank with its siblings. Gazing outward to the presence of water. For the river and the rocks and the invidious weathers were the sediments of angry gods. Where lodges this child past living? Who commanded before we were us?

"Them bones belonged to that girl. She was three. They come from the fort."

As she says it she stands and climbs up the bank. When she arrives at the cabin where her parents have died Billy rummages the air for sound. Cups her hands behind her ears. Then down the hill and house to house and while visited meat has been cooked. The settlers themselves not the cookers. Dishevelment proliferate. Dirt floors rutted. Animals and rodents basking. While not searching for skulls she finds two. An adult and an infant on a nail that's been driven in a door freshly sawn in bandwidths. With the onset of fear she walks outside, final home in the line and she's done. They've built them staggered, misaligned at the base of the hill, but privacy and safety won't blend. Not in a land you've invaded.

Behind the ultimate cabin lay their graves. This last house in line is open in front and the backdoor removed from its hinges. The what, that it, has taken the doors and made makeshift headstones and markers, as if Billy wouldn't know these were tombs; ten bodies above ground, the remainder buried shallow, the ones of which I speak half eaten, for they inhabit a country predacious. The bodies gallate burned but unswollen. The skullwork she finds is crafted for her. She or whomever would find them. Had they fled running east and returned courting failure to unearth an unspeakable horror? Though what has taken their lives hasn't done it whole slaughter for it is nature that has toothed on the ten. They are tethered by hand, ankle and waist, loosely, but joined the same. A nexus of the dead plainly resting. They appear to be me. To be you. Having learned of their deaths after death had informed them and seemingly not before that. Assault with your reason this bellicose world and you'll quarrel that logic in patterns. Circles can't reason themselves. And there are things so craven they hide from your thinking until your thinking feeds their being. After that they are craven no more. As declarants of attention lavishly given the darkest of machines enliven. Evil is always the wake. Cease running and it covers like meal.

Billy buries where she can and has to. This isn't the wrath of the tribes. The skin of the bodies blue-pooled like the dead but their veneer is nonporous and smooth, excepting the eaten offended. It was clean, preplanned and absent of arrows and not a trace from a horse in the dirt.

"I wanna find somebody."

With her words there's a hawking behind her. Mason wasps buzzing theatrically. A child is too young for this. Any other child, not Billy.

"Hey! You! Who is there?"

No cough. A visitable region, does not open behind her. She stares at the greenery with patience. Nothing charges, no hawk, but a greentwine knife she draws to squeeze in her palm. The blade is of bone and the handle thereon and Sarah has sharpened them justly. She's paralyzed with a killing uncoming. Why say you thus my child?

"Goddamn this fuckin world."

It is the only one we claim.

Tiny body, rogue mouth and back to these victims who seem chilled in a dormant vapor. How so, beyond conclusion. Had a particular citizen crazed with a bite sought to destroy them eachly?

Difficult work for that him or that her for they would never dwindle rapidly. Yet they're equally murdered in shares. Unscathed and unmarked in their sleep. The largest and strongest of the troop in general was Abijah and there he lay. Dying first as a resistor should. Their protector, the spokesman of the seventy. He'd failed in his job against their tormentor; his musket at arms, cocked to fire, prepared to defend after dying. Waiting defense or else?

She's a day into the work when Billy realizes their eyes won't close themselves, her shifts contested by gelid lids, as if she moves about in a gallery. Billy builds up her fires, aligns them, exhuming the horde by hand. Simple shovel-pitched rolls from the shallowest of burials and there, reemerged from the brink, as a member of the dead she dozes. Pulsant blazes, a sacrarium, Billy in the center, the dead arranged in firebent columns. Billy never puts them under.

At dawn she walks east with a woodframe pack. Her straps made from peccary hide. No motives for her actions run riot in mind and there is no person to judge her. No hawking in the bush, but by that day's end, the polyrhythm of a human on water arrives to stare at her tracks leading east. Embryonic from the river, as promised, it embanks the birchbark canoe. Long strides, heaving breath, certain things are determined. Overland the girl and her mark. She is followed for a dozen miles. Turning back to the homestead torches are lit but the bodies are left in their columns. The flesh won't last the night. The predators are invited by the sound of the voice and the homes individually burnt. Soon they burn as one individual.

*

Billy's family, the three that she chooses, find her sixty miles east of the settlement. In or near the Cascade Range. She's requisitioned from the valley as Sarah has taught, chewing cud and stippled with filth. They close on the girl in the wagon of their deaths, believing the meeting predestined. Billy recalled the man smiling. He said nothing, lofted Hank, the boy pale and wrapped tight in a shacto, as he coughed, grinned, then coughed. The mother said something spoken as a prayer, a reliction leaving barren the scene. She said "I pray for safe passage for ever'one comin" and Billy responded "ain't nobody here. Damn sure ain't nobody comin." She smoldered Billy with spiteful eyes. Told her husband to jog past the girl. "How dare you pick her up."

"I ain't fleein from a child out here. She'll die but her memory won't."

"She's not a child but the likes of a fiend! If she boards we're damned to the soul!"

When he struck a tooth cracked like a branch. Her lips separated then fused. The woman rebounded, scuttled back in the wagon, pleading for the anointing of blood, for her god to hear her cries.

He said to Billy "she don't mean that."

Hank coughed and his father loosened the jacket, she protesting from behind the flap.

"Hank'll worsen if that devil boards as you wish! He'll hack himself into chunks!"

The clapboard bangs and again she is there with a message she's received from the infinite. Back in her seat the words that she says are glottal and muddled with low-pitched rancor, in the victimized spirit of the pious. The husband says he's sorry he struck her. She responds "God is my armor." The father attempts to explain.

"She thinks she divines what comes. You're welcomed to join us here. We ain't headed to a particular place. You chose young to be on your own."

"I ain't chose a goddamned thing."

Hank giggled and hacked when he registered the words. Knowing only another was speaking. It was the selfsame cough that had taken her parents but the blood that she saw never came. Even in a world priding its misery, certain things give way to the child. Choose sand and snow in black and white and sand and snow are the same. For the innocent darkness is strangled by light and a human is never quarry. Pleasant places beyond and before are those places where everyone goes to exist. Billy is not this child.

The years she is with them they are aimless, the man and the woman dowsing by choice like gabled droplets of rain. Rumors of gold and cattle and credit, which the father, disaffected, abuses. To keep his face from allurement and family alive he begins to travel by night, on plains and roads and paths and byways, oft cut by their own pure diligence. They invite the night and such will proceed, for what is trimmed from that cloth tends to travel in dark and in dark Threadbare flourishes. They enmesh thanks to Dampier. But before their demise on those saltblank flats the mother makes a decision. Two weeks prior to the death of the family an attempt is made on a life. Billy awakens with a razor to throat and the mother astraddle her body. An exorcism is imminent. That, or Billy's throat will be cut.

"Offa me woman! I'll kill you!"

Billy catches at her wrist, knees her on the father and he rises to defend his wife. The girl makes no comment. Within the hour the wagon is clankingly progressing with hymns from the lips of the father and the demons of Billy entrenched. Hidden like they need to be. Intend your best and then, amen.

8

"AND THAT IS it from front to back. Baptized in clabbered shit."

"That's the story," Mox says. No questions.

The two relax and laugh and stare at the other and there is sound in the wind and that sound is the river and there guardedly creeping where her voice has storied she can smell a storm that's building. Under foot the snow has frozen, her breasts obesely peaked with cold, their ovate shape cajoling. Billy gleans from the glout of the tracker, the finite at her feet. A certain famine in the eye of the beholder. Metronomically Dampier's prostate thumps as he mulls her face in study.

"They're cold goddamn you Mox. Stop oglin my fuckin titties."

"Sorry I offend you Billy."

"I ain't offended. I'm fuckin cold."

She covers them the best she can. Chucks his chin and laughs. He's a solid-needed figure before her and the wetness runs between. The color of his hair she cannot determine but she wants to straighten those curls. Mox's hat at a tilt with cold watered eyes and her guts are fired to fuck. She is a girl of perilous action and the dead man makes it worse. Dampier is erect and lathering from his penis in a stream disunited like a branch. Billy sniggers and says "I will. But gimme some time to amuse it."

"I've a hammer on my heart like a ballpeen."

"That is accurate. Let's bury this fucker. Stink draws things that eat."

"Be more'n glad to help."

"You'll help cause you wanna fuck me. That I comprehend."

"I can't pretend you ain't there."

The sound of coming sun no matter its height is the sound of water boiling. Billy ponders an east engrossing. Holds her worshiping face up to it. What would be buried will not be, that day, nor night, nor day thereafter, if Billy is the one that is digging. She has mastered the changing of mind.

"This fucker ain't goin under. He deserves to be eaten or rot."

"Hereabouts it's one or the other."

"He was shit before I shot 'em. Back to shit he'll go."

Already wolves gather with determinable yips. Aposematic in purpurate mists. Their priestcraft enabling dawn. The two living, the man that is dead, are then married by a buzzard en masse, its smalt-streaked eyes disgruntledly seasoned from a gantry of dissimilar rock. It lights entirely too close for their comfort, a link in the chain back to soil, Mox watching its funereal intrusion. Resolutely carrion bird.

"Fuck. They're done set groupin. And him not startin to stink."

"Why Mox! What foul language!"

Billy climbs to their camp. Mox doesn't. He places his hands on his hips, as if Billy were a thing to determine. The tracker she's gunned lies nearby to foot with a cavity where the masseter was. His stare a sickly reflection adoze. Steady eye. Nothing he sees. Mox lofts a question that goes unanswered for certain stars have garnered his interest. Betelgeuse on Orion's shoulder. Then disgust with the world throughout, for he's here not there in firmament arms, but from those stars his origins. *God or god not* he thinks. Have the furthest reaches deposited humans and abysmally turned proceeding?

"Hell, I'll bury you," Mox then whispers. He wonders if the soul has departed. Gives the man a kick. Wants to know if the judgment was held. Is the tracker burning in hell? He's known the heinous, the approvingly religious. Dampier Mox is confused, if both are either or neither, then decides he knows nothing worth mentioning.

Billy watches him think and then realizes Mox is posing for burial. Searching about like a crone. An old woman looking for thread. Let the man do as he wishes. She drifts west to empty her bladder. Pants down, skirts high, the snow licking her sex, smoke rising as she releases. Billy inspects beneath. "Their world in a fuckin pouch."

A shape scurries through the snow with a vermicular slither. Makes sense of its path and leaves. The creature lends its tack for with the advent of sun comes the storm she's smelled through the night. Dampier's gimlet, offencing the ice, whacks to dig the grave. Curt strokes percutaneous through the hoarfrost skin and then depth with a handmade shovel. He digs while burying himself. The tracker watching him sink. Dampier reaches to close his lids. They resist, frozen, the flesh won't shog, Billy listening and knowing the stare of the tracker is the reason he won't dig.

"Dead fella is doin his best."

While bouncing through the last of the droplets Billy notices tracks. They are deep, reversing, searching for something, weighty rider, heavier horse. The poundage of three big men on a mount of significant girth. Beachheads of snow heap around the prints. Alike placards of thin cracked ice. When she panics the snow erupts on his body as his horse does the same from its ribs. The avalanche of drift snuffs her to waist, miscellany of body asunder, rotating Billy to stomach and chest. With her haunches displayed he clutches a thigh and drags her past his feet. She is lifted by her throat, run close to his body, flagmatically then away. Nose to nose she's addressed with interest from a face as hot as dross.

"You..." He starts then stops, "were intending to piss on us both? Billy, do you know who I am?" She replies "him" then "you." Threadbare says "yes," then labels her head, saying "eyes" then "mouth" then "nose" then "ears," before a hand slides down to her groin. She is supported by her sex and held. His hair is long white with a nape-tilted hat and vulcanized eyes minus gesture. Opaque like a reredos screen. His pupils are open, there sucking, the empty space of peace therein co-opted by a thing other than rage.

"You're Billy. But not a man."

"Can't you fuckin feel that I ain't?"

"I feel no thing remembered."

"Then you'd be the first to admit it."

He smiles expecting her pepper. Billy's tilted and her throat is released. She slams face first into his wide chest. To cheat her weight she twists her head, but there is no thudding there. Billy mumbles through his necklace of bones.

"He's done gone."

"I knew Mox would bury the man. That tracker would've killed you both."

"It's your fuckin coin that caused it."

She is scraped down his torso to rest on his hip until her feet touch solid ground. Her forehead to his pelvis when straight, as she stands in a terrane of stones, its smallest as wide as a stipe is long and he in the snow flat footed. She looks up into his mouth for the words.

"But Billy, you did the killing."

"I fuckin done it and they's killin as yet."

"Yes Billy, as yet there is."

The blade is tucked in a scabbard the size of a crawlway for rats or a drain for sullage. He demonstrates then watches her reaction as he cleaves a stone in half. Kneels to meet her face.

"Jesus God Almighty," says Billy. "I ain't had but a minute on earth. There are few yet summers I remember. No easy days I recall. Do whatever the fuck you wish."

He's poetic as the poet is sane, for few see our world throughout. Know it for its fixity and where it is sharp. Understand that the world doesn't know us. Its scabs are our hearts. That is it. Her words he finds beautiful as the words she has spoken and he's noticed her use of *yet*. Twice over not begging for life.

"Not but a minute on earth and few yet summers recalled?"

"I said remember, not fuckin recalled! I ain't tradin verses with you!"

He says "few yet summers you remember."

Threadbare translates, his language deceptive, not the same luster, same tone. In his eyes and breath a feline curiosity, smitten with what she has offered. As smitten she offers more still. Fear of what comes. What is.

"You smell like red and silver. What I reckon them colors would smell like. And blue, yes blue, some too."

"Blue?"

"Uh-huh. I said that."

Day completely upon them compounding. Dampier has entombed the tracker. They listen as the body is covered, waiting for the prayer of Mox. That thick set muscular voice of understanding with a plea to all beyond sight. Too much time elapses, Billy then reaching to his face, outlining its features before tapping his head, delirious with the coming of death. She says, "blue. Your eyes look blue."

He catches her hand, puts a finger in his mouth and blood lets down his chin. Instantaneously Billy's unconscious. She is placed in the snow and then in the sun and then on a tier of rock. There in light, through a pall of moans, she's enlaced with other stones, so as to stay where put. She seems a sacrifice left to a beast from acedia who cannot catch his own. Threadbare fires above his head sowing her body with crystallized granules of powder, percussively spent by the chamber. It's a missive and not a suggestion for Dampier to arrive posthaste.

As he mounts and rides towards the backlog of storm Billy's digit is chewed and swallowed. Her in him and him with her.

9

WHEN HE FINDS Billy on the altar of stone he sees that her finger is severed. Right index, through the topmost joint. Wye-shaped wound, ebony bone, piaster of droplets about her. What has bitten has positioned the hand in her groin like a maidenhead evulsion symbolic. There's a circle in her vestment there. Mox handles and studies and wraps it in a kerchief and with the pit of his arm applies a modest pressure while iteratively checking the flow. What camp they've made they return to. She's as light as his thoughts on their deaths.

For an hour she sleeps on her bedroll before waking to curse the finger, a runagate pulse in her head and hand as she turns her face to find him. He's behind a scutement of horned mass-stone, heaped and projecting ledgy, scrutinizing the plain for that malleable assault, weaponized and anlaged to kill, the sun announcing its presence on the stroke of his blade as he rotates, finesses the strop. Downstroke, rewrap the wrist. Return the knife again. Residual dust from the sharpening, patters on the shale like rice.

"Dampier. I say Dampier."

He stays with the horizon and ignores her. Says "yes" and then her name.

"You don't want him that close. Not him. He's done what he wanted and left."

"Whoever they are ain't through. Your finger is gnawed to the knuckle."

"It ain't a they. It's a he and I asked for it. Put my hand right into the cage."

"You done what?"

"Too close. I felt it."

"I can see what is comin from here."

"It was him that climbed in the wagon. By God he lit the snow. He burned it, come up from it. Snow, it don't light."

"I'll kill 'em dead when he hits this slope. You got the talkin fever."

"You're more likely to grow pine from rock than cap that motherfucker."

They examine their bodies, those accumulate wounds, since their day on the great salt flats. Each person no longer themselves. Changing wholes where cruelty is common. Pieces of flesh underneath their clothes have been purchased by land and men. They are less than they were and shrinking. Lost weight, nerves skittish and what thing moves is a seedling for Threadbare's form. Ten million wraiths of smoke. And not one is erosible before them. Each thing lives and each thing seen is a living breathing affront. Dampier makes Billy paranoiac. Like a child bathing and the stoppage of splashing and the parent gone from the room.

During their reeling he trots southeast. The two in the rocks designs. The idea of Threadbare grows from a barrier of sixty miles distance maturing. He enjoys the landscape with an artisan's eye, phallic cacti with glochidium barbs. A whirligig beetle in a snowmelt pool and he says "you're not from here. Tiny bug, you are misplaced."

*

Rain changes to sleet then snow. Billy's fever gradually rises, the evening there as the mattery wound colors white, but the white is the fleshless bone. When Dampier overlaps a fold of skin Billy screams and blanches.

"Sorry."

"I ain't fuckin dead!"

The front poststorm arrives with its cold, though Billy perspires as the sun sets.

"Hey," she says. "Dampier?"

He's pacing, searching, for any material to build a travois from scratch. Crude rig but he's trying and doesn't hear Billy while snipping his piling hump.

"Dampier Mox, are you there?"

Billy's head is atilt with her chin raised. Domed rocks, their undersides. Above her stare phonolitic, clover-green capes with their gadgetry hovering infatuate. Billy motions to that earth inconceivable, where it speaks in cracks and fissures. That intercalation of ticks. Geological years where the chicane of time hasn't waited on humans being, or any other being respiring. Age of stone and mystery and bedrocked soil. The shifting of continents awake. About our creation she thinks, and within Billy fever adduces, the ideal soul within. By this she's imprisoned by rapine seas aromatic and drown she will. She sees a skylark suspended in sound and the words in her mind, they hold him. Then comes the blast from his musket. Followed by his footsteps receding. He is then athwart her face and body with a soft painted pride suffusing. Billy asks *did he lope right past you?* Realizes the words weren't spoken.

"The fuck he did," says Billy and Dampier repeats "we've meat. I shot an antelope yonderway."

She asks for a smoke and in what seems like hours a butt is placed to her lips. Lit by bloody hands. They are his and then they're Threadbare's. When Billy is conscious sufficient to speak she sees what's put before her. He wants her to eat in that moonphase scape, the gutted animal trimmed in chunks, the work of an infantile butcher, whose birth was the last of his seeing. He's dressed it near her bedding and its blood is saturate sand. The shale coated with gut. Billy's offered the lungs. Hacked and fried and they look like dung and the pronghorn isn't beast. Attribute something else.

"Good shot Mox and I thank ye. Please take it somewhere else. I'll trim it back right for what we can use, but you'll have to wait till I'm able."

"Sure shot. But I ain't no dresser."

"It's an art I learnt from Sarah."

"And a thing of necessity dear."

From the plate of her bed she cannot move though she tries a handful of times. Going rigid she tenses and gasps for air and there's a wheepling sound in her throat. The same as the dying proclaim for the living if thinking the dying will live.

"We gonna have to fix it Dampier."

"Understood. And we will. Why ain't we dead? Here ain't hard to find."

"We're interestin livin I reckon. Time'll come when we wished we weren't."

He reasons his options. Those he has mastered. Exposing the neck of his shirt, he displays a wiggling scar. Puts a finger to its middle to show her. On his knees, she can see better.

"Shot myself cleanin a shooter. It punched through the fat and come out. I's stupid to be what I was. The meanest ain't often the sharpest."

"Don't let this get in my arm. It ain't got nowhere else to go."

"This scar was cleaned with whiskey, and a bullsnake brand orange-white. But the man that done it ain't here."

"Make due. Make due," says Billy.

Moiled eyes black rimmed above her expletive, as her arm hits his pocketed hand. She's already seen him clutch it. Relief can be apportioned between them. He puts his hands in the air as she pleads with her eyes, grimacing through her words. "I want that fuckin booze." The corkthumbed pint of the chalk-white mash is extracted and the stopper released. It's brought to her teeth and she downs a hefty gulp and its level shows glass as it drains. She blows the smell of the liquid in his face.

"When I'm shut go on and do it. I'll be down for a spell. Never been much of a drinker."

"I was suggestin. Waitin your askin."

"Mother God in heaven ain't you precious. Revealin that scar and all."

Forty-five minutes and the fire as was is a magnified set of flames. The rocks haven't changed in aspect. He's chosen four, coal burrowed them separate. Before he draws her hand he'll select his cautery and perhaps that decision is simple. Uncovering the four he looks. A moated stone selects Dampier. It heats black, whitegray, gradates through hues and he slides it from the fire with a shalepiece. "Mox," she says. "Yes Billy." It's the talk of ataraxic slumber. Billy's hand is pulled across his hip and vised between his knees. Dampier spits on the stone and it sizzles. He smells the stench of his own saliva.

"Alright then my dear."

With the blade of his knife skin is removed in what light he has as fire. Infection advances but there is healthy tissue, pink and blood has reached it, beneath the roup where her system defends. There are scars in the palms of her hands. As with one, so is the other. She's come to this world with them both.

"They ain't enough skin to do it. Can't wait for more to grow."

Mox encircles the weeping joint. Gathers what flesh will gather. Enough to cover the wound. Billy shifts when the cautery is seized. She's awake, not sober, but feeling. He's wasted her drunk preparing.

"I can't hold it that long with the kerchief. I'm usin a stone to do it, cause a garden of stones lay about."

"Fuckin do it and stop your talkin!"

When he presses her eyes roll white. She can't smell the skin burning but listens to the hiss with the sizzle and Dampier's grunt. She dismayingly wails to mute. She has a physical body, then a vaporous spirit, in a sequence above herself. All at once she is everything painful. And then she is nothing without it. Another self then completes where light resides, Billy floating right to it through ossicle comets that inject her womb and rattle. They birth by brisance and tail and body until their girth splits Billy to chin. She the prime mother of drifts that calve as Billy reblends with our world. Back vulnerable from where she has been. Returning to Threadbare's Eden. What is fluid surely enters the cosmos. What flees simply enters itself. Both are revealed to Billy.

"It is done. I done it," he says.

"Let loose my goddamned hand."

10

"AIN'T NO NEED to drag any further. You and the meat and myself a pullin ain't makin but five miles a day. And that from dawn till dark. We need to make another plan."

"Get us in thinner snow."

"Nevermind. Stay where you are. I feel like a rake for askin. I drug eleven in a row and twelve is started. I'm gettin tougher with every step. Gimme a minute. I can do this."

"Sit till your heart is content. Sun's bright. I feel better."

Billy's hand is infected but her body makes due as constitutions are wont to do. As before this place no comfort. Far from the cities they've made this life and in living this life they've chosen. Iron isn't native to earth. Iron is of igneous birth. Harden what comes as conditions demand it: from their Green River camp he's drug three leagues west, following a gill then the spoor of a wolf with its tracks of limulus shuffle, likely shot by the ball of a hunter. He then sees the platformed doyen. For two hours he stares at the gravesite. The scene is wooden, carved and empty. Warriors given to deified care. Mox searches for what he can use. Two lodge poles are frozen in a drift, bracing the rostrum of a subordinate chieftain. The doyen's left untouched. There are too many bones swarming the scene and men have been slaughtered here. Few have proper graves. He finds an eremite's trench that has mingled with the spirits and a hairshirt chewed to pieces. Someone has hidden from something. The webbing from the shields lean eastward. Frames too rotten to lash. He takes his collection to Billy. They have the makings of a sled rudimentary. She instructs and together they build. Billy shows him how to dress their meat. Weakens with the effort and sleeps. What he's provided has made her feel better, but she's worried they've offended a minor creator by blaspheming an apparitional fraternity. She thinks the wolf they've followed omentic. The animal has delivered them there.

"I don't believe in them heathen gods. And I ain't took nothin from that chief."

"Heathen gods were conceived before yours."

"Reckon we'll see what happens."

"The choice of seein is ours."

Before leaving the camp where he's buried the tracker Mox gathered what he could, gorged their hidesacks, with sufficient water for the week. Billy's cauterized wound was suppurate and festering and he worried as he strapped her in. The travois as comfortable as spikes. She asked in her delirium if he'd spoken at the gravesite and he responded "which place do you mean? This'n here or that'n last week?"

"Here. Where you trailed the wolf."

He said "nothin was said" as he watched for movement, though no one came or went. The wolf vanished as they arrived. Distal tracks that faded to nothing.

"It was the snow, the ground, their things and us. What I needed was throw'd in the dirt. Them shields was in that trench. I took the lash from the trellis of that big chief's bed. It'd been there fifty years. I wasn't gonna get a thing. That rawhide lash made a tie for them runners and that was what I needed."

She is adamant, stoic, widens her eyes. Raps his hand with a callow visage.

"You ain't never alone. Not nowheres. That's a thing worth knowin forever."

Eleven days in the bit with the poles on his shoulders in snow of a depth inconsistent. Like nature can measure commitment. They have the meat dried jerking, hidesacked water and Billy strapped too tight. For her the travois, a vehicle primitive, becomes a sled then a sleigh of two hundred pounds with incessant modifications. Half runners made of wood. He starts, stops, eats a handful of snow, loosens and tightens his knots. *It doesn't look like a fuckin sleigh.* He cleans her sex when she menstruates. Washes clothes in a gullied source. Protects Billy to atone for self. Their water is low, but sufficient, brackish southerly sinks, clearest spring on their fortieth mile. While roaming southeast, he lances her finger. It drains and Billy improves. An hour later he thinks she is dead. Thought dead before she speaks. For the last two days you've given her your meat. You yourself walking on water. Eloign and away. Abstract. What she says Mox makes his own: *Dampier, please listen to me. You're starved and weak and I in a shell on your back as the dead in a memory. There are pictures of oceans you think you see and their waves are the joints of gods. They crash and crack as the short-lived gather and you think your past is speaking. They congregate. They press. They stare. Each gazing toward you on that beach in the surf before they're pinched from their solid existence by a voice that returns you to me. You stop in the evening, make our fire, and adoring, nurse me to health. You realize the inclines are peaking. Foothills, then mountains, and home. As you unwrap my lashing you talk of our house where you'll take me to live and prosper. You melt snow in a pan and bathe me. When my legs are spread your face turns away, yet you clean with a touch that I feel. If they follow, who follows and what will they see; those dragmarked tracks three feet wide and the socketed remnants of fire. Your triage, a singular patient. There are bandages proper and sloppings of mine for scavenger's noses to sniff. They trail, their distance interest. You pack my hand in snow.*

You freeze it, warm it, until you see tears. You're sorry and you're forgiven. There's a veinlet of color next to some rocks and I know there's a root that resides there. Buried shallow for water is scarce. You lay me down gently, circle the sled, then dig till the root is exposed. Where it grows will come mushrooms with rain. You slice, I chew it and grin. It is spicy and quick, making lobes of the sky, my skin igniting and burning. I'm greasy and know that I stink. Above this, near that, the hum of the heavens. You allow me my high and laugh. This is what I had to do.

*

Twelfth day and back to the beginning. Mox camps early to test her. Her body's been through the worst. He unstraps, grasps, lifts her to balance. She's unsteady, sticky and smells. The transport is stained with her urine.

"I'm filthy."

"Done the best I could. Your womanly time come eight days back and I thought you was bleedin to death. Blood and piss don't mix with the cold, but I kept you from sorin up. I was respectful in case you're wonderin."

Billy is jovially offensive.

"Another man woulda fucked me senseless. Cocked me inside out."

"Billy! My God!" She laughs. "You know I'll protect you from that."

"I know. I know. I'm playin."

"Keepin southeast we'll cross the Little Snake. I was jailed in Kentucky with a Comanche. He knew the rivers hereabouts. If the passes ain't clogged there's an outpost. It ain't American and it ain't on this side. We'll get you able to cross."

"An outpost of who from what?"

"I don't even know if that fella was Comanche. He whooped

three soldiers, sodomized a whore and after that, they brought 'em in. Whores have the right to complain."

"You'd think a whore'd charge more for sodomy, but keep it on the menu?"

"Even whores read the Bible you know."

"Proper point. A commendable response."

Days go by, Billy strengthens, the weather clearing, blotting low pressure. The pair occupy a hinterland region where a heap of bones lay cragged. What was driven lay in there to die. There was a stream unseen, then a barrial ruin, followed by a pediment marker. Here began the Arapaho's land. On the slope in the gravel with its alluvial fineness they sink heel and hand to the wrist. Billy sees it first, mentions it second, directs him to the slovenly hulk. It's been placed without thought, this elision, omission, with its strength and impregnability. No passer would think to know it. Until stumbling upon the colossus.

"What the fuck?" says Billy. "What is that?"

"Don't know, but I reckon we'll visit."

"There, where that streambed narrows. Let's see what comes and goes." Billy takes his eyes and leaves them. "Yonder jail of trees. It looks like shagbark hickory, but ain't a stick of that shit around here." She cancels the musing, wipes her tanned face and imbeads a better position. "Right there, them boulders have a clear line of sight to whatever the hell that is."

"Federal garrison maybe?"

"This land ain't federal U.S. This is Mexican claimed."

This is what they see: it's of timber construction, the footpoles silvern, foisted prior to the tribes enjoining. Cut by axes and fires in the hundreds. The fort smokes from its crannies and as the lashed poles weep they agitate, secluded, with their rumple-headed tops bleeding smudge o'er open dominion, an empery of leviathan peaks. As if in secret it was built forever, to burn afferent to sky and space. Its haze is blacktan to Billy and Dampier until the redborn sun adds white. From its coign of sky the fort is splash-bathed by rays from a liberal roost. Its entrance illumined and Gothic. Mattock-hewn stakes have been driven at an angle around the base and there they smoke. As if noshing psychotics might push from inside but never lean from without. Need the plague pass this to wander elsewhere, for affliction worse here resides? It peeks through the crenels and pushes on merlons as calamity unbridled short traipses. No sentry on the parapet lately. But if something does come it is obvious. A steep cirque must be descended. A horse-trampled field then ridden to its front, straight ahead to a gate tree-walled. Here the prison contrarily smokes. The approach they can see through the trees.

Immediate to the entrance are men that toil and amongst them men with whips. They trot canting from a portal hidden from sight on horses with Mexican brands. Enrooted pesthouse thugs. They're notably agile, though bulkily dressed, with arms in slipshod motion, their bolting whips in crack then rescindment, off a choice of rawboned backs. "Goddamn you sonsofbitches! Goddamn your births to the man!" This report is for taciturn men, some feeble from the lash and they go to their knees as their guardians urge them proper. Flaccid in the muck they rise to commence with filth embracing skin. They are prisoners imprisoned, antipodean, for they are beings imprisoned by space. And a formidable mix they are: most white, few blacks, native or other, but there's a present quartet in extremum; tracked barrow hiding Mexicans cannibalizing the dead while fleeing from Threadbare's chase. They've no clothes at all, though in assemblage there are various wearings. You see homespun cotton, heavy ratteen, a plethoric in a decollete blouse. A cresset of iron dangles from his belt and his fierceness is regarded as menace, though he speaks in an altered tone. The skin of his neck pitted black. He's a weldment from a bedlam dynamic. Lights a candle and wears it on hip. His face argent like the prison's supports, the man coming and going as he pleases. The he-she digs for aught to be busy as he wags his tongue at his lovers. When the candle on his hip in the cresset is extinguished from a bend this way and that, it is dutifully lit by a guard, the he-she asked "what more?"

Those bearing the prison for eighteen months tend to the cattle in shifts. With reprisal over other prisoners they've earned a limited freedom. As the slavering beasts snip late winter shoots, these men sit high in their saddles, doting no particular thing. A trustee they favor sits pumping his cock so his brethren have stories to tell, this heresiarch belligerent a known bestial romantic, whose familiars stand guard as he rumps them. Whatever cattle return his glare. The man will rape what walks and divide from the herd and this herd is a pool of the wary, and there is nothing in this place not chanced. Depravity is encouraged and bartering with scruples will stand you up on stilts. Good men are lackadaisically tortured. Niceties clandestinely fibbed.

Shrill whistle from the teeth of a guard and a charwoman steps from the portal. A horse kicks at her head and she feints. Svelte and lovely in a time when she cared. While serving the prisoners from a teakwood bucket she tipsily sloshes the water. Now and then a pitched schiller, a coin unburnished, is paid for services rendered. Right pittance for she's birthed a collection of children without keeping or naming the first. Sated, she invites them to dig. They watch her leave, return to their ditching, their minds flivelling through women, recalling orgasms, although pasts, will never be present. Their forever place is here.

"This is a slaver. They're cuttin the west. Takin cues from the Spaniards I bet."

"To go where and what for exactly?"

"The Pacific Billy. The ocean."

"Why? To see it, turn the fuck around, come back to where they started?"

"Convicts maybe? They got their own clergy. There's a collar in the ditch just a diggin. Poor fella. Hell on earth."

"Hell is buildin it here. They's at least three nations to slaughter these fellas and them with a smokin prison."

"We can travel due south, avoid this…"

"Please, don't avoid us."

The voice stands them in the boulders as regardants, to the length of their vision the prison in smoke, the pair like a couple on a beach, the other men in the ditches toiling in their sea, digging to drain from nothing. And nothing drains where they ditch, their picks breaching like fish and back underneath and the couple means little to them.

11

DAMPIER MOX HAD his gun on a voice before the voice had a shape or meaning. The accent carried in the smoke and the wind and the profile of the wind as it blew southwest took the words in another direction. A bush shook and rodentia scattered. Clicking misfire. Another. Two weapons. Double clicks, no caps and Mox's focus is no longer on the voice he has heard.

"I smell them horses," says Mox.

"I should've killed you for twice you've offended!"

With the squib of a pop Mox's pistol disjuncts, springing back from his clutching fist. Fragments of metal blister the skin between his thumb and the wrist and he sucks at the wound while searching for others around them. Billy knows what waits isn't singular.

"Another shot padre. Here it comes. That I consider a miss." The accent is foreign, malicious, as if the words have been effectually practiced.

Billy and Dampier are tiresomely fronted by men they cannot discern. Thrumming hailstones like instruments sounding. A burry felt tempo of clunks. Their gyve a wall of ice. When they step, the tempo, it changes. As they shift, their feet empattern icewhorls and the largest ice amulets bruise them. Nothing shows in the boulders and there is no cover, behind them a calamitous gap. An inheritable sprint to doom. Still the men in the ditch, they pick and shovel, spragging the muddy snow. Alike hooks and tenons that ground them. Their mortice the earth at foot.

"Son of a bitch," says the voice. "The weather in this clime is preposterous."

"You're English?" Dampier asks. The response appallingly rapid.

"Irish goddamn you! But hello to you both. Mims Nickel is there behind you. The only outpost, facility and ward of a state using vagabond, slave and criminal labor to go nowhere in particular slowly. We make triply sure the state of Missouri is somewhat thinned of its roguery. They send them here to improve their behavior or meet their demise by choice. I am their warden and keeper."

Billy asks "who the fuck are you?" Through the sprue of a rock she can see him. A red admiral flies that path. Orange-red wings bright on snow. Her yet-born nettles dormant. Billy wants the voice dead.

"Forgive me young lady. Aten Mire Conquin. What a mouth you have."

From behind a boulder he speaks. A hetman ensconced in ghouls. They are three horses deep to conceal this Conquin, defending crooked in a staggered formation, they secure what doles their pleasure. A giaourscarred trio, this infidel lot, half Arab, tongued Berber, Moorish Spaniards, stowed for Missouri by Catholics, with the promise that America is holy. What it became was a hive of the scurrilous. Ire is as ire condemns. Ten priests would be found with scimitar wounds. Priests that would bugger no more. One of those eunuchs is digging. Working in the ditch by the fort.

"These are my jackals," said Conquin. "My trinity. Obedient to me."

Billy sees parts of a face. Dampier the fingers of a hand. Both see becketed pommels. Reins dense as nodules on pine. Saddlebows pressed flat from their leaning, as if the men ground searched for any suggestion on the state of evidential impermanence. A lonely chore indeed.

Billy says "we ain't in Missouri."

"We are not even close to that state." The men stop but Conquin continues. They phalanx, contract, boulders blocking boulders and no one can flit or move. It is to shoot through orbicular stone. "But your government is young, influential with the sovereigns, this Mexican presence about us. Powerful men are concerned. Senators and the moneyed, et cetera. Mexico will release particular holds in exchange for American favor, especially to a state near five years old and bordering hostile lands. They've a small population, your newborn Missouri, and they strain every brigand and fool, chance they west or east, north or south, any location inconstant. They hang and shoot as many as they can and the remainder visit Mims Nickel. Wave of the future my dearest. Prisons imprisoning elsewhere, in lieu of keeping them home. My name, have you heard, well of course not, this isn't my country of birth."

"You ain't got no reason to retain us. We were passin through."

"Pardon me, ahhh, Billy, correct? I am the law and the sayer until you're clear of my purview. Besides, you're safe with us. This innocent distraction has saved you. Though not convicted by Missouri you are here. What shall I do without that?"

"We both understand Mr. Conquin."

She turns to Mox, convulsing, screaming, "stop includin me in your shit!"

Dampier Mox attempts placation: "Billy, please. He'll kill us."

"The fuck he will! What he'll do is jail us! The motherfucker gets stipends for captures!"

"She's brutal," says Conquin. "What a peach!"

Their phalanx breaks and channels. He steps to the pair on a florid wet bay, reaching down to shake their hands. Neither hand is offered. Looks are given, he to them, they to Conquin. It's a face that is practiced from carousing, his hair to middle back in a frowzy red tail with a tumpline decorously hung. The remainder of the sling is about his waist and there are sections around his wrists. Hides are his ensemble. The seams stitched inward like a wealthy corpse and he's a dexterous surgeon at this. His eyes intend you harm. They are that blue and his skin that pale so when the vein in his forehead pulses the words from his face seem rhythmic. You're irate if it doesn't fit together. Billy looks at his birthmark. Must.

"Ah yes," says Conquin. "Take it in."

The stigma is congenital, grooved sincipital, what the parents have given the child. From the cofferdam of womb it has come. The word **MIRE** tattooed on his forehead. **MIRE** on the father before. Of no importance is its tint or dimension. All excluding white are the same.

"It is what you read my dear. The way nature includes we beasts. A gift I think, from my illiterate father. A present from the great beyond."

Conquin looks to denounce the sky. Wags his pallid finger for emphasis.

"Why would blood hand that?"

"Yes, yes, exactly Mr. Dampier Mox. Since-birth terms I guess. In a word this life is declared, is it not? I am a natural defect of and by nature and there is nothing to be done at the present. As for you, you misfits there. Well, usually these bounties so called, are taken care of by western elements, out of reach of our facilities here. There are wilds sufficient between the Nickel and the ocean to end one's life by wandering. Nasty terrain it is. But look at you and what you've accomplished. You've found our fort without effort. Over the last two weeks ten or so seekers have mentioned your regional presence. And you dear Billy, you've peaked his interest, to be preferred by the most tremendous, an ogre who speaks in erudite phrases but hasn't come to visit. Yet, thanks to you I've befriended that regent so named in conversing here. Without dying, for I've nothing to give. Oh, how are your wounds? I was afraid to ask, though my hospitality has no limits."

Billy somnolently recedes from position. Catching herself on a peonage stone she crosses and uncrosses her arms. There are tears on her cheeks and through the splutter of hail she designates Conquin on horseback. Hears the clangor of shovel and pick. She rubs the stone. The razor is there. Quick sprint and this will be done. His trio of guards watch a condor in flight and Conquin hasn't straightened in the saddle. To enhance her furor he clownishly turns, his words from a head in reverse.

"Give it a try. I'll still collect for these bastards will cut you in twain. Your lower half will enthrall them for days. Your head I'll deliver myself. Not the way that man of yours wants it, but Threadbare will be glad to pay."

She whets the razor on the face of the stone. Back and forth, forth and back. The sparks from the blade redacting. She is lost in the violence of fit. To herself she slurs anechoic. "I'm gonna slice your goddamn throat."

"Billy, no more," says Mox.

"Listen to your fella," smiles Conquin.

She replies "this is for you."

By a signal from a guard three others ride to them and their parley increases to nine. Billy stops dragging the razor, the sparks countermanded to cease. Conquin is unarmed and Dampier Mox makes a note in his mind of the vanity. The rabble that has come is a dire triumvirate thighing weapons of slickshot bore. They're the talent beyond his trinity. Incarcerated here since the first tree fell with myrmidon eyelets fixed. They can't glower without being instructed. To their left, the first, a man of sixty, has no ties to family. He's been convicted of robbing for his destitute brood who perish to the member post trial, for the judge chairs the board of the bank that was looted and to recuse his authority was odious. He pays no mind to the pair. The sere one in the middle is a mutant. Misleared with a head like a cork and eyes that bulge and weep. A scrofulous man of enlistment. He removed the eyes of a demanding lieutenant when the officer asked him to spell. He's of no known age or place of birth, but remembers there was heat and sand. When Billy ventures a glance, he nods to Conquin, squeezing his crotch. He says, "cunt, hey cunt, I'll furgle ye second after Tottern fucks ye first!" This Tottern on the end is a study. What bloodinesses here are told. Harried to the north from Chihuahua, Mims Nickels' where Tottern came. Riding northwest from the blade of coming Texas he'd pursuers and a decade afloat, laboring on dreadnought's decks. He's a mender of armament, a sturdy-body smithy, a linguist besotted by ale. Gainful bellows where the wages were constant. But he'd leave if the plunder decreased. He has a penchant for sodomy and rape. His tendencies the dead and the dying. West of the port at Tampico is where the Admiral's daughter was found. A swineherd thought she was a bundle of milpa, his sow bringing the man her foot. The word *damsel* carved on the sole. To the shell of the Nickel Tottern rode, then walked, to inquire if asylum was accepted. Analogous decisions he cites. Conquin is addressed in the language of the briefs and their descents he recites in Latin. Tottern adjudicates brusquely. Conquin, overwhelmed, relents. "No, no asylum," said Conquin, "you'll live your life on the face of my stamp." If Tottern escapes his bounty quadruples. Threadbare honors that sum. As for the Admiral the man is conveniently drowned, his son the last of the family, and this brother seeks to avenge. This man is a being resolved. After making his contacts in the state of Missouri from his home on the bay of Tampico, the city receives a bludgeoning. The hurricane is immense, though stalling, and the son is unladed from the bay. He's found bobbing with his father, the Admiral, rope-tied in a warm embrace. What an irony beyond proportion. The blood oath on Tottern erased. Now Threadbare holds the link.

*

What gave whelp gives violence and there are too many men to face. Dampier tempts a glance from individual trustees, from eyes beneath his oilslick brim. He gets Tottern first as the Moors return to their intensive condor search. There's a complete cessation of assailable hail and that pack, astatic and many, sits in silence to wait on words, the man of sixty who has lost his family purloins Mox's stare. It says *I beckon be the first to die.* Mox draws with his opposite hand, the pistol snagging for the weather has grimed its surface and the leather holds its arm. The old man does not twitch. His resistance untroubled, little more than a grin and Mox obliges his wish. Through the chin a shot well aimed. Tottern splattered with gore. "That angel is better off," he says. "Nothing left but the bitch and her razor. You wield it honey pie!"

As skull and brain are wiped from his face the mutant assists with a kick, the older man no longer a burden, as his body repulses and jerks. He lands headfirst and they look and stare and cannot do the thing that ensues, the mutant yanking his sidearm to fire, his shot meant to startle for the men have been told the pair will be held for their bounty. Dampier is missed by a foot, the stray of the mutant whanging dicrotic, expanding as they quake and titter. The trinity's boreholes are on them. Pointed in specific directions. His head and the head of Billy. Conquin has nodded them forward.

"Thank you Dampier Mox. He was a miserable drain on morale. Why just last month, right above his pallet, he attempted to hang himself. He fell with a thud then cried! Ruben made the worst mistake. He brought his outside into the Nickel. Said his children would visit in dreams. I said there is no leniency here. No passes for the deadest of children! Dream or no dream, get them out! Daddy, I'm hungry! Daddy, I'm thirsty! Daddy, mama isn't breathing! Has nothing to do with me! It made for a sensitive man and I'll regale you in giving him death! That having been said, don't shoot his horse, these redmen are hellbent traders! They sell their beasts with whelks, teeth flatground, but what can I do, I am here?

We've got to have mounts and meat! Jesus Christ this is civilized slavery! I'm running a prison here!"

Dampier reloads his pistol in the face of the men that will kill him. Here's a thing confuting the horde. With robust strides he clears for his dying by removing Billy from harm. The boreholes follow young Mox as Conquin dottles his pipe, Dampier transfixed by the meerschaum bowl because thereby Conquin has wished it. Offhorsing, the warden gets behind Billy, the woman limp with fright; Conquin excitably permitting his loading to see what Dampier does. He levels and fires at the mutant. His headback extravasates. What realm that he knew isn't his any longer, other sunfast realms in wait.

Conquin squeezes Billy, puts a hand on her breast, chiming "two of the negligent dead! You've been hired Mr. Mox! Congratulations! What a fucking performance!"

Brimming, the **MIRE** on his forehead reacts with the beat of his heart, throbbing in an umber that devolves to the blue of the eyes of the keeper so pale. He's excited and Billy feels it, the two dead men the cause of his protrusion as he slips and regains his feet, saying "go ahead when you're ready," the volley of shot a conflation of lead more salute to an emir disembarking. Not a man in the horde even shuffles. Neither hoof nor leg embends. Billy and Dampier collapse in the hail where it rolls like a child's shot toy. Conquin scrapes from behind her and cuttingly instructs "please sober to your current position. Such games tend to quash our boredom. You understand our isolation of course."

Fifteen men saddled aft riding include six uncoiling whips, others priming to reload shot arms. A fusty green haze, tinged with beige, floats above their heads. Smoke from the fort and discharged weapons sorbs the air throughout. Conquin gives Mox his option.

"Finished with your playing Dampier?"

"Too much. That many," he answers. He is flat with his face in the hailstones.

"Thank you men! I have them!"

Billy's lucid, her temper decreasing. "Why don't they simply shoot you?"

"A cogent inquiry my dear. I welcome you back from your brink. Truth be told from time to time they enjoy killing each other. But if they consider invoking a legislative terror, well then, there's a dead me, which I say is somewhat dismal. But of course, there is the other." He oscillates his hands to twine them. "Out there gets worse than here. Hereabouts imagination, is limited, infrequent, refuted. Do you understand my position? See what happened to Ruben? Couldn't keep his dead to himself. And of course out there is he." Aten Mire Conquin in parturient silence. He maintains two hands entwined. "What world you hazard unknown. Whereas here you're safe within. Can see and know what's coming. As secure as if a child."

12

BILLY AND DAMPIER lose their days and nights in the tunnel and in their cell. Leeching voices cringingly heard. Allocated as if their own. Ambiguous hail, it taps up tunnel, like codes from a crust annealed, the pair in that ambit above greater depths, where conspirators reek of unkenned tellings and the two in a keep above them. Mulish speech outside their cell as sustenance is rammed through a cut-out. "Gray fuckin food for you. Grab their drawer. I'll fuck you here." Rough housing, squealing from a corridor encuntment. Eight fingers drop through their slot. When balanced the woman on the tunnelside door says "roundsman, in my ass! Your spunk in my fold makes me sick!" The cantilevered whore and the sodomite roundsman exchange grunts and the frame and the crosspiece toggle jostles and loosens within. She says "yes, right there" and "I detest the others" and "you have the largest cock." Billy says "goddamned men. Five words will hoe your garden." Mox patiently watches the fingers. They're red then white then red. He's been blinded and punched and selected for beatings but his pizzle is taught with blood. Embarrassed he hides in the dark of the cell and therein enough for a dozen. Their room, this section of the fort at Mims Nickel is partitioned by earth and ice. Rearward the pair is leaning, Billy in a corner, Dampier to her right, like rain through a bower their backs sopping wet and to their left the crudest of loo. Beneath its chinquapin lid molds the waste of years and above that midden in shit: *Lo, what Barabbas we ain't.* The attic message of mucronate point terminates by a door unlocked. The fingernails of the kept, broken and blooded align from ceiling to floor. Around its frame, overheading the axmilled door an alike enation there grows. A human heart is nailed to the trim. Mugging like a rubicund face. Separated, unaccounted, dispraised. An unusable stony pump. Welling nothing for whereto well?

Dampier ripens the farfetched belief that a day and night have passed. Like a spelunker lured by light he crawls on his hands and knees, clawing at the black as if it will tear, speaking as the darkled speak, not knowing the shape and size of his cell is unique as Conquin requested, eighty in varying poses. After ten minutes fingering the walls and floors he listens for the breath of Billy. She stoically nudges him past. Her words about sleep and permanent night, about what she does when there is no light and there is no light within. "This man Conquin'll rid us."

"No Billy, he'll trade on our presence. Then we'll belong to the other."

"Go the fuck over yonder you goddamned fool! You think that's any better?"

"This'll be solved. I promised."

"Solve what? You stupid ass! What we know for certain is a whore is bein reamed yonder side of that fuckin slot! You can barely see her fingers but the fuckin is clear! Go jerk your meat by the door!"

He goes to the bottom of the saucer shaped pit in the center of the cell they inhabit. He offers the gruel, "no thank you." She refuses to sip their water. Malodorous in a yawning dish. His idea: the cup as a tool. Dampier digs and picks at the wall. Twenty minutes and his fist is through. Firping sound somewhere but it fades. Nosing the aperture he smells cooking meat then fists through the hole to warmth. Barred window. Late evening. Compline. Strafing light on his reached through arm. Curving that arm it is there. A stew of pork and beef. The synchronizing scent of camphor. Decussate light from the shape of her body. His hole then filled with directives.

"Take the clean water firstly! You're nigh three days without it! The majority don't tally usin the cup and some never claw an inch! Conquin declares that's the funniest shit, to jail a motherfucker with the key, while leavin the cells unlocked! You're the first to figure it out! Durin the day he opens the tunnel to thaw these deepest cells! Once roamers with sachets, perfumers you see, come north from the coast and he got 'em! Sat in their cells six months! I finally had Tottern tell 'em to dig afore the wall mended itself! They never thought to check the door! Cells'll droop and drip, then freeze midsummer! Goddamndest clime on earth! He had the first prisoners diggin down here and it amblin past ten below! Them fuckin brutes was shirtless as apes! Hot as hellfire down in it, while up yonder lay froze in feet! That, I do not understand! If you might, explain it to me!"

Mox says, "I don't know," the length of his arm retrieved within before his face is in the hole. In that room her skirts are to neck and she senses he wants to watch, another behind her standing and grunting and his eyes they see Dampier. Hawser rope scars allotted on his throat. Acne brands of a spherical nature. Brazenfaced, occultly feminine. He clutches at her hair, shoves her head in the hole, as her hands brace left and right. Dampier backsteps a stride as she hurls insults behind her. His mind a tolling shambles. The entirety of her skull wallows at the hole, her john wildly jabbing, kneading the flesh on her ample hips and spitting where his shaft she's taken. It runs from her anus to his plunging. He's a man of years with galluses hanging, a vulpine starer either sexed. Torturedly his lust is bled by invective and he at his culminate seeding. The man says, "it's gonna do it."

"Fire that shit on the floor! Or that teeny knobkerrie claimed as a cock I'll reduce to a nub for life!"

"Turn roun' bitch and gimme your mouth! I ain't shootin my fuck on the floor!"

"You sure as shit ain't dousin my tonsils! I ain't a goddamn cultch for your oysters!"

"Stay there," she says and Dampier does. He couldn't retreat if he wanted. She pushes and drops to the balls of her feet before her suitor is rudely dismounted. With her balsam glistening and her bosom-tucked skirts she turns to frig his sex, a series of pumps and his sperm jets fireward, greasing in the flames with her saliva.

"Get the fuck out you bull seeded bastard! Pay Conquin my tip this time!"

She spins her inveigher. He exits. Mox has watched and learned, the woman a harridan with the coarseness of Billy, her extensity of traits he prefers, Mox a foot his side of the crazing hole when the woman calls his name. Lumpingly Mox is there.

"Hey," he says.

Rejoinder: "best livin I can make and ain't fuckin ev'ry hour? Man and pussy don't part."

"Were you the nice lady in the slot? Them was your fingers I reckon?"

"Yep. Yep, I's that lady. The roundsman that dropped your food is the chaplain for the prison here. He mumbles and prays, absolvin your sins, durin the actual plungin. Otherwise, the fucker won't do it. It is a queer profession indeedy, but the man won't touch my roast. The good chaplain prefers the brown-eyed gravy but I hafta instruct his pourin. Ain't humans sour-meant to confound you, if they be humans a'tall?"

"And the food? That food there?"

"This here is for shares. Stew enough for ten. The water is to sup cause it's boiled, but there's dirtier water throughout. Its sick'll make your guts run thu' your fingers, if only to escape its drinkin."

Other statements are made of a general interest before the woman says "imma goin." She pauses aggrievedly searching, as if an ungotten gift were misplaced. She is then from the room and the tunnel at large and Mox hears the order she is given. She responds before it is finished. "I'll fuck 'em, yes, but not till mornin cause my pipes are as raw as hide!" Another query from somewhere aloft and "yes, they're both awake!" While the woman is gone he enlarges the hole with persistent heelfirst kicks. With cool water in his cup he gives Billy a drink and when it's drained she says "I thank you." Back into her corner to sulk. He dips his cup, swirls the liquid, drinks without first testing. The concoction reacts on his tongue. Denudating the buds of his taste.

"That there is for tendin to bodies."

Billy laughs, snorts and coughs. The woman has returned to her room. Dampier appears in the hole. "Sorry, wrong bucket, forgive me."

She sees what he's done to the opening. "You wallowed it good. Ya'll could crawl through. Ain't you gonna eat?"

Both say they aren't hungry, the woman's head through the hole, where she nods at Billy dimlighted. Then back to Dampier's face. She says "give me that arm of yours so I can pluck what pinscrap lodged. Then you Miss Billy, let me have that finger. Your hard sumbitch, what nubbed it, is ridin about somewhere. Men are posted to summon him in."

"He ain't none of mine! He kilt my goddamn people!"

"Well, whatever the case they ain't no sense of the rot takin your life. Need to see if it's black and don't you worry, he'll serve justice in time."

"We ain't bad people," interrupted Dampier.

"That justice ain't referrin to ya'll."

Mox rams his arm to the lateral muscles and inadvertently touches her breast. She allows his thrallment for it holds his attention as she lances and plucks and greases, clean sutures arrayed in a fantail pattern while his hand works at her breasts, sliding between her legs, her skirts on her knees and her womb adrip as his fingers slide in and twist. No pain is felt during his procedure but another comes for his handling. The woman closes her knees to trap his hand, saying "I gotta suck this'n off. Keep your hand where it is. It's fine. Suckin cocks is like brushin my hair." When she squeezes, Dampier, he winces, driving his fingers the same. As she takes the stranger into her mouth he listens to the woman inbreathing, intent on hearing the finish. There's a growl and a grunt and "I thank ye." She then yanks at a finger on the arm she has nursed and inserts it with a limpsy glide. Billy is inattentive.

"Keep that'n movin right there. I'm loathe you see to suck their pricks when they come to me that young. But they finish in thirty seconds. Give Billy somethin to eat, then let me have her hand."

"Come in here and do it."

"Nope, nope, Dampier, I can't. Miss Clarabelle ain't chose death. Last time I touted deception, I was pressed against a Tulip Poplar. Close near to Frankfort, Kentucky. Now I'm fucked daily for life. Don't screw your sister's husband. Not when he's runnin for governor."

"Ain't Missouri exclusive here?"

"My sister and me come from Dora, a farm on Bryant Creek. She went east lookin to court. I followed for an equal swoonin."

Clarabelle asked Billy to please oblige her and Billy cleaned the bowl. She then returned to her corner, saying "thanks," without conviction.

"Billy, she'll see to your finger if you'll put it through the hole."

Dancing chiaroscuro that crossroom vent with the fire on Clarabelle's side. When Dampier shifts there is light. Mox can see that Billy has quit. Knees to neck and arms enfolded, forehead to arms enspliced. Lax mouth, bottom lip extended. Ravening desire for pity. The melt, though winter, was wetting her back as she cursed her farcical youth. What clear future isn't.

Clarabelle won't clemently relieve her as she places her head in the hole. Dampier tumbles back and away. Scarifying she frenziedly screams. "Get your fuckin hand in this openin! A pus-swolt wound shouldn't kill ya! Gimme that goddamned finger!"

Remonstration arouses young Billy. She's obedient when sense has been made. She's bulgy in the corner then stands. Asks Dampier to move. She kneels and presents her outstretched hand. Billy is uncowed, determined. A shaft of light responds on her face. Tear washed cheeks but a stilling muck black she has smeared from head to neck. As if to hide from death. She has worked in the dark withstanding the cold and there's a finger ground symbol on her forehead. A cross of skin with a p reversed. Her sinciput emblazoned like a servile god, therein that vaulted chamber. For if, and when this hardship stops, it's the choice of the ether to stop it, their commands averted like clouds. Go peddle your words where hope presides. It is flailed past dying here.

Billy is unafraid, embroiled and seeking, no earthly place preferred.

"Listen, Clarabelle, is it? What's he want with us?"

"Conquin says that bountyman is comin. Says Threadbare'll split the pot. You're both familiar with him?"

"We know'em. See this bite?"

Clarabelle comforts where the couple doesn't need it. Neither enter her room. Billy should adjust by knowing femininity resides in this quod where they're kept. As if that should matter to Billy. The girl wears a symbol of her own creation, though the two in her midst have ignored this. Clarabelle is frightened and shows it. Softening her tone she mentions escape if Billy and Mox will accompany.

"I know about the money that's due. Five-seventy-five is temptin, but it won't do me any good to betray you, for when we're fount we're all three dead. Either way, someone'll come. That comin ain't our choice."

"How're we gettin free from a prison wantin people to escape? We're caved to rot and your leverage ain't shit unless your cunt is bein tupped."

"Billy, shut your goddamned mouth and stop actin your hairless age! I got the onliest cake worth eatin hereabouts and information will be forthcomin! And it appears Conquin won't rape you, which means you're safe from rape."

"Aye God! You're loonier than nighbreak bats! She's a whore in a fort Dampier!"

Billy yawps, embrowns to dark. Slams down and fumes in her corner. Dampier continues to listen. Wants to know what their risk entails. Clarabelle, this precisian of sexwork fidelity ruefully wags her finger. "Mox, put your gourd through the hole. I ain't that, but what there is." He rams his head and shoulders entirely inside as the woman displays her wares. Scion of a race intemperate. Middle aged with hair streaked gray. Her eyes dark and the fire rubenesques her. The dress is the same as the day of arrest and it wasn't a rag in court. It's now a murmur of hardstood swathing. Her long skirt of green with a white torn blouse is covered by a vest of blankets. Hips well muscled from trulling. She's a diffident beauty and with a tilt of her head, he realizes her years are few. She sees that he sees and the woman is embarrassed and demurs from his stare and that seeing. Drudgery has pasted where reality inflicts and the sores about her mouth are pursy. Clarabelle is twenty-three.

"Listen here Mox, my middlins are a mess and I need to rinse my mouth. Gotta visit Conquin in the perch. And don't fret for he's always impressed. At the rate of his drinkin I can get what's needed followin my ass or a hand. Might glean the place of exchange if that mongrel ain't ridin direct. Of course, what I get might be lies."

"He'll come," says Mox. "He wants Billy. Thank you for helpin us."

"Take the us outta that Dampier! She ain't done a goddamn thing!"

"Damn you little bitch!"

Clarabelle with her stricture remains by the fire but wants to lunge through the hole. Her fists are spruced with red. Don't test the girl symbolic. You can't decipher her cryptic message. When they mark themselves without proper reason the reason is in the marking, which Billy refuses to speak of. There are annals where history stops.

Billy says "invite the whore in." Clarabelle refuses the offer.

*

Cold sphery night in a courtyard bleak. Variegate starlight is held and reduced then abandoned by comets streaking. Known colors that you name ersatz unused and you forget how things defy you. Prisoners mill and ask for favors. She responds that Conquin has called. While she winds his stairway the game begins separate for men with guns. Five trustees propel the match while Conquin, in his nest, is above them. His quarters built high, higher than the walls, so he can see and decide and harass. He's already at work as Clarabelle ascends and Conquin ignores her knock. Snapping his fingers a croupy trustee looks and Conquin says "run him. Which one? The larcenist bastard. I'd claimed his mother's bay for my rides."

"This'un?" The trustee points. Conquin replies "yes, him."

The boy of sixteen was devoid of English and a year for his theft he has suffered. Murraine from his hunting, transferred through the meat, has settled in his system to blind him. It is gradual, pronounced, then steep. In an eastern portal, a squat door for egress, he is joined by a tribal accomplice. Their mother has been gunned while sacking her water in a meatcamp Conquin has raided. The bay was the mount she was loading. The boy of sixteen is spoken to gently by his friend and his brother and his charge. In Shoshonean he is told that first shot survival will not bring a second. His sentence commuted outright. The alternative, attainable death.

Clarabelle listened to the banter of the men. Cursed Conquin for permitting the gantlet. Without welcome she pushed through his doorway.

"Must you insist on that game? You're a man of stature and most devoted. It's barbarous, indecent and cruel."

"I don't have to insist because I am this game. Emmit! Cut him loose!"

Clopping his feet the Ute is released but he has not queried his path. His accomplice and brother adjusts him serenely into a goading, headlong dash. He has warred and defended and swears at Conquin to fire until his lead is finished. A hirsute vest skinned from a bore covers his torso to waist. In his mind the vest is impenetrable. This impulse as strong as belief. He trips and gains his feet, anxious to run but he stops and turns where Conquin can see him clearly. He challenges the keeper to fire. Youth and no light bilged from the moon ever as quick as he. Bestridden some rocks he picks a round stone and slings it at Conquin's perch. It rises to mark but misses his head. The warrior is blindly fortunate.

"I like this little fuck. Better than a man that quits."

Admiringly Conquin lays grievance. Against the boy and his youth and his arrogance. He's otiose in grabbing the weapon. Five years ahead of its patent the smoothbore diffracts in its case. Belgium made and inscribed with care: *PARATUS* in kern, the Latin projecting, as if its firing were a terminal point. The end of the need for casuistry. What wrong made right inherent. At any speed or condition, sun or black night, Conquin could lead and kill. There were men he'd shot neath the cowl of night with a ball that seemed suspended. They ran to its waiting then dropped. Illuminatingly drunk he takes it in hand. The sprinting brave gone askew. He's fifty yards afield when Conquin notices the case has been thoroughly damaged. The tallow from a candle has spilled. The silk where charred is a feathery white and Conquin says "who did this?" He sniffs the air, the Ute is thirty yards further, the barrel wiped for there's gunk on the Latin, Conquin polishing till it gives back. "That savage dexterity is firm in my mind but I wager he'll run on a rope!" He admits Clarabelle's presence. "Oh you, there you, am I correct, will that non-seeing fucker run straight?" Clarabelle looks and correct he is, the last cloud that night rehoused northwest to molest the moon no more. The plain is given to light. The tectum of sky revealed. A celandine moon with cantankerous grip vomits its shine to earth and there is nothing you cannot see. Still Conquin casually wipes. As patient as the growth of a tree.

"Will you have a tumbler of spirits? I'll load whilst you sip your drink."

"He's shimmied from the straight and is headed for them boulders where you had them two pent in."

Conquin looks and "so he is! The shrewdest of eyes you have in that head and I'm done if he gets in there!"

The weapon is gravely lifted. A pilule of metal is rubbed by his thumb and a sight clicks and extends, the dorp of boulders a hundred yards distant, the brave assisted by shouts of direction and he knows the rocks will protect him, there detected a shinnying light, like children descending from trees. The Ute will use their cover to furtively find the river. His cohorts will remember he was the first to succeed, though Conquin to date hasn't missed a man in the gantlet. One has been slain in front of the rocks and the Ute will be his second, the fire of conviction everywhere present until his hand met the boulder, and blind or no, Conquin was bereft his challenge. The brave halted and spun to boast. "Oh me, oh my, fuck yes! A death defying, arrogant bastard!" He fires, there's a roar, his left arm elevates, unbuckles from the joint without bias and such is a hideous thing. He goes down with a sigh but held to this world. Lying flat he chortles his prayers. Cloudy faced Conquin then yelled at his men as lacteal boresmoke congealed.

"Wait you ingrates! That was my shot! See if that arm will bleed him!"

Impatient the horde in front of the gate awaits with glumness the order. A lull then the brave is standing, the Ute bloodprinting the rocks with his stump as the vim of his prayers increase. He is chanting the name of his mother, pallbeared by the stones in a sanguineous manner and her name there wailed to export him.

Sluggishly dragging his feet, the brave swaddles the wound and walks toward the fort and Conquin is elated on sight. "Look there Clara! He's bloodloss confused and wants to come back home! Go ahead, you bastard fucks! The coup is yours to have! No shooting! I keep my word!"

The trustees had the main gates opened to defile with trotting ascesis. Their arrangement of weapons began with a maul and increased with a marshaling sharpness. The brave reversed his stumble and ran. When he stooped, he fell, the appendage on the ground, and he gathered his arm to defend. The fronthorsing trustee laughed at the tribute and heckled and faulted for Conquin. He slid from his hip and across the raised pommel a pistol he has concealed. It was miniscule, quiet and their melee would tamp it, his shot would be swallowed by sound.

Conquin says, "look at that man." Realizes the shooter is missing. He then reloads with quintessence and beauty. Like the motion is a rite required.

"Tsh, tsh. Disappointing my Clara."

"What of disappointment my dear?"

"The best do abound with betrayal. You can't trust the Irish for shit."

The throng reined heavily and paneling dust surfaced the brave and boulders. Conquin's shot has landed. The offending trustee feels something pass through him and where his footing was surer it weakens. He remains in the saddle with illimitable breaths until those breaths are gasps. Glimpsing the hole in his chest, another says, "Mackey, you're kilt." They watch death invest in a cranberry trickle, the pour from his chest and back staining halos, though what is felt is insensate. Conquin has severed his spine. Another inrushing boots this man Mackey from his horse and life and memory. His animal is hazed into their paltry remuda. It lifts a hoof like a woman being kissed. From the parapet Conquin's plaudit. Machicolating like fiery missiles.

"Three cheers for me! Two dead! Check that fucking Ute! Deceased! Yes or no!"

The matricide Plapus who has drowned his own mother dismounts and walks to the brave. Eyes open on his back gurgling blood but the flow from the stump has stanched. Plapus says "reddy, are you dead?" Perplexed he walks from the grouping horses with his beetling forehead bunched. "Naw sir! Reddy is livin!"

"He's yours then boy! Send him!"

Plapus imperatively muses a second before plunging a knife through his breastbone. As if the choice was a virtuous blading. The Ute's penis is removed and shoved in his mouth and they giggle and consider their humor.

"Gentlemen!" The men face Conquin. There's a blue on the moon, which is sapphire. "Never-ever a shot after or before any of the shots I include! You do not fucking shoot! We keep our oaths in here! Otherwise we'll harbor unholy resentment and stray from God's own path! The blind heathen was bested and failed, but Mackey cheated his death!"

Leeward of his weapon they cautiously defense with horseflesh and eyes asiding. Eight horses in a line with their riders on foot walking behind their necks. Conquin's sported their numbers before. Amongst them were whispers of the infidels' fate when it came to the whims of their warden. The boy named Plapus, the matricide toper, suggests that the fort be taken and they respond he should take it himself, a Dunker called Virmach telling the boy that his needing to thorn unseen quarry was the equal of hunting oneself. Plapus goes missing the following day and each of the days thereafter. Spiders awaken this warden. In the deepest of sleep their shuffle as ambient as the spuming of creation itself. He hears everything.

Back in the perch they have settled. Clarabelle's opinion is heard.

"Two more dead for the reckoning. Both downed in moonlight dark."

He has attempted to forget she is there, but she speaks from the middle of the room. She impregnates his solace with the harshness of presence and bloats the room disproportionately. Conquin blows through the bore of his musket, rag wiping some oil from his hand, lowering the sight by pressing the pilule, lightly and then with force. As he cleans and examines the weapon she uncomprehendingly stands there waiting. He cannot ignore her to leave. The **MIRE** on his forehead raillery light as he scolds the woman's invasion.

"I completely forgot you were here. Never speak first or enter my perch unless invited or trailing my lead."

"Perhaps that pickle would prefer a man's ass if my presence offends your lordship."

"Ah yes, your American incredulity. So Clara…"

"Clarabelle please!"

"I humbly beg your pardon. How many transactions today?"

"Six with the chaplain but I took my time with the pair as you asked me to do."

"Any interest from Mox in your love?"

"He diddled me through the wall. Fingerfucks like his hand is a duckbill."

"Billy is rather incendiary?"

"She ain't more than fourteen and has run the west. Yes, she's a tit combustible."

"With proper incentive might she ply your trade? Diligent lay that you are."

"Mox'll have to die first. He might be overprotective."

"Yes, our Mox, I think he'll be next. Maybe run him on Wednesday or Thursday. We're rather overcrowded here at the lodge and it appears that fellow who brings in the water has also delivered the plague. We've compromised environs about. I'm considering a cull of the symptomatic fools. Perhaps I'll walk them through the parvis yonder under ruse of cleaner air. Let nature and the elements and the beasts dissolve them and maybe the rest won't suffer. Did you know, in Europe, these plagues are instructive, but here the openness will cure it, by feeding it human flesh. No reason for all to be crowded and sick when a few can fend for themselves."

"Won't that weaken protection? The tribes'll see 'em leavin the Nickel."

"A few will do for the exodus. Besides, the buffalo drifted. The winter, where mild, has drawn them away and perhaps they'll graze northeast. The savages will follow the herds."

"All won't follow them fuckin big cows but there is another solution. Offer that bountyman an interest for protectin where prisoners can't."

Conquin was pacing from her left to right in the twenty by twenty perch. Then the warden bit his own tongue. Spat blood in a lunate suffusion. He coughed and gathered his wits. Raising both his hands he framed her face and kept that face from movement. "Clarabelle, put your eyes right here." Bladefuls of iris in founder. The table's candle chisels their shape. "Clarabelle, my precious, with that man, we'll deal as infrequently as possible. Case in point and fact concerning the pair and this is how I see it: by releasing those two he'll spend their lives toying with each in turn, until their graves are covered and crossed. Otherwise they'd be released. Not being an issue for Missouri."

"He ain't partial to the money that's in it?"

"For her he would fuck his own horse. Dampier Mox was his primary interest but he seems to be taken with Billy. Otherwise, myself, I would've already plucked her or had you both together."

"Have you seen 'em?"

"No, I haven't. But there are those who have and all remember the day, the time and the details. As if the race of man were held collective while Threadbare impressed those louts. Their stories are grand to hear, but disturbing in the company of ladies."

"But not to a man like you?"

"I'm refined my dear and will admit I wasn't reared on potatoes and liquor. Lesser beings' games hone survival but there it stops for me."

"You mean killin and what it accompanies?"

"No. Simple control o'er my kingdom. Intimidation. Extortion. Bribery. I hated to shoot that boy. But an example had to be made. Go lie down on the bed."

Clarabelle does as requested. It's a triple cot frame adorned with lowered posts so while sleeping he wouldn't be shot. Not from the courtyard below. He removes his shirt, his exertions bold smoking from body, mouth and clothing. She looks at the dish-shaped whelms, the bruises yellow and black, their nucleuses burned with wax. Unblistered is the nape of his neck. A patch on his back right shoulder. The remainder welted and whealed. Someone, whomever, has done this to him and he has received it willingly. She comes to foot to sit where he writes and tousles through his missives. His flagellatrice hasn't responded.

"Is that love? She got in her licks. Never seen a man that whooped."

"Of course it's love. She's a lady like you. Miner's wife from the Sangre de Cristo's. Powerful winch who obviously learned not to fear my tastes. Quite the complex pleasure. She struck quick then I struck back. Don't be jealous my precious. I dispatched the harlot on the night received. Watched while the wolves consumed her. As I said, complex pleasure."

"You killed a whore, left a husband to pine?"

"Indeed I did. With him as my witness. A fuck fast world it is."

"I've seen worse than you. Boosted their wallets for pleasure."

"Yes, I'm sure you have."

"On Threadbare. Rumors or outright lies? Any of it true a'tall?"

"Mere tales Clarabelle. Some are valid. There is color in the boldest lie."

"May I hear the truth?"

"Can you hear the truth in question? May is a month for warmth."

"Anything to quell the drudgery."

"Any tale at all?"

"Truth or lies. It don't matter."

13

CONQUIN SAID THREADBARE'S selected pursuits knew no border but what wroth knew and those boundaries weren't held by land. His chase was an issue prosaic. He researched a bounty, its peccant provisions, the how and why of offense. Back in those months of Iturbide's reign he recessed in Agua Prieta. Here he decided to pause on the bounty of a poet who feasted on children. His poems were ascribed to source. Threadbare recited, read through his verses, ten quatrains entrusted to memory. The swath of this pedant, its catamite splutter, stretched from the pines of Franco Louisiana and was slated to end in Sonora, Threadbare pushing the poet north to the desert and there the wordsmith stumbled. His tracks were a drag, shifting maniacally, and Threadbare knew he was dying. It looks in track like it does in person. Tristful and bolderously weighty. He gave a Mexican fossick a ten dollar piece to search for the poet's remains. Told him if or when the body was found to cairn the spot with stones. The fossick said your deed will be done. After waiting an hour he followed. Casually walking his horse. In their camp that night he scrawled the memorized quatrains in ink he'd leeched from datura. The hide of a civet his tablet. He corrected the poems, augmented factotums, becoming a nidus for souls, for the duped wanting words to transfigure, though Threadbare's command would change. He told the fossick when the corpse of the poet was found, to take the corrections Threadbare had made and shove the words down his gullet. Wedge the scroll in the simpleton's throat. As deep as his fingers could manage. "Seguramente," replied the fossick. Then Threadbare tripled his payment. Warned him for water was scarce. "Con cuidado," said the hunter. "El desierto es un sueño permanente. No hay palabras en èste."

The next to draw his attention was a looter and a robber of lower class means but popular offense with his people. He took as he wished from the wealthy and able, fording and refording that uppermost river, going north to commingle with the southwestern tribes and there invited to trade his plunder. The militia was summoned, but their podgy bulk made them partial to bivouac and comfort. Their Mexican officers, in the matter of this brigand, were the capital's studious elite, though they tended to war by candle. A month then a year soon passed. Enlightened Europe printed tomes of revolt. These crossed the Atlantic, shipped into the gulf to embolden clannish guerillas of the ilk of the brigand himself. As his fame superseded his ten man army his legend would become his undoing, for martyrdom was Threadbare's forte. He waited for a break in the pattern of the bandit and he stopped to spend his monies. The first and last time he would do it, the last and first time he would try.

Threadbare followed the brigand to the port of New Orleans, going west from there to the place he was hiding his wife, child and their valuables; disbanding his group while he bought up land, attending that business with cash. He purchased waterfront acreage from established plantations, filing his claims with a notary, behaving as if to remain, ten Mexican bounties and five in the states hounding his every transaction. And Threadbare had claim on each. They were contractually generous, redounding with riches, a substantial retirement for a man deemed mortal, but a heteroclite beast has been hired. To Threadbare pelf means books and weapons, what food he will need for the day. Extra coin is given as alms. Seeing him, it doesn't make sense.

On the day of the replevy absent of courts he confesses at the church of a prelate before hiring a woman for company. Threadbare is behind them on a tree-lined path as he strolls with the harlot to the edge of the ocean where they enter a copse of tamarack. Incult screams, two quick thuds, and the bandit runs from the copse. Threadbare buries the woman. A misogynist excludes any haste or the bonus for his head to be punctually delivered. Threadbare will take his time. His mastery the ticking clock. He's desirous that prey sense its demise. Perceiving the hours as sand.

Separate from the logic of a standard cuffing or a shot to snuff his life, Threadbare is a man of invention. Back to the wife and child. This woman is as bold as the bandit she has wed, taking their son into Baton Rouge where she shops as she pleases with scripts of remainder for her husband will right the difference. In these days there were Baton Rouge merchants come northeast with Mexican holdings. They knew of her husband and to them she spoke Spanish with her vanity arriving before her. She scrutably milked for attention, Threadbare listening to her brummagem speech, shading himself beneath the ambient moss, its hood besteading as a greygreen protector as he waited for the heat of the day, when the shopkeepers closed for an hour and the deserted street would be his. He watched the woman with the child behind her, the pair leeringly rapping at the shops that were closed, their louverslanted windows and *REVENIR* signage unacceptable to the woman as posted. She'll tell her husband they are plotting against her.

To their hostel he follows them smiling. The building is a safehouse the bandit has purchased to evade his incessant pursuers. What the citizens would recall were the quandarized sightings and the jaunty demands of the wife, the child as unmemorable as a petal of clover having fallen from its other three siblings.

Threadbare walked through the door of their opulent room

and tore the two from their bed. Placed a lien on the bandit to collect them.

"That's just another murderous tale! My God Conquin, there's a child involved! I'm not impressed or overwhelmed! For Godsakes, finish your yarn!"

Conquin laughed when Clarabelle spoke. She'd interrupted when the story was embellished. Rumors nurture to fact. What she wanted was a painting of an earlier time with the reason and the justice taken from a people who hired a ruthless servant, when they each had more than enough to spare though reluctant to spare a crumb. She wanted Conquin to prefer the bandit. Wants a victor and a burning parade.

"And when you're done tellin there lies a dead whore and a wife and child have perished. It don't scare me a bit. That type of passion ain't studied no more. As for the whore she's another dead whore."

"I never said the pair would die. I'm not sure for the thing gained multiple parts. Ordained and unique as is reckoning."

Conquin walked to the window as she drew the knife. Sliding it back she left it, the blade nicking the side of her breast. *Not yet, not here,* she thought. "You said he placed a lien on the bandit?"

"I did."

"You have my interest."

"The truth, I suppose, is his."

He strapped the wife and child on two separate horses and led them northwest by night. A thousand miles later they were dumped from imagining into the actual of what he had planned. Those plains a redoubtable ocean. The woman and child were foully accoutered, but they had not died of exposure. Fed and watered throughout. Grubby faced and exhausted they stared at their abductor who motioned where water should be. About-facing the horses he told them "on foot it is easier to live, for you can hide where horses cannot. Avoid a chase," he said. With the clothes on their backs he left them. They found water and then they found plain. In a week their shoe leather failed them. The bandit had nothing to lead him. What relevance would law include? He was wanted and Threadbare as sire of that wanting chained the hands of the bandit if found. There was a clue surrounding a Pawnee's sighting but the bandit was a southerly concern. In the pitch of the night a woman and child expansing polychromatically, were beings traipsing as spirits, no more or no less than a membrane of life and evidence that life has evolved. Another crinkled and deceasing fluorescence. Plodding specters and ghosts on the plains they inhabit are as they themselves will be. The Pawnee could not help him.

"He dropped it? Lost interest? Quit?"

"The bandit?"

"Yes, of course."

"His undoing was confusion for there was no one to ask and no response would be given. Live or die, who knew and cared. He, himself, alone. The abyss is itself unrelenting when your world is empty throughout. No more did this man plunder. His mind and his martyrdom tenuous. No relying there. The bounties were rescinded on Threadbare's word and with that the bandit excised. He never had nor would exist. What stories were told became others and others became those tales."

"No capture, bodies or heads?"

"No need of the former and the latter is illusion. We're speaking about Threadbare's honor. It was told the three had vanished. Better yet, been absorbed. What they were became its own fiction. Said gods of a whimsical realm. A story the night disgorged. The only one we know to tell."

14

CONQUIN GATHERS THE culled at dawn. Assembles the group in front of Mims Nickel where the brave was issued then murdered. Here there are men with evident symptoms and men suffering from others. A soldier much affected by the grasp of the sickness has seen this malady prior. Wizened veteran of America's revolt. He remembers those warm weather camps, the lessons of a Prussian physician, the sinewy rifleman knowing if grouped he can serve the men with the ailment. Before abandoning his cell he asks to see Conquin. The interview is granted, the old legs climbing, he emphatically arranging his thoughts. Conquin says "stand in the door. From there you can speak, go ahead."

"You gotta clean the enclosures, boil drinkin water and bury what the body rejects. Fewer'll die in a month. I seen this afore, lessons of war and ain't them the blackest of clouds? The dyin'll cease if you heed me. It'll pass if measures are took."

"Then Paterson my man, remain at Mims Nickel and I'll appoint you exclusive counsel. Director of shit and piss."

"I ain't here to be heckled. It'll get worse. It's somethin adorin a home. When the cold gets gone it'll strip this place and disburden you of your works. Your arrogance embittered your ignorance, till both as one are the same."

*

Conquin is cheery and has not slept and is pendulous on his bay before them, drunkenly and agogingly wanting their deaths for he's selected the expelled himself. As for the veteran's infraction he cannot recall what he'd done, what caused his transfer. "Paterson, what did you do?"

Paterson steps forward from the line of the affected. "Filed a pension from a county of slavers. Not bein a slaver myself. I wasn't raised to hate."

"You're a blackamoor lover? Mims Nickel repays you. You're free to resume your equality. Go coddle your imbecile slaves!"

Paterson, the apotheosis, shuffles foot and bandied legs: "Conquin, hottest hell is your just deserts but I refrain my judgment on that. Bein cut loose with the lepers hereabouts will more than make me glad, cause what freedom there is ain't here. I'll die in the cold enjoyin the scenery. Fuck you and your goddamned prison. I ain't got strength to holler."

Conquin is taken aback, but wishes to part good termed.

"Always remember here at Mims Nickel you're welcomed to roam as you please! There's never been a bond on any of your lives and as proof these men are free! Beware, the passes are icy this year and I wish you all the best! Paterson, have you a rebuttal?"

The malnourished bend and stand, myopically aloof and hurting. Too much time afoot. Paterson is ill but angry. Sparring, he gives context: "free as you say and free as we choose wasn't the freedom I'd minded. I took three British balls that sit in my chest but I never swayed in them fields. There was more liberation twixt the blast of them muzzles than any of my days hereabouts. We're free cause you know we will die. Better to die out yonder. Better to die by him."

"We thank you Paterson for your sacrificial flesh!" He peruses the motley assemblage. Paterson's eleven glare back. "You intend to lead them Mr. Paterson? Look what you have to work with!"

They're a ransacked scald of human flesh. Ill-kempt.

Transmogrified. A gamut of bodies grieving. They are counterfound humans, silhouettes contrapuntal, inferential, bewildered and tottering. Paterson responds from their center. He need not be lionized.

"Well Conquin, I don't know. I was born to a mother my birth did steal. Saw Delaware become our first state. I'm at a loss as to what you'll accept. I ain't much for oration but if you insist them heights seem easier than here. Each can go where he chooses. If not, I'll be glad to help him."

Paterson stomped his foot. He gave a muffled command whose caesural bars deflated and rose again. The warden's mount snap reared, his chest to pommel, the bay giddily simpering and spinning, avoiding Paterson and Paterson susurrant.

"Ho there boy! They're soon to be gone! Your scents offend my animal!"

Amongst the evicted is a former slave whose catarrh rale his wide chest. The man is nineteen stone, six and one half feet, but his cough halves his height like a scythe. The knees of his pants sequester his fingers as he twists the innumerable patches, stacked and resewn and so overly mended his fingers allude his flesh, as if no knees within. Paterson patted the width of his back, watched the skin turn calcareous gray, the former slave said "thank you, I'll be alright. Gimme a minute. We'll go."

"Take the time you need. Look yonder, the sun is peekin."

A lackluster ochreous pelting of rays displants the gloom immediate. A man in the group says "that ain't sun, that there is a penitent moon." Eleven laugh, but one cannot, the ex-slave says "my lungs are bleedin."

Four years earlier the slave tossed his owner from a window for selling his wife. Before the event the slave wouldn't speak, he did what was asked and excelled. He was waiting for his buyer to offend him, that offense an admittance of debt, the plantation owner claiming her selling a message received from angels. His

God undeniably managed accounts. Transfers of human flesh. His reward, defenestration. The gazebo broke his fall. After breaking his neck. Since there was no witness to convict him, there wasn't a slave to convict. The wife died of fever on a sublet plantation, the escapee fleeing to Missouri where he stole a spool of thread, the knees of his pants needing mending. The white judge enjoyed his coughing. Being a consumptive he went unhung and it was hoped the man would suffer. In Mims Nickel daily he has.

Next to the ex-slave in those vagabond ranks was a vaquero adrift from his outfit. He took the wages he was owed, shook hands with the men and kissed his father goodbye. More adventurer than vandal he followed the rivers and the high mountain creeks that fed them, until Conquin saw him sleeping in a glade. He approached to converse and the vaquero asked smiling if the state of Missouri spoke Spanish. Conquin replied that Spanish Missouri sold but its nobles he knew. They were housed in an estate entitled Mims Nickel, those palatial grounds due west. Tottern translated, laughed, then chided, the boy given a decade. Fourteen years old but his months at the Nickel were few for the sickness as culprit, arrived to level the prison. Mumbling in Spanish he has told the ex-slave that the illness was a woman who wore a bonemask with a robe of russeted silk. When her feet touched the ground her hair filled the cells and if it touched you the symptoms resulted. The ex-slave asked Tottern for an adequate translation but the trustee has failed to explain it. Said the boy was scared of confinement. A month prior to Conquin's expulsion of the sick the ex-slave has comprehended, and with Paterson's assistance they act. The vaquero and black with the blessing of Conquin winter camp in sight of the perch. They dig their own hovel, drink running stream water and bury their waste in compress. Others decried their efforts. Paterson asks to join them, but Conquin replies "no father, another has been sent that is well." The trustee he handpicks spies and reports and after that expulsion is imminent. Conquin wants the three of them dead. During the interregnum they cut strips from their coats making masks when forced inside. Other plagues they duly expect, their pitiful filters enabled by hecklers with quotes from Biblical plaguement, before Conquin stitched a mask of his own.

When Tottern himself seeks the source of the beldam he questions the boy directly. Is the hag floating her curse through the Nickel something sent from below? The vaquero responds with frankness.

"No es una bruja. Es una belleza. También, es un perdón."

The ex-slave and vaquero do not have the symptoms. Consumption afflicts the former. Our vaquero pretends he is wasted. The beldam avoids them fully. They're spared her touch by leaving.

*

Voluminous distance, the dozen gaze east, morosely stamping defiant. There on the plain with Mims Nickel affining and a melisma of voices about, crescive squawking, a cadenza of bustle, then Conquin addresses the fort. "Shut the fuck up! Let them see!" The twelve have a plenum of range outflowing before the mountains await them as told, their imprint geometric like fundament scaffolds where the attrited can climb to the heavens. The agnostic tumble from sky. The expelled, the men that are sick, should fear if sick or not, the plain and the snow and the woods in succession pocked with inequitable hazard, before the foot switchbacks to climb. The disciple amongst them, their purveyor of hope, raises his hands to assuage. When Paterson speaks they listen. For who or what will they listen besides, though Paterson's voice is subdued.

"Here on the plains or in yonder ridges the eyes of our God won't dim. There are people we'll find that're eager to assist and though sparse these men can be found."

Conquin applauds, his trustees too, as the warden sketches their predicament.

"But these men, their camps, you'll see, are beyond the legs you have! Three quarters of you will die in a week! Said legs buckling like fawns! And I pray myself, that your deaths are the harshest for inviting your pestilence here! Manson, please forward these estimable parishioners with the tip of your quirt and boot! May your memory fade and dissolve! Fuck the lot! I hope you all die!"

"Move motherfuckers! Go to it!"

Manson enacts to start the droll column by striking with quirt the men in the line who sit for they cannot stand, the piebald surface upon which the men walk corrugated from the rains that have passed. They shuffle onward, incarnadinely impoverished; this Manson small, black headed, a dark beard and he's vacant of humor, flip or otherwise; rarely seen on foot or in bed, a harpy tattoo red bound on his neck and the artist has fed her with leeches. They dribble from her rectum, circle his neck before returning between her cheeks. Part bird and priestess, afeared in this company, Manson exhorts her salvation, says the harpy alters perception of what a woman should be. When he found the rank bawd to tattoo it, she embossed it then gave him the clap. Manson cut out her tongue, sliced off her hands and he applauds these mitts at the men, slaps them like toasted leather. This Manson, trustee, iniquitous human, will receive his absolution. Remission for what he can't do. Not for what he has done.

When he sees the ex-slave pausing to cough he assaults with a notable tempest.

"Hey you! Goddamn you boy! Stay with the line or I'll carve me a piece of that black to roast on a spit!"

"I ain't under you Manson." He coughs. Blood down his chin. "My keeper is me and these men. You come offa that horse and you're dead."

Manson doesn't respond. He quirts two who're dighted like skeletons, their palpable spines revealed, his strike imprinting a fleur-de-lis and when they yelp Paterson reacts, as Manson tugs at his pistol; the ex-slave, tremendous, fractures the line, his hack heaving with auding and echo, heightened with tension and rage. He steps athwart foul Manson and the stricken men, the trustee whirling his horse, doffing his pistol to fire. Conquin pulls up on a singler in boot, shoots the air and Manson ceases. The keeper then climbs to his perch, the Belgium there encased, the weapon irrefragable and loaded, for the probing of commenceable death. Conquin lifts and kicks at the window, selects and taps the pilule. A Mississippian named Vill is shot while supported, the ex-slave and vaquero attending. The man's head constringes to nothing but thrapple for his skull is a belch of spray. The wrists that they hold crack once and crook and Vill is never again.

"Better off done," says the ex-slave. "I'd likely take a ball myself."

The vaquero acknowledged what he strove to relate then gave the victim his due.

"Fue Vill. Vill de Mississippi."

Later that day Paterson halts at a stream larded with an infantile geyser, the sulfurous water holding no shape from its abysm beneath these men. "Piedras," said the lowly vaquero. Paterson responded, "can we?" The ex-slave additioning "yes. Make a bath. Get these men warm." After rocking the geyser infiltrated, and though it seeped it held and smoked. An hour then two and the temperature plummeted and when the ex-slave is replaced at his labor his cough has sapped his strength, the community of men more than the jailed and Vill is missed for his wit. When one has to rest another steps forward and there are those who cannot move, these men speaking kindly if they cannot work and there were others who prayed forthwith. As they finished their casement the boy vaquero hasn't faltered nor will he sit. He walks across and he sees where the horses have watered and his words are a bleeding remote, jumbled in the ears of the men. Paterson knows what the boy has found. Doesn't need to ask any questions.

"Them muddy prints is from unshod ponies. Light and quick for dispersal."

"Could be any or several riders. Could be no rider a'tall."

"Unlikely," he responded and the ex-slave nodded and they were there as there is solvable, currently solvable not. "There are riders on the backs of them ponies. That patch, them prints, they're backward looking. We're followed and tailed we are." Paterson takes a branch from the roiling stream and selects a mottled hoofprint. Colored wine like the hoof is bleeding. "Somethin substantial rides that one."

They group and those that cannot rise anecdote related subjects. Like circling pagans with beggarweeds broken they point to discuss what comes. They tandem here and there; "it is this" or "that" and the boy vaquero says "no, obscuridad." Without an article, "obscuridad." Not a man pays him any attention. They should've paid attention throughout.

"They're paints. One tribe or another. Wouldn't think they'd try us here. We're diseased and they know where we are. Eight miles from the Nickel or better I reckon and what've we got to take?" The ex-slave says his peace, lowers his chin and Paterson wants his name. He replies, "it holds no earthly significance. Here or otherwise." The ex-slave then wades the stream, the light briefly diffusing with its syrettes of beams, his arms around the last of the rocks they will need with the hem of a moon cumbersomely wending and if not for the trees they could see it. While he hefts the ultimate stone there are those that are pensive amongst them. The vaquero appears at his elbow. He reaches to his face and to the black's nose. Two plague masks soggingly pile. Their expressions can now be seen.

"No son indios hombre."

Addressing the black he looked back at the men. In a phalanstery mortal they're arranged about Paterson as if something approached from without. He has no answer but knows what is said. Save wonder no response is given. He then says "it is some thing." Some thing separate from men without food and beings exposed to nature, their torsos drawn and burrowed with eyes steeled like lentic fish, trapped pooling in isolate circles.

"Some thing?" asks the black.

Paterson responds with meekness and confusion: "some thing or another I guess."

"Okay then," but his cough steals his words and places his hands on his knees. Nonchalantly a palm is lifted for the vaquero not to cross. "Son, please wait on me." The boy trips headfirst in the water and for him the black has meant it, the vaquero believing for an instant, that the group was planning his death, he being the halest amongst them. When he rises kneedeep he rose contrary and his tone of distrust was translatable. Death on that tongue, negated reluctance, as the conflict rushed through a funnel. Any and all in spin. The black said "enough" and remanded to hacking as the vaquero brandished the jackknife. He lunged to pith the black's fleshy back but sliced a seam instead, the ex-slave coughing furious and then he isn't coughing, his feet spread apart to receive him.

"You ought not fight from the water. We're about to build you a coffin."

Raxley Hide is weak from effusion but knew the vaquero would die. He intervened from his back with two round stones lying beside his head, Hide as ambidextrous as a bluedeep squid and the stones are the size of plums. He came to his hip, threw right handed, and the jackknife landed on the bank, the vaquero closing his fingers. As the second is launched the black said "boy," both his hands going to his knees. No cough nor blood nor sound. The ex-slave rubbed his chest and waited.

"Enough," said Hide. "We need you. Not one, we need you both." On the bank that opposed the fracus, Raxley Hide hip sat for their eyes. When he had their attention he begged Paterson's pardon in dehydrated febrile speech. "The boy ain't seein tracks. The boy is seein track. Them is Threadbare's prints. What you deem as three ponies is a weight solitary on whatever the fuck he's ridin. He's rode it up and down the bank. Know'd where Paterson would bring us. Now listen big'un, and the boy there also, cause I know you know what I'm sayin. They's eleven remainin after Vill got his. If you result the death of the other, Paterson is left to defend us, and him beyond his biblical tally. We're eight mile from the Nickel, but the Nickel can't thwart what's bearin a course goin west. You see if I don't make sense." Raxley Hide then softens his speech. Mother's lips to the ear of her baby. As he prepares to finish his statement, a jointure of blood and sepia liquid leak downbody and drool from his calf and he feels it and watches and turns. Raxley Hide then says "I'm fine," before speaking to the vaquero directly. "Young fella, cross to my front. Stop sloshin the hell around. You get cold and you won't get warm. See that I mean to help ya."

The vaquero obeyed, the jackknife resheathed and he crossed to stand by Hide. In broken English he made amends, to the black and the men and the conflict as seen was accepted as past and done. No other contention here. Both Hide and Paterson commented on the actual, the worth of what men will do, and in that doing for others.

"Glad that's finished," Hide said. "They's enough brutal comin to quell, without us addin our own. Threadbare'll kill us for sport. He won't waste his powder. Conquin don't know shit. Cause nothin would charm that bastard more than to watch us killin ourselves. With that, although, it ain't gonna stay, I'd like to try and eat. If I can tab enough gumption we'll dig Vill's grave and those that are able can help. He's a Cath'lic I think and would want a stone so the Cath'lic god can find 'em. That's a good thought to have. Is there a decent weapon amongst us? Asides the boy's sticker?"

Paterson produces an old fireflint relic from a diversity of parts he's smithed. Seems cognizable to damage its shooter. He says "this'll fire straight but my powder is wet," and the debate on their arms is clotured. Hide smiled and said "sun'll dry your powder, but we better not take the offensive, partial chance we'll be outgunned."

Laughter in that pack and that laughter is degenerative and exanthema dark oppresses, dampens speeches and bodies and hopes, a man called Leekes asking for water before repeating the name of a child. The vet Paterson fills his palms, takes them to the lips of Leekes'. With that sip they remain, staring at the hands of Paterson, the last name summoned the child in his mind and if he or she were able to hear it, would they know their father has passed? As if in summons their lives were maintained, whereas his, this Leekes, has left them. There is symmetry in what you forget. Recollection a periphery otherworldly.

"Seven left sick," said Paterson. "Leekes went on to go."

Hide replied "that number'll shrink, but you're doin what you can Mr. Paterson. The boy there also and you my friend, ya'll are what's keepin us breathin."

"You're welcome," responded the black. "Though I ain't quite well myself. We're beyond bein in this together."

"Puedo ayudar," responded the vaquero. Any boy left in him departed.

Paterson handed the pistol to the ex-slave and gave no instructions to follow. To the vaquero he pitched the powder, the youth squeezing and smelling and fawning the sack like a periapt baglet of indistributable magic and he searched for what he then found. The granules were spread on some fulgurite crust still holding heat from the day. Vill's body was an easy carry, the particular issue concerning the men becoming a Leekes deceased. The vaquero thought his spirit hovered. With interspersed pauses of Spanish, his conviction was convincingly eloquent. The vaquero and the black would leave him. Paterson walked the two men into the dark and waited for the black to cough. A runlet of blood stained his cloak and he said "I won't stop bleedin."

"Take your time," Paterson responded. "You fellas go west a

couple of miles, three or four would be best. We gotta take dark and cover our tracks, attempt to confuse if we can. To rightly know how I do not. Conquin won't stray from that perch in the Nickel, cause he's got them two he's trapped. His best choice is that, but this world tends to wrong such security and choiced wishes. If Threadbare finds us, we're dead. If that happens, God bless you both. Go east, stay paired and pray."

Paterson asks for the weapon with its ulcerated rust and says "you'll need to foray with this. Son of a bitch, I'm sorry. You got the powder? Of course. You're ready. Won't shoot spread on that crust." He smiles at the men and covers its firing, the cleaning and what they can kill. "It'll be human and big. Fuckin Manson'll be settin somewheres. Expect as expectin is breathin. Said afore and I say it again." The black takes the pistol and hands it opposing, shifting Vill to his other shoulder. The vaquero receives the shooter, unsheathes and offers his jackknife. There's a round robin laugh from all three men before the vaquero and the black take leave. Their steps snowcrunch and the steps they take are an obsequy for the man named Vill. And yes, his tomb lay marked. The black and vaquero then wait for the dawn and the crepuscular brings conveyance. Like retted hay he does not sound. *Some thing* was there, then it wasn't. The two are never heard from again.

15

PATERSON UNROLLS THEIR bedding. Encamps them shoulder to shoulder. Their bare skin he then bathes with alacrity; diarrheal streaked flesh and there is blood in it all and he has stripped the clothing of Leekes. The men, they do not complain, approve of the warmth it gives, the rag of Leekes' shirt and the leg of his twilling dipped into that geyser sulfurous. A rock is removed to drain the bloody pool and what they've constructed impresses, the hot water leaking and running beside them as Paterson adjusts their pallets, saying "men, get round the edge. Put your feet in the water and soak them." As they submerge their bluing feet there are sighs, moans and thank you's. He responds with "fine, we'll make it. Look there, keep your feet deep in. In a moment I'll bathe you entirely." His breach is then plugged and as hot water rises the men are denuded of rags. The ones able to undress do it themselves and the weak that cannot are assisted, these argonauts sublime in their innocence and it does not matter their guilt. Baptized they're scrubbed and cleaned of their filth and wrapped and swaddled like infants. Three are so gaunt an apishamore holds them but the others are enveloped in bedrolls. Their putrid water is drained and it runs to the stream in a sorrel gush like sewage. From Paterson's pack comes sourdough bread loafed and spread amongst them, he entreating the men to eat. They grasp and nibble their shares, drinking brought water from a pool upstream for war has brought Paterson ready, though the man is as ill as the rest. This Paterson behaves as Jesus. We sometimes think we do.

"No shame in your struggles men. Eat what bread is here. I'm gonna wash these clothes and dry them."

Snow arrives and its chirruping upon the rocks threatens but does not stick. The temperature drops and locks below freezing and the wind is spasmodic then dying. Peremptorily the weather changes, balmy hint in the slightest of breeze, a front from the south but the ground remains cold as two rise to the bath for warmth, the night melding together with a coalhole blackness and there is no fire, only Paterson, he sick himself as is known to the men but he thrives while he suffers and moves them, each man half his size. They strain in choreography like netherworld combatants and what din from the mouths of the men has nothing to do with their sickness. By dawn two more are dead. They've fallen from their blankets embracing themselves to trap their souls within. Paterson blames himself. He weeps and is stunned with inevitable defeat and has words to place the blame.

"Didn't see 'em come outta their blankets. Too goddamn busy otherwise."

Raxley Hide is the man to counter. He has seen this pain before.

"You done good for them and us. We're dead to the man without you. His name was Silens, the far'un Scripts. Both Missouri born. Silens was a reprobate, Scripts a mankiller but they seen what peace you delivered. Here, by death, is finished. Nothin else that plain is known."

Hide had improved during the night but he alone in that starveling caste. There was dignity amongst them for the briefest of time but their bodies are ruinously ailing. Paterson kneeled to converse with Hide. No other can speak nor come to an elbow and not one could dress themselves. A rustic dutch oven Dravidic in origin was sketched by Hide and built. Paterson lifting the stones. Assisted by the weather and the squelching of the cold the dovecot of rock was ingenious. The clothes of the men nearly dry.

"I can't do anymore Raxley. They're clean and dry and though they'll sip water, ain't a morsel of bread stayin down. They were dead with the routin by Conquin."

"You done plenty Mr. Paterson, though hope ain't here, there is somethin and it ain't quit."

"Guess you got your grades in school?"

"Never even been in a church. Daddy taught me to read and write."

Paterson disrobes and the sickness of his body is lewd as filth is misery. He pauses then says "I am covered." The man walks into his shins and then to his thighs, submerges and the cold is layered, the strange of a thermocline two feet below, invigorating but freezing as he stands on the bottom with the cold high stream to his chest. He goes under then rises and clambers up bank to the gaseous covert of steam. Paterson feels threatened with time. He sinks into its warmth and stands for the sun but it has no interest in Paterson; a bore of ululation disrupting his wishes and though the grizzly is distant he hears it. Raxley Hide says "there one is." Paterson watches his body smoke. The lines of his mallowy palms. Unhindered by death he thinks. While around him these men, tunica and bone, are a machine without a working title. Their limbs overlapping with color starved flesh and he's amazed to see Hide's equilibrium. Sick but agile and he a young man and from his canalized hands they drink, for he expects the living to continue. Hide says "I'll tend to you."

"Thank you Raxley. Thank you."

"It's my duty Mr. Paterson. You sit there. Take what warmth you will."

Paterson laughs, says "I'll stroll." Hide replies "that was a grizzly. There's blood and death in the air." Paterson replies "you're right. Holler and I'll come runnin. I ain't goin very far."

The old man dresses, walks west from their camp, but is unrelieved by the movement. It's not self-pity, that's a futile condition, for who or what is lenient here? He simply wants a moment alone. When a milch of white smoke directs from the Nickel there is firing followed by silence. "Yonder they signal. There it is." There what? An antagonist arriving? A parlay between Threadbare and Conquin? Paterson cannot decide.

"Paterson! Hey you Paterson!" Across a snow clogged veldt he turns to see Hide and the youth is beseechingly calling. Raxley Hide has tracked him there. Paterson has wandered dangerously afar and he was worried for the morning was passing. Hide comes to Paterson and Paterson to Hide and they slow to a crawl from exertion. Arm on shoulder, Paterson on Hide.

"Sorry to do that Raxley."

"It's alright. They're all gone."

"Ever-one?"

"It is us. Any thoughts?"

"Not a one brims the rim of my cup. It does not floweth over."

"I know somethin. It ain't but one thing."

"What do you know dear Raxley?"

"We ain't gonna be two for long."

16

AFTER CONQUIN SHOOTS Vill they walk from their cell. Dampier and Billy revolve in the daylight like dervish somewhat confused. Their earth has transcended attributable to former but singly by crude design. There rise before them robustious high walls that are garrisoned by men afflicted, quotients within themselves. What is burning around them smokes from the top and that smoke is the air they breathe. The pair listen to chatter in gashes of tongues and they array and English they hear. Someone says Conquin is brooding in perch refusing to walk amongst them. He fears that his prison is dying. The warden sits and drinks and receives his food by pulley from the wall outside. These meals are prepared by the last of the weal who can cook and boil his water. This kitchen a half mile east of the Nickle and he sights them with the Belgium and dares. Invites these men to desert. He's been following the vaquero and the black's example without crediting Paterson's advice.

The remainder of the Nickel refrains from pure idleness by passing its day in task. Some sweep snow into heaps of refuse thrown from the bowls of the prisoners, chamberpots dumped on the detestable mound and the swine find the muddlement precious, gorging themselves on the fecal-pocked snow and the syrup of the sickened inhabitants. Along with the sweepers work a pack of boilers who stuff fired kettles with linen, swirling the mix with paddles from boats next door to the blocks of the butcher. Conquin has placed them three feet apart wanting someone to be murdered. When dripping white sheets, damp and stained shirts, emerge from the kettles for twisting, intentional guts are arced. A boiler cuts his eyes. He submerges the linens, apprises the butcher, the warning met with his own.

"You're mistaken my friend. Twas an errant fleck. I'd be cautious quavering blame." The boiler then back to the butcher. "Your fuckin head'll look good on this paddle."

"That's enough! I'm tired of your shit! Fuckin test me and Conquin'll deal you!" While the haranguing trustee basks in the glow of a reprimand hardly accepted, the butcher snaps his fingers. His companion stands to assist him. This erudite scholar of Greek and Latin spent a year sequestered at Cambridge and was received by clergy at Yale. With a doctorate of divinity he shipped back to Missouri to begin his labor of arson. He burned thirteen churches in a hundred square miles before his father found his journal and betrayed him. Page one, introductory paragraph: *the conflagrations are my personal homily. My audience the ash that results. What more can a prophet admire?* He admitted that the words were copied from a text written by a Connecticut rector. The arson he interpreted as "needed. No humans perished. Just wood."

Billy watched the scholar climb a splitrail fence, armed with a dibble and hammer. He's regarded with the direst of boredom, insubstantial in a homespun, shoeless state and as drained from emission as others, the butcher and the boiler unwatching the scholar until he took from a pocket a blade for skinning and addressed a witling in Greek, the assistant of the boiler saying nothing to the scholar as the arsonist cut his throat, a spate of carotid spewing through the laundry and that which was hung became art. He dropped the dibble and the hammer. Didn't need them.

"Oh fuck," said Billy. "He seen it."

The tone of the blast in that ataxia pending was the boom of a cannon on bell. The hips of the scholar held his smooth hands then the base of his spine revved forward. He broke backwards surreally, a tableaux from Hades; like a sketcher seeking men unbroken, before breaking them in pencil from spite; their imagoes unalterable perfection, as if unbent humans shouldn't be.

Dampier Mox and an awestruck Billy hid behind a pallet of stave. There was a bustle and shrug from this and that prisoner, but if anyone stared or sidestepped the scholar neither Billy or Mox had seen them. An erudite man but learned no more, the back of his head made junction with his heels, like an O, but he would not topple. "Fuck me," said the warning trustee. He snubbed out his smoke, turned his dun gelding, to pigstring the scholar's ankles, as if the spilth of corpse would flee. Another approached with a length of waxed line to tie to the pigging by hitch. The warning trustee remounted the dun with the lariat looped about pommel, the body bouncing and scattering swine. Beneath the portcullis it was dragged through the gate and released by the mound for the dead. This bilge a slumgullion of plague-dead indigents stinking in a pond without outlet.

"Billy! Dampier! You two!"

Conquin waves from the perch, mouths "my shot" and clatters down a handful of rocks. From his back to his front he passes a finger, yelling "whew, whew, whew, did you see that? Held together by guts!" He selects another digit, screams "give me a moment!" and ducks through the door of the perch, tripping on its portal with an intoxicated stumble, laughing so the Nickel might hear him. When he returns with his composure he is back in his spot, rummaging about before airing both hands directly above his head. Lowering them slowly past his broad shoulders he claws the air like a rodent. "I've allowed you an escape!" Hands back he claws some more. The castrum stares wary and long, every set of eyes on Conquin and the Belgium as every set of eyes should be.

"He wants us to watch it founder Dampier."

"Billy, it's done foundered."

*

Before their release Mox opened the hole for trepidation the door was guarded. Clarabelle said it was. He asked Billy to crawl to the kitchen. She said "that's what he wants and if gainly misfortuned I'll be raped, knifed then shot, instead of solely raped." Dampier maunders a second, replying, "Billy, he needs us alive." Whuffing and flimsy and on tenterhooks wary Billy climbs through the hole and into the kitchen where Clarabelle cooks and serves. She, from there, is as lost as he and then finds a tunnel intersecting, the walls sectile, melting, but sturdy. When in front of the door of their cell she says "it ain't nothin but opened. That whore-friend of yours was informative." Billy swings and bridges the portal. They stand entranced in the banking reflection, light diminishing down the colon of tunnel. "Billy, don't get us kilt."

Clarabelle is listening. Conquin shooting. Between blasts she summons them upward. "Come here! I was comin to fetch you!" Several stanchions have been posted in the tunnel they walk, elongating and stiling and pinning the ceiling and again his officiate blast, guns unknotted in the holsters of men but never a shot besides his. Their footfalls stop at the courtyard. They remain at the corridor's mouth. Clarabelle mawkishly eyes them. As usual in the melee's locus.

"Come on! Here! You're safe between shots! Conquin is stoned to tumble!"

It was here that the witling and the scholar were murdered before Billy and Mox could join her. Clarabelle was truckling beneath the fire on a rigidified platform for laundry. She had a basket of shirts and cotton drawers and was snapping them without reservation, her own thoughts relieving her speech... *"and I reckon there's one less arsonist scholar and idiot to daily gander... though the arsonist... he wouldn't fuck me... but Lord a mighty would he yank his prick… a gettin stiff as a Methodist and all I had to do was read in a foreign language… naked in a tongue I don't speak…* and this… oh this… is his dryin line originally built as a gallows… though drunk or sober nary was hung… for that smoothbore Belgium'll hit from that perch in the dark and yonder is the ladder… climb the fuck on up!"

These gallows cum washhouse cum laundry are pressed in the northwest corner. Dampier and Billy scale abreast crates and walk through a hidden scullery. Conquin's cookery prior to plague. In its rear is a ladder, on its sides curved sipes and pans to collect rainwater. The pair climb the stout ladder and Billy is first and Clarabelle requests they yield. She lowers the plunge and the pair ascend and there is Clarabelle blowing through stockings, threading both in the ovate noose. Pausing, she smiles and her banter resumes and thereat an opinion on the dozen: "that Paterson bastard is screwpine tough and won't let them others suffer… not before God in the heavens… cause I got to know him in his time at the Nickel and aye God them stories from the war… you'd reckon we'd never create this nation fifty years back you see… and us out here west of the purchase with a Mexican claim to boot… and there's country enough for a world… a prison for Missouri is some such shit and this goddamn place is a tomb… and I'm scabby with hate for that Conquin!"

Clarabelle's soliloquy need not a listener but her words are more than ruminative. They listen for something administered, for and against their keeper. Some calumny to cast as aspersion and with that purpose escape. To where or what place they know not exactly, but Mims Nickel will be vanquished.

"…no… you're here… but you ain't been here… you ain't seen it comin!"

They insist she speak on what's come to bear, but Clarabelle conceals whole truths.

"A few of the sick were exiled from the Nickel to return from whence they've come. Hereabouts that is death. Though Conquin has been drinkin and as a right guilty Catholic he sent 'em a savior named Paterson. The worst of the shit won't flinch that fucker, but my, the bunch he took!"

"That ain't got nothin to do with us!"

"Billy." Mox touches her shoulder.

"It's got everything to do with you. Yonder in the corner that cart of the dead ain't gettin no lighter with bodies." Clarabelle decreases to a whisper. "And truth be told I was lookin to that as our means of escape from here, but we'd prob'ly get dead all three. So I studied on goin one at a time but don't none of us want this plague. And what with one missin and three of us talkin he'd know we was up to somethin." And then as instanter *he*. "And ain't nobody slippin past him, if the bastard ain't amongst us already." She then breaks from the pair with foreshortened precision, a gap between calculable horrors, be it Threadbare, cholera or dysentery, the former more daunting than both of the latter and "you two mull it over and let me know if you got any notions to soothe me. Ones bearin east of Conquin's shooter and this shit that's killin the Nickel, but I tell you onct we're free of this place the healthiest has gotta shear off, get Paterson fount and stopped, turned to wait for the others. If we fuck with direction or get lost on an errand them mountains ain't a place of forgiveness, and back here pity is nil."

Clarabelle descends the ladder as if her yarn was the ultimate cleanse. Billy asked gently if their bounty was rescinded but Clarabelle dodges the question. As she breaks into the courtyard three trustees abruptly stem the woman. She banters with the men and her message seems vital, her confreres nodding their heads. The last was Manson, the unsayable-sayer and his parcel of time is lengthy. He gazed down to the woman with his hand on his swells, grunting with pleasure and grins. Enthused, he stared at the pair, whelm then convincing as is often the obvious and they know to evade him if possible.

"Shit, we gotta go."

"Dampier, my dearest, we do."

"What next then?"

"A wager?"

"What're the odds, our bet?"

"That Clarabelle goes straight to the perch and repeats ever' word she remembers. If she don't, I'll flash you my middle."

"I won't be seein your middle."

After hesitating she walks to the butcher, the man there shorn of an arm. He hands her the chops with his left, the concretia of a gutted shoat on the rack and he waggles his tongue at the whore. She then skips to the steps of his perch, Conquin standing in the door to seize the meat, which he throws through a beamlit breeze. He then pushes the woman inside, feral dogs on the meat and she in the perch and he affixing his stare in their empty direction with scorn and exophthalmic eyes, they and unenviably them alone on the scaffold biding their time, scanning for holes and breaks, a read from the prison's descant, those voices rationed by air. They shouldn't have fallen for climbing the scaffold for they've become the stage and its occupants. Billy and Mox are seen by the Nickel and espied by another outside it, the man admirably watching from a hillock with an unimpeded view of the pair. When he sees that Conquin has closed his door and Billy and Mox are frightened, he collapses and drops the spyglass, the lenses released in a dishabille style but landing upright in their case. The toes and the scalp of the strayers from the fort rumply accompany the lenses. The case's inscription reads: BELFAST: LON GILLY & SONS, ESQUIRE, 14TH DOWNS. Threadbare's obtained it by securing a bounty, a trencherman, cutter of whores. Within the last two hours he's observed our Paterson attending the boneghost men, making jokes about the antelope Threadbare has hidden and how Hide might need to consume it. These driven and salty unorthodox men have a blessed quintessence about them, an allusion not lost on Threadbare. Also illumined in their jovial speech were the warrants that neither possessed, whereas the vaquero and the peaceful ex-slave have been found in a codicil of infractions, mostly created for him. Threadbare could link any wan sin weakened by years of neglect into a reason to hunt as he wished, no color nor creed about it, you'd be traced to the gates of perdition. Truth is rare but these men have impressed him. Paterson and Hide will survive.

While individually boxing the toes and the scalp he intermittently glassed his interest. They came from the scaffold to converse with Manson, a man suited for exploitation, if Threadbare could draw his affront. A verst or two from the pile of the dead would do if Manson would come, the man a callow and grounded murderer Semitic with thirty dead Semites in graves. And though Manson himself was mother-born to the tribe he was a patricide also of fame. When his father beat his mother for displaying a menorah, Manson responded in blood, he unable to awaken his mother. The child was nine years old. It was the first time, but not the last, that a governor requested a trophy. A severed head was asked of Threadbare. The governor didn't want to see it, having nothing to do with the electorate.

Trembly the riverine thickets shook, the klaxon of hooves charging their spark on the stone at the base of the hillock. When he came to his feet to scratch the second address his corolla of pencil snapped. He decided to route them in unison. Tearing open the wrap, its interior cloth, Threadbare palmed the toes of the strayer, put them in with the scalp of the other, amazed at the pliable paperboard walls, the enclosure for his gruesome receipts. He implemented the sharpened remains of his pencil to longhand a fluid address: JEFF CITY, MISSOURI-CENTRAL ROUND. TB in the center above this. With his sour stench surlily wafting, the carrier hove into sight. The animate wind bested his scent and he could not hide his coming. Threadbare thought of his parcel. Someone back east would hold his payment and he knew the name of that man. He argued with himself on adding a note and then said "fucking money. Fucking goddamn everyday money," he trepanning his heel in the dirt.

Though hugely there he backed from the trail and waited for the rider to pass. Unflagging fabled beast. Why do you wait on me? Just abaft of the ears of the horse of the rider Threadbare stepped forward to flank him. Placed a hand on the withers and slid. He unsaddled rider and mail. Mims Nickel's particulars and undersize parcels littered the stonerent ground, the rider sailing past the croup of the hackney and doubling when he hit the trail. His nose struck his knee and the grousing began with a "why in the hell did you do that?" as if Threadbare had stepped on his toe. The bountyman went through the mail. He took updates and names of coming arrivals and referenced his list of recalcitrants. From state posts there were requisitions, which he ground underboot and held. When he'd pilfered the laden he added his parcel by cramming it behind the bedroll, the hackney freezing jejunely, Threadbare stroking its neck. He moved frontward and kissed its forelock. It needn't have lowered its head.

"This horse is for dancing. Not delivering mail. Why are you riding this animal?"

"What?"

"Distance abuses the hackney. Why are you riding this animal?"

"It's what the fuck they give me to ride."

Threadbare cracks his knuckles. Uncunning stupid boy.

"Buy yourself another. This horse should pull with a team. Or serve as a mount for a child."

"I ain't got no money for a goddamned horse! Now I'm breathin thu' my mouf to speak! My fuckin knee attacked my nose! Ain't you seen it bust?"

"Burst."

"What?"

"Burst."

Threadbare answered, restructured the sentence, made his point but the point was missed. He lifted from his shirt a jangling sack and hovered so the boy would humble, he sufficiently fearful already. He saw, said nothing, then apologized, as Threadbare doled the coins. Thaler, a decade of salary. Thaler from the century passed.

"Look mister, you…"

"Do what I asked, exactly as I asked it."

"I ain't drunk enough to see you."

When the carrier awoke the hackney was hobbled, the plane of his nose perfection, cotton stuffed to staunch the bleeding. In the swale below a rough-legged hawk disinclined to know he's present. Genuflecting over fire he has not started and with a weather eye out he vexes. Touches his enfevered temples. Brays about bad mescal. The postman says "I dreamed it off. But I won't never buy it from a bow legged woman with a cough and big milk titties. Where's my fuckin boots?" His boots are impaled on a scrub oak branch eight feet above his head. The mail is on the hackney in commensal order, trepannier pressed and waiting.

"Aw hellfire," the young man says. Away from the fire he tugs at his pants to inspect his organ for clues. He looks for scratches, blisters, traces of any of what has occurred that day. He stares at the hackney, walks behind her, lifting the tail to inspect. The hackney is amply offended. Takes umbrage and shifts the soil.

When he bolts past the gates of the Nickel he refuses to stop for the night, catapulting their parcels against the portcullis before retracing his previous path. When it hits their gate the bundle explodes and the warden demands retrieval. Four trustees swing the iron doors and the mail is lofted for Conquin. He sighted the Belgium on the path of the postman, led him by twenty feet, the unerasable dank protective, heavy and humid and moist. As he galloped aswerving toward a lessoring moon, he's a boy in arrears for its shedding, as if that light is owed him. Conquin does not fire. As is right, some light escapes.

17

NO MESSAGE FROM Threadbare within. Conquin despairingly smokes. That flutter in his chest from his mother. A radical leaping throb. Uncharacteristically Conquin ignores this, the windows closed in the deaerate room; Threadbare giving the night, circling the prison as darkness intrudes, watching the west in its dying. He builds autochthonous fires north and south, east and west at a seven-mile range. Fledgling blazes elementally daring. Fires Mims Nickel can see. They are like drone burghers, churls on peaks, as if the distrained were sent to emplace failed light on the hummocks for an Argus come up from the sea to feed. Not a man on the parapet invects these pyres and therein fails them entirely, for these symbols are signs themselves, the world drawn from the ware as it is, the fires growing larger until no fire is seen, bloomed from the night like cereus. He's petitioned to show you his place. "Here I am," the bountyman says.

Threadbare eats little, lays down these warnings, close-loops the fort and is gone. He selects the tracks of Paterson and Hide, their curvicue yent profoundly wide, one man helping the other. They're traveling southeast at a plug horse's pace aptly searching for settlements. Locations of rumors extenuate. Paterson then carries young Hide, the furrows in the soil and glaze of cracked snow tell of a support increasing, he light then heavy as Paterson exhausts, before Hide is brought gently to earth. Threadbare has given them life. He trots his horse due south before sensing the others, backtracking to muse on their reason. Other horses, other riders close on the pair and in their primitiveness, which, to a tracker is beauty, have been reading their path like himself, a study as accurate as his, signifying the men are alive. Threadbare leaps from his horse to decipher their mark, ferruginous pawings from their animal's hooves, the frogs of those hooves stained red, the white line through integument completely unshod and these horses have been at the geyser, having ridden from the fort and Conquin. Due south, southeast and within a mile they supplant by scattering largish, dispelling immediate attention. Five horses, five men, three circling back, the other two with Paterson and Hide. "No, no, no," he says. All five are nearer and next, their gaggle of tracks lining catenulate, deceiving as the competent will. He gazes left, then right, directly behind him, prepares to outrightly receive them. Snap of a twig and it starts.

When the lance hits the horse it pierces the ribs and protrudes through the opposite side. Another strikes the poll, inflicts damage on the skull and the mount keels pasterns together, as if roped and those lines yanked from under. It lands with a thud but he sidesaddles clear, leaping and scudding in snow. Being hunted our hunter responds. If he returns to the horse there's a natural breastwork, yet he refuses to offer expectance. He hears chatter, smells tiswin, listens to their tongues, a mishmash smattering of Shoshonean with Algonkian and thereinto, the bastardized screeching of the wild, its convex tones apparent. This positions his foes propitiate. Threadbare knows to the man where they are.

The warriors are waywards denounced by their tribes and Conquin has paid them in vice. Their tertian drunk has been rationed in days so the warden might numb his true sentiment. "Find Threadbare, his money and kill him." Amongst the lithe band are a Comanche and Ute with a Pueblan long crazed syphilitic. He has a brother who loathes their Arapaho companion but has enough sense to conceal this. Each man is dishonored in the presence of his people for a variety of horrendous infractions. They've chosen to drift and have found one another in the centrice of the Mexican nation and the Apache have threatened to kill them. Wanting fresh horses and to trade stolen mounts they've stopped at Mims Nickel to barter.

While they scan vestigial lumps Threadbare counts their steps. If they were sober he would've been dead. But he's any other theriomorph or caprock prominent in rangeland mimetic of any, mundane as he scoots into a bank of powder, formless as human in the embrace of the drift as the first of the Pueblans comes looking. The brave stumbles while searching and cannot react when Threadbare permutes from the drift, his subjacent thrust from the antler candelabra burying in groin and anus. When Threadbare removes it his face striates, the trident then run through his neck. The Pueblan's brother fires an ash tree shaft caught by the bountyman's thigh. Threadbare releases the Pueblan, breaks off the shaft, chasing the brother through the knee-high snow till he slows, the warrior in surrender and "surrender to what?" asks Threadbare nonchalantly. When there is no answer after mothballing seconds the fletch is rammed in his nose, the ash flexible, an eye pops out. The ganglion of cording is cut. Threadbare pockets the orb.

The Comanche, Ute and Arapaho warriors stand witness to their brethren's slaughter. They've not enough weapons by choice. Armed light for a singular man. And what that is lacks nominal clarity for these men haven't words to describe him. Conquin said Threadbare was an oversize oaf, a marksman though his eyes had grown cloudy. Said the warden: "he's a penchant for sleeping through moons. For liquor and boys and lekking for men and he couldn't light a fire with flint. His constitution is hampered by multiple goiter and he is generally sluggish and daft." Conquin has prepared them for death and should've listened to his own translator. The man said to Conquin "shall I give them the truth?" Conquin replied "fuck no. They'll never leave the fort!"

The opposite now stands to defend. This is no tyro as seen. Here no servant of vice. He is nigh wholly else though partial to human and only that for a biped is he. His sum total breadth is a fatuous lie conjured from the throat of the warden, for before these men stands *it*, an interplay trapped between nature and not, where fragments of man and myth become yoked for the pleasures of idols and gods. The river Styx has swept inland and the levees have failed. The cargo waiting before them. Taking to earth for his excise. Here stands a rootstock impervious. The *it* regathered in one. Inevitably they heir his approach. He is awake and loud with silence.

With their shock and confusion as to his appearance Threadbare has time to position. He splits them and spins them and pushes one back and their choice is encircle or run, he in their wheelhouse as they scurry back farther, the ground changing as mutates their steps; lumped muskeg with stones, peat that is fuscous, the braves stumbling then righting by hand, his tipped antlers displayed as he draws a thin knife with a circumflex blade for deboning. He orders and purges and motions them forward in the tongue of his youth but they hold. The Comanche squawks something but the others won't budge. It is Threadbare who answers this leader. As if the language of the warrior he held captive since birth and is his sole means of acquaintance.

"These two will die for themselves. You, you'll perish for Conquin."

Snorting prayers they apologize skying, accepting sliced throats, the docking of ears without even losing their balance. Like simulacrums of death with bodies of straw and their mouths sewn shut, eyes open. Seemingly requiring an abject mercy when Threadbare is the thing being hunted. They expect that their prey be disposed towards forgiveness like the Christians in the churches they've passed. Nightly in towns with repellant imploring sins and black thoughts are admonished. White Jesus, white God, white ways and white people composed in buildings and tents, with contrition as simple as words, though nothing seems simple in dying, or in the death this ferryman brings.

The aftereffect is Threadbare stands winded when finally the men collapse. He gives them their scalps and ears. His reward for their own fileting. He limps to his horse where it bleeds the packed snow and sits on the still warm beast. Threadbare sponges the wound in his thigh with a strip of depilate pelt. He takes the circumflex blade for the removal of scalps and slices the wound in a circle. Without the vivisect flesh the ironmongered barb can be seen in its pocket of muscle. Less a change of expression or a parting of lips he meditates on the tissue he sees. Blood black in the overcast day. This ghastly chore is averted by the hardest but to Threadbare the wound is his and no other can claim his interior. From the abutting of bone the head is then freed. The oblanceolate barb he sniffs, tonguing the blood on its tip. He laughs and throws it behind him.

As the night chips day the sun remains hidden, the rocky orogeny and hostaging clouds withholding the light from its source. He rifles the packs of the braves. Uncorking their tiswin he drams his wound and the building of fire is begun. He boils water in a plate made of tin. Cools it and tiswin is added. Again he rinses the wound, stitches with a catgut strand, his pulls tearing loose for the adjustment of body causes a weaving of knees. He tries a second time and succeeds. A small slit is left open, a hollow reed inserted, the drain keeping if Threadbare is careful, but he's not so he lashes it down, his blueblack thigh wrapped once with leather and again until his foot goes numb, the man loosing the drain and throwing it away before stitching the wound to closure. He bends back his needle from its suturing hook and mends his bloody pants. Stares at what he has done. Begins again to insert the drain. A clean linen patch will hold it in place and Threadbare knows the procedure. He's ashamed for losing his temper.

He hunts for the barb that has pierced his thigh and when found he unsaddles his horse, the dead carcass stripped of its equipage and the barb a rendition of others, six more that he keeps on his person. Threadbare makes a decision to walk. Every last weapon and applicable tool is thrown on a blanket and considered. Hight of a pack from saddle and rigging complements what Threadbare requires. He copies a fishpack his grandfather wore and remembers himself before this, when the impasse was family and friends. Peaceful lessons from his father and mother.

Threadbare recalls a traversable pass where a cascade of water falls westward. It's east southeast where the plain gently rises before a brief stand of larches marks entry. From these larches you can hear the falls, the Comanche the first to scend the pass when the rumor of the horse drew them east. Threadbare is prepared to travel through the season while Mims Nickel depletes its stores and the ravage of affliction is completed. He will then come for Billy and Mox. They'll separate themselves like the black and vaquero and Conquin will keep them alive. The coins in his pocket says he will.

Threadbare's staid from his wound. The plain about millpond flat. Then the early March storm develops, a blue murder pitch with a black and bruised luff, contained by the winds that produce it, sailed from the mountains where hailed. As fresh buds peek from deciduous flowers this high mountain desert, as an act of conation, becomes a morning wine color that arouses. He already knows that the braves were sent and in his limping he ceases to limp. As the light floods before him with harmonious reach Threadbare sees Conquin's features. Blue on white and white on blue. He's up in his perch with a smile to the west though he's struck the deal back east. Conquin's made agreements with periphery authorities for the capture of Mox and others. Handed false bounties and paid. This means a legion, men in their hire, need Threadbare to coffer his papers. Every bounty he owns is a price on his head and gold has changed hands to obtain it; for with a thousand plus bounties between the two coasts a hundred of these are major, yet they stretch from Chiapas to Maine. There are those who oppose his monopoly. He a chiliad criminal himself. A thousand souled bounty afoot. Mims Nickel there in wait.

18

"Y̲O̲U̲ ̲W̲A̲N̲T̲ ̲Y̲O̲U̲R̲ cock sucked before I have to go back?"
"I need to keep watch for those savages. Make sure a head is brought. Imagine that fucker locked down."
"Conquin, he's already dead. Five on one and killers at that."
"Did I ask what you thought Clarabelle?"
"No, you fuck, you didn't."

Downward the honeyed sashays. No prisoner desires her favors. Conquin's made a vow of protection after the bountyman's death. She'll require his assistance through certain mountain passes and from there she can dump him and leave. He won't hurt her in the fort or in the mountains therein because Conquin needs his sex and her service and Threadbare won't kill her while accompanied. Adequate pressure insures this, as inadequate delusion breeds fear.

The warden is hoping they'll decapitate him cleanly but his eyes will stay open when cleaved. He considers those eyes as he glasses the plains for the five who have not returned. When they shape in lens regardless of order he'll decide if the Belgium will reach them. Conquin says "he's killed at least two. If not Manson can help with this business while I remand his head to a pole. What the fuck is Clarabelle doing?" From the corner of his vision he watches her work, she lifting her skirts to look at her feet, from man to man through the helots. In a catenary bend she flits through the yard, climbing the gallows ladder, to where Billy and Mox await. She asks Billy if the girl has a bonnet she can borrow "to defend against light and whatnot." Billy throws a pebble through the noose, glaring insanely at the harlot.

"A fuckin bonnet! What the hell are you?"

"Calm down. We're leavin the Nickel. By the end of the day or tomorrow night or in-between sometime."

"We can do that now you bitch."

"Billy, Billy, no we can't, not without a shot bein fired."

Billy knows the game, the deception at hand, though the details are murkily hidden. By staring, she asks without asking. Clarabelle continues disclosing. Dampier sitting quietly miserable.

"Conquin has officially released you. Threadbare is fuckin dead. Savages were hired, I seen 'em, watched 'em, paint their ponies and bind their hair and they were sober-hateful bastards you bet. Wore elk-skin shirts and not a man wantin pussy. By noon his head is here."

"Clarabelle, pardon me, will you?" Dampier Mox stands from his heels to present a structured argument. "Don't that mean that Conquin'll own us if he ain't promised our necks? To fifty other men or one don't matter cause my killin ain't goin away. Don't leavin invite the hunt?"

"No, it does not," she answers.

"How exactly don't it mam?"

"Because Billy, my dearest, a hundred other men got paper on Threadbare dyin. And if the man lives, which mind you ain't likely, them hundred and a hundred more, will do him in a matter of days. He can't make an example to stop it. You've been traded for him and that price ain't bested and that makes you of little value. Some bastard could come for you separate, but I'll wager prob'ly not. Threadbare has been outwitted. His monopoly no longer pertains. Conquin has made the deal. He's strategic, a man of brains."

"He ain't what you call political. Strategy don't mean shit. He bought and paid for those bounties, cause the job gets finished when he has 'em."

"Why Dampier Mox! Have faith in the warden! He has done you a favor!"

"He ain't referrin to Conquin," said Billy. "It'll snow on the sun before you guess his intention. It's what dark does while you sleep. He ain't closin an eye."

*

Manson has watched as Clarabelle spoke with an interest as pensive as she. He thinks her dramatic and laughs to himself as he smokes on a cheroot and saddles. With his red harpy ink and her connubial leeches Manson seems deuced by the years. Countable years they are. As if the mordant tattoo and what it portends feeds from his flesh and veins, his black hair and beard losing their sheen like the raiment wooled skin of a stigmatist, spavined in Erebus' pit. With marginalized legs and a spleen overconfident he trots his mount through the gate. Conquin yells and Manson stops. "Take this, take this here!" Four miles hence he lays back in the cantle and tugs on the reins to stop. Briefly reconnoitering he walks for five minutes then positions for the brave's meander. He's southeast of Mims Nickel in a strath of high grasses with bearable cover afforded. Though the river is a trickle they will water their horses and graze them on the winterized grasses. He hasn't thought beyond that.

Manson submerges in a brake of sacahuista, his knees unwetting in its dryness. Conquin's weapon he holds aloft. Down on his stomach he cannot see and he wonders how the bear grass invaded, this far north and the spring held southward and he asks why nothing has grazed. Why things as submitted seem far from place and in error and Conquin then speaks: *Manson, they're besotted with drink. Shoot them from largest to smallest. Their bossman, the Comanche, is peculiar. As instructed they'll return in that dry riverbed. You can line your retreat to here. Fuck their bodies, bring me his head. Take what you want from their packs.*

When the clouds grow cerise, their middles char-cinder, dark wrenched like skerry where the waves have abandoned what form contained at sea. Manson rises to his feet and vomits. As he composes to administer his ambush, his mount slacks to a guttural whinny. The animal is tethered west of his lie in a trimming of stone and burnt timber. Bone clack but Manson denies it. It's a sound insignificant like water or flame or a tree nature felled in the loam. Like a bolt scorching granite from a garret in heaven or the sound of an angel's pared wing. No crack that concerns grave Manson. Imperiled ignorance is deaf. Denial its nethermost region.

He makes an incautious move aft a wind-yerked tree where he can slue in any direction. Not readying himself he slumbers, before drowsing in sullenness again. When he wakes for a drink from the trickle of river a hare and a crow are watching. Like mantlepiece statues a wing and a shoulder touch and they are contented. With a pink-eyed harrowing and corvine reticence they sit glary like malevolent twins. The have seen it stalking you Manson, its appearance enclaving these opposites. Its tracks are in the mire by the trickle of the river and it has slurped and removed you from relevance, its ken disincluding your figure. It circled and sniffed while you slept, seeing you alone ever foolish.

The pair mock Manson obscenely, for the heinous abounds you see. It is sensed to existence like breath. He says "who is not here is alone. For me or more me, we are here." No Manson, you are not him.

With caution Manson lifts the firelock. In sleep he's clogged the bore of the barrel by scooting the weapon forward. He raises the stock and the dirt falls clear and he decides to bet on a movement. To trace a hummocky, receding declension. He thinks he's hemming them in. Rooting in his pocket he grabs a chew of raw betel, pleased when the dope-nut restores him. His fear-drawn nausea recedes like a sickle, that blade held above by a thread. The unscalable recess accepts him. He has to walk back to come up. Manson, you know better. He's ordaining your circuit, scoffing your measures, glinting from cover like a beacon. You think there is more than he. Only he, and he is behind you.

The figure stands in relief at the top of the declension, in the spot where Manson descended. Lauded by the north like a surface thrust gift from Tophet or lower depths. He's half shaded in relation to those high desert mountains, as if he were an anchor to hold them, a kedging lone hook across the face of the world caught here, come to ridge, held fast, awl-armed gods claiming its chain, their teeth round the links for the contest, as back to their lair they traverse. Idyllically dusted with death. Here light and more dark equal nothing and the sky is so bright it is black.

"Goddamn me. I'm beggin to die."

Manson ascends the declension. Realizes he's been herded and cornered.

He slogs to that pocket of timber, the stone pugsmeared and mended; the marble insculpted, blocking some bleed, its cordiform shape having bled there. Is it magma? Some other earth's blood? There's a hard right turn quickoff the trail but the animal hasn't whinnied or sounded. Perhaps he's sedate in the cold. Manson notes the tress of a tail, the back unsaddled, the head dipping forward, it stands and that weight is supported, the withe-bunched rods hacked from the growth where the timber was scarred but sturdy. The front shoulders, back haunches, were pierced by the withe, like rebar rammed by hand. Two bloody ends are supported by syncline, the other y-racked like a spit. The horse's head has been lobed to the left and right, bilocularly crushed and neatly separated with a leaf-shaped stone from a dead-weight heft of a hundred and fifty pounds overhead.

"Jehovah, cleanse me, I'm dyin."

"No Manson, he will not."

Threadbare stood in the trail between Manson and the Nickel and there is no help to summon. He's proud of the feat with the glandered horse, blood to his elbows and streaked on his face like a sabbat novitiate come dawn. Manson was girded with his choice of weapons but he couldn't stop staring at Threadbare. He patted himself inanely, showing no clink would report. He raised Conquin's musket to the cirrus clouds and there he fired the weapon. Delaminating his layers weapons fall footly but the bountyman does not move. Threadbare's presence has stolen his wits.

"You're Threadbare. You're head is intact. I rode out to check if you killed Conquin's hirelings, but it appears I'll return on foot."

"No need to hurry Manson. I've studied you from afar."

Manson's fear-propelled guts erupt. He wipes at his mouth, turns back his head, but the trail is an empty condition. Threadbare was wearing a nosegay weskit and that vest lay folded mid-trail. He spins to his six but nothing is there. Revolving the weskit is gone.

"Alright motherfucker! I'll play!"

A schlock-bladed lance hidden by the Pueblan separates Manson's short feet. It sticks and whangs and the top strikes his head, lacerating from the force of the whip. The Pueblan had wrapped and buried the shaft near the site of his very own death. As if the man would return to claim it, for a realm where warring prevailed. What conflict found here apparently substandard and now the weskit, loosely attached, flagged in Manson's face. In a single revolution he was frozen then spared, the shiny black lance of walnut with weskit stilled and his temper exploded.

"Come back to your spot and you're dead! Motherfucker, I'm goin to kill you!"

As he walks to Manson his hands are raised and he's shirtless but his arms remain bloody. He's too close and has lighted too fast, a doppelganger punched from a mold. He passes and turns within a foot of young Manson, guttate, blood spotted, resuming his position exactly where the vest lay folded.

"I won't move Mr. Manson. Will your lead be wasted?"

Half-cock and the weapon is a soothfast load until Threadbare offers his guidance. He says, "Manson, you've plugged it with filth, so why don't you piece and clean it. The ball will sink and fail you."

"I ain't about to clean this shooter. When it's broke you'll kill me and run."

"You're already dead. Take a few moments. No better deal than my promise."

Manson tilts and shakes the barrel. Looks at his foe to confirm.

"Manson, the musket won't murder the shot. Weapons don't know they are deadly. What will murder the shot is you. Manson, please pay attention."

"Them's your last words I reckon. Damned if you'll utter another!"

"Should have's and did not's aren't equal partners but either will presage a future." Manson thinks on the offer before screaming his curses then refuses to limber the firelock. To even lisle through the barrel and see. He sets it and primes and rams down his packing and aims at the chest of Threadbare. He, still guiding, extends his long arms and flexes to crucified pose.

"Manson, don't shoot at my chest. Aim at my head so when the ball does betray you it's likely to strike my heart. You're forty feet away, no better. These things have to be ordered."

"I ain't listenin to more of your shit!"

When he fires there's a whoosh with an ordinary flame, an orange light ejected from the barrel. Manson's face is scad-worked black. His beard is alight and burning, having Threadbare's wisdom for comfort. He says "Manson, while you slept I assisted. The barrel has been gently warped. It split when you wasted your shot on the clouds and you've successfully ruined the weapon. Shall I smith it, in secret, for Conquin?"

The vicious little man with the harpy tattoo grapples with his booted pistol. It's sufficient for killing if aimed with precision but

Manson isn't precise. He's a curtain of hair and jitters, tripping on a futtock john-boat straightened when the river ran high during flooding. Regaining his balance with pistol in hand he marches directly at Threadbare, the first human to ever attempt this, the bountyman childlike, saying "come to me" and Manson calling him "you!" When he's ten feet nearer he's ten feet distant and Threadbare says "in my head. Put it where I tell you sir." Manson's followed the weapon since it came from his boot and he walks it to Threadbare's face, his impulsiveness again stealing his wits, he placing the end of the snub-nosed barrel directly on Threadbare's lips, the double-barred teeth like horseshoes grasping and the barrel sinks in to its hammer, a wink from his opponent to astonish. Two magnificent palms clap Manson's shoulders as the orotund presence overwhelms him. Manson then enters those eyes, their weave a nexus being of colors where Manson reflects his own. Threadbare's scent is that of an infant fresh washed come to an ethereal world. Utopic face inviting. As if a lotioned innocence was slathered on his aspect and why should death be other?

Conquin in his perch thinks he hears a shot. "Yes, yes, distinctly a pistol." He considers the time, the smudge of black clouds and then questions himself for security. "A false charge, merely a calving, its origin from the east. Could be the mountains or thunder?" Perhaps that or some other, a forelocked stone, tipped from its ledge sounding shotlike, its echo a pistol unleashed at the head of the man who should have fired it. But these things are vast and deceptive. Conquin returns to his listening.

19

A TEN MIRE CONQUIN pays no heed to the breaking of the gate with his coming. He thinks Dampier Mox is splitting rail kindling to restore the fires of the Nickel. As prisoners irrepressibly stream from the fort they debut emaciated like a line of dense floss, progeny becalmed and cerement dead without illusion or jounce in their steps. A shelterbelt of inaudible penury. Cartilaginous urchins of woe. Unenshrouded with speech, harboring before, with thereafter as unknown as prior.

"What the fuck are those men doing?"

Conquin, he knows, but will not look, the stout horse of the Comanche with its rearward stabs stoving the open gate, automata and rupturing to splinters, the beast roistered soundly of its own volition without a word from its zealous rider, he sitting in the saddle hissing phrases at the prisoners in a language unspoken for centuries, and they then fear the same. Hypnotized mute, hands on their ears, with bag-pouched cheeks of pure scarlet, geodes of red-rimmed eyes. They entrain from here to viler things and what spirits entoken are not. Beg, pray, do what you will. Check here, do what you must.

When the hinges are destroyed the gate buckles inward but the horse won't stop until told. Threadbare and the beast then approach. Clip-clop on the gates of the Nickle. The head and the shoulders of the horse Conquin sees but Threadbare is spelled adumbrate. Conquin thinks the animal an inferior grulla until realizing the man is mounted, forcing the beast to a swayback stance with the weight of his body and weapons. Then the lustrum of moonlight includes them. The ears of the horse are at twenty-one hands with an eye opaquely clouded, the other eye searching for water, its nostrils out flaring like screams. Threadbare studies the walls of the fort. Smells the drifting smoke. He releases the reins and the horse finds a bucket, siphoning the liquid upthroat. When the bucket is empty he nuzzles it over, the beast's skull a bloody rising, his snout puce-red with discharge.

"You'll be fine my friend. The blood will stop when your dander recedes."

He deteriorates his temper and tension and is sorry the horse will die. His stirrup then tugged and released. Its opposite yanked the same. A young lad circles the bountyman's horse, lucid though hungry and sick. Ward of the fort but not a dead father, his fear seems of minor importance. He seeks this man on the floor of the fort. Expects to confirm the rumors.

"You're *it?*" he says while staring.

"I am he," Threadbare responds.

The bountyman's appearance is irrelevant. The child has seen worse in a dream, Threadbare's fucus the entrails of Manson with aperient feces excised. He's painted like a gutrack on broadway. Hellsent that jujus prevent. A kowtow demon that guards the dark lord enticing the Christian to falter, lest their savior guide them to light. That being said the child doesn't care, hunger and disease his reality. This rumor on horse is yes, nightmarish, but interruptive of his waking pattern. A question then from Threadbare to boy.

"The keeper?"

"Yonder in the perch. You come to the Nickel for him?"

"Whomever. Just now he will do."

"How bout' me? Is there a price on my noggin?"

"Not yet. And please don't place one."

"Reckon I'll be on my way."

"Best you couple with somebody helpful. You're nine or ten I guess?"

"I'm ten but there ain't no decent a-dults. None not shittin themselves."

"Family?"

"Daddy is sposed to be here but the fort kinda took me over. What I thought as daddy is dead."

Threadbare smiles, motions him next, removing two coins from his pocket. He says "here" but the gold is refused, with an overturned palm like a bonze. What is money in the world of this child? Shall he purchase further abject misery? Some type of privation less vicious? A favor then asked of the nightmare.

"I don't want no money. Ain't earned it. You'll make me a goddamned target."

"You'll need it when you get to a city."

"Don't worry bout' that. Weren't raised taken charity, though I'll ask a task from you."

"Ask it and surrender the Nickel."

The boy considers his words. Wants clarity, objectivity. He says "take this fuckin fort and put it in the dirt. Burn it till it fries like meat. It took family I won't remember."

Threadbare honors the statement. Counterweights with a fury his own.

"It will be as soil underfoot. Mims Nickel was never here."

The child slings with fash his head at the perch to the keeper who has watched and decided to take his own life with a leap. As he ruminates Threadbare gazes, the horse of the Comanche buckling beneath, trembling to its cannons before landing cheekfirst, leaving Threadbare standing in straddle. He asks forgiveness for killing the animal by asking the animal's forgiveness. Seven people hiding timidly in the folds of the fort then sneak through the gates he's destroyed. Billy and Dampier aren't amongst them. On the scaffold his presence arrests the pair, like their souls have been drummed from their bodies, windlassed through brain and bone.

"Hey big salty! You like to fuck don't cha?"

Clarabelle calls from the corridor of cells with her skirts rolled high to the navel. Exposing her sex she walks to the man soliciting with a rankled staccato, she stopping and posing and rubbing her cunt, her hand plunging between foot-split thighs, to rest a finger on her anus. Trailing from her rectum she skips to her clitoris after dipping in her moistness briefly, enough to show she has. Reaching to his face she plants her scent by drilling in Threadbare's nostrils. Clarabelle's proximate to a bone-crushing squeeze. Barred teeth that halve mint coin.

"If it ain't hard after that, my man you are Greek."

"Did you see the child to whom I was speaking?"

"He ain't of age to handle this pussy!"

"Nor to see and hear it offered."

The backhand is meant to knock her unconscious when she reaches between his legs. It also breaks her jaw. She crumples in accordion fashion. He looks to see if the boy has seen, but the child is out through the gate. Threadbare lowers her shift and skirt. He returns her comfit breasts to bodice then laces the front of her blouse. She's leaned against the felly of an eight-pound gun and strapped to its duledge headfirst. With a kerseymere strip he repositions the jaw, fingering so the mandible fuses, an archimandrite phrenologist cowled with entrails whose practice he acquired in faery, or a gant middle world purblind, where the feverish nomadic cant innocent victims, their numbers a line curved endless.

With Clarabelle secure he audits the fort to design his raze ensued. From a portal on his left someone screams from the dark, foot charging and yelling his name. He wields no weapon and has no clothes so Threadbare passes him by, the veronica leading the man from what light infests the ground at large. The yelling stops and the delinquent vanishes, from Threadbare's environs no sign of the man as he kicks loose the tomahawk's handle, wraps his fist around its orriflame neck. He lifts the kindling wherein the hatchet was lodged and shakes the chips from its face. The delinquent is coldly watching, nude and unarmed from the butcher's foul pen and he would stay in the dark if he knew. Shunting himself in peace. Billy's seen him advantaged by others. She wants to assist the delinquent.

"He's crazy as hell!" she screams. "He ain't gonna hurt nobody!"

Threadbare gives Billy his undivided attention and when he does the man exports, his carillon of blasphemy in the brogue of the Irish met with the log pectorally, the man's feet in the air, then back on the ground, his forehead scanned for the **MIRE** of Conquin who's imbibing catatonic in the perch. When the tomahawk falls on the naked delinquent it takes his head, both of his legs, the limbs and the head then thrown at the scaffold where Billy and Mox are praying, finding God right then and there. If not one they commence begging several, their pleas unanswered by them, as Threadbare responds to their pleading. Composed, his audit concludes, with decisions that time will obey. He walks the boundary of the Nickel's interior walls, past fraise and reductive delineate shadows, an incongruity of exits he blocks, with green ash timbers and white elm poles, notched bull and ponderosa. When he arrives at the gates, their frame annihilated, he lifts the splintered doors and leans them. A pinchcock he bends from a spring he has found before he throws the clamp behind him. Too simple and easy. Won't work. He renails the frame and the hinges and doors and when they swing the pinchcock is found. Pulling the iron spring straight, he bends it to the shape of a U. Punching out the locks from inside. One end of the U is adjusted to pierce then looped through the other and tied. Handtwisting the spring is plaited, though the doors are below his standard. Too loose for Threadbare's liking. No gap or escape. No hope. No thing other than him.

With the rising of the sun he's pounded in stakes behind and in front of each door. Billy and Dampier have patiently watched while Conquin blacked out after midnight. He audienced the dismembering of the delinquent trustee then lay on his back in tremors. Awakened much later by the bungstarter's pounding he came to an elbow, requested his mother, unaware when the kettle came forth, Threadbare tilting the boiler of the washers, rolling its mass until centered, like a lumper intent on destruction. Into that kettle went bulkfried grease and the oil that burned in their lamps. In casks from their stores gunpowder was dumped and another five gallons of booze. Six spades of manure to season. He's a luculent warlock admixing ingredients for the paste to paint these walls. By the bucket he sloshes to the height of his body and it burns anyway so burn it, the kettle soon empty and Threadbare with flint as he lights his combustible paste, the fingers of flame sexed by dry air and there are four who are trapped inside. Dap your own devil amongst you, though Threadbare drifts to a memory: it contains what Threadbare was. It's accrued for the flames are accreting; back then his school eaten by fire adjacent to Reykjavik proper, though not close enough for its firemen, so his village fought it alone. He was a child and as a child sleeping, when the embers ignited his house, their mansard roof lavished with flame when the boy was awakened to help. The school sat atop a steep rocky escarpment behind the home of his family and pasture. His father and another and a generation more having built it as a shelter from insuperable winds when the island was a braise of illusion and ikon, when their sea had a terminal drop. Threadbare's parents wet wool blankets to drown where the flames burned brightest. The smaller bursts were the charge of the children, Threadbare at the rear of their line, lifting the bucket with a gripe on the handle from a well stone-lined and shallow. He recalled his deep cough, the wind changing direction, the ice in their rockyard melting, and he slipped in the mud between. Smoke and flames and a leavening fog and the school burned in exeunt clouds, the fire begetting and parenting its own, the fuel of its being commuted to cinder from the need of fire to burn. Origin and origin alike. Engendered primordial spark. A first thought in the welkin God cannot recall and from nothing came something forever?

Threadbare questioned whether brother or parent placed him in his bed that night. He was left with a hound of an indecent breadth that smothered his rugose cheeks; his face striped, black lined to an elderly depth and no child lay underneath. The boy he had been was dead. Threadbare born from the darkness. From a cataract of overmuch anger or abandonment while his family protected their lodging? How serene for us to consider. He simply became himself. A flagellant sly with a whip of glass bone and he pounds and he pounds and he tears.

When he returns the banging is deafening, Mims Nickel an inundate flame. The hinges he'd repaired and the plait of bent lock are clanging and his fraise work loosed, the doors receiving bludgeon from a body that strikes, the shots redoubled with effort, inclined to invade the fort, a structure progressing towards nullity and so burning the heat becomes wind.

"Sir, when it does break through, could you kill it as soon as you can? Appreciated, since this is your doin."

Some voice and man grown there, Threadbare watching that growing when the gate flies inward, Billy shrieking when the horse hits a strung javelina abandoned by the butcher to rot, passing back by Threadbare and the owner of the horse and Threadbare is amazed it can run, the beast croup to face in flames, searching through the fort for want of relief for Threadbare has bathed it in paste, as it stood doing nothing but waiting, expecting its rider to mount, that owner now standing inches from Threadbare, the material of flame himself. Burnt shoulder to the white of bone. He does not allude to this.

"Joe Potts from Alabama. You lit my fuckin horse. I brung 'em with me for my sentence cause they took a year off if'n I'd pull the dead-cart. He was hitched in a seam outside. You slung your shit thu' the wall, didn't see 'em. You ain't seen me neither."

Red hair singed black with inhumanly body this Potts from Alabama. Doesn't tremble, show fear or care. Patiently they observe the beast streaking orange, showing blue and Potts is irritable.

"He ain't got a fuckin chitin goddamn you! Would you be inclined to shoot 'em?"

"Take my weapon sir."

"You tote a two-hundred and fifty dollar motherfuckin shooter and do you gander I'm healthy enough? Can't you see I'm done near charred?"

Prisoners have heaped a hayrick with snow and the horse charges for relief, deftly stumbling but regaining its hooves, before sticking to the wall of the fort; blinded to pinion like a river through rain and does that river know its raining, its form the very fall of the water, the body and head of the beast betrayed by a tail not incurring a burn, the ungulate erecting the prolongation like a crank that sets it in motion. It trots forward miraculously and the pistol is offered and the beast steps huffing from the fort, smoke signaling from its sockets like censers.

"Shoot your own horse," he says.

"You're the cruelest motherfucker on earth. Gimme the big'un then."

Potts insists before his wish is granted. Threadbare hands him his musket. Potts boxed back to land. He has words, a weakened request.

"Please sir. It's gone too long. Your musket'll bust me in twain."

Threadbare looks at Potts on the ground. The weapon remains in his hands. His lip is burst and again he asks, but the sentence is blunted by Threadbare. "Please sir... it's gone too long... *too long for what Mr. Potts? What exactly is too long...?* The deplorable pistol then shoved in his mouth. Threadbare insists he stand. Potts comes to his feet with the pistol on tongue, his teeth on the barrel and chipping. Potts blinks and wants him to do it, for reasons abundantly clear, he extracting the borehole to his chin before spinning to fire at the horse in transit. When the shot hits the beast in the matins east light the top of its skull peels hatlike, the mind spraying like the brain can't hold it, the horse somersaulting near the pile of the dead, the irony exclusively Threadbare's.

"Thank you sir. I've a wife. Reckon I'll find her now. I am sorry, my mind is hazy."

Potts is led through the gate. To freedom or chosen affairs. Shortened waddle like the years of his life, its own sentence of coming and going; missed footing, black thoughts, the emptiness of hunger, though that rumble in his middle won't fill. Death swabs night as it sits in the darkness inhaling and waiting us all, Threadbare raising the pistol for the fourth and last time, same number as lowered again. On the ultimate stay with a hundred yard think Potts turns to Threadbare and waits. He begs termination with outstretched arms but the pistol is sunk, is holstered. His course not ventured as Threadbare refutes him from his position in the burn of Mims Nickel, the fort now choler with fire. As it releases to rage its candent body, Joe Potts drops dead by his horse.

20

THREADBARE GIVES BILLY the briefest of inclusion with a look and a nod to affix them. They watch him judge Potts, sickened by the treatment, but neither will move to attract him, the flames of Mims Nickel a hundred feet high and the perch and the scaffold afire, their consummation by flame at hand. The prompter Threadbare ingathers his weaponry and disperses on foot outside.

"We can't see 'em, but ain't, ain't gone."

"We gotta go or smolder right here."

"Yep Billy. Okay. Let's go."

Clarabelle would've used them to shield any trouble that would've saved her life. That they accepted but the woman was unconscious, her head cut loose from the gun, Mox hiding Clarabelle deep in the tunnel, her breathing confirmed with the smoke of her puffs emanating from sootblack lips, other woodsmoke driveling from the walls like whines and she was safe from the fire, but not from him, though the bandage round her jaw he had fastened, after setting that jaw with care. While being saved she awoke to cajole them, the woman lowing her predicament in the tongue of the wastrel Billy knew she was.

"Get the fuck offa me," she mumbled. "I tried to suck his dick and he broke my face after askin bout' a goddamn kid."

"He don't want your cunt!"

"Billy leave her!"

Aten Mire Conquin sobers enough to willfully scale his perch. Above the domicile smokes a flat bast roof with a cushy steaming joist. When it snaps he leaps to another, to his right a sixty-foot plunge. Before they enter the tunnel Billy watches him scramble up onto the perch, the **MIRE** of his birth in the varicolored light expressive castrated bravado, above the pallor of a weakening heart. Hand to chest he takes a breath. When his boots begin smoking Conquin brings forth a sword to slash at specters and foundlings. He screams "he, he has found me!" Billy sees him trip, but it could have been he jumped, though Mox said the sword flashed after. He told Billy he had glanced, a blink more like it, Conquin pulled through the bast and into the perch, the warden sucked down to extinction; yet in such light with its bascule of dawn there was fire and smoke and sun. The miosis of the pupil might deceive you. You'd need to search for bones if you could. However, seconds are precious, and into the tunnel they descended, with Clarabelle's body in tow. After she was left they returned to their cell with nothing but fire above them, enough light in that dark and they know there's an outlet for Conquin was the master here.

"How do you know where to dig?"

"I don't know where to dig."

"Not knowin and him don't mix."

"He's gone or goin Billy."

Between the timber and the fire that consumes them they hear the nicker of a horse and a shot. From the bourn of the Nickle leaves the gallop. Listening they know it's a stopstart rider but what rider, which person, unknown. The north side of the fort then crashes. When it does it is felt with an onerous concussion before the smoke from the tunnel disappears, floats into their cell before draining. They smell its horizontal movement, wind past their noses like the slamming of a door with smoke on the back of that breeze.

They claw at the wall to their front. Mox turns, muses and listens. They walk back through their door, look to their left, but that leads to the floor of the fort. To their right goes deeper with a sharp curved turn and they notice that smoke is escaping, penetrating where smoke should not, a white skean above their heads dressing them noxious as they sink to hands and knees, coughing and crawling and reaching ever forward to a right turn back and then a drop. The wall is solid, terminal, they dig and fail, but Dampier has reserves unmentioned.

"Get on my shoulders," he says.

Billy brings him to the ground and positions his body then stands on the small of his back. From here she can reach the joint. "I don't need to go any higher." With stabs of her finger slush falls on his head and thereat another room. Chunks of ice, choice meats and a pisaller of liquor lockered, cooling and staid. Conquin's own special bodega, his system of tunnels ground ice dependent and he the archon of confusion in their digging. The warden found it comical that every comfort needed depended on inches of ice. With heat it peeled back to a tumbledown house of extensions and corridors ad infinitum with another, then another, still teasing. The caveat, it never peeled back. Unless one burned Mims Nickel.

"This'n ends right here."

"Don't know where I am, but here ain't burnin, which is currently sufficient for me."

"We're pointed at them boulders you reckon?"

"Go in and see for yourself."

Billy bends and flexes, crawls and adjusts, ash drifting through a slatboard front and Billy is then inside, dropping down from Dampier who straightening behind her can see the top of her head. She looks for a door, no in or out, he twisting through the hole and into the locker and there is room for two their size. Dampier kisses her cheek and grins, the wall from which the couple has descended melting as they stare outside; three fronts with slats nailed inward, the Nickel burning, extirpating to their rear; from behind them then the pop of a wing, a sullage partridge in collision with a slat to their front and when it hits the bird falls and is there.

"Runnin from the fire," she says. "Look Mox, look right there."

Above their heads is a hatch easily sprung by inverse weights with ropes. They pull and a side releases. With his help she ascends through the drop and into her choice of tunnels. Sitting back on her haunches she touches the ceiling and though packed the dirt is dry, cool to the touch like rain soaked hair and she lowers herself back down. She says "we'd do best to pry loose a board and see where we've got ourselves to." But that's a thing demandingly seen, where they've arrived and where they're going, what's behind and to front the same; more a dark accursed world of Midgard fanatics and vipers that feast on tears. Stay where staying has delivered. For there's a quarrier sketching your movements. Selecting rot over flourish with a merriment sorted in a skybuilt tower of wishes, a reposit bunching the thinnest of air in a place too evil to conquer. You believe when must is decisively final and decree when wants are stifling. But what comes in the dark won't come with your sensing for it waits for you to smell it, so close that scent your own. You're enswathed inside what Threadbare has planned and it is he that is there untold.

"I ain't scared of what we'll find. Knock them high ones loose."

Dampier Mox pries the nails inward from the topmost board and then the second. From chest to foot he's underground. Quietly he works the disjointed blade, part of the locker buried above what was once a hoarfrost floor, excepting these vents secured on three sides and in minutes the slats are in hand. There's the smell of the burning Nickel. That indefeasible bouldered space. He says "Conquin's possibles were shoved through here, but I do not know what the tunnels are for or where these tunnels are goin. Anyhow, we can hide..." she then interrupts, saying "fuck your hidin! I ain't sittin in this locker till sundown or time thereafter! We can get the fuck out right now!"

She puts an elbow in the vent and proposes to lift and when she does they hear the lope. Billy reenters the vent. When her feet hit the floor he is there. Without dismounting he sits in the saddle, creaking and spluttering the leather like voice and he shifts and cabals himself and the saddle and the horse he himself has selected, the mount lifting a hoof to its belly, its cannons as wide as a posthole, truly a hugeous beast, the equibalanced horseman holding standard in the vent where its residents suspend their breath, the chaplet of scalps then dropped to the ground and rue the day you screamed when they hit, the bloody pelts in a wad as his horse quarter turns to launch the filthy wreath in their faces, thirty tokens on a buckskin string. Yet another board shatters with the strike. When it splits they're open to him, four hooves there canting in an imprecise circle, his manner like the mother of a child gamely hiding, thinking *son, my son, I've found you, by knowing your favorite spot. Seek and hide elsewhere.*

"My God," whispers Mox. "We're dead."

"God ain't here with him this close."

Mox wants to backtrack to the floor of the fort and if Clarabelle is there he will carry her. He pitches the suggestion to Billy's right ear and Billy replies "we'll wait. Clarabelle's scalp could be on that string, but damn if I'll look for her head."

The eastern gate of the Nickel in similitude plummets to the plain and their locker reacts, sifting and panning dirt and smoke, a break and a burrowing low above their heads that could be animal or man. Their vents filter sand, surging their bodies, sparks riding the frisson of wind and there develops proviso to form: less a mile distant, where miles seem days, the hunter, their need, sits mounted, observing as the fort reverts to the soil wherethrough it came to be. He's a compound, a pact, between overawed nature and the despair of underbred beauty. A formidable assay, an experiment, what creation refused outright, so he's dripped to the earth biding his time, through that space in the teeth of the rarest of heartache, though he cannot replace himself, for he is also derived from the very same vein of that fire raining Eden as we, if ever that garden lay fulsome, from there he's been harshly ejected, along with the us that is him. He himself, that permanent dark, as if color has bled into the earth's skin, for his colors are red and gray.

Billy says "there he is."

"Where is there?"

"Yonder," is pointed.

Like a memorial to the fallen he waits. His animal, as mounted, the same. Doesn't whip its tail or pitch its head as they watch the fort's displosion. He releases the reins and waits some more and an hour then two intrudes. With the ogive arch of the sinking sun the fire makes a schism where the fort once was and still they wait like poilus. The day is short and winter is there, the fort throwing its rabid lamping, but still they wait through night, the next day coming and in that morning no sleep for Mox or Billy. Behind vented windows their chins and eyes as there outside as in. They question his existence as it pertains to what they see before them. While reasoning through exhaustion both decide he's intent on reordering position. He wasn't there. Then he was. He was a mundane clump, another pile of prisoners, perhaps the corpses of the scalps at their feet. And there, look there, to the left where he waits, those stones could be a horse and a rider. What requests their surmise surely gets it.

"I don't know Dampier. It has to be him or not bein him is a thousand other things."

Just then in her confusion sunlight hits the vent and when it does there is movement behind them. The body of the partridge flown in from the fire straightens out its wings and trembles. Tweet of birding clamor and it lives. The bird flies between their heads through the vent, their vigil on plain broken asunder and when refocused on their man he isn't there.

The ocean and land through time and folly have seen what man can do. They decide where we go, how we get there, one a fluid carpet washing stalwart shores while the other makes the ocean that will wash it. There is no choice in being themselves as Threadbare's choice is Billy. And that little woman-girl has grown impatient so out through the vent she climbs, on elbows through the mud and the slush to her knees before standing to take her measure. The boulders on her right are the rocks of their capture, the fort burning double walled behind her. All has been hewn beneath the natural landscape and there is nothing that does not blend. That source of stone where Conquin has found them extends to the vent, ceases as stone, the vents shaded by rocks that hide them. The burning fort she can see but doesn't feel. Its center is chaste, unalighted.

When they debouch on the plain Threadbare walks his horse north. He can see her through the ruins of the Nickel, Billy standing, studying there. He laughs when she sees him and flattens with his spinning from the mount he's acquired in trade. A cropper wanted mules and not the single draft who in body is three mules standing. Threadbare offered five, a sack of horehound candy, but the cropper wanted six and gold. He said "the Percheron's strength would best eight mules" so Threadbare brought him eight. But no gold or horehound candy. Eight mules for the Percheron even. No deal was struck but he was close to the Nickel, the cropper's scalp on the buckskin string. He came west to plant, to trap and live, but the cropper's never heard from after.

"Stay flat Mox. He ain't seen us."

"Suppose he'll go his own way?"

"Which way is that?"

"Not here."

"No, I don't suppose that. You shoulda stayed in the goddamned locker."

Billy splays her arms, puts her cheek to the earth and touches his fingertips. Dampier's searching from his chin for a weapon, if any, in the rocks, on the plain or with a body. With a sixty second crawl there's a pistol sitting poised in a heap of depucelate snow. The wroth of a blizzard has gathered the drift and churned it in a batter of filth, the glint from the barrel resting encima an admixture of brown and white. A boulder shields the size of the drift from his eyes and Mox cannot see the man. He says "I'm goin for that pistol" and she says "go" and he asks if she'll watch for Threadbare, he viewing every move they've made, both their lengths stretched flat on the platy high desert and he on the Percheron's back. Yet Dampier Mox is cautious, crawls two to three strokes then stops.

"Go get it," she whispers. "You're fine."

The hand clutching the pistol is placed on a slope. Downward as decoyed bait. A hidden shooter was firing at Threadbare. From this vantage an enfilade smartly achieved, though his crossfire was merely a shot, the shooter ridden down and murdered. What remains is his hand and the pistol it grips, the arm and the body scattered, as much part of the drift as the snow packed around it and Threadbare's left them this weapon. Mox calls from the safety of the snow and the rock as Billy backs into the vent.

"It's a trustee! Parts of a man! Pistol is good I reckon!"

He looks to her and her finger is lipped. She crawls back onto the plain to search. Billy stands. He is not seen. Nothing on that gibbet of wind-scoured tundra except Threadbare and the embering Nickel. Again he's unmoving, is any shape seen, though close enough to hear them.

"You ain't gone," she says. "I feel you."

Dampier wrests the weapon from the hand of the dead and finds the bag of shot. The trustee's head sits close in the snow, demarcated as a skull inferior, his eyes plucked to whiting watching him work, Dampier saying "sorry" to the head, Billy's pliant yielding his work. She is there with Mox before the echo of the scream and against the boulder in person. Threadbare, bogey, with heels rib-locked is bearing and curved like a jockey, closing the furlong in seconds, he then masting priapic straight, without angle and his chin leaves the Percheron's neck and as he bolts through the smoke of the fort he acknowledges the keg of powder, the kindling burning near. Threadbare's halt is admirably brief. Adorned for Billy is he: the Percheron's unsaddled and bedawbed with grease, painted ewers with eyes and tongues, from their mouths more blue with tails of orange and his head is smeared with white; the horse's blacked eyes like bodement zombies, a look of generable horror, nay lowers realms inquire him. What's painted in vase, what comes from the ewers extends to Threadbare's body. He's wearing the skin he's brought to the world with boots of hide to knee. To his cock and hips he's a black pollute blue with a zagging belt of orange. All else is amplified black, as if the blood in his veins was so, the man slicing himself diagonally, from shoulder to thigh and the slash of wound pumps dinning through bloodbunched locks, the hair resting chest and back, its tenacious muss enmatting like a corpse in a tomb for the once defiled. There is nothing to notice on the broadest of plains except he and that horse and their barbarous appearance as two becoming singular. Their isolism yells you deaf. They are radically execrable, an image unsought, what thing known prior before partnering humans contrived their own bare truth, other arabesques of liewet speech, to eternally deceive themselves. Threadbare here, is a cleansing terror, spiteful of lies himself. Strange that he wants young Billy. As if the purest of truths lay in her.

Threadbare wants them to come to him. When they step from behind the boulder Mox pitches the pistol to plain.

"Okay Billy, this is permanent."

"Fuck him. Let him come."

The Percheron snorts, sucks and neighs, throwing its head like a brick. Rheumy equine eyes. His muzzle jetting its wind. There is no matter between Threadbare and Billy and there is no noticing Mox. No *why* in her, she refusing to fear, as she picks up the weapon he's thrown. "C'mon, motherfucker, let's end it." Billy's green eyes and cloudberry cheeks are ridiculously colored violent. The haunch of the Percheron sinks, the isosceles of dust from his duo of hoofs never touching Threadbare's skin. He levitates, stops the horse, the dust enveloping the man like fog, his animal without lurch.

"A goddamn show," says Billy. "Nothin but a fuckin dance!"

When the kegs of powder release and expand they send their flash towards Threadbare. He'd decided to turn southeast, shortening his charge on the pair. When the coitus of fire gains a top surfaced keg it immediately ignites five others. From fifty meters out its Arcadian fury the equivalent of surgical sleep. Its asperity feeling him nothing. Threadbare's slammed to the ground and the Percheron follows, wobbles for a moment and collapses. They watch the man wheel, wait the Percheron's stunning, both down, they check their own senses. Dampier Mox is temporarily deaf, blood dripping from her nose like the punched. She wipes it on her sleeve and speaks.

"I gotta go see if he's dead."

"I heard enough of that to say no."

"I'm takin the pistol with me."

He is prone with lachrymal bleeding. Hemorrhages mouth and nose. Other tiny incisions on that blownblack corpus like slices for wind to filter. The cut on his chest requisitioned for Billy bleeds but not profusely. It fills his navel, sluices to pubis, his stomach sunken, not expanding. Other blood from his hips bleeds to the ground and no breath in his body care lift. His lungs like spoiled and torpid bags and no devil now dead equates. Threadbare is the same as the child of a mother. That mother the child did bear. How size the bearing of evil by mother when every mother bears some evil, when sized in everyman's breath. In the mirage of a river you'll easier find current than a breath from a thing less evil. Now you see what Billy sees.

"This close is more than upsettin."

"The dead seem small. Not him."

"I'd feel better killin him further."

"Billy, that is dead."

"Dead on skin ain't in."

Billy can't stop shaking. She fumbles with the powder and fidgeting drops it and Dampier won't help because he can't. It's a desperate act to desecrate the dead and the sin of the act is unforgivable. He won't adjust his oaths to his liking.

"Billy, before you shoot 'em again…"

"I ain't fuckin shot 'em once! You thought he'd take our surrender! Does he appear the cuffin sort?"

When she doesn't fire it is always remembered, the marvel of his body unforgotten. It's merciless, hateful framing. She is touched in her sex from staring at this man and Mox is breathless from watching. Offended to his very core.

"The throne has cast its judgment."

"This pistol could improve his death."

"Leave 'em Billy. He ain't no Christian. I'll be damned if I bury a heathen."

"I wanna slice his throat like a shoat."

"I ain't providin the knife to do that. Let's catch Paterson. He'll move slow."

"If they're movin a'tall," she counters.

The saccular prating of the rocknested chicks is a sign from God to Mox. A positive omen reckoned. They find the nest, touch it, and stare at the birdlets before Mox is tagged by their mother, the jackdaw matron relocating her home as the Nickel combusts and burns. She pecks him on the shoulder, twice on the head, before the message is fully received. Billy and Dampier make a traveling pack to walk south for their night in camp. They are then in the open but find a rock sash where they shade to hide their movements. Unrolling their bedding in the line of rocks they choose the caudad end, facing the north in case what comes, what closes is separate from him. With their bedrolls together their requiem sleep arrives by lying still. One dreams of her, the other of him, Billy seeing him rise from the dead.

There are frangible stars at the foot of the storm when the Percheron routs from its stupor, their proximity to moon before the clouds waft over so close you see their centers, what suns realized therein, spaces unceasing between their tips and with your finger you can trace immensity, the vastity of deepest dark, profounder things not us. And in their fail of light with the coverage of clouds the horse he examines in trot. He wants to see if the Percheron's foundered. If an injury sustained will show. The hooves are ministered, limbs squeezed rudely, the Percheron passes the test. What light from the fort prods them both and they are on to other things.

21

SHE CALLS TWICE but there is no response, her jaw carding the pain through her body. Touch the bone in your jaw. Feel the damage. There's a contusion on the back of her head for she's slid to the L of the tunnel. To her left the bodega of Conquin. Light from the clear silent day. With the kegs reporting she surfed down the tunnel, riding mud and ice and with that momentum was piled in the angle's turn. Clarabelle is coated with the filth of her sledding, a sard and black effigy with no one to help her, a damsel in a corner of mud. Sensorially, she's unhurt.

"Cocksuckin son of a bitch!"

When the blood in her feet circulates to feeling Clarabelle stands and asserts. The muck disrobes itself. She emits to the floor of Mims Nickel. No fort she knows is there. A crater where the kegs in and exploded and a days more burn thereafter. A pool bubbles with cresylic greasing and in that liquid shapes. Bobbers plunk and return to the surface. As Clarabelle draws closer the soil becomes heated. She sees the pool is lined. This catch she will not touch, the source of its heat fumes from the depths like the torch of an imp in hell, the demon holding his flame rather steady.

"What the fuck has he done with the people?"

The face that perks to the surface is the head and face of a prisoner. Disguised and compromised by the heat. She looks and revolves with the slowest of turns and is startled but doesn't yet scream. Before her are the trophies as left. Four bodies he's staked on the plumb, as if a line were released from the heavens and the shafts through the bodies thrown down. They are headless, armless, legless and neutered. Impaled on the points of the compass as his other fires before. What remains of Mims Nickel smolders in stations and is gathered about these trophies. They squeg obscenely with the southwest blowing, like semaphores calling the dead.

"Conquin! Billy! Dampier Mox!"

No answer or why would they answer? What response to this?

"Gone. Just me. Right here."

She recalls a depression where springwater gurgles somewhere behind the boulders. Unchurched rolling stones. Mother jackdaw awaits when she comes in range and Clarabelle is flogged and ousted. After drinking then cleaning as much as she can she hurries her way southeasterly. Intuition stops her in minutes. Something she's missed at the fort. She talks to herself to counter the urge but its strength is undeniable. Back to the eastern torso, her respite brief and dreary. When Conquin emerges from visible ground, he demonstrates from the front of Mims Nickel. One hand in the air and then there are two before the warden calls her name, she as inferant to what he is. As predicted, they solder together.

"Conquin, I admitted he had you."

"No, no. I fell. Nothing more. Awoke in the night right there. Within paces of my cache of weapons."

"Were you buried and hiding?"

"Of course not! I tripped on a joist in the perch. Tumbled, hit my head. I was lucid enough to enter a tunnel. This hole is the eastmost exit. I heard you walking and almost killed you."

"You keep muskets in that pit right yonder?"

Together they reverse his steps. Conquin tries to slow her, to prevent her from looking inside. When she does its an empty dugout. A lid studded with tangled nails. The frame itself is four inches thick and there is nothing stored within.

"Conquin, you ain't got shit!"

"Not another word for I've prepared for the eventual. Two miles east of where we stand is a caisson covered with rocks. Inside is a pistol, musket and shot with an oilskin hamper of food. And on the first river down from the pass is a pram recently hidden. It is tucked in the reeds near a killdeer nest. As I said, this was eventual."

"You eventually expected this?"

Permit your sight this focus: calcaneal dragmarks from the heels of four bodies and that path is bloodied sand. Their torsos pierced by lances. A limb-rife cauldron perks. It contains what the torsos are missing. Revelations occlusal this. A holocaustic map of dreed. Still arrogant, Conquin will fence.

"Yes Clarabelle! Eventually this! The elite of this world sense mayhem! Chaos with its strict assault!"

She speaks to keep from listening. "I know you know," she says. She needs Conquin for crossing to safety, refusing a contumely direction. "You still appear fine burnt on your edges. I see you've bathed and dressed. You defeated the bastard. He left."

"As usual I went to the spring, to tidy my personal appearance. Ahh yes, also, look here dearest, what I've kept on my person throughout."

From around his neck comes a rosary, the prayers replaced by stones. Diamonds, silver and rubies, terminating with nuggets of gold. They've been delicately drilled, but even so damaged, are a boodle of comfort to manage. Unsure, she asks if they're real.

"They are payments owed past due. I took them from the safe of Missouri's own governor and that man has accused another. He shook the jewels in Clarabelle's face. I am personally sly and have power to feed it, moreso when others deceive me. The man hung was my replacement. I stole the loot between drinks and dinner, the safe being practically opened. The other was immediately arrested. A rather shallow political fellow."

"They have to suspect you Conquin."

"Why would they think it was me? I volunteered for the wardenship here."

She skews from the topic leading Conquin away. Her breach disincludes him.

"Someone wrapped my jaw. You didn't even ask me about it. Billy and Mox..."

"That has no bearing! All have gone on except we!"

"I suppose you're right. But Conquin, can you deny his impact here?"

"He's done his job and left. We must do the same."

"We can't. He ain't gone."

"What else remains to harm?"

"You remain to harm. We're a shovel nigh scooped as long as we stand here. Prob'ly, even if not. That motherfucker is thorough."

"I've come in and out of the Nickel throughout the whole ordeal. He's done what he wanted by razing the fucker and hanging these silly trophies. There never was much to him."

"You been awfully goddamned drunk. He done the spread of this place, planted your ass, bandaged my jaw because he can. Torment ain't a bother when you're dead."

"Well Clarabelle, dear, do you think he wants us living?" He glances askance at the sun-dazzled world and then says "that he must."

She replies "he wants you dead. Myself, he does not."

"Well then, here we are."

"You know Conquin, I knew you had a purpose, asides your cock and tongue."

"There is reason in the water of my ideals for it includes the smallest things."

"My God, astoundin arrogance. As if Jesus plowed your fields."

He wants to hunker in the boulders for the rest of the night but she refuses with the torsos staked. Conquin sets them alight with what he can find of the parts of men dismembered. Their flesh ignites, burns carnelian red; the cloche of bones, their tops pipe-steaming, are heaped on the plain in the dent of an aster where a chunk of debris has skipped. Wood oil bastes the pile. The brazier consumes their flesh.

"Clarabelle! Come from the rocks! They arise the sweetest stench!"

"Fuck you Conquin and your blasphemous ways! God's watchin, knows and sees you! In his image as others sought! They deserve a Christian burial! We shoulda had a prayer!"

"Then you should've contended that task! Come, pray this instant!"

"There ain't no need to discuss it! You've burdened us yet again! Their souls'll cross the river to await us, yonder side, perplexed with grins!"

The frost that coated their blankets was a cold attended with rum. When she took him inside her the bottle was empty though she begged him to squirt on her thigh. She feared pregnancy and travel and Threadbare and prisons and has dreamed of the four in unison.

"You left that shit in my guts you fuck and me with a broken jaw! I done had my period and was clear of a baby and now you stole my peace! I'd hafta jump and wash and jump and wash till there was no water and the ground was droughty to get myself near empty!"

"Our trip will kill the child."

"I got pregnant onct by smellin a mule! Goddamn! Just don't talk!"

*

As the argument cools and they fitfully sleep Billy awakens Mox. They're twenty miles farther than seeing Mims Nickel and they've commenced their climb in cold. She stokes their fire then removes a log to read the tracks about. She's as alive as unfrightened is reasonably living in a sensate world of danger. Billy expects her end. Though no date on that trust she knows or delivers to the follower tracking them daily. There's a primrose of fire on a southeast peak and its asloped and horsed and close. Three, maybe four miles distant.

"Mox, come here and look."

"Look at what?"

"Our world as known. World of you and me."

"That's a touch wordy. You been readin my Bible?"

"Naw. I see what I see. You can't go flippin forward. Not with this here read."

22

BURNING LAKE OF night with its blackest pitch and their sky is bedimpled with stars. Before dawn he rolls from the woman in blankets for his penultimate look at the Nickel. His last the memory of it. Like an ancient physician forborne the body he walks onto the equable plain. Eastlook arrives your day. Hieratica of dying stars. Is their skin the skin that you wear? As much you as they are them. Conquin, sir, bear in mind that today is your acme friend. What you once were and your unborn child mere units of a pride destroyed. He awaits on the eminence of peak. On the promontory where you'll travel. There is sun on his snowdamp back. Fond and patient like a path without curving. Its lie through yonder dark. You wish you'd hidden that boat. Wish there was truth inside you.

"Clara, come on, let's go."

"But the comforts of ground are eternal."

Their palomino has a saddle one can ride with a quadrangle of packs around it. He requests then demands she come to her feet and ride her lethargy waking. Her chin bleeds slightly and her knees are cut from their abandon of the day and night prior. As she squats to piss where the two have slept the liquid smells like ore, Conquin's semen dribbling from her enlipped gape, making eyes on the face of her urine. Her jaw pounds and his bandage is gone.

"Goddamn you Conquin. Damn you."

"Come on now! Let's go!"

He has a clear brogue, reassuringly confident, looking to the woman from the withers of the horse and smiling with inclusive patience. He pats the saddle, "sit right here," as she sips his taste from her mouth, grinding a finger across her front teeth to erase the lingering jissom. Then, right then, she is more than a whore and more than a mouth of succor. Clarabelle is something needed. Through the wince of her jaw she speaks.

"You hurt me bad jammin at my face, knowin my jaw was broken."

"That's why I switched to your pussy. Twiceover, if recalling correctly."

"There's hell to pay for that."

"I burned those men like you asked."

"I ain't talkin… fuck! Nevermind!"

Snow and ice threaten what sun they are given and their day is uneventful. They find a stream reversed in its run from a crag and follow a trail beside it. Clarabelle looks back at the Nickel. Aten Mire Conquin does not. Either with a heart stomped black. Best to deny ever-ever being and accept the front of this; their proximal nights darkened long colds with ice so dark it congeals in fists to make their horse erratic. On their fifth day east he bolts with the thunder, fifty yards later a foreleg snapping in a kiva ditched for snow. Rising trilegged he attempts to scramble and Threadbare shoots him twice, the blasts eternally roaring, the horse instantly dead, though touched and stroked by Threadbare. His places his hand on the pulse. Roughage of beats then nothing. He then climbs from the floor of the kiva.

"What? Conquin," she attempts to slur. Conquin does not move.

The couple lay poisoned in a vapid sleep with their whiskey drained between. The skittish palomino hadn't been hobbled when they found a cave to house themselves deep enough to damp the shots.

"Who is about?" Clarabelle asks, without caring who is above them.

Threadbare kneels between the pair. He sits the night watching as if such devotion were expected, whether or not, his wakefulness takes their lives. When Conquin's scalp is stripped at dawn she's awake, but the woman doesn't sober, as he trims and rips and hangs. She thanks Threadbare for her bandage and though he is scalped, Conquin doesn't stir.

"The rosary?"

"Around his neck."

Threadbare removes it, stokes their fire, tells the woman "your horse is dead."

"Can I not go with you?"

"That, you cannot do."

"Well, why ain't I followin Conquin?"

"The governor wants his rosary. Not the charm you wear on your neck."

"Shit. Well, okay."

Threadbare then slits his throat. Never a twinge from his body. He offers the woman his knife for what imagined ables. She takes it, puzzles and holds it.

"What do you want me to do?"

"Walk east or take my horse. I've nothing to give but that."

She looks at Conquin in the fire he has stoked. Primogeniture bold on the walls of the cave unnoticed while they drank: long bluestem grass. A kestrel hawk. Coatimundi known as chulos. Other ideogramic worlds. From the paintings her eyes range back to Conquin. The warden's head is gone.

"He couldn't sober up for death."

"But it came. Chose. Dealt."

"What if it comes for you?"

He looks to the woman, sighs with impatience. Becomes a fairing for the wind in cave. In thought he considers what Clarabelle considers, that she should follow Conquin. When he mentions rosemaling the children have fingered, he says "believe me, their impressions are deeper. They prefer drawing flowers in red." After this, he responds to her question. "You're holding a weapon that chooses. Does the hand holding the means, know the refrain of that meaning?"

"Shut your goddamn mouth! There's more to life than death and riddles! You speak to hear yourself!"

"Just as you say Clarabelle."

He points behind the woman.

"The flowers are there. Their blooms much deeper. They unite the back of this cave."

"I said shut your goddamned mouth!"

"Just as you say my child. After you, come, we'll see."

TENDER

"The dawn."

"Sun'll be nice if there is any. October's been a month to forget."

"October is gone Dampier. She had the first on the left of All Saint's Eve and the second on the first of November. Ain't nothin but tempest in that. Let's eat a druid when that dark'un falls asleep. If he ever sleeps again."

"The druids were a people Moba."

"How the hell should I know that? A hardworn midwife dumped on the plains and Billy my only business. Since '25 they birth 'em prior, bring the kids out here grow'd. I wouldn't tote a baby this far."

"You ain't birthed in four damn years?"

"I gen'ally keep water and holler with the women. They do what work gets done. Afore' I come from South Carolina it was almost four a week. I tended whites and blacks and any betwixt and aye God did folks fuck then! Hereabouts, screwin has stalled."

"You ain't learned the Mexican tongue?"

"Not nary a fuckin word. They like their priests and prefer other midwives. I ain't tried to break in. Then you and Billy settled like fools. Though I reckon it don't matter, an American twot or a Mexican twot look the same with a human squeezed headlong. Apache twots do to. Twots the world alike. Aye God, the beauty in that. Though goobers tend to differ."

"Thank you for your vileness Moba. We ain't goin nowhere."

"You'll enjoy it a partial fuck less if the Comanche come offa these plains. They'll skin ye from heel to asshole and make leggins outta the strips. If not them you're a season at most from Mexico City sendin soldiers. For no other reason but to whoop you."

"Other things I consider," said Mox. "What we know is there can come."

*

Billy had the twins in the fall of '29 thirty-seven minutes apart. They needed help. Moba was sent for. She the sole midwife northwest of Austin who speaks no tongue save English, Austin southeast some five-hundred miles, the trail fraught with inseparable dangers. Moba is sixty-years old. She rides her speckled donkey the twenty-two miles northwest from Reckingfort Soo. This latterday cluster of adobe and thatch since leveled by the ranches that owned it. They've built a road on its back, fenced that long stripe, Reckingfort Soo has dissolved. What was plain became homes and homes came with settlers and their bones and that dust buries deep. As if to aver their existence herein these pages are read. Play witness to the birth of their twins. They before Texas I imagine. The first whites in that panhandled region.

"You time 'em Moba. I can handle the rest."

"They ain't two comin Dampier. Twins is one and the same.

And your handlin of Billy is what got us here and the Lord, you're white as a egg!"

Moba swabbed Billy's forehead and does as she's asked, a supine Billy with a sheet above knees lying on a cornhusk single. Flat on the floor like sunlight. Their lonely sodhouse near the Punta de Agua north of the Canadian river. Dirt in her hair and mouth. Through a fourteen—hour labor she has grunted and cursed as the twins took their time to adduce. The first of the sons, the swarthy boy Torq, came to a crown and stopped. Moba said "push" and she did. The lamp extinguished with his birth, he born unto dark, swamped with this beginning he was soundless.

"Move Dampier," said Moba. "Light that fuckin lamp."

Moba grabbed Torq as he exited the womb. She hung him by his ankles, holding the umbilical and popped him on his cheeks till he wailed. Moba asked Dampier to trim his navel, but the father's busy retching in the doorway.

"How bout that othern Billy?"

"He ain't quite ready Moba. He's holdin to the sides in there."

Following Torq's liberation he is given to Billy. Moba rubs his body with a square of wagonsheet and a howl from his chest laments. Billy kisses his lips, tickles his soles, the yellowtinted eyes and bruise colored skin harbingers of a health that is failing, though his death won't come for years. Death wants him to remain where he is. Wants him here and tanged with a hate for others decreed by his very birthing. I'll suggest who will come for him.

"Wind your timepiece if you will Miss Moba. I want the minute and second."

"It's wound and tickin but it ain't no clock. It's busy endin our lives."

Brother Latham was birthed with the minimal pronouncement, Billy sipping her water and drawing her smoke when his head slid free of her cavity. She reached between her thighs, pinned the baby down, while screaming for Moba's return; the midwife in the open webbing her skirts, watching Dampier search the grass. She bounced and shook her haunches, clearing her thighs of drops.

"I'm here Billy. I was peein. You had the lil' bastard without me!"

Torq lay in the smoke of the cheroot coughing in a crib separated from Billy. His brother whimpered and cooed without crying, sliding from his mother like a calf. He has analcime skin some rouged. Torq turned his broad head to focus the noise but the smoke in his eyes was blinding. Lamp smudge and cheroot burning. Avast what woe they will, but neither helps this boy. He has hives from the sheet of the wagon she has used and alone in the crib Torq will stay.

"Billy, this'un is perfect. Like warm udder milk. My Lord!"

Latham's swaddled in a cotton shirt. Placed in the crook of her arm. Moba leaves the umbilical, reaches for Torq, but the infant refuses her grasp. He smacks at his ribs with tiny black fists and screams and she smiles and vies for his affections by changing to the voice of a Titan. The boom attracts his attention.

"He don't want me, nor nobody else. You want me to tidy your middlins? You ruined this here mattress."

"No mam. Get Torq. Give 'em to me."

Moba disposes the packing of birth and inspects the infant's navels. For fault of the light Torq is placed on her left while Latham gurgles on the right. Billy studies the twins, their heads on her shoulders, countermanding what twins should be. They are more than nothing alike.

"They ain't a damn thing similar," said Moba. "You'd think 'em birthed outta two separate holes and they won't be playin no swap tricks. That'n couldn't hide in the dark cause he glows, but the othern can't see enough light. Why the fuck did he come forth purple? You musta pinched 'em, squeezed 'em to birth. Ask Mox if his dangle is broke?"

"Dampier's penis is fine. He's flogged me the whole damn time. He's the first and only dangle I know."

"One damn man Billy Mox! They's twenty I done forgot! They're harder to find when a lady gets older, the wind flappin the laundry and whatnot. You're a might wallered out yourself. For such a young woman that is."

"Moba, please stop talkin. I've recently brought forth twins."

"I'm here to support, to soothe."

Dampier Mox doesn't watch the first feeding, fear increasing his rounds to a schedule, Kiowa ponies circling their homestead, the riders leaning headward in the saddle, cutting the trail for sign. They have followed Moba's donkey, behind her instepping, concaving the grass in places, a bevy of warriors alarmed and intent on a study of the trail before them, who has come from Reckingfort Soo. For the last three years since escaping Mims Nickel both tribes present and wait. Check the margins of the homesteader's place. Four times a month they sit on the horizon, no alteration or change in the stoics of pattern since Billy and Mox's arrival. They came with the clothing on their backs, a subsistence lacking human dimensions, somewhat improved after three long years and the Comanche and Kiowa haven't killed them. Refuse to steal their stock. Take the grain from their rudiment cowhouse. Something other keeps them at bay. He, this other, has come from Mims Nickel to trail at a reasonable distance, seeing where their wastes were buried, as if any could hide from him. They knew he was there and knew what he wanted, but a tease of pursuit was given, Threadbare snuffing their fires while they slept, he drawing in the dirt, making snow pillows, placing the cold at their feet. He was there, then he was gone, present quotidian for the steps of their journey until Billy left a message he could have them. A silver maple was the tree she chose. With trembliness she carved COME TO ME, her gravelly whisper into springnight dark, "come on, come in, you fuck." But Threadbare disobeys. Absent when the pair builds their lone sodhouse northwest of Reckingfort Soo, a place in that time of itinerate nomads, deanimized from their travel on plain. Desultory they encroach through plackets of haze, outliers classed in doom. She refuses Reckingfort Soo, as if contact would soften her core. Billy has to comprehend that they are alone and Dampier won't question her reasons. He of a similar logic. *Who lives without threat isn't living she thought.* You're as alert as your primary doubts. They stop at random where Billy requests. In the empty near the Punta de Agua, they simply cease, then begin sodding.

*

The east is ormolu when Mox walks in, a goldblack light sneaking on the prairie, Billy asleep on the singlet. Moba Threnody has cleaned her, flipped the soiled mattress and sits by the window with her pipestem. The twins are docilely awake. Each child has found a hole in the sod, there fixing his stare like a handmade doll, Mox wondering why the light attracts them. On this, their very first day. Do they know what they are in becoming? Or are they trapped in a world unchosen?

"You can touch 'em Mox."

"I don't want to wake her."

"You won't. They won't break. If they broke we wouldn't be here."

Moba exhales and looks to her fusil. Leans back in her chair to speak.

"That first'un Torq is hideous beef."

"Surely ain't pretty now is he?"

"Then again Mox, they's other things to be, asides bein fuckin purty."

"I'm sure he'll turn 'em over to find 'em."

"She wasn't happy with you fuckin around. Missin the whole damned thing."

"Moba, if they come and the five of us die, you won't think about happy dead."

"Them Kiowa woulda kilt me a comin. They did not me and will not us, so let it the fuck alone. What do they want? Your riches? A spot in this half-assed house?"

"You're the one that warned us Moba."

"I warn of all comers awake and asleep. What wants ya'll ain't the tribes. Besides, I'm deadly with this fusil. And I ain't a sore shot neither. I expect to be looked directly in the eye by whatever chooses to gut me. Death'll get me back home, offa these flats, hereabouts ain't fuckin habitable."

"Like us, you ain't worth robbin."

"They could steal my drink or want somethin odd! Menfolks love their oddment! Lord, the things I've done!"

"You've had too much odd already."

"I married big-cocked men. That's what wore me to frazzle. That sixth'un almost kilt me. Goddamighty the peter on him!"

"Did this here all go good?"

"Babies comin outta mamas ain't lackin in sufferin. Good ain't a apt description. She's alive. Your sons are too."

"I'm gonna sleep for an hour. Will you rouse me?"

"You damn people with your time. I ain't gonna need to rouse you, that ugly baby will. That lil' fella ain't tolerant."

24

PANG FROM A rumor in repeat, he's been sighted in the town of Juarez. He swam the river onto its north bank to stare at a state in burgeon. Coming. Wanting to be. In the past three years since halting his pursuit he's been an idler, a trader and a murderer. With the Yakima he has camped and learned to weave net, with the Creek to make blades from bones. In hostelries numerous from west to east he's avoided the whites on purpose, often trotting through parties and scores of lost families like a divider of necromanced seas. They call after. He doesn't call back. If a word was forced in the narrows of a pass or in the windings of riverside forests he refuses to speak in their language, implementing amalgams of various others to the scorn and confusion of many. Some become bold and he allows them to be, though this ambivalence isn't to last. Early in the year 1829 he fires the houses of a Mexican village. When troops are sent from the garrison they fight it with buckets and shovels. Their lieutenant colonel is a placid man whose family resides in the fort. He believes the flames are the fault of the weather as he believes that Threadbare is fiction. When he remains in his office during the encounter his family comes to abide him, three sons and a wife who is frail. By morning the five are buried in the desert, looking inward, a circle of heads, chins swiveling without collar or need. Lachrymose all except Threadbare. "Hush, hush," he says. "You're fine." He tells them to speak and he is attentive and their father begs them to pray. Says nothing to Threadbare directly, he as if fiction still, too horrible yet to consider. No threats or payment is offered. Watering the five he waits. With a sun insentient he squats next the youngest, a boy of nine who is smiling. He says "son, which hand is your preference?" He responds in English, says "sir, my left." The hand is freed, water given, the boy told his village is gone. "Child, dig if you wish, if you want." Threadbare then departs.

Three weeks later a lawman named Timms is surprised by Threadbare in camp. He's been sent by Austin to search for the body of a relative, a stranger to Timms, though it's work and the man is dire. Threadbare hears his clanging, cresting a hill, unknowing what Timms will do. There he sits his horse like a totem, an orphic, arrhythmically violent and shocking. In a pannier he has marcasite samples, their grinding alerting Timms' horse. The man is at his fire eating his meal and what a sight for the lawman to grasp. "Timms, I'm coming to you!" Into his world he rides. The Percheron is adorned with the heads of the villagers like an apprentice of Minos on earth. In amongst the strings of the humans that have melted is an intervening swineherd necklace wrapping the Percheron's girth, an eight foot strand of decapitated pigs hobbing the mizzliest eve, their mephitic and execrate shimmy, in liminal dreadful bounce.

There's not enough night for this lawman Timms for there is enough moon to see.

"The Lord be my witness," he utters.

Timms crosses himself and begins counting prayers on the beads of his in-hand rosary. Threadbare is reminded, thinks this is funny and commences to sing of the sea, an aubade of a bloodstone vessel held fast on the curve of the earth. The ocean in song is an ocean that boils, clasping the hull of the ship in spin to pull the crew beneath. A shipwright drowns in the process of waves and he croons of a love that is lost. On the surface of that sea, for unanimity is not, there is new falling snow that spits, on Threadbare and Timms the same, as the Percheron enters the firelight. Threadbare surveys, dismounts and nods, but Timms, he cannot speak. He shows a long pistol, a musket and cruciate that twists to become a blade. Threadbare talks to appease him.

"Do you know me Timms?"

"I do. Don't want no trouble neither."

"Is my appearance, uh, off putting? These things are attitudinal."

Threadbare's shawl is of the hair of skinned humans with a face smeared minium red. Timms is unsure if his eyes contain color but their ocellus is as black as their pupil, with a mane the white of fresh paint. His stomach has been scratched by something he has eaten and its blood is on his arms and chest. From his elbows down is a black-ash rub that glistens with an oil he has added. He appears to be limbless there. He wears the pants of his trade from his voyage southwest. On his waist is a drooping and padded hack-belt so gnarled and gory Timms gasps. He recoils from the fire, steps back.

"Where were you going Timms?"

"I ain't got no fight with you. Is them the hands of children?"

"Some. Most are not."

"Goddamn you man! Look here! I ain't been churched or forgiven enough to not burn eternal forever. I'm dead if I stay and I know it."

"Don't leave the light. Come to me."

"I don't want no rub with you. I'll go. We weren't even here."

Words and signs are the clothing of mind and this man has spoken volumes. He says "how can that wish be? Us not even here?" Threadbare sits flat, extends his long legs and places a calf in the coals. Timms watches him roll a slender cigarillo and is presented the pouch but refuses. "You're a nice man," he says. "We weren't even here?"

"I ain't a reader. Don't wanna trade thinkin."

"You're trading it knowingly Timms. And have no concern for

the man you seek. His scalp hangs nearest my heart." He taps the scalp, smiles at Timms. "This hair here. The reddest."

Timms is encouraged to walk to contentment but is kept from taking his horse. Thirty minutes hence he redirects northward to confront the predicament before him. The firelight blinks, its bittock of flame in relief of Threadbare's movements. He draws closer to a hundred yard span. Threadbare shoves his arm in the fire, withdrawing a log to signal.

"I ain't livin outta this. Won't beat it."

Timms passes the time on foot and awake watching the bountyman sleep. He cannot kill from there. When Threadbare stands and stretches, he screams "young Timms! We begin!" His horse is then slaughtered with a shot. His packs rifled from interest. When the wind begins tumbling in Timms' direction, the speller of a child blows past, herein sketches of birds and prey, and though Timms is a study reluctant, he has perspective, an eye for detail. From his lefthand boot comes his cracknel and jerky, chewing till his mouth is dry. The wind from the north then defeats its stale counter and downwind conditions are steady. Threadbare smells him there on the plain. He triples the size of Timms's fire and it saws and the stench in that heraldry of blaze wafts to Timms in seconds. The lawman decides to close. He has seconds or years awake.

"He ain't gonna do right by me. It's ugly or nothin with him."

Threadbare has apportioned the lawman's mount, the meat spitted and braced and cooking. The stump of the carcass engorged with mesquite and it smokes beneath sizzling haunch. Threadbare bitts the shank, the paloverde flexing, reacting, holding fast as Timms approaches.

"We'll eat in an hour Timms. I need you to gather wood."

"I ain't eatin my goddamned horse!"

"Then there's more for me and mine."

The Percheron is straddling the head of his horse, hoofing the obloid skull. He back-kicks it ten feet, chases it down, the sand trailing the blood of its rolling. Timms lowers his pistol from the shock of the sight and Threadbare is pleased to see him.

"Timms, dear sir, you're vexed. Leave your shooter on me. Don't consider my horse a target. He's liable to kill us both. Let him play his game, though your horse's head isn't shaped like a ball. I think he's gravelblind."

"I can't take you in for what you've done so I'm gonna end this here. You made a decent bondsman onct. What happened ain't up for discussion."

"What has happened is that I'm here."

"By sorry means you done took rotten."

"Rotten as relates to what Mr. Timms?"

"I said I ain't fuckin wordin with you! Step to the right of the fire!"

"Mine or yours?"

"What the fuck does it matter?"

"And what is to be done with your wife and child, Mr. Timms from outside Duckett? You've the house and whiskey to vend. That lumber won't pay for itself. Best take me home to collect. Spread a pallet by mother and leave me there and I'll dandle your junior on knee. As if creating the boy myself."

"Enough! That girl has tipped you! The rest of the world has to bear it! Them lunatic fuckers in Reckingfort Soo have you to thank for their deaths, cause that little missy resides there!"

"Billy isn't in Reckingfort Soo. Commence with your killing and hush."

"Ain't a thing in your blood held sacred."

"Timms, you're in my blood."

Raise the pistol. Audile tension. Timms repeats what he must do. Repetition like a child quoting poems. *Put the bead on his forehead, a ball through his brain and he's gone for me and many. Put the bead on his forehead, a ball through his brain and he's gone for me and many.* The wind it abases, plicating from distance, as if offended forces gather, unable to enter their purview, the hair of the bountyman pliably blowing from the wind at his back to his face, switching, changing due east, the tail of that white sufficient distraction for Timms to miss his shot, firing the ball in his shoulder, where it sets in meat and bone. An unfazed Threadbare laughs.

"The best mustered is a dent Mr. Timms." His face is a recess hiding disinterest as he inspects the lawman working. With bumbled grabs he seats his next. Shakingly primes, reloads. The bountyman peruses with patience. "Take your time. Aim and don't falter."

When the Percheron gallops through a Timms that is firing he breaks his jaw, his leg, and is then led easting with an encomium tongue in command. The horse arcs and turns to sniff Threadbare's shoulder, to kill Timms in his wallow on the ground. He is intuitively sent into darkness, Threadbare calling to the horse for placation, to keep the beast from crushing the man.

"Wait," says Threadbare. "We'll last him a bit. Extend his pain a little."

The beast trots neighing and his muzzle is rubbed and Timms is asked to roll. "On your back. You can get there." When he refuses he's placed with his face to the fire and his shoulders are broken with stomps. His hamstrings sliced and crimped. Threadbare removes his shawl of scalps, piles them by his feet in the dirt. With a caramel greenknife from the bisque of a potter he lances his wound for perusal. Exterior black, pecten of muscle, abut against bone but clean. Leaning sideways he allows inspection. "You missed by a foot Mr. Timms." The fragment is extracted with the smallest of pliers, the wound seared with a fire-heated blade. The nibs of the pliers are of the bones of small birds. Here a masterly craftsman has labored.

"Timms, I've an idea. Let's make use of your shot. There are elements of conflict a man must conserve, while others wash with the rain."

Threadbare pops the ball in his mouth. Ejects the lead to his palm. Apposing the shot to the fire, the fragment is branded with thought. Crucible, mold, pestle and snips are secondary to the man like books. Wares, threads that attach. The ball is flat on a side from the stop of his bone but the shot will be rounded again. He stokes the fire, the crucible is whetted, the ball studied, melted, cast. Recouped from his comb-shaped wound. When the cupular bottom has cooled, the new shot drops perfect to palm.

"This is acceptable Timms."

"I'll do it," slurred Timms.

"My pleasure."

Timms is given his selfsame weapon with the ball he's already fired. The Percheron stands behind Timms. There propped he lolls unassisted. His injuries prevent him from remaining upright so he is lashed from crotch to waist. Threadbare uses his pommel as cleat. The Percheron supports him, steadfast in wait, Timms hanging on his ribs from the saddle, his gun loaded and given to squeeze. Timms is confused and argues.

"I shoot you and he drags me to death. If not, I can't walk. I done missed. Can't do this again."

"You've other options. Think of the given. I can help you decide with a favor. Let me untie you first."

"I don't want no favors! You do it!"

Threadbare unties him, dismisses the draft, Timms collapsing to stomach. He need only pull a three-pound trigger and he's jerked about screaming to do this. A small temple of stones is stacked for his wrist, his arm supported upon it, the gun laced in the hand with the fingers that bend, his head leaned on his shoulder for aiming. The sun has risen. The sun they find. Buss of a cloud from replica night recusing the heat of that star. Fourteen paces are counted due east. Threadbare wingsides his arms and the man is as large as a body can be with the emptiness. He sees Timms is unconscious from pain. The other goes to work.

There are eight of the men who see the fire burning as it confutes from an origin singular. They know what they see is one fire, but as it hops they think it is two. These Americans, hunters of game, have been tracked by Comanche for weeks. Discovering Timms a man in their brood recognizes his errand from Austin. They find him by a fire, without carcass as fuel, snugly wrapped with his head on his saddle. He's been attended, set, left with a note on his chest he cannot touch. It tells them to emplace this man Timms in their knacker-worn transport for comfort. For salvation, whatever they bring. Timms has heard the grind of the wheels. Awakens to stare at his saviors.

"Surely, be gone," he whispers. "This is no thing of yours."

"Mister, goddamn, who left you with a note? Ain't you…"

"Leave. Leave. Leave."

"We can't leave you nowhere's from nothin. Who the fuck kilt your horse? Why the fuck is its head on a stake?"

"I know what has come and is here."

"You want us to abandon you layin?"

They are haggard as shibboleth humans. Gravure prints inculpate. Cornucopian painted misery. Diapaused creatures of woe. The man that speaks is the only man speaking because he is the man that can. The rest bemoan within. Confiscated amongst themselves. Embrocated, sweated with gloom. What color is the color of pursuance. Besides their knacker not a horse is amongst them. As harsh as it gets thus getting.

Timms says "abandon me layin. Damn you to the man, go on."

Profaning instructions they take to their bottles and by late afternoon are camped. Timms warns thrice more, exhausts. Sleeps then wakes then begs. With a blasphemous cordon "heed what I say, for if night finds you here you're dead."

The sun sets bringing night and with the following day there are truths intending truths. Eight heads on stakes but Timms is untouched. The ghoul unit circling his bed. He there in its center protected. Threadbare's note was used for the wiping of the ass of Timms's luculent questioner. He wouldn't obey the lawman's imploring and the others could not appeal.

The platoon of Comanche knew Threadbare was near and therefore stalled for a day. The knacker wagon was taken with the mule in its trace, though Timms was left to fend, he hearing them yapping, the Comanche presaging, that eight sets of eyes watching him die were double that count in lieu. The heads would stand guard until Timms could rise, what mind he would have by then. There is night then day, his screams they recede, the weather clearing, sedate as reason. Strange pattern this time of year.

25

TWO YEARS ALONG after birthing the twins and Billy keeps Moba busy. Dampier says men should provide and protect; bring meat, do chores and cherish the women, lift where the burden is heaviest. The women heckle him fondly. Then Moba has the stroke in November. In six weeks time she's healthy enough to return to Reckingfort Soo. Thinks she's a burden to Billy, though Billy wants Moba at home. In a battered surrey they probe through the Soo, Moba sick and frightened with her failure of body and they've come to collect her possessions. Her speech remains clear but stilted. Lacking flow from word to word.

"We built that house brick upon brick around the share of our things. It was summer, tragically hot."

Billy's heard the story before, the aged converse through their years, while the young have the pasts of the born. Moba traveled from the east with her house in tow and when tented unloaded her furniture. She brought a man no longer a factor, living in the tent they pitched, shaping and shaving the malm into bricks, the walls climbing around their possessions. He intentionally minused the door of the home so their things couldn't be stolen. When he went to draw water in September that year they found his bucket at the well, but didn't find him, his footprints dragging northwest, as if her suitor wanted her trailing. Moba tracked him from Reckingfort Soo to the Mora, through modern day Watrous to the slopes, the massif of the Rockies preening before her when his shuffling changed its complexion. At the base of the North Truchas Peak he began to be led by another. Moba reversed for home.

"It's a hell of a bed I brought," said Moba. "We best knock down a wall."

"We won't never get it out, least not the frame, through that window of a door ya'll cut. Torq! Come offa that brake! Stop fuckin with progress and sit!"

Tiny blackheaded Torq in the rattletrap surrey is pulling at the improvised handbrake, the lurch of the mules quite comical, gazing at his mother to test her condition until Billy roars him still. She hands Moba the reins and reaches behind her to thump him on the nose and shake him. She slaps Torq to his shoulder on the lap of his brother as Latham climbs Moba's back. He lands on her knee saying "horsey."

"M-u-l-e-s," says Moba. "They're m-u-l-e-s."

Inside her own head she inventories. Moba thinks if they can borrow a buckboard and horse they can be back at Billy's by midnight. They've a section of spile to punch through the wall. If the women can pendularly swing it, the bed can be tugged through the gap. With a half frozen mouth, numb left arm and a soricine glare she turns, Moba looking at Torq with threat, the message sent to the boy.

"Torq, sit nice with Latham. Moba ain't spry no more. Me and your mother is busy."

There are twenty small houses of similar design. Moba's sits on the end. From conflict twelve lay empty. Two here, three there, no legislate pattern and there are spaces to fill that won't be. Beyond the homes there's substantiate prairie, an afflatus to few for what comes off it engirds the worst of fates. The plains have lost their allure, what desire they contained in the first place, not found in the people undead. There is no mail and rumor is scant for the settlers who call this home. Their world is devised with exordium dawns, each instant a second inferred, such inference harshly concluding. Be damned your comfort here.

His voice booms from the back of the surrey as Billy is unloading her children.

"You ladies best abandon that spread of yours and get to town this week! Reckingfort Soo won't last till spring! The General will see to that! A plague worst than locusts descends on this place! Biblical! Biblical judgment! Heed what I say! Be gone!"

Billy deems his leaving a positive. Has heard his diatribe prior. She listens to his words, dismisses them quickly, her months as of late sublimely irreligious with a god that sounds like her twins. As an infidel, this sustains her.

"We'll be payin you no mind on this fine day as you go about your fleein brother minister. Do remember my flock in your prayers."

"Sonofabitch," Moba grits. "The only fat bastard twixt here and New Orleans on a diet of pie and poverty. The select seem to fatten their waists and wallets in the middle of fuckin nowhere."

Moba watched the pastor waddle from his house then wait until their surrey was halted. He'd come to her twice on nights in high summer with his penis hard-biting his zipper, a quart of good rye on his breath. He had a wife and five children he'd irreluctantly abandoned for the heathen of Reckingfort Soo, two of those children from two other women, with warrants for extortion submitted, by six congregations thus served.

"Come this August the redmen will burn us! They'll have Mexican gold in their pockets!"

Billy knows the pastor was a reputable slaver before his call to the fold. She hates he exists and corrects him: "if they burn us we likely deserve it for ploppin wherever we choose. The day the Comanche and Kiowa submit is the day we're gonna leave, cause fools will come behind them. Till then I'm willlin to swop 'em a steer or a sup from my freshwater barrel."

"Mexico pays better'n a steer or a drink from a damndable barrel! And if it ain't them there's more on these plains to wipe you and said party slate-clean! Billy Mox, you listen to me! Five years of luck are gonna run dry! The Lord has told me it will!"

"I have to hear you pastor, for indeed you hear yourself!"

Latham squalls with the heightening of voices, squirming from Moba's lap, pitching to scoot in the dust of the street and when he rises he looks like a fryling. The boy clatters the spokes of the surrey, rounds the corner in a dudgeon of tears, there his brother is standing with a gallooned lamp, the wick removed and a frown smudged black, Torq dumping the oil in his hair. This sends Billy into fuming hysterics, the minister continuing his blatting, though he's quickly astride a paint. Departure won't save him from Billy. His sermon has moved her spirit.

"Moba, can you help me please?"

"Yes Billy. I'm sorry. I ain't no use."

"You're plenty use to me. Excuse me, reverend, sir!"

"Speak damn you! I'm leaving!"

"Listen to me you shit! It's taken five years without the help of the weather to collect a herd we can manage! A sufficient beginnin supposed! That havin been said, we ain't gonna quit, so go about your business and find another town to hide your head and prick! Tell Houston or Austin they's plenty of room for any sumbitch that'll come here! As far as we know our lease'll be Mexican and land is what we're after!"

"That's nothing but a hoax woman! They want you Mexican, Catholic, speaking their Spanish or you'll be enslaved or murdered! They don't want no Americans floating out here when the states want the land to the ocean!"

"Stop damn you! Right there!"

The paint throws its head, the minister unseated, his horse desirous to launch him. He holds tight with his reins twisting right, the fatman remaining atop. Billy secures his headstall, hisses and the paint removes him. The pastor lands on his rump. When he gets to his feet a snell leaded with ball slides to his palm for quirting.

Her pistol is bared like a fist. Mashed in his face, there held. The twins cease fighting, don't know her irate, their mother intending to kill him.

"You won't be strikin this horse. And you won't be hittin on me. Ain't nobody gonna scare or evict us. As for you, get the fuck on, before I kill you dead."

Billy lowers the pistol. Allows him to speak. He'll have the very last word. She doesn't want her weight on the weak. Especially this pious arbitrate of duty meaning well if gaining control.

He says "Billy, the tribes have eaten Mexican soldiers since Reckingfort Soo came to be. War, it shall consume you."

"You're sayin the tribes eat humans?"

"To the very last woman and child! I have it on authority as true!"

"Then you, dear reverend, have suffered too long without a decent thought in your skull. Please go wherever you're goin. If you don't leave your ignorance might leak on Moba and the twins. I can feel it on my skin standin near you."

"If Dampier Mox shoots the wrong game or forgets some toll come due, you won't never realize they're on you! Not to mention that bunch in Chihuahua! They've had enough of this Texas shit! They know you come from the east!"

"They didn't come from the east. They come down from the far northwest. Reverend, you leavin your wagon? That shuckstompin mule in the back? The onliest damn thing you done since you come was build that flatbed yonder. That and try to screw me."

He looks at Moba, nods and prays. She herself won't feign him control. He says "I'm traveling the paint, take the wagon. That mule is crazy to bite." To spite the man Billy asks for a blessing, the dimwitted minister vain to give it and in so doing is victorious. Latham's eyes are weeping with the burn of the oil, he watching the minister's movements, wanting to pray like him. His brother is the polar opposite, Torq chidden, openly scoffing the verbage, screaming "no, no, no, no pray!" When the minister is finished Billy thanks him fondly for creating their legalized marriage, with documents unquestionably false. His school of divinity and pithy red seal the work of Moba's ink. He says "blessed we are in becoming. Blessed for the protection of *he*." The minister then doffs the wide brim of his hat, its circumference and dome faded from sun, as is the raglan of coat he wears. This visitant on plain then rides east through criterion swale, disk-shaped plants with a caravansary of peak behind him, the squlchy suck of the paint's clout-hooves sinking in mire that is drying. This river hereinbefore. The pastor sees where horses have crossed. One large breed, especially in depth, has sunk to the knee with its rider, a proselyte of multiplied size. The minister checks the track, his own grog blossomed hands, and thinks of the hands of his mother. How the woman moved blind about the coldest of kitchens in a morning laced with darkness, a mutual converser to a child not there though she talked to that child for years. Dead brother. Live sister. Dead son. As dead as absent can be. He left her in that kitchen and did not return, his mother saying "Thomas? Thomas?" This quotha of sin yet expressed.

"What mortal thought is your disease dear reverend?"

The reverend faces the voice. That periwig white of head. A canthook of bone rests in his hand as the day then its night interjects. Compline's hour is here. The reverend asks "what've you come for?" Knows the deep track is his mark.

"Why, solely for you," says Threadbare. "I'm here to lead Thomas home."

26

PARCHED SUMMER THEN September and without rain two families home Reckingfort Soo. They believe as credible ineliminable hearsay that the provincial governor will burn them. Light the prairie on the Llano Estacado, raze it north to the High Plains' flats. When north and south of the Canadian River smoke is seen partitioning, the governor is the immediate villain. No concessions are made for a prescient maker, who neither impressed nor offended by man, and from his own fulgurate sky, sent a balden of storm upon a Kiowa, where unquarriable flint has surfaced. A solitary bolt from that saturnine firmament kills the brave and the grasses ignite. The water starved prairie searing from drought became the tender of an incubate maelstrom. Wind rose from the west and in feeding the fire raced between the Canadian River to the Punta de Agua due north. As it squares, it chooses its map. The push of the blow its direction.

Watering Comanche saw the smoke at noon. They've seen these fires before, their analect history on paper and tongue speaking of a time when our world was afloat and into its center there drained, such gape becoming the Christian's hell, though from that sieve their gods, one of nature who sets the world alight, regenerating fire after fire. The trio of braves bound at a trot to the reach of the augmenting blaze, sweeping down its eastern side. When they gallop northeast of the Mox's claim they're trotting on the nape of a herd, redirecting the heads of two hundred bison into a caucus of five hundred more, spiraling and turning their inferior body north with the assistance of others. These phantasms adumbrate join from the smoke, there and not there, present again, like a life in its finish or a wind unabraded seeking relative form to claim it, for a breeze without friction is silent.

Dampier watches them hail from the smoke, the band in riding stagger, on purling horses for in that light they seem as gold to him. They conglobate patient as their fathers would do, these holandric men of plain, humans locked in time, of a state encoded and including the land as gift and killer alike, so much a portion of the earth itself that ahorse they appear as vergers, ordaining excogitate shapes. With a suddenness the band exhales from their leader and their chieftain shifts and calls, ripping up turf until he sees Dampier on his horse confused and lost. When he reaches for his weapon the chieftain expects it and overtly extends his hand, clucking and throwing his chin at the fire to announce in Shoshonean that we under fire are the same. Dampier cannot accept this.

"I can't do nothin! These here is my cattle mixed in with them buffs!"

The Comanche converts his phrasing, Dampier screaming alternate orders, as if yelling will make them clearer. He's been thralled by the tongue but attempts no greeting. The Comanche laughs and resumes. Hoping something might get through.

"Qué estás haciendo?"

"What?"

"Hay bisonte y vaca en juntos." He gazes to his left then back. "Pero, en esto momento no."

"What?"

The chieftain stares at Mox. "Nada Mox. Nada Mox."

"I don't understand. Shit!"

Insinuatingly the Comanche raises both hands. Mumbles "hmm," turns and gallops.

Dampier's cattle wander to pen. Five have been added by count. Four beeves he's acquired are range wild beasts with black-tipped horns bent awry. A bison in the stand in pullulate need paws at the ground to entice, the bulls in the lot inching to him, lowing and scraping and pitching their racks before the bison who swings a red and swollen organ oozing pale yellow and crimson, a wound in its abdomen from a former collision for he was once the plinth of his herd, cast upon this bathos of desolate plain to breed through will, suffer exclusion, and excluding pain realize, his alien place amongst others. The Comanche thought the bison a bull and in faulting returned it to pen. This they quickly remedy. Six shafts in rapid syncope beat take the bison's legs; Dampier and Billy, she coming out to him, go numb at the edge of the splitrail fence as the bison thuds to his stomach, limbs cracking like the spelch of an oak. Other cattle step back but do not excite, the bulls amenable here, for the bison would've slaughtered them thoroughly.

The chieftain, his sons about him, whoops his disgust and queries. He knows Billy is paying attention. His own two sons are not. They watch the progression of fire upon plain and refuse to look at the whites.

"Qué tonto! Lo siento! Me hace mucha falta! Es tuyo ahora, quieres?"

Billy assists her husband. Dampier's beyond his limits. He's sitting on his horse in the midst of the cattle. Billy unlatches their gate. Its rickety gripe is spastic with creak, his carpentry lacking in seasoning.

"Dampier?"

"Huh?"

"He put a buff with our cattle. That's the buff they lanced. He says we can have it. It's tough."

"Ask him…"

"They're done gone."

"I'll let these cattle graze. The fire ain't blowin to us."

"Not right now it ain't. Hard ever' day ain't it Dampier? Makes livin life rather *tenuous*. That there's the word I wanted."

They drag the bison from the pen with a mule called Earnest and to the best of their ability dress it. The leanest of the meat is sectioned and packed, drug across their yard into an excavated cellar dug within a week of their building. Here on shelves of her own devising Moba has placed the following: orrisroot, cannas and chervil. A hundred pounds of field potatoes. There's a dulcet of fruits in jars of clay and neither Billy nor Dampier have the slightest inkling where the midwife secured the lode. It was dug, empty and then occupied and to that they add raw meat. The carcass lay stretched on the plain. The stored meat they will not smoke. Impediments will promptly close.

Dampier and Billy and she on a donkey then bundle their cows southeast, telling Moba they're moving the herd, the cows smelling smoke which makes them want water and the sun in traction will not set as it burns through sculling clouds, a rose and pink fog-bow drifting them to water in mass and the herd is anxious, higher winds dissecting the smoke from the fire as the flames exhaust their fuel, it tiring in quadrants of dry streambeds as its numerous tracts are cinched. The couple lose one other. There is too much smoke to see. Billy sits the donkey and waits. She says "Mox, I'm right here."

"Come closer! I can't hear you!" He rides into the streambed, spins his mount and in that bed five others, a bull and four cows scudding the draw past Mox to drink from a pool. He can see her listing on the donkey, as if the weight of information Billy must impart is too heavy for the head she wears. Again she speaks as he touches his ear, the cattle blathering, chucking hooves, sufficient in decibels to drown her speech, Billy then by his side within seconds, the donkey petulantly roughing the drinking cattle by ramming their slurping heads, kicking through, instead of around them. She says "Moba has the babies and the fire is contained so why don't you ride 'em down? Ask how long they burn." Billy knows for eons they've fought or dodged them for she's seen it on lithograph stone. Happenchance is a constant to these warriors in herd, mere grizzling sobs of earth. "Ask 'em to help us Dampier. You gotta talk to these men eventually."

"Billy, they're Comanche."

"I know what they are. They think we're cursed senseless for livin amongst 'em like those in the Soo who're stayin. We're alive cause they think we're cracked. They choose to leave us be. If we die, no one'll ever know. What else is there to respect?"

Dampier affirms with a sullen gesture. Spots the warriors working stray bison. Eight braves bareback on ponies gait heaving, legs nude, free hair horning. They are scriveners with words on scrip by hoof, plunging in the face of that scrubland fire before retreating to heckle its fury, the breadth of the blaze irrespective of containment smokes out, then flames again, what beasts emit bison pursued, though they've nothing to fight fire with. They seem minikins dusted with magic, graminivorous riders in flame.

"Welcomes here are presented daily. Ain't a damndable one that pleasant."

"What's tame won't matter in cinders. This'un might burn us yet."

"Indeed it might dear Billy."

From the streambed they see a line of teal to the south that holds no fire, though the sky there does jail smoke. To the north and west the sun is aging, there obscured for the fire still burns, the braves dancing on their horses or standing to battue, their day dream bright as they flush what hides, the fire in battue without them. The smoke adjusts, mandating inferno, the braves on horseback chasing the bison like boys in a furnace lit room, back from the fire before the ball of the sun bleeds them through open embrasures, outlines abridging but seeable. As their huntways are checkered in abstract vortice twenty bison are taken for winter and the Mox's drift to their skinning, for they've botched the one they attempted, while these men are preeminent bloodsmen. The fire sees them exit the streambed, the bulls and the cows to their front, the pair with their herd stepping northward. At their homestead a blaze has risen to knee, twenty by ten, decreasing. It burns close to their house, the unfinished corrida and it hears their children screaming, the door of their house flying inward in shards, the man entering the room with Moba and the children and he is known as is foretold. A familiar he relishes the seconds of shock for their pleading and their begging and denial. *How can you be with us?* Torq leaps from a corner to wrap around a leg, biting his flesh to protect them. He's flicked to the floor and Latham goes to him as Moba is thrown through their doorway. "Take me," she moans and he says "later" and she is drug in the cellar with the bison, headfirst against raw meat. She's sequestered there with a pierce and twist of a marline to remain. The fire watches him bend it, transpose himself and look into the empty passage where the twins are choking on fear. It is here he pauses and waits. The fire rescinds to stubble. Licks at the base of their ramshackle pen before snuffing its digiting flames. He watches it flicker, weak without forage, before stepping through the open doorway. When his blade reflects they freeze.

Latham says "the man chasin mama." Torq says "ya, está."

*

Billy talks Dampier into joining the Comanche and their cattle are permitted to drift. They're issued stone handled torches of tarred ascender, d-shaped clubs of oleaginous wood that when lit will burn bright blue. Until there is clarity the chieftain sketches in the dirt and the pair finally understand. Within a ten-minute gallop they are backfiring flares as others cover the wall, the fire selecting a five mile stretch to open another campaign. As they backlight and their torches extinguish the handles are left where thrown, tossed asunder in navigable grasses, found post fire or in a thousand years or never discovered again. By the set of the sun they've dammed the blaze and it wars against itself, its grassy fodder soon diminished. None in the party will speak of what's done, for what will words describe, hours in mount against the lees of a burning that if choosing to flare tomorrow will singe by storms' desire. Why discuss the hollowest victory? The expanse is victor here.

Dampier finds Billy on a hillock where a line of buhrstone sits. It is sunk like quatrefoil cabbage. Her donkey grazes north of the millstone where the rock has stopped the fire. Behind it untouched prairie. The buhrstone cloves, trenched shoulder to neck are like sundials, gnomons to shadow-feign days, or the beginnings of a venerable edifice. Says Billy "up yonder he wanted these dug. To cut and sell to granaries. Haul the fuckers to God knows where. A section of these bastards is a hundred pounds light. Count five times that to pay for your trip with him and two womenfolk loadin."

"Your daddy? Where ya'll come from?"

"Yep. Another scheme. Another bloated fuckin idea. You couldn't get one dug with six men helpin. Four mules to tip it over. And when you did the wagon would split, the axle justly wrecked. We had him, mama and me. Hank couldn't do a thing."

The Comanche ride to them but will not speak. What they know has passed the Mox's, whereas what they've seen was sensed. Circling their mounts they whistle and point, disaccustoming need for language.

"Reckon your donkey is funny?"

"It's done its share today."

"It appears to have burned itself out. Easier seen at night."

"Could start back again." She stares at the assemblage of warriors. "They see somethin we don't."

Two of the men in the impassive band ride north behind the buhrstone. Twenty-eight more search in alternate directions for fires that light but die. Nothing resurrects. Without the whites the Comanche would've ridden the burn to its protean absolution. Permitted the fire its path. Billy surmises the elder Comanche are discussing this point intensely, yet to offend their God. They speak of how it's been used. What effect the blaze has wrought, the revenant forthwith who now has abused it, with this illy surtout smoke. Like a coat it covers whereas needed and he's moved within that needing. They already know he is present. Know he has used it to move.

"This burned close to the house. I didn't think to check till now. Moba knows what to do."

"One of these braves would've warned her. They ain't never affected that woman."

"They need not a-ffect you. Dampier, you amaze me."

The Comanche break. Then they ride north. The brave who has noticed, a copy of an elder, comes to the pair with a question. Without Spanish they struggle but try. Dampier is attentive and humble.

"I'm sorry. I don't understand. Please forgive my ignorance."

Billy stares. She says nothing. All is unveiling to her.

His father who is sporting a uniform cape from the kill of a Mexican officer intrudes to arbitrate. From the dark he is there and his son with the others as if in dark exchanged. The elder is a veteran of Mexican skirmish and of Spanish before that time. No tribe exists that doesn't know war, amongst themselves or others, this man realia of its consummate practice, honing war to cementation. He has transported hunger into southern jungles where he raided and prospered and cached food and his sons are present this night. Snatches of English he carries. They were learned from the prayers in the missions he has burnt for those words were the last of their praying. Build your temples on alternate mounts. Not in the path I have chosen.

He says "horse is large. You have this horse?"

Dampier replies "this horse. This here is the biggest we got."

He motions for the couple to follow his lead. Hastened, but with iterance, he signifies tracks, Billy's donkey slowing her pace, she behind her husband and the Comanche elder and there is no moonlight shining; smoke wafting and their voices she hears, the brio and rancor of starlings unnerving, flying in counter to the stalesmoke mist, Billy jumping as they yen their shrill. The moon waxes but its purity is drowned and again, the moon is assaulted and blanched, removed to a tint nigh cold. The peneplain and its scape becomes less pronounced and she is boxed in gloze ashimmer. Billy, herself, alone.

"Who is there? You, Dampier?"

When it comes it's amassed like disease. The figure rips her from the donkey as the Comanche lights the boll to show Dampier the track, where the Percheron has waited for its master. Four heavy hooves like the buhrstone clover, its rider expansive to sink it. The singed plain shows his footsteps ending backhouse, at a door scattered like potsherds.

"Billy! Hey Billy! Come here!"

Both listen, await her arrival. No light. But moon. No answer. There is no Billy there.

27

SUN IN THE east with a sky autocratic, from the canthus of eye he sees this, the smoke darning like moonstone candy, Billy's donkey behind him in wait. Dampier is told by the elder Comanche to refrain from riding impatient; to stay his horse at a distance and approach from the back by foot, to recline on his heels. Draw the pistol you carry and hold it before you as another will hold his same. Dampier attempts to get this: "so I do?"

"You do," says the elder.

"They're done kilt. You know it."

He replies in Shoshonean: "there is light in the east. This is what I know. You'll go forward here."

Dampier wavers with his read of the sodbacked house, torn between this and searching for Billy because he already knows what he'll find, her body on the plain and three more here and he feels no other is living, not on this prairie or ridicule earth, his presence a barbarized ulcer. Dampier can't be without. Without her and what they've made.

"Moba! Boys! Boys!"

No answer. A step, then a halt. His weapon unnaturally lowered. As his horse finds the trough, it flings loose a rail and slurps at the water he's left. His steps shorten, up on his toes, not doing what the elder said do. The rear of his home is no different from day when he rode to water his herd. Sodbrick of ecru with surplusage weed that has dried and cracked without moisture, here receiving the heat of the sun. There's a window he's cut with a piece of glaive Billy found on the prairie last year. The curtain is drawn to the left. Is he able to summon the dead?

"Threadbare! Sir! They ain't but born! I'd like to have my children!"

Around the house, sweat running from the band of his hat and he's riling the flesh of his cheek; pressing, stresspressing, with so much sweat that a streak of wet sod lay behind him, his pistol in his left and that hand surely quaking as he knocks loose a marly deposit. As it crumbles it sticks to his arm. When he gets to the door there is no sound but he peers and there is her cot. Its corner draped by a quilt. In the center of the room is the table Billy built with the whiskey he bought from the Gulla, a freeman who plied the Soo. The jug is tipped but the cob is replaced, with a cup of tan clay beside it. This vessel is empty, liquor drunk, with the pipestem of Moba extrorsing, its length extended by an islet of light and the horse at the trough is joined by the donkey and he needs for the pair to quieten, his ambience their slurp with the voice in his head but there is no answer offered.

I am goin to die.

When Dampier goes in he raises the pistol with the bore to the ceiling thus neutered. He's hardened from the work of the plain and its labors but not for the killing of men. With a lengthy stride, long and around, he moves like a turret deep right then left, and when back right his children. They sit reconciled, uninvolved, their backs against four feather pillows. The cot is cattycornered, the twins in the shade and a sunbeam of light has found Latham. He is jabbering but the boy is asleep, as sound in the slumber of the immortal, as mortals unhindered by age. Torq glances at his father then speaks, as if another has filled the room.

"Him nighty. Latham not died. Pop, him gone, take mama Moba. Her screamed, but then her went."

Dampier goes to them, gathers his children, kneading their bodies for injury. Latham moans, awakens, whines and cries as Torq rudely stares at his brother. "No, no, no. Why Latham blubber? Him say big boys don't! Him say lanterns burn bright blubber and big boys not no lantern."

"Torq, what else was said? Did he say where he was goin?"

"Big white head with Coo-manch cluck. He give me a mark for bein good. Him not mean to Torq. Him say Latham is real bad. That Torq much nicer than Latham."

Dampier takes them outside but his scent is there. With fear his scent throughout. It's the smell of a gesture on a face pain sealed and the skating of wind over graves. A perceptible oaken and venin. The scent of the place of the loneliest being and in that place no other, as in that place denied, where diabase sands are mercurially heated, the joss dancing with claws that retract. It is the smell of this earth before fourth day light, post Biblicist days of darkness. He is in that room at the top of that building where storeys have taken the light, though he awaits for your watching down there.

"Stay here with me boys and think."

"Think" and "think" refrain from his sentence as they take their thinking poses. When Dampier kneels Torq steps back striking Latham in the back of the head. Torq straddles his brother, horseheeling his ribs, before Dampier yanks him rearing, releasing when he's clear but on little boy feet Torq tumbles through the door to his stomach, his shirt then coming untucked. Dampier sees the dressing, middle of the spine, six inches from his belt the bandage, its raveled edges frayed inward and red. There's a trickle of blood from the patch inundated, the habituate blood and sweat of little Torq making round the patch to drip, seen only by his father and the man who has set it; the latter branding the child for life, the former giving him breath.

"Latham, stop cryin." Calmly. "Throw grist at the chickens. Go play. Torq, stay where you are."

Latham minds as directed and his brother does the same, remaining on his stomach while his father oversees him, Torq placid till the patch is removed. When he squirms and yells, saying "him goddamn you!" Dampier is taken aback, his father sitting on his legs to read them: four in number, four inches apiece. Tattooed in black, there inked. They are permanent, stenciled with habile digits by a paint coerced from a linden, its pulp brought west from east. Around the Percheron's eyes it is also implemented; matching thick yellow rays of the sun in rise to the horse's yellow iris, the rays worming down his snout to his nose. A sunbeam bright this is, while on Torq **LOST** has been etched. **LOST** in unquestionable black.

"Him knows daddy and mama. Him follow you always, forever."

Latham chased a pullet through the back window curtain and the hen pecked at Torq and his branding. He gave no reaction and made no fuss when the bird left his back even bloodier. Dampier craved fleeing, but running to where, with Billy and Moba to find. He sat on his cot to think. Poured from the whiskey and drank it. Latham came through the door to accompany his father, passing his brother in exit. Torq said "I goin out there."

"That chicken'll die," said Latham.

"Torq can't catch a pullet."

Latham lay back on the cot. Dampier had another then another. Twenty minutes passed, Dampier mildly drunk, the mare returning to the trough to slurp, the donkey shortly behind her. They drank, the obstruction offensive, the pullet submerged and glaring. Torq entered the enclosure, yelling at the animals, sinking his hand in the trough. He retrieved the soggy pullet and threw it. As if to flour it rolled in the dust.

28

THREADBARE DRUG MOBA through the nubble of prairie then selected a spot of vantage. They are a mile and a quarter from the homestead, he watching the Comanche backfiring. When the braves were close he erected, Moba on hand further broken unconscious from the lick of the knifegrip given, he explicable on the plain with the nightfires burning, like the clingstone pit of a fruit. There without cover, perhaps lurid to Comanche, stood this flamethrown Magus with ward, brought flailing by otherworld onager, to walk where others would burn. Knowing or not, the Comanche ignored him, Billy within yards of the pair on her donkey, a legitimate haze of smoke without deference in and around the two. Threadbare wanted to be seen but wasn't.

Moba awakened from the dropsy of concussion with gules before edematous eyes, those slits to the world barely open. Her face is swollen, neck twisting, muscles lauding with ache, the colors she sees her captor and kin so he becomes these shades approximate; indelibly white and flaxen, blue with the gray of an almshouse wall and the strewing green of grass. Moba whispers to Threadbare exactly what's seen and he replies "you've been hitting your head. I've seen my face in the run of a brook reflecting the color of night, though day was pronounced upon me. The colors you see are for the patching of heaven or for things that grow from the earth. On me, they've nothing to accomplish."

"It's what I'm seein. Has your head been hit? Ever been struck this hard?"

"Yes, but caused by a brother and sister. They sought a horse I could not ride. On that horse I didn't."

"Stop pullin. My legs'll walk. Cut loose my goddamned ankle."

He obeys and she thinks she's dead. What else could this man be? Threadbare before her on a plain familiar, enfolded by a night of heat; fires here and there and demons on horses accruing amongst the blazes. She's athirst in a lake of fire and flat and his hair is bechamel white with eyes of black dissension, no damage from the stroke can she feel in her limbs because she has no sense of feeling. Something in the punishment has left her sensate but only in sight and speech. No tingle below her neck. Must be her salvation. Moba thinks *heaven will follow. For the moment I am his.*

"Is this hell? Did I get demoted?"

"No, but it will be Texas."

She watches him divest his clothes. His corpus is a printing of scars and burns and where the bite of frost never healed. On one foot is only one toe, but he maintains a normal gait. There's the scarring of a rope around his bull neck that has festered to worms and back, the joint of a finger rooted through the wound has removed necrotic tissue and was left somewhat to fill. His left shoulder is stricken with gangrenous black but it does not seem to bother. You would never know he cared. His eyes teem with an apposite message, from other threads, immovably divining. And with that warmth he turns to Moba, sitting naked on her pelvis as her breathing breaks rhythm and the woman attempts to amuse him.

"I ain't gonna be much of a fuck. I think I shit myself."

Threadbare grins. She doesn't smile back. The scent from her oyster is as foreign and remote as Dalmatia or the North Atlantic.

What we have here is a ritual, he scaling ratline through webs of dim light, where skin to skin he can feel another human as a sail feels the touch of its wind. He takes his blade and opens her clothes, slicing and peeling Moba to bareness but he doesn't look in her eyes. He throws them to the side in a pile for his torches and stabs the blade in the dirt. He runs the tip of his finger down the bridge of her nose and she sees it painted there. It's hieroglyphic, a bird of known breed, broken by his features but present, the last she'll see on this earth. Moba knows its song from childhood. Threadbare knew this was so when he painted it.

"A bobolink. Yes?"

"It is."

"One sang to me as a girl."

"Again it sings dearest Moba. Do you see it in the colors you have claimed?"

"I see it for what you are."

"Let it come through the last of your hearing."

"Do what you will motherfucker. You ain't paintin a memory for me."

"I've watched you cross from Reckingfort Soo. I allowed you to travel my plain. You've been trimmed from feeling but your heart still beats. I can see it in the blue on your throat."

"Stop expendin your ample time."

"Your quality I rarely encounter."

"I'm forgiven. Leave me be."

"For what?"

"For you."

"Ah, yes."

Moba studies the way he has mounted. Sitting on her thighs with his penis and testicles snugged inward to perineum, the hair of his pubis kinky and stained with blood and grease and sweat. His body is extensive, unatoned and avenged by a soul manured in tears. Nothing is linear about him. He is plot and plat and curve.

Man and woman and the pietin image of human hurt received. And on his face, there painted ideally, is a bobolink songing its meekness. As if Threadbare were present at birth. His sortilege bordered by what she remembers and into that memory transpired.

"*It* forgives Moba," says Moba.

"Forgives you for what my child? You're as perfect as *it* ever made."

"There is forgiveness. *It.* God."

"There is whatever Moba requires."

"I'm frightened."

"No need. No need. You've led your life. Now you're with me."

In her thoughts she's with Edgar her third drinking bourbon and the rink of the sun is setting, beneath a Bald Cyprus in the west of Louisiana and a colony in Texas awaits them, she holding his hand as the pelicans dip and the topic is *what is forever*, the water stumped in that swamp from the cutting of firewood for people much like themselves, mettlesome bugs attending in hordes and Moba says *Edgar, I think I'm with child* and he responds *we'll settle, but westerly, not here, not in this place;* he touching her arm and *the least must be signed, though officially business has started;* next day Edgar with his brace of pistols and a singular suit of black, boards the pirogue to pole through the inlets before a portage quite near what is Sabine Pass, where he trades the brace for a team, a cart with mule in trace, Edgar northwesting towards modern day Houston, where a Karankawa avows without illogicality that Edgar, without responding, will pass north of their settlement on the gulf draining Trinity, which Edgar refuses to do; a week then a month and a year then passes before Moba pays out their rental, takes washing for board and food, loving the man like he cannot return for a part of her being is maimed, perfecting his loving through absence, a similar spell making ice from light and of the child, what of their child? In the maze where deities sleep. There was never a babe to begin with.

She cannot recall where she went after this but there was always a hand to touch her; a love, some peculiar, most vapid, one or two with unkeepable oaths, their edicts valueless stiver. She buried men that loved her in the soil and in harbors and she went to a funeral on a ferry, by dumping his body off port. Undefiled her time transpired on earth and her sallies became incessant. A profluence of bodies piled up. Threadbare's watched Moba for years.

"You know what I done?"

"I do."

"Is the sun up?"

"No, it is not. There's light, but light without sun."

"No sun. No sun. Indeed."

Threadbare stands and redresses and leaves her there frightened, the Percheron asleep in some roguery wheat tossed amongst indigenous grasses, he of profane size as he rests on his flank and you'd easier hide a river. When he whistles, the Percheron startles, rising like a whale in breach, humus of soil adhering, he shucking his coat and it sounds like a bat on tin or a hammer coaxed keelson. A landrail alights on his back. Sniffs where he's rolled in the wheat. When it takes flight with a hindquarter shimmy Threadbare watches the bird, its riparian sense to where water will be and by its flight he isn't equal.

"Go to her," he says. "You do it."

The horse with preciseness reads where he's walked. Sees her bulbar form in the grass. Moba Threnody is abed in the rank of her body and he's positioned the woman for death. As if Moba were already in casket. She speaks to the horse as if he were human. He comprehends what Moba can't say. The horse is here to vindicate nothing. To absolve? No, think not. With his jangling bits he elevates backhoofing, the Percheron's skull blocking fire and sky and what allegiance he has is behind him, Threadbare lustering in the grass amongst the Comanche, bear grease being rubbed into leather. Threadbare cleans his hands and chisels whetstone before chinking a bobbin he's broken. He's had to sew his pants again.

Moba says to the horse "I've seen your tracks, knew you belonged to him. That hoof there leaves its mark."

On Moba that mark is left. Along with twenty others.

29

BILLY FOUGHT WHEN Billy was taken from her donkey but the emptiness refuted fight. She hit a creosote bush with edaphic perimeter, baresoiled like radiative earth. Her head began feeding the dirt, the blood and wax from the skin of the bush suggestive of fresh crushed lemons. Thrashing and gasping the wound opened more, Billy rolling to her stomach to vomit. Blood to eye and Billy is blinded. Is there war between plants as there is war between humans, her mind firing and asking its questions, and why is this subject of interest when the bane of my life has returned? To this man I'm a flea beneath his pressed thumb and though I writhe I am going where he puts me.

Billy gets to her knees, then palms, then to standing, to make his figure and steps unite. When she does he kicks, Billy flips to her back, a beatified saint in crisis, the man squatting to look at her face, pushing here and there on contusions, abrasions, a fracture that grutches her sinuses. He cleans her wounds and attends her needs, the glug-glug from his cannikin down her parched throat, branching faceward where the creosote rubbed her. She is held and her nose is straightened, his apology in a recognized tongue.

Billy bounces in saddle through an august day, the flesh, muscle and caul of her guts bearing the pain of the motion, her hands enshackled at the base of her spine and her feet ironed the same, held with the wisp of a pin. Halved on that saddle with a covering burnoose, its purpose to shape her figure, so she'll appear as a package of goods. As if anyone will notice or care. If there is that person, she will be Billy, working her bindings and by late afternoon they've loosened and her hands are apart, the smell of night fires in the collar of her sark and Billy cannot recover, her limbs engrammic with life. When circulation returns it pricks at her feet as her skull conspires to break her, the skimming of numbness a threatening pain and beneath it flows her blood, its awakening wire brushed skin.

"You there? Is somebody with me?"

From the canter stealing her breath the Morgan slows to drink. The water croons to the surface with a gurgling melody and around it the prairie is greening, its vivifying accomplished through the natural pipe, skeins of water running like faucets. The horse drinks, grazes and drinks.

"Comin off. Horse don't move."

When she lands forward a shoulder dissockets. She makes it to her back, looks at the sky and waits for the water to reach her. In the shade of the horse Billy angles her head to lap from the miry effusing. With her fill she lolls to the right, there the trail the Morgan has managed, winding forty miles west before another five north and the horse has been here prior, as she has come through herself. Years past now when she said "we'll stop. Soon, but we ain't stoppin here." When Dampier asked "Billy, why oughtn't we settle, in or close to Reckingfort Soo?" Billy gave the man no excuse: "yarning citizens and loggerheading bastards can decide to waste their days. I ain't wastin mine with visits." From her chosen isolation she's become sibylline and it doesn't appear she denies this.

"Okay horse. I'm gettin up."

The Morgan won't drink or graze with her touch. Billy knows where she is and says it. She's been here before with her husband, though another with a noisome fidelity has made Billy Mox his mission. He seeks to possess her like a well holding ink, surrounding what's written prior to words, this suitor drily adusting, the Percheron's hooves in churn.

"You're wet to the knees lil' Morgan. West end of the Canadian, huh? Shallow run after drought though ain't it?" Billy peruses unworried. Examines the flora and fauna. There are jojoba and ocotillo plants known to the Mexican desert. "The plants that'll hurt you sprout where they wish, specially the fuckers that do."

A jenny with its bag brimming with milk haws then walks into view. Contra sun, the donkey repeatedly sounds and the Morgan perks its ears, she standing astutely like the jenny was born from the light of the sun onto plain, her shape unique to the Morgan and Billy and haven't we forgotten our shapes; like gods we inflict, disfiguring others, for they're the shape of our larger selves. We're ineradicably soiled and if one God long since was he done with humans. What watches us mince is we. Therein apprehension's non-existent.

"Mama donkey on a goddamned plain. I bet the Kiowa have missed you."

The horse walks to intercept the jenny. No scintilla of evidence others are here except the gametrail all have traversed. She hasn't been milked, the teats moistly reddened, where she's brushed the longstem tops. Billy approaches, yanks at a teat, and the jenny yowls orgasmic, her colostrum indenting the soil. While getting to her feet Billy sees the wound, proximate to her tail and weeping, castigated by flies and crust. Eight inches of bite and chew.

"Motherfucker. No, no, no."

The Morgan and jenny bolt, neck and neck, the horse eluding, a length then another and the long throaty rumble from the Long Tom releases its action, the blasts on the steppes ringing chicanerous, a darkened black misery, groundfelt; the Morgan and the jenny gasping for air as they sink to their deaths paroxysmally, wheezing and gasping for air. Billy holds herself down with the burble of the spring as acute in her ears as their function. With fistfuls of grass she makes herself ready, the pain in her shoulder repentant with anger and "goddamn, motherfuck you Threadbare!" Rising pleatfold straight Billy sees them at a furlong, the jenny and the horse both dead.

"Billy Mox! Atalantas! My goddess!"

He's to the north, his call in thirds, Billy as in sight as what's been killed, and when she screams it the woman is finished: "I know all four are dead! Fire and make me fifth!"

He has his hand in the air for Billy to approach where the trail becomes ramous and fades. In the fist that will grasp Billy gathers her bindings and announces she's coming to kill him. She has a hand with which to do this.

"Come to me tiny princess! I am yours!"

Billy Mox is still attentive. Sharp enough in the face of what Threadbare is doing to realize the shackles held in hand were fashioned from the andirons of Moba, requisitioned from her house in the Soo. With her one good arm they're lifted overhead as she walks to his contemptuous stare, close enough to notice the framing of his jaw as it hinged in Athapascan: "…stun. Do not kill her…" The brave solemnly stepped into Billy's blue shadow to strike her across the shoulders. His warclub is of millet, tuckahoe braided, the rootstock sufficient to bludgeon. The brave watched and allowed Billy's felling, before Threadbare caught her hair. He laid her gently on her back and was curt with the man he has brought to assist with the rite.

"I said no killing. No hitting the ground. In how many tongues must I say it?"

30

Awaken leaden and the talk she hears is Athapascan, Shoshonean and Siouan intermixed, an amalgamation of the three in repartee though his response is direct and infuriate, a loud negating followed by quiet. Billy's senses vegetate from the strike on her spine but their speech is from below she thinks. She's held aloft, platformed on a type of proscenium amongst the dead in their rotting stages. The legs that secure her osier bed have been cut from the curlicue twist of a pine culled south of the Niobrara River, hoisting Billy higher than them, others dressed in feathers and bones; their headdresses, maniples and escutcheon woven on skin paper thin from sunning cathedralled, the newel of their stilts their ladders, for no God will deny them entry. *Here, no others save we.*

"No price?" says the brave.

"None whatsoever. If you ask me again no forgiveness."

When the brave speaks English Billy twists her neck to peer through her osier bedding. He walks forty feet west to venture a glance he can use to masturbate. The brave's head has been shaved, grown some and cropped, before a razor slicked it for lice. She can see where that razor has skipped. Billy knows the word "lice" in the tongue they are speaking for Threadbare suffers the ailment. Her death isn't imminent for their banter changes tones and more familiar tongues she hears.

"Billy," he says. She's attentive. Chin to chest she looks at his face. The brave is sitting as shade for an ungrasping light that jealously bathes him with streamers. She sees the scars on his chest from his dance with the sun, going into the hinter as a boy of twelve, not returning for twenty-four seasons, the desolation required in the mind of his father for the boy to become a man. For the brave to emerge as a warrior. Billy considers this so.

"You're Sioux?"

"Half. I offered him triple. He means to have you alone."

"And that for the life I've been given."

The Sioux's father was Assiniboine and his parents shared Siouan but he's adventured south for revenge, assisting Threadbare with Billy for the grounds where he's placed her are sacred to the Comanche people. Sacred though he thinks. Two springs past trooped Comanche came north to take the bison of the Sioux and the Mandan. There was a clash on the White that bristled to the Badlands where the Comanche found the brave and his camp. His sister was raped and the bivouac erased and the living left in their dying. During the attack his parents drew water but the pogrom was the couples' undoing. Aged and lame they were not seen again, the Sioux relating the story while lying.

Threadbare stands listening to the brave. Remarks when the Sioux is finished: "they told him that mourning was nature's idea and it forced you to wait on its seasons. Made you gather your camp and flee from your place, though nature remains when you leave. It has its own sense of humor, though nothing seems to amuse it."

Threadbare speaks while coiling a lariat. He's softened his weave with the pounding of a greave found on the northern malpais. His subsequent plans disinclude the brave who has made an alliance intact, promises he cannot keep; the truth of the tale not the epigram lie spewed from his mouth for Billy, the brave actually inviting the Comanche into camp to replace his father as sachem, offering his sister as bait. When two of the Comanche who weren't suspicious came to retrieve the sister, his father quartered the men by horse, the son then banished for life. When the brave climbs down from speaking to Billy he scales a knoll to defecate. Up and over, earshot close. Threadbare tells her the truth. Threadbare wants him to listen. With fluidity the bountyman explains: "you're desecration here with me, but the man squatting yonder is desecrate. To himself, his people and man. What it took to convince him to follow your donkey was a busking of tisane and whiskey. Touch me and you know I am what is me. Touch him and he's what's given. Falsehoods, untruths and dung."

Yet Billy Mox won't allow inattention: "you've blasphemed the Comanche by roosting me here. You're a goddamned liar yourself. So since you augured my people!"

Threadbare dresses his rope with a gyre. Beds it in his open kit. He then dusts the length of his body. The brave departs to recline and drink. To connive, reviled as is. In the pitch of dark night there is fire on the plain for the man won't camp with Threadbare. Won't mingle in silence and fate. He takes the brave, that milt, in ruminative care, Threadbare speaking more truth.

"What we have here aren't Comanche. Around you my kills, my work. I have built and adorned them myself. Each man should have a site, irregardless of condition, of his very own making and choosing. A vision, here infernal, and this place exists for you. You rest on the very last bed. Higher than others you see."

"How more insane to aspire? How the fuck can I not give up?"

"Lay there on your altar little Billy. I'm giving you purpose, you know this. Without me your days are, how shall I say it? Doleful, triste, pathetic."

*

The northwester that dawn is of a chestnut hue, the wind gaining speed but assenting to a front and that storm rushes to them from the baldies, southwest from the cold Atlantic, barging but the weather stays warm. In the cave of that night he comes to her. A freshet that's falling glistens on his skin as he pisses on the stilts of her dais, saying "Billy, I'm climbing to fuck you." As he screeches through his frenum, the call is satyric; Threadbare, aberrational and warding, appearing behind his back, catching the brave with his chin tilted up, nowise to his rear and when his fist goes in he narrows his fingers to secure him, the brave lifted by the stretch of his anus. He carries the man on the stump of his arm to his camp, a thirty-yard walk, and there he dumps him screaming. The blood rills from his crack, between his long legs, a vole in his foodstuffs next to his fire sprinting from the fright of his landing, the rodent running through the dark from the anus of the Sioux taking leave of the violation, the vole's tracks colored wine with blood.

"She won't be touched or handled by you. Such is not negotiable. I'm finished with the help you've given."

The brave moans and is torn an inch here or there but won't answer or acknowledge the comment. His assaulter goes to knee. Threadbare scoops a handful of coals. Rubs his palms as if they were lotioned. The feces and tissue, blood and stench, sizzles and roasts on his flesh. When he can stand the brave quickly departs and the Ute resolve his case. In the rocks bulwarking Capulin, they skewer said anus and leave him.

Billy listened to the clinking of coins. The brave mounted his horse but could not ride and in his choosing to walk she watched him, he leading the animal north by northwest, Billy seeing him blush on plain to a scatter, that mantling of man and horse. He thinks nothing of his days as rendered, the Ute supposing he's abducting because abduction is the rumor Threadbare has told their headman. Billy ponders his death, envisions her own, the Percheron's snort a provoking distraction as Threadbare stands in his saddle, the torso of the giant elevated to waist above the sagging osier cot. He inspects his weave, perturbing with his weight, refusing to look at her face. Threadbare wishes to see like Billy. To convey in humanly terms.

"He's a poor example of his people. I see my bite has strengthened." Threadbare touches the bitten finger. "Had I a mantuamaker or the equal in skill I myself would dress you better. The others hereabout are gaudy in death while you are clothed as a pauper."

"I ain't yet fuckin dead."

"And you shant. I am unfinished."

The weave abruptly splits, his hand going through it and a hinge of reinforcement gives a splinter. It's six inches long and five less wide and it buries with his pounds like a railspike, perforating at the palmside wrist of his right before tearing to a stop in the muscle. A tunny hematoma births through his pores, his eyes sweeping the given horizon. Threadbare's study is the versal, what roils, what we are while being ourselves. When done with his thoughts he pinches the barb and reverses its path by tooth. A draft takes the splinter, lifts it ever higher, and to him this is premonition. Threadbare lowers his body by fractions. Though he moves small, the man is enormous, as the depth below dreams is presentiment.

"I beg your pardon," he says from beneath her. "There is something in that wind."

"It's the wind," she replies. "Just the wind. Ain't but a single kind."

"Again, your pardon Billy. This is not the case. There are a trillion breezes in a solitary wind and one might bend a flower. Though the wind sweeps forth whole oceans."

"Leave the work of thought to stones. Stick to other matters."

"And look to you for that response. More profound than the words that provoked it."

"Fuck you. You're dead when I can."

Suddenly he's asquint and walking northeast, his hands

cupped around his eyes like lorgnette, an ursine figure at two-thousand yards and Threadbare knows it's watching, muring on the plain at an equidistant height goading onlookers take notice. It is lilac-grey in the heat at that distance as Threadbare returns to his saddle, rising back above Billy's prone figure.

"What is it? What do you see?"

"The horse considers it bear. But it saunters like a man and we can't smell it, though the wind brings its scent right to us."

"I cherish your unknowin. I'm fuckin joyous with your confusion."

"This thing will come for me. For me and then for you."

Billy's womb is his brace and spot, the two fronts collecting their winds. He tilts the Long Tom slightly and the man that is bear is at fifteen-hundred yards before stilling. Threadbare grooves to stock and site. The thing as sighted becomes orbed in an ether of dust and sun with gigs of walling gusts that prevent it from being seen, more a regnant of what is illusion.

"Billy, if I awaken, will you please console me in this. What I'm seeing is a first for me."

"I hope it closes and murders us eachly."

The concussion in her ear takes what she can hear before Threadbare surmises a hit. He drops to the saddle and the Percheron frets, unmoving until Threadbare parents, with a heel to his ribs and they're gone. He reloads in transit caressing the weapon and thinks that the brave has returned. Though he would never approach as the living.

"He sees what he's done," Billy says to self. "What haunts a man who is fear? That out yonder does."

She lay alone flexing where she can, watching pervious Threadbare searching; he trotting about the spot where his ball has struck, a mastaba of rock he's slain. He dismounts, strokes the impact. The bountyman is unsure. From forty-five hundred feet she watches him stall without conciliatory track to guide him, for what has gone adrift? A thing begirt by a power that is? Apparently Threadbare shudders. A remembered paternoster is repeated. What further imaginable evil contracts to check them evanescent? It's come before behind Billy in that great northwest and in repeat it's come again. Yet a third visitation is expected. Save that for another time.

31

DAMPIER, WITH NO other choice, will keep the twins at his side. A decision they will recall. Their mother, their Moba, who loved them utmost, have been removed and *he* has removed them, what peace remaining evicted. The world as known presses on feeding and its residuum crumbs won't guide you. He'll have to invite you to follow.

"You're both gonna go with me."

"Moba, mama and man who is white. Him cluck-ting," said Latham unrumpled.

"All 'er unawaked," added Torq, before he spat in his brother's face.

"Stop it! Goddamn you Torq!"

"All 'er unawaked! Unawaked! Unawaked! All 'er u-n-a-w-a-k-e-d!"

With a shred of croker sack Latham wiped at his face, the twins enisling their father, he seeming the size of his grieving, the emptiness superabounding, their questions about mother and Moba and living and *why weren't we with them* and *why won't you take us to fetch them wherever they are*; you, our father, the man that avoids us to offer the plains your stares, to resurrect when auroral light floods you; you, not *him*, that noumenal draughtsman, nigh muffling the actual as real. But still, Dampier, does not act, neither Comanche or Kiowa or Apache intruding to betray the trust he won't give them. For the present he considers the tribes are the cause but knows it is he, their accuser, who will never be sate from Billy. He's tasted your wife. Such carries.

"Okay boys... bedrolls... some sheeting. Torq, you get our water. We'll take salted beef and chard for today... no, no, for the week, maybe two."

The horse is caught grazing, sturdy and young and they can triple on his spine without gallop. Dampier gives the reins to Latham on the withers, he in the saddle behind him, while Torq frustrates on the croup. There's bloody debris and shreds of torn clothing rolled tubal behind their cabin. When they discover the body of Moba they're at thirty-six hours and wilting. She's been sectioned by coyote with a menstruate tugging, her identifying parts rather sallow, what intenerate pieces they find in the grass confirmed by a scalp in some rocks, her hair colored gray with a prandial gnawing, and out from the light it came, ominously glaring at its finder, for the discoverer is none other than Torq. He screams "daddy, her head is here!"

Dampier tells Torq to cover his eyes. The boy picks her up by the ears.

*

"We'll dig a hole to bury Moba. Ya'll sit on the blanket. I'll do it."

Latham said "dig a hole, but wait on the blanket for daddy."

Torq adds "collect her first. I fount her head right yonder in them rocks. Latham ain't found shit."

Dampier doesn't hear the dialoguing twins. He brings the parts he has found, three-quarters of Moba, eyes crossed seeing coeval, her final absorption a blank. Moba's narrative has ended. Finished. They will never realize what she was.

"They can't see this," he whispers. "They'll know what we become."

The twins, they know already. To the west the commencement of montane slopes and he selects a scenic rise. To his east the boys at two hundred yards and he booms to bring the animal, his rifle and shovel burlapped vertical on a quarter of his lee side saddle. The wind blows from the south while the children lead the horse, the shovel his tool to bury, his rifle waiting its turn.

"This is the spot you two. Look at that spring, them flowers. Pretty place as any."

"This is the spot," they say on cue. "Rocks at the spring," says Torq. "We're big and can tote 'em to Moba. She got plum' eat up!"

Dampier shovels through exhaustion as his whelps watch and carry, rehitching their movements like gabbling fowl scaling posts to feed on corn. To their right declines a blenchwhite sump with its till including headstones. The ground is moist where water shouldn't be. There are mallows, crocuses, nasturtiums and orpine and someone has etched a sign, its bottom planted and hoisted in rock. With his voice almost hoarse, Dampier pronounces the word: *HECATOMBE,* dissipatedly visible. So inclined, life has sprung forth.

"Don't stray amongst them flowers. Them don't grow together. Not even with a tender hand. My mother… nevermind," he says. "This ain't no place for fondness."

Moba is interred and rocked with haste for Moba is dead on the plain. Torq watched his father arrange her corpse while Latham simpered then cried. Neither inquires until Moba is buried. Then Torq, leeringly, offers perspective, with levity and seriousness both.

"Hole is too deep. Hell'll hear us. The devil'll send him then."

"It's well dug. You're both big boys. Thank you for your help."

Latham collected a handful of dirt and tossed the soil above him. It blew into the face of his father, who asked either to speak to God. Latham searched Torq and Torq told Latham to "Godtalk, we gotta find mama." Latham nodded affirming: "go back to Jesus mama Moba. And back to them people too. Them buried neath' them flowers."

Torq looked at Dampier and turned to the sign and his father furrowed his brow. Neither child could read nor write. Though a child isn't slew by living.

"That word means bunches of flowers. Flowers grow best where it's moist. Around the spring all and any might grow."

"That's a damn lie," answered Torq.

Dampier doesn't respond. He pauses, says "come on."

Lengthy ride, same grouping and the boys fall asleep and the signs are increasingly jeering, Dampier cutting and figuring the clues he can catch in proportion to the circle he's made. They align, saying "I am here." With his children strapped to his waist, Dampier rides for their homestead.

*

"Wake up boys. We're home."

The twins climb from the horse and clamber to their wagon, footing from the tongue to mount it. "No, get the drag," he says. "We need to blend in if followed." In their first months here the Kiowa had smallpox and they'd given them beef for their children. Billy's idea, not his. The travois was a gift to their family. This sled was made from firkin barrel shaped from oaks downcoast, more akin to the frame of a curricle, than the sled it was meant to be. Lashed with mule deer hides in omega-shapes, it was surcingled and cinched like a creaky old saddle and its sound was a wagon rutting, its body rheumatic and worn. Latham said he knew where the "draggy-draggy" was because they climbed it to look for braves. Falling to the ground meant something would eat you but they never determined what thing.

"Can both of you drag it to me?"

"We're too little," said Latham. "It's heavy. Stinks like moo cow poopy."

"We're three years old and big," added Torq. "Three is almost grow'd."

"See if you can get it to here. I'll do the rest while you tug it."

"Okay then." Again, in unison, like actors recalling their lines. They pushed it to the ground from inside the house planning in twinspeak phrases, part English with gestures and proprioception maugre the size of their bodies, a dialectic, an anodyne smoothly assisting and only they could understand their banter, their father observing when they did get it moving, as he packed every weapon they owned; Moba having purchased a gunsmith's pistol forty days in Reckingfort Soo. With a month of black ice and limited trade he offered the iron for half, Moba paying his price with additional sex, the gun smithed from a large game musket and compacted to a pistol's frame. Seven pounds to the ounce, .52 caliber, extra iron melded to hold it, for the boremount cracked when the smithy test fired it before the handle split in two. When finished the carrier had to holster the weapon in a scabbard backfolded for a rifle. If the shooter missed the target or the desired shuddered flinching, the ball from the cannon would unwieldingly arch in a parabola defiant of natural law or the physics holding forces at bay. Like the shallow pond skipping of a piece of deadly slate or a weighted limbthrown rope, its vector was largely unknown.

With their chore the boys ceased worrying. Dampier, alone, did not. In a shoal of dry bones he'd found on the prairie he selected the rib of a bullock, making washers to cheat his harness. With their animal fit snugly into the travois the twins were told to board. Torq bounced to his rear midriffing the drag while Latham sat at the bottom. Both boys then turned to watch Dampier as he fingered their separate bundles, calculating where water would be.

"Latham, scoot up, move next to Torq. Directly you'll understand why."

Dampier mounted the horse, negotiated turning, until he found the path he'd reversed. They'd made no attempt to hide their escape for it was wide and scarred where burnt, Threadbare and another with erratic tracks, like seeds grown crescive to harvest, planted for Mox to find them.

When he finally unloaded pounds of waste tumbled from their horse's rectum. The travois remained untouched. Expertly the dung traveled beneath before curling and smearing the bottom, where Latham Mox had sat. Latham and Torq made faces. Dampier turned to speak.

"That's why you sit in the middle."

"Okay daddy," he answered.

"Big stinky," Torq said and giggled.

"Ya'll keep a crisp eye on our satchels. Make sure nothin gets lost. That includes you boys."

The trail is like virescence in an ocean. Threadbare wants them there. Torq and Latham on the drag are modestly dusted then caked like nyctalope idols. They harden because hard is required in the ruleless heart of that day. The boys stare at the prairie when the dirtclouds lighten as their father flushes north intersecting a trail out of Reckingfort Soo from the south, what fear then left at odds in his chest for a man must be destroyed. What has taken Billy says "come take her back; your wife, their mother, my charge. This starshine path will guide you. We're here, where that path terminates."

32

BILLY HAS FEVER but will not sleep. Refuses to close her eyes. A watery fluid leaks from the wrists. Her runnels of brain oppose her. What reason the woman can gather, enacts inside her head: *they'd be horror'd before me if he'd already killed 'em, but here I lay clacketing chains, with a tink tink tink of my wrists and ankles and the sun up yonder with its white-hot surface and earworms slinkin across it. Hey you Mr. Sun, with your bridepale face, I ain't gonna look right at you. Black dots on your edges and I'm blind with cryin and I cannot open my eyes. Why should I see anymore?* Billy thinks someone approaches. *"He'll see 'em comin, go to 'em, watch 'em sit by their fire, sleepin in their blankets in starts. He'll give 'em pieces of my clothin, traces of flesh, until Dampier is delivered to his altars, to me on mine"* and then there is night and with dark the sound of his dragging; a body, a human, heels leveling grass, grading where Threadbare takes them. She knows it isn't Dampier, too light for Threadbare pauses, his breathing staccato and labored. He says "do you need water" and "not from you" and "damn you to perishin hell! Motherfucker, let me loose!"

"Be nice. I've a reward."

Billy can't stay awake. She sleeps. Threadbare doesn't.

*

With dawn the warmth is acoustic. Wet from the rain past night.

Something in the grass is offended, its changeableness draws her attention; the eastern sky irised with encaptured humidity and their malapert wings are their prelude, this aviary of dove and quail; the lanneret creaturing, bombing their center, killing two with one pass and the gallowbirds enmesh to mend where those birds were flying, closing the holes of the recently fallen, though the strikes of the falcon are prisoning. When he purloins a quail at the side of her bier Billy looks down the length of her body. By knowing she doesn't see it. Her clothes are in tatters, pulled from her torso and strewn like words of faith. He's perforated the weave of the bier, bringing the fabric down through it, slicing in strips until Billy is naked before the inflaming sun in its rising. She wiggles her hips, squeezes her buttocks, no soreness there from rape. He adores her gypseous stench.

Billy doesn't recall the water he's given but smells the soapweed incumbent. Threadbare's cleaned her while she slept. With her head alolling the retable sun agilely reduces the grass. Something crops intentionally towards her. Threadbare watching it feast. Billy looks to her left and right, the face dead sexing between her legs with harshness and untenable tongue, for he's wedged it to please her spread. The boar below Billy is dining on guts, the pig entrained by family, the male double their size. When finished he sidles and pivots, content with Threadbare's provisions. Tusks bloodily rise with a steric sniff, the male eponymous evil, groundworking at the height of the grass.

"Now leave us." They do as he asks.
"It ain't gonna stop," she says. "Goddamn you take this head!"
"I've marked Torq, the darkest twin."
"Don't say his fuckin name!"
"I gave him his life. I'll come for him later."
"He may be sent for you."
"By whom? You? Would you send blood?"
"He may come of his own accord. He ain't like me or his father."

"Neither are like you both. Latham knows where my hundred are buried. He's seen the flowers I planted. And men don't come for me." Threadbare collates his mind for the poetics of verse forgotten, verses lost. He reaches for a screw of paper, there a sentence of incompleteness, some thought or another composed. He sings "yes, I am loved by him" and Billy finishes the song.

"You are far from salvation sir. There ain't no god who'll have you."

"And neither entertain you."

A catspaw is lifted, he picks at his teeth and Billy says "I… am… not…"

"Not fucking what my dear? Torq will leave you for shinny and whores, or any soogan offering devil. Such will be his sonship. Though I'll come for you all in time. Take you one, then another and no one mind will recall you ever being. Like drought fraught by blood."

"Come round so I can see you."

"You, you talk to your friend. He wants to eat your pussy."

She renarrows her eyes against the light, resourced enough to recall.

"This man has come through town."

She knows the hair and the face and though his eyes have been punctured they glisten like paillette trimmed. He was a chandler and vendor of scuppernong brew and its medicines by annual occurrence. From west Mississippi he bartered with tribes, his muscadine whites for passage. Threadbare met the chandler on the southern plateau riding north to Reckingfort Soo. The man presented the gold of the sabra merchant, the chandler admitting "I kilt 'em, goin north to the mission and him to the south with goods for Nuevo León. Shot 'em without even thinkin. If you'll let me live, cause I know who you are, I'll split the coins in shares. You already got my bounty." His head is placed between Billy's knees. The aforementioned coin for Threadbare's bribe he sowed on the

Camaron River, northeast of Anahuac, in a tiny aldea late summer. His apologue of deed is there still told because I've sat in a bight of that gulfrunning river and heard its telling alcalde. A claimant who keeps his coin. Son of a son of a son of a man Threadbare gave a piece safekept. I held it in my hand twenty-eight years gone while buying mescal from his brother, crossing the border from Catarina, Texas on a big roan horse from the ranch of a friend the border took with its vice. My recollection is somewhat vague. I was then unscathed and unreasonable. Who isn't at nineteen years old?

Miswandering voice and Threadare is close but refracting a tone communal. She has no idea where he is. She waits, looks to her right, there he sits on a lower bier, crossed legs in a serpentine bend. Strangely yarded, albinotic in light, a tenant on the bed but there without body, for the dead he's thrown in the grass. When it hits the boar, groundrhythmic from vega, disentangles the grass and attacks it, an aitchbone ground in broken-mirrored teeth like a bosket of perlite fragments. Billy shows her disgust and he sees it.

"They, well he, will eat what I throw. His palette runs the gambit."

He hangs his legs from the stave of the frame and dallying swings his feet. Redid are its corners from the binds of a kiack and though strained his pounds are held. When he leaps to the ground it brockles the swine and there's a cacophonous shrieking repine, actuated from the heartmeat of boar, the swine darting north through bunchgrass split from its brooming by touches of wind; other quarry, other places the boar will behold, increate, where presence deflects. Hitherto preterminal as we are us all and he with his dark staked bibulous suck affronting through the carpet of prairie. Where to waggle from that maze inbuilt? On and on the plains continue.

Threadbare glances to Billy, says "your bindings are loose. Inspect your neighbors if you wish. I've placed them according to title and rank and if they countered my efforts. Though you, dear Billy, outrank as the highest. Though that head is my personal property."

He jumps from the ground then again appetent and his second leap frees the head. It trampolines from the side of her bier. Is caught like an untreed apple. Pitched into the grass and left. It is at that moment she chooses to look and there are thirty of the canewoven bier, extending farther than her own palliasse; eight steps apart, conchoidally scripted but ceiled no higher than Billy, no matter rise or fall. No smalldoer or inferior excavate has routed the posthole depths, for there's only a tang of inches between the first and the last of the tombs. They seem looseherded with needlethin contrast though no two beds are alike, as were no two men confronted. She sees slabcut risers and yokewise braces and a strand of voile in the wind, before her shoulder relaxes her abdomen, which Threadbare says is a strain. A peculiar litter four beds east has a saddle squareskirted for a pillow. There are spangles like tlacos or fobments fresh minted that glitter in the shilpitted, lightboiled skull with horseshoes turned down on the corners, snubbingpost its rectangular frame. Crucifixes octally abreast. The Percheron whickers on the yermo behind her for he knows the gunsel who lies there. Threadbare assists to allay curiosity though Billy doesn't care for his stories.

"That's the sole white man amongst them. Those are the shoes of his dun on the posts. The braves shoe their horses with bullhide. I've seen them sapped to the hoof. It's good that they know what the coming invasion refuses to learn offhand. Though they'll have to have metal to win. I was reluctant to put a white in their midst for they knew what whites never will. You need your kind close to you."

"Didn't help 'em with you though did it? White nor Indian neither?"

"Another matter entirely."

"What matter is that? Dead is dead."

"I shaved his white nose and cut out the meat and stuffed his face with gold. What you see glittering there, is the coin in the mind of a flourwhite gunman who took from a church its almspouch, before the Godmen gave me his bounty. Praise be that Lord of hosts."

"As if that makes you more. Some collar payin forth vengeance when such is the Lord's to have."

"I seek joy where men can't hide it."

"You're eternity is growin short."

"And you, you're here with me. Where I put you. Where they'll come."

Delirium heat shatters what cool adsorped to the humid night as passed. He destroys the beds by size. His jimsaw clasps each of the posts with a double-wrapped catchrope on pommel, the Percheron tugging in hacks of labor lathering the beast in minutes, Billy watching through censured tears. Threadbare directs the horse single handed, with the Long Tom's buttstock fixed, massaging the spread of a thigh, the man as tolerant to the folly of coincidence as a desperate prayer by heathens. For if he is not the scourge of God in his heart is a love amended, like the quake of the earth in a colony of lepers and them not gods themselves? Make that in an image profanely just. If rubble atop, man moans. Go afloat on the Lethe to forget your past, for in the bramble the shore is afire. There is no sense to make. Have you more going out than you have coming in? Do you know? No, you don't.

"Tear it down," she says. "Put it'tall in the dirt. I do not give a fuck."

Hairsbreadths of light and the lanneret watches Threadbare in his element. The Percheron insistent between stirruped legs that every bed must fall and man be stomped beneath hooves as wide as fronds, breaking bone and crest and shield, as the confusion is pieced from chaos, chaos turns to riffle, clinging to the skin of its ordinate master who flat on the spine of his steed, re-erects his posture paretic, as any man of the horse is more inhere than not of a soul irreducible; than what he's built for Billy, with nostrums thus concocted, as if in and of those tilling earth searched for bones themselves, and who will find what for they dig, for they are dust indenominate where panicgrass sprouts and no man will dig for them, and what whist and fash valgus goon searches slagheaped hells? Not a one. There is no searching for it's fallen to hoof and him aboard his steed, the veins in the neck of the Percheron throbbing and the arteries like conduit piping, Threadbare the bole of a tree atop like a transept supporting the world. They exhale. Dust then settles. Threadbare bowed like a godwit waiting. Whispery plain shakably employed and Billy has watched in rue. Seeress she sees all. Drunk with a rage that impregnates. The destruction looks Godlaid. No human on horse would attempt it. But they have and their work is done.

He waters the Percheron heaving, pulsebeat of blood in light recaught like a pictograph enwaxed by ancient stylus on a mountain of wax in dream, the horse drinking from a sump dug close to Billy with Threadbare resting in saddle, a workscout relaxed having hired his brood and their ferry to the other side. He is pleased, ragging his mug, in a blackcloth soaked with smiles, an evocation misanthropic behind him. For two hours they yanked drugbreathed with rage, the place appearing as an armory befallen, what the hordemen left the defeated, so what's killed won't kill them later.

Billy remains for they haven't come yet but he knows they're closer than not. Threadbare begins his arching, like patterns in wet cement, heartracing the Percheron in medial dressage, closing half circles with lines, giving ground to her bier with full sordid singing while watching the falcon make dives, scauping like a board driven nail.

"Don't kill that fuckin bird you shit! Ain't but two I've seen!"

"I'm looking for his nest! Don't move!"

Gone she's alone and her body craves sleep and she must give in to need. Why not remain on her litter? He'll find you wherever you run. The dream is as instant in a mind that's fatigued as a body purchased by death. A single cloud hovers and it's enough to shade her and she sleeps like the passing of years, glaciers sliding over Billy across the vast plain and Billy can feel their cold, at large wryly invading. They inch slowly, millennial, but she is much slower and in time they gain their edge. On the firn of the glacier closest her dreaming sit those who have gone before her. Though he cannot speak, her brother is there. "Hank," she says to the boy, he pneuma cold atop the glacier with breath a melamine white, petrichor scent in the air. The sight and smell of life before birth and if you remember, you shall. She strikes sacaton grasses and her legs are like trunnions but the glaciers begin melting away, a petrifying sunset falling due east and what light Billy knows comes from there does not leave reversing, the wash from the glacier in the melt that's occurring becomes a wave that lifts her struggling, swimming amongst the dying, every hand that can grasp reaching her throat until Billy is drowned herself, sinking to a bottom filled wholly with rushes, when alone the dead relenting, and she can swim herself, up to the surface of a plain that isn't and the ordinal commencement of a world where arcanum voices ring, comprehended like the sound of rain, Billy treading there and she is first human and what's clattery loud is silence, as if the voice of God was her. Lavastone bobs about, suspended on the surface, red and hissing and what God voice, becomes that hissing there, the ocean changing red from leviathan vein, Billy swimming in the blood of her maker. It is then that Latham says "mother" and Billy is stymied awake.

"Mother! Mother! It's me! Looky here!"

When the twins walk beneath her Billy was thinking the heritor kingdom her own, then she felt the burn of sun parboiling and saw that sun close-reining, its blisters cornada and her nipples raw pink and she thirsts for the sump where the Percheron drank and she wishes for things less rending, but they aren't and never will be. "Latham, I hear your voice." Dampier was forced to pigtie the twins while he cut for Threadbare's sign. Secure on the travois for all of five minutes they worked their bindings loose, sliding from the drag to the grass, Torq having listened to the tales of Moba, of how her very own father found game, by locking his hounds at home. Dampier left the trail that was hooved by horse and pursued a trek of deer. Within an hour the boys had found her. Meandered on the scene like sheep. She wanted to turn them away, but their father was nowhere in sight.

"Lemme get down. Stay there."

"Why're you naked mama?" Then "why're you naked?" repeated.

Billy toothed a strap then released three others, shimmying down the opposite side. For the children naught is unordinary as they devise in the tongue of the twin, Latham asking Torq what's the pile in the distance, Torq replying "mama's clothes." As he points Billy walks to them, conscripting an arroba of wood, flipping back the posts until the skeleton's clothes can be shaken of the skeleton's bones. She dresses herself in the rawhide breeches and the pull of a rejoneador, the man's javelin in Threadbare's arsenal. She looks a leatherized mystic in flowerstrewn pattern shirring the spirits at hand. A millermoth lands on Billy's injured side and she invites the moth to a finger. Patiently lifts it to space. She rolls up her sleeves and cuffs. Creates a culotte, turns it to ankle. The vinous stained pull she likes.

"Hey mama! Big horse! Look yonder!"

By the time they see him his heels are cocked back with the rowels of his boots spun outward, the primary blast circumfluent explosion, it and hundreds of others, kindred echoes inarguably pinging. The Long Tom fires again.

Billy screams "DOWN! DOWN! DOWN!"

It's a game to Latham, but not to Torq, the high-grain shots in ten-second intervals tearing loose the bier of Billy, the frontside bezelling to expose the back before the litter falls to earth. Threadbare untwills it with a quatrain of shots and the wind in his face hard blowing, declining a hundred yards out. The fractured posts seem horned astillados, like makers of wounds long healing. Billy crawls on her stomach to shield her two children, Threadbare dirking a seed from his eyetooth, eating the seed like a swallow.

The three are given their time. Threadbare sits on his horse airily observing like a borough watching a city. He shot the falcon, disemboweled it, and has searched for its bezoar magic, finding some and then none the same. Disherding its feathers he whisks their topends to make a trivet with four of his fingers. Guiding with his elbow he fans the feathers and thinks of the falcon in flight, how he in his mind isn't grounded, though his clouds are the color of death: white, yellow, yellow-green then black, and so goes the flesh of man.

"Lo siento halcón. Tormento." He looks at Billy holding her children. Pure, his quiet reflection. He's torn and crazed and fugued with violence but chaste in the focus he garners. Not one amongst many but singular, condoning no other to match him. Disfocus intent of light and nightdark and why have the stars that shine? For there is just as much him as the light from each star as there is just as much dark around it. Aren't we each manifestants of both? He takes the blood of the falcon and with vertical streaks paints six across his face. His intolerable appearance is explicable. At the end of summation is he. His cosmodicy Billy and family.

"Billy! Show me your children!"

He progresses on the back of the Percheron like a paste through a tammy sieve. Except for the bunchgrass snapping underhoof there is no sound but Billy, her calls bringing the boys to their feet, no place to hide out here, a child on a hip and another to her front and they're running against the sun, Threadbare increasing to a trot and a gallop casting a lengthy shadow, scabbarding the Long

Tom to brandish the acero of the rejoneador with his javelin, giving the reins to the Percheron's withers, the acero and javelin across his pommel before the javelin is stuck in the ground, bending and whipping and flexing its body with the whang of a sallygate shut too short and the acero then grounded behind it, Threadbare wanting his hands on the three, disowning the weapons collected, Billy looking at the face of Torq staring back as he watches Threadbare's closing, the horse aborting its rangy gallop before commencing an earthrent plunge, lowering its head and snapping, Threadbare and the Percheron at four horselengths and he leaning to his right for Torq, the three running as fast as their legs will carry when Dampier simply comes to his feet, directly in the path to the left of his family when the .52 caliber bucks, hitting headhewn muscle in the neck above breast, Threadbare unhorsed with a putative cry, his ribs giving the last of their wind, the Percheron raiding the meters before him as if his master remained in the saddle. When he falls from the horse he hits the back of his head, twitching his limbs to stasis.

Dampier permits their sprint to safety. Reloading, he watches for life. Blood wells and he steps ten paces closer to inflict a wound in his chest. Quiet breathing, stertorously rumbling. No breath is heard after that.

The Percheron pays no attention. Leaves to return again.

33

THE PLAIN AT your back is yours for the keeping as you count the beats of your heart. You smell bluestem and side-oats grama with a cocklebur lodged deep chest, a tobacco brown seep from your neck and bosom and the blood paints your body through grease; adorned like stelae you are, the light in your eyes growing dim, your lashes long for they are your mother's and not of your father's ilk. In you there is little of him. I say none of his voice you're hearing, your mother calling in speech like a gypsy, that voice a billowing sheet, a blanketcoat placed underneath your head for Torq has put it there, Billy jerking the child instantaneously away, that Romany in ear the speech of the twins for there is nothing that dies in their world, you a known entity shot from his horse before their father shot you again; killed or not killed the warp of adults, there or not there a child's, an ameliorate complex presence if the swart of your spirit isn't seen, for there is more than tableau for Torq and Latham and both boys know that you live; if not for their eyes, alive herewith, and ever increasing to swelter.

"Billy, take 'em outta his reach."

"Latham, Torq, stay with me."

Who stands about shades the warm sun but they cannot remain with your body. Both your ankles are tethered and you're pulled to the pile of biers you have created. Dragged like a matador's kill.

Billy says to her husband "he's thoroughly dead," but he doubts your face, its color, not the type of dead he's seen, the kind he desires is where you are dismembered and mixed with the dead to burn, though Billy won't have you fragmented, won't own that deathbed warrant. She says you'll remain to rot, like "every motherfucker he put here. There's worse that'll do what we ain't doin and these children should see 'em up close. For more than half a minute. Dampier, bring 'em to me."

He's triple half-hitched your feet to the travois and you're all but ready for pyre. He takes you back, Billy kneading the knot, the slide loosened and her scent is there. Gently she lowers your feet. Torq and Latham unafraid of your body. You've done nothing but die as they watched.

"This here is the man that stole the family I had before your birth. It took place on the omen of salt, years back, but the day I remember. You dream salt, means the world is dyin, though ain't it all dyin the same."

You are then seen as different. They touch the skin of your face, hands and neck, and their fingers are tinged with blood. They tell their mother that red is inside us, then consult in tetchous twinspeak. Torq asks to kill you again. Latham wants your boots.

"What good is this doin mother?"

"Let 'em see it in cattle and then in a human and maybe they'll know it's there. My folks raised me to fear it and that there is a waitin calamity."

"It ain't natural for them to know it." Dampier sits on his horse watching them probe you, though you yourself can't feel it. Latham is poking your ribcage. Pressing his hand he looks at his brother, but his sibling won't look back.

"Ain't it natural? No? As if he might rise? Dampier, he ain't comin back." Her anger flashes like cobra or krait. She is palmy in the heat off the prairie and her eyes and that face are in contrast, the soilure of her skin and the stature of frame in sockets of eyes candescent, as if the ordered world prostrated when glimpsed and the woman is glowing from torture, her hair blonde in streaks and ragged, requesting his pouch of smoke. She asks him to roll it for three of her knuckles feel broken though her shoulder improves. "Nothin hurts to pain me really. Though my head is swollen. You see it?"

"Christ Jesus," says Dampier.

*

You're left to rot on the prairie. Billy takes a lock of your hair. Snips it while Dampier is loading the children and then kisses your cheek and you twitch. It is slight, your palmdown hand. The one hidden opposite Billy. She doesn't notice, farfetched that you live, why notice a twitch in the dead? Squatting, she bends to your ear.

"You're burnin in hell or you ain't. Fuck you for not bein better."

An interpenetrative dreamscape obedient to rule comes to your comatose body. Therein a perfect life. What humans think they'll have. But yours is different somehow. In yours there's a spitalward crowded, a faceless nameless lazaretto; the bed you occupy in the dream you are having cold until touched by hands and they are anyone, everyone loving… then it is night and their speech is Shoshonean, two women hefting your ankles, relocating your body by order of the satrap One Arm Torch. The Comanche chief wants you hexed by women whose sons you've murdered off warrant. He's asked these mothers to trap you, in aerie dimensionless space, to vex your spirit before your flesh passes through scavenger's bowels. You, eternal, Threadbare and prairie and none living will know you've been. These sarabbath females, with incantations, will step and seal your closure. They'll ask in prayers affianced in dark, to permit your entry there, where light is strangled whole. Here no other souls in throes but yours darkdying lightless.

The women struggle to get you moving. Drag. Rest. Drag. Losing their breath they stop in the night and use your chest to sit. The younger of the women plops on your ribcage and points at the disarray, the highway your dragging created. Having pulled you through a cup in the plain they'll need to drag uphill. Their trek is as wide as your arms are long and makes it easy for the scavengers to find you, since dead isn't dead enough. She suggests they roll you shoulder on shoulder upon a muledeer path. The oldest of the two wants the early morning moon and the younger answers efficiently, repeating that time doesn't matter, for she's witnessed a goathawk in a tree of tascate where neither thing should haven, where neither thing should blend. She thinks it's their sons instructing the mothers, ethereally unkinking their doubts. She recollects thirty years past when Threadbare made a memorable example, she a small child that knew some white words for the missions brought them their Jesus. The man that came had a badge, not a Bible, speaking to her father with a summons for he knew Threadbare was close. Her father told the lawman that Threadbare was near but their quarrel and summons was white and he would have to take him alone. In that year One Arm Torch was a youthful warrior of thirty, he and eight others with this eastern lawman rode to find Threadbare skinning, cleaning and drying his hides. The mother sitting on his ribcage thirty years hence followed the party to snoop, hiding in some creekside groundsel. The Comanche left the Georgian lawman and Threadbare invited him down. There was an attempt at an arrest but he wouldn't submit so a parlay was then decided. Pistol on pistol the contest. Threadbare offered a sixty-foot shot. The lawman replied "you're to be questioned" and Threadbare "I'll answer your query. But first you'll take a chance." The Georgian compromised. "I'll do as you wish, winged or dead, I'll get what I came here for." Threadbare pupillessly faced the sun with the creek at his back to catch him. He then winked at the children in the groundsel. "Watch this," silently mouthed. The lawman that faced him backed twenty paces and trembling, loaded his weapon. When the hammer and frizzen met to ignite the ball flew tragically low, Threadbare with arms wide spread, a huile in each of his hands, like a hierodule inviting a troupe to the temple for a sacrifice including their kind. The ball hit his pelvis and he jerked ingraphic, the shot burning and tearing his pants. Dull thud and crack of bone. Threadbare made no sound. He then took his own pistol and limped to the man who was hanging his head and waiting. He put the shooter in his hand, raised the tense arm, saying "fortify my friend. You have to account for drift." The Georgian replied "my shootin is done. I hate what the fuck I do." Threadbare sighed, took his horse and weapons, cuffing his hands to his front. Asked him to remove his boots. Threadbare sent him east on the Llano Estacado, the children rushing to camp, with what they'd seen from hiding. But Threadbare, he called after: "if he is assisted by Comanche you'll suffer twice his fate. Your families doubly that." From her seat on his ribs she said they understood and nothing was related or conjured, only falsehoods shared. Threadbare then finished his work. Left a hide for One Arm Torch.

The one standing and listening has alternate scenarios of acts unleashed on women. Grotesque, horrendous things. She walks into the dark but is skylighted there as the other remains on his ribs, before scooting to the mass of his chest. She's heard the story about the bars of his teeth, thinks there's value there. She calls the other from the dark to see. Similar things she has heard. She gives a tug on your dewlap skin. There isn't enough to open your mouth and "if we take his teeth, his soul will escape through the hole." Her confederate replies "I'll do it. His dark soul is solid."

Two dirty fingers pry apart the jaws, twist and settle and probe. She presses down on the tongue and the bars discharge and she can feel where they're daily released. There's an anterior groove on both of the bars where his fingers or tongue unlock them, where he clicks them back in place. Bringing them forth she hands the bottom to her friend and they knock them on their knees, deciding they aren't substantial, excepting the mouth residing. The extractor says she felt something else. Wants to go back in. Same two fingers with a sweeping thumb and then her fist entirely. Her index finger burdens the epiglottis and the body thinks it's swallowing, the ball from the pistol coming forth, sliming between her fingers, its pathway impaint upon it and half one side is dented. They don't notice his chest or nasalized wheeze, for they're inspecting the gobbet intensely. When Threadbare blinks he tastes the emptiness of mouth, the blood from the woman's withdrawal wanting to force a cough. He abdominally respires as they display their bounty in a profiting moon that's shining, forgetting the dead behind them, as Threadbare opens his eyes. He sweeps the banks of his gums. Pleaching stumps of broken teeth. Jagged enough to cut you and where have her fingers been? He meditates on peace then smacks his lips and *she's been threshing ryegrass*. One Arm Torch has bought this Creek from the Navaho who got her from the Mexicans. *She's made them think that rye will grow in drought, on rock or sand. There's not enough water here. Not with a dry fall coming. They'll never make the crop. There are penalties for such sad lies.* He then says "rye" in Muskhogean, but the women aren't paying attention. *I didn't kill that woman's son, the woman who sat on my chest. She claims no blood Comanche. She shouldn't have lied to the chieftain."*

The elder woman warbles her tongue, a bird then coyote enrobed by wanemoon gives riposte to one then the other. Threadbare listens as his pulse increases and the anger in his chest subsides, his wind difficult to grasp if anger augments it and he knows they'll know he is living, though they sough with their prizes and he lets them. He thinks the wound in his chest will harass him for life but the hole in his throat is treatable, perhaps by that sightworn nympholept hag east in the Antelope Hills. She mended his back with maggots and oxtongue when the panther called Haint dehorsed him and the Kiowa begged for the hide. When Threadbare recovered he gave her the skin, but she wanted no trophy actual and present that Threadbare himself had slaughtered. In Caddoan she said "your ways are death" and "I've extended your time amongst us. You will never leave this world." She wanted Threadbare to know that his hemming awaits by an enigma in carom his equal, native from the vault of the earth; here it glances and grows to descend sojourning when Threadbare is at his weakest. He emptied his pockets and left her hovel, she bathing her home in smoke. Routing what Threadbare brought. The dregs of his visit in memory.

The two mothers strip Threadbare's clothing. He's patient while they work, asking questions about his horse. It seems to appear then vanish. There in that slype of rock and sage, is that the Percheron standing? It is dark, perhaps it's nothing. But it's jelled like frozen water. The oldest says "no, those are rocks." His reputation cloudbursts and as they are in dark they prick and rumors rain. "They say his horse speaks ten tongues. Rides clouds with nostrils smoking. Was bred from the steeds of Satan." Unerring, ill treating, they begin their chanting, the eldest stationed at his feet, the other by Threadbare's head. He allows it for quite some time. With kicks and taunts and a caning of his body they sit before recommencing. Quiet breathing, whiting their eyes. They are denizens removed to a land where mind is a syzygy of darkened tunnels, of damascenes acred black; an enemistad in all these nights and unawares they chant at his hips, each with a hand on a wound, so when Threadbare reaches to touch them he robs their exhortations. He gathers them close in both of his arms and considers his words inquiringly.

"Pray on. Ask what hears you. I would like to know myself."

His injured throat croaks the interest. They struggle to see him living. This side or any other.

"You've assembled here for me? My spellbound maidens chanting."

34

"DAMPIER, WE OUTTA go east. Decide on another location."
"It's been a week and the prairie has cleared. We ain't got nothin but a hock of venison. I need to hunt cause I ain't gonna slaughter and the stores are all but empty. With this fire and you…"
"Me what?"
"You shoulda allowed me to burn 'em."
"Nobody knows he's outta commission."
"They'll know soon enough."
"I shoulda took his teeth."
"I know you took some hair."
Billy ignores him. Decuples from speaking. She wants to ride into town.
"I've had enough of here. Let's go into Reckingfort Soo."
"To do or see what exactly?"
"Whatever, whoever is there. I need to hear other voices."
"Best to go on Sund'y. I can corral the cattle. Billy, Moba is dead."
"I miss her like I made her myself."
"Sun'dy then? Sun'dy? Yes?"
"A fuckin cow don't know the days! They eat and shit the same! Stand around outside their assholes! Driftin here and there!"

"Billy! The twins are listenin! You ain't no cow to know!"

"I'll be damned! Sun'dy then! They don't care what I say!"

The twins are at a table scratching with a quill. Together they scream "fuck!" Dampier says "there you go. They ain't heard a thing."

She loves everything about him, but about that frustration in leading the life they've chosen. Dampier wanted to settle with Billy and Billy would go no further, this banlieu of drykiln prairie a home that called to the woman. The hunt they suppose is finished, terminates to begin anew. Another phase is only beginning.

The night they returned from the burial grounds Billy wanted Dampier to fuck her, her fingers clutching the unpaned sash of the unglassed window frame, her bottom lip bled by her teeth, Dampier gently inserting his member, though Billy wants to be fucked, needs to be back on the salvific bier, redeeming the hurt she has suffered from other hands upon her flesh, pressing her buttons of bruise, with the sting of the sun on the tips of her breasts and it is not Dampier she is fucking, late night with their children asleep, the travois still hitched to the horse whose snaffle clinks with his drinking, his teeth grinding in rapine beat. Billy asks Dampier to seize her neck and feels his instant softening. Billy then seizing herself, grunts and he erects, his indicate shot profound in her guts with Threadbare's name on her lips. As he sat on his cot in the sterile darkness with corporeal hate for his father, their sex is viewed by Torq. His nails chewed back to quick.

*

The following day Billy walked the plain with the twins and their peck of questions. She brought newly risen bannock from their claybrick horno and a sweet they preferred called charlotte, bannock with molasses drenched over. The day was cloudy, sticky, with their hands in the charlotte so they rinsed them in an indigo seep, the water stagnant, blueticked, with aboveground bugs skidding on the bluegray surface. She has her gripsack, children and plains. After eating Billy revealed it, from the first of her days in the verdurous northwest, to this moment by the indigo seep, all given to the twins by their mother. Threadbare irrefutably condensed. Though she spoke on their level she didn't balk darkness, avoiding the innocent slain, but not his slaying logic, random though it was and would be. The boys stretched in the grass out past the burn with tiny fingers behind their heads. She saw Latham yawn once and Torq said "stop" and they listened and heard without ears verboten for their mother spoke in truths. For she, truism, is a jacklight mute, her work laying asprawl lies exhausted and those who lie their days. Nothing profound in this. Delusion keeps us sane.

Latham understands as his age requires but Torq gazes elsewhere. He asks Billy if the tree on their way to the Soo casts shadows throughout the day. He says, in a statement, not a question, that it was always night beneath the branches, she responding that the pinoak was planted and must've been watered daily. "Yes Torq, shadow is dark. There is light and then there ain't. Shadows are peculiar bout' suns." Torq asks "mama, has he sat there, afore daddy kilt 'em with the gun?" Billy replied "he has. Like you, sat and wondered." Torq seems to understand. To him, his mother is inheritrix, positioned in his personal dream, he birthed from the slit between her legs and thrown in the grind of the world, a place where their tongue is ungoverned and no one wants them there. The natives consider them touched. They're alive because Threadbare chose her.

Latham fends with his own inquiry, loaded with truth's mundaneity: "you've only kilted that man?"

"Your daddy sent 'em to Jesus."

Torq replies "that ain't what he as-ked."

"The man is dead," said Billy. "Gone."

Cirrus clouds entangle above them. Mother with children and the boys from she mere integers on the prairie. A wind that is chilly wants to get colder as Billy circles the seep, a waterbug gliding on the alkaline water rangling the boy's attention. Hers is taken north. Something stands tall on the prairie. It does not move and is nothing to the boys and is a thing there fixed for her seeing. Some searcher seeking distance? It grows from the surface, from miles, an ideation epigeal and Billy standing antic to buffer Torq's inquest, unable to watch or stop what comes on the flotsam of grassburnt plain.

"Boys, gather your things."

35

CROSSING EAST THROUGH a canyon to the Antelope Hills the rains fell to fall on him, his neck dripping viscid and the subheart wound aching benignly compliant, as if no shot had entered; Threadbare craning, adjusting, lodging his chin to protect the hole in his throat, the effort making him dizzy, frenetic the Percheron's pace, leaping brushtops and clooting with equine rage so it appeared in the mud that horse and man had reared from terrible depths; a polyphonic horse and rider, intoning a consentient unhomed tracer mellifluent in echo chamber. Follow them not dear reader.

He finds the daycamp of the Mexican hostlers. They are well past the grazing of any of the settlers and east of the Mox's homestead. These men are searching for bulls, owned or nativeplain, the capeas of upstart cities gladly paying for afternoon death. When they see him he is seen inasmuch as any other is accepted as flouncing from prairie, vianding with coffee about their fire, rolling nicotiana dissected and plucked near a swell in Pinto Creek, its intersect of the Rio Bravo, riding north like legates snared from stone dungeons and they are auctoritate violence in pack. Men best left to musings and works apart from stable minds. Fluidic channeled hate. Here no need to control it for their lives are not in question. Though Threadbare senses weakness. They are dead where they stand like billhooked lousewort, though he reins to exchange their speech. Ragout chewing, hypnoidally staring, they jut their jaws with a brume in the air as a smiting by hail commences.

"Una fábula… damnificada…"

"Ya nooo! Me importa un comino… pero…"

"No más," says the third. "Es un mecanismo oscuro. El origen oscuro lo mismo… but he'll keep that darkness checked, the men yanking their pistols as bullwhips uncoil with their strikes like iaculi darting, the tips of the whips conical jasper and their cracking snap one, then two, the last of their speakers a man superstitious thinking Threadbare has come for the souled, whether lemures or wakers sent by the heavens he's the meed these men have earned, an anagoge found in the script of their lives as they assemble for his seated appraisal.

Threadbare scoffs at the bullwhips. From a trot to a run the Percheron is spurred as he reaches for the brim of his hat, the first of the men to the left of their fire watching him grab the cap, raising his chin reluctantly higher and Threadbare knifes his throat, his horse through their fire without leaping or flumping as the grin in his neck beards fluid, Threadbare back with the palm of his hand on his head as he grabs his cap, spins it, like skeet it inclefts in the air, the last of the rustlers discharging their weapons and their aims are an absolute hit. The hat receives two holes. He reins right, turning one-eighty, faces them where they stand. The two hostlers reek of fear. He's the wicket whereby they must pass, Threadbare more bitter than usual.

"Es una gorra," one said. "No hay sangre por dentro."

They are shoulder to shoulder on the skirt of their fire with its embers of jacinthe in shreds, gratuitous lights about their feet, arc-curving when the Percheron strikes them, trampling hoofs to chest, a singular rustler succumbing, bashing his skull on a footstone for drying his boots by the fire. The survivor of the charge has injuries sustained that will not take his life. He can stand but refuses to move. He asks lenience from Threadbare for selecting his path and grovels in Threadbare's tongue. Dismounting, he finds his hat. First standing to relish the acumen there, he squats and hears his confession. Responds in English to test him. The man is a linguist now rogueing. Choosing to waive his could have been he's become what he has chosen.

"Where did you learn these apothegm?"

"The Cluniac order sir. From the script of the heathen and my words are not pithy but honest for my tongues are many."

"Is the language of my homeland difficult to read?"

"I was exposed to your language in Rome, no more, the library there…"

"…made a father and monk without simony searching for wildrange bulls."

"Sir, my faith is lost. I heard nothing but me when in earnest I begged, cadging my maker to offer me solace when none could be found amongst men. Such has led me to this. I do not want what I am."

Rain and sleet encumbers. Snapping his fingers the Percheron sobers and the Cluniac covers his face, wincing for his sternum has hairline fractures with a stomach that flips from concussion. The man is lifted, his clothing adjusted, swept of its mired ordure. Threadbare sees to the needs of the rustler as the Percheron circles in range, the grasses enwired like rust.

"Forgive me Father," says Threadbare. His countenance is effective, sedate.

"What should we do about this? About the lives we've chosen to lead?"

"Exactly," Threadbare replies. "I see where this is going."

The Percheron hears the whisper. Fain to wait on his signal. Threadbare offers in Latin the sepultured unction and the Percheron is animus rage. When he rears the man is thrown under, the frogs of the hooves welding inward, plunging like curia justice, the Cluniac's forehead crushed. He rears again but the body is hung on a hoof, dancing in rallentando.

"God remained quiet again. You must not lose your faith."

36

SHE SMELLED THE blood on his horse and the scent of the man but would not step from her hovel. With a versicle curse he was welcomed. In Caddoan and Spanish she gabbled "Threadbare has come to see me." He asided the jambtacked rawhide door, ducking and necking the wound, the hag with her hands on her hips, a sciomantic abbess in a leanto hovel who quotes the herbaria for pleasure. The hide of the door flaps back. Sizing Threadbare, she begins to doctor: "we'll use soapwort smoked to prevent catarrh. That will weaken your system. Elder bark tea will relieve you of poisons. You're piss will be red, but not bloody. Then betony and borage for your brain and breathing. Ineffective if you had a heart. I'll suture your goddamned neck. Also, for sleep, we'll use hellebore and dittany soaked hot in the waste of a…"

"Just suture my fucking throat. A poultice or two if you have it."

"I do. They think they've killed you."

"They know I am not dead. As you know that I am here."

"Not all. She holds a part. As usual, your arrogance precedes you."

The crone won't face him from the dark of the hovel. The walls are speaking to Threadbare. She is there somewhere in her ark cohering before the rawhide door floods light. His order demands a particular balm with a barbless fishhook threaded. He doesn't notice when she walks past. Neither does he sense her return. With catgut she works from his back, nimble in finger and wrists, her fire without reason except for her cooking and it is stifling in the sparing hovel, hot wind through the walls with a stile in the corner to a nowhere ceiling imponderable, around it ciboriums filled, every color and others of unforeseen need, the hagwitch dogged with potions. Silently she stitches his neck, will not come around to his front.

"We'll pack cobwebs and henbane over these holes. Imprescriptive sawbones say. In moderation what heals is the man. The soul? Well, the soul?"

"The wound below my heart can stay. Like birdlets in slatted nests, three balls have found homes in my ribs."

"You've had visions on the plain with the woman I see. Showed her your altars and slayings. By her womb you shall recede."

"Stitch, goddamn you witch. I'm not your whoreson proper."

"Or you'll do what to me?" She waits. There is no response. "Off with your clothes then bed by the fire. I need to bathe this flesh. You're too fucking tall for my work."

With the catgut hanging and the fishhook buried Threadbare slowly undresses. His vestment a slicker from buffalo hides and the clothes underneath hides too. She makes her way about the starkness with eyes in her fingers, referencing a codice by touch, saying "nepenthe, not for you. You'll remember completely you bastard." She then comes to his side cowled to her chin, theophanic in a den syncretistic.

"One ball in and out you say?"

"I did not say. He shot close. A ball has been removed."

"Air from your lungs escapes. The more that flees less you. Only so many breaths within us. No tare to count that number."

"Need I apply for more? Can you see or not old bitch?"

"My eyes are unlit lanterns."

She removed her stitches, palpated his throat, making

comments on the taking of food. He said he wouldn't chew until his body healed, yet that wasn't the answer she sought.

"Such healing could lapse eternal. We'll do as originally said. Clean. Stitch. Poultice. But your heart will maintain its burden."

"It comes as it comes but it's heavy with Billy." Threadbare sighs, relaxes.

"Your ire is your weight. She's terminal. Did you know you scar like a child? Inside is a heap of damage."

"Be at your work, not talking. A summation of your shit will suffice."

"A summation it shall be: with racking and bewailing come densest dark and light resents your presence."

Threadbare doesn't respond. A comal with a drain in its center is stilted above her fire. With a basilisk hissing and forking ejection she spits into the orifice. She pulls back the cowl as if to see but her eyes are tattooed sutures; twin black crosses and hemicycled reds with lashes that snake through the symbol, a paramour of darkness in pawl, their notchwork the dankspan of vision. What sederunt prophets speak from in neuma to council the endtime seal. She is the depth of a black river running.

"You haven't been born from the flesh."

"I need spikenard," the cronewitch says. "These eyes, do they bother my master? They were given and taken not by my actions but by thoughts I could not see. Here it is! It hangs on my breast."

She gaffs with her fingers, retrieves the spikenard, a bag almond in color.

"Don't plant your deception inside me."

"You demand an interest I do not claim. As if a carrion bird would want you. Dead or alive you're fucked."

Threadbare grabs at her wrist to define with the physical, she then on his opposite side. Recowled, but her garment is listless, until her hands shoot from the sleeves.

"How dare you strongarm me."

Threadbare gazes at his palms and the skin is moist from where he didn't touch the crone. He is pleased she lives by facet, on a plane of hue and cry, where the screaming for blood has given presentience, searing her eyes to our features. The hag rests between human and that pealish loud ringing of the apostrophized disappeared. There, but then she is not. Like emotion on the back of your neck. A vapor solidly forming. That incipient fringe more horrible than blindness, where illusion is coated by skin, thereby no illusion it be. She has no fear of him. What can you do to a thought?

"Threadbare, you are impermanent."

"Changing your outlook on me?"

"I'm reconciling having you here."

The smell fills the hovel and the acrid scent burns her fire bright orange.

"Why am I dizzy and sick?"

"I am wafting fraxinella."

"The throat," he growls. "My throat. I've no interest in your fucking witchery."

"Everything else is completed."

"No more of your goddamn butchery. Am I free to leave?"

"Why would you want to leave me?"

He puts his fingers on his wounds and they're sewn. Three lead balls from his viscus are panned and melting back to liquid, her fire cutpursing the dark. His head pounds like a ballpeen hammer. She isn't there, then she's atop him, the time in the hovel racing, the witch pitching a semenic liquid into the middle of the smoking comal, it sizzling and beading and Threadbare's inside her as she holds his hands to his side, her strength now fifty of him, rocking her gape on his erection and balls with her cunt eely slick as castor, a font for agnostic seed, she lifting her caftan, the pudenda there youthful with a waist in supple rotation; she, this crone, reversing her squat to open her anus to Threadbare, he spitting on his fingers and wetting his tip before the crone sinks down on his shaft, the brunt of her palms receiving her pounds by his ears as the man thrusts inward, her laugh that of another, the jingle then heard by his ear off-fire as he looks to define that tinkle, from a bracelet his mother once wore. He then spills in the rectum of someone, be it Billy, mother or crone. It was a body requiring his lust. Threadbare has to sleep.

He awakens by the fire without a fire burning, clothed, no crone about. There's a giggle in that blacktime sheave. Threadbare is banded by darkness, the stile to his right rising to ceiling with its ampulla and ciborium empty; no concoction, decoction of root of althea, wood sorrel or burrs for eczema, coltsfoot or tutty for eyes. She's left a resin of mastic and resensive arient wrapped in a nankeen pouch. This is in the dirt by his feet and by those feet a message. She's spelled it in coals that glow for his reading, the ovoid embers flame hot: NEVER THIS WAY AGAIN. Threadbare rakes the message. He gets to his feet and through the rawhide flap before returning for the mastic and arient. The coals there reassembled. Threadbare tugs at the stile but the steps won't budge. There fastened by intangible cords.

37

THEY LEAVE THE twins with a Freemason horsetrader in a Reckingfort Soo in decline. Haw Plil is twenty, an invariable woodsman come west from his home in Vermont. In the trade Plil's selected are chimerical men, handclasping circadian goons. Agents of Mexican and American origin and mountebanks concealing waxed hooves. But he, this Plil, is a dutious man, what ethic he chooses, he grasps, for thirty years hence from the time of his arrival in a Reckingfort Soo growing tumid, Haw Plil will mount and ride, due east to assist a nation in combat, its rebellion within its own borders. Plil will be a private, fifty years old, who's befriended a Confederate major, a former neighbor in Reckingfort Soo. To July, 1863. Gettysburg is in a glut of heat. The armies encroaching for action. Though it will rain on the fourth it doesn't on the third and on July the third they'll meet. Plil and the Confederate major. Third day of a battle culminating. Plil's behind a stout wall on the crest of a hill, his friend ranked and stepping across an open field, lessening his breadth by dismount, he gives his horse to an orderly private. Longstreet watches him do this. His chin resting in his hand like a gorget. He already knows Pickett will fail and that Lee will take the blame. Though Longstreet blames himself. *Pause here, who be you, pariah or antiquestion, in the radical flux of the fire? Here ecpyrosis on a mile glabrescent, angeling and deviling and my friend in declivity marching to take my life. We enweaponed in heatmirage, demoniacal awaiting your arrival. The major is awarded with a doubling of life and a pistol ball in his breast. Plil is shot once behind his stout wall and Haw Plil doesn't recover. The major is assisted by Hancock's surgeon thirty yards from Plil's prone body. Said body will accompany the major, crossing over Confederate lines, but they do not retreat with the masses. He leaves July eighth with Plil in a box made of pine and wrapped in fulling.* The time and place isn't marked on his headstone but the major brought him home in his carriage. Haw Plil is buried in Dora, Alabama in the plot of the major's family. His lapidary stone reads 51. Haw Plil and 51. He's a dead Union soldier, the only one there, and a miscreant broke his marker. The Confederate major, a solitary man, took his life at ninety-seven. Weekly he visited Plil. My grandfather Arbie knew him as a boy from a row of company houses, for the war broke the major financially. He mined coal through his eightieth birthday. Arbie hunted with the major, sitting on his porch, listening to the stories of Reckingfort Soo and his friend Haw Plil the horseman. Arbie once asked "what of Shon Plil?" The wife Haw Plil brought to Reckingfort Soo when it was they and the Mox's and the transients. The major nodded at my grandfather's query. Brooking his tobacco like gnawing cement he switched the wad to his cancerous jaw, swallowing the juice it produced. He leaned back macrobodied by the clutter of porch and said "Shon, his wife, Shon Plil? She never left Reckingfort Soo." Arbie asked, "did she remain?" The major replied, "never left it. Stayed as stayin is perm'nent. That notsleep kind of forever. Praytell to infect us eachly. And ain't that the damndest truth?"

*

"Dampier, they'll be fine with Shon and me. We aren't going anywhere."

"It'll be a day, maybe two. If they're trouble confide the strap."

"Won't need it. This is our primer."

"Don't allow Torq... well... he'll get..."

"...started. Dampier, I know. We'll handle it."

Haw Plil stood in the door of the house he'd chosen, which was any of the dirtfloor hosts. They looked together the length of a street that is vacant and the twins are staring at Haw, their father behind them with a Morgan spline-legged Haw Plil has traded for friendship, while his Virginia strain trades war. The Mexicans want his horses for upcountry militias required to battle the tribesmen, but these lies are casually buttressed. They'll be used for routing the whites. Plil's corral is Reckingfort Soo. He's learned the land, its mode of grazing, buying forty hectares on promise of deed, withholding his better stock, until the deed is produced and delivered. You can own what you want in this barony of solace but Plil wants the title to prove it. He grazes where he wishes, trades with the Comanche and has cribs bulging with forage. His doors stay locked at night. He often doesn't sleep. Plil never asks what they do with his horses. By not asking, his business is growing.

"And Billy?" Plil asks. Demurring.

"Is two miles thataway." Dampier points west then retrieves his finger. "She's waitin on me to come to her. Done said bye to the boys. That thing we done, well, Billy suffered, afore I was able to help her."

"No need to cover it twice. I completely understand."

Dampier swabs a drop of sweat on his nose and "I ain't sure I do."

Latham and Torq leave the conversation to venture down the street. They see a speck due west like a cenacle built to house black specks oppressed. When they wave in its direction it doesn't wave back and neither do the other black specks. Which speck could be their mother? Dampier calls and the boys stamp dust to the feet of a waiting Plil who is smiling. He says "we're fine," Torq twisting his pants, Plil looking and "how may I help you?"

"Seein if you're gunned, but you ain't."

"No, I'm not gunning."

"You outta be gunnin cause it'll get dark when the sun don't wanna shine."

"Learns early for a boy his age."

"He wants to draw the Bible." Dampier looks into the face of Torq. Arcana, bed you there? "Says he wants to sketch it from front to back. Says he can read what it says. That it ain't the shape of the letters. It's the only book we own."

"Fascinating," Plil responds.

Dampier leans past Haw and into their abode. Shon is sitting at a table for appropriate dining if your floor isn't packed dirt, her fingertips drumming a felucca model divined by Haw and built for pleasure with a frame of blackoak reeding, trimmed and whittled and pared. She's worked loose the lateen rigging and wants to murder the crew, staring past the ship to the expanded room and the hunks of a wall Haw's recently demolished to make Shon as comfortable as possible. A pacifistic hand rubs her rotund belly and she is hiccoughy, icy and waiting. Evensong on her lips but it's crude.

"Shon. Hello. Billy sends her regards."

"You can both regard them in hell. I am pregnant, getting pregnanter, and the goddamned birds will eat my flesh if I remain out here with this baby. Tell the horsetrader there to give you our will, but oh, we're lacking there. We'll be willing broken down nags. Fucking heat and interminable days."

"Nice to see you Shon. Looks like you're comin along. It'll be cooler soon."

"Goddamn idgit. Goddamn," she says. "Go ride your fucking range."

Dampier stares at Haw. "You're certain this is okay?"

"Of course. Her mood is light."

Shon Plil begins reciting from a Psalter, the scripture she makes pornographic, replacing the verses with bestial concordance before adding human receivers. Emphasis is placed on a donkey named

Buck and the twins laugh at her language, Shon swilling flasked bourbon with a dangerous lean in a chair imported from Paris. Capping the tinselly container, she screams "dinner'll be served at six for the babies, but there's booze whenever they wish! Drink up you tiny bastards!"

"Shon, please stop drinking."

"That I cannot do, because that would make me sober."

"Haw, are you sure? They can fend at home. Might be safer than here."

"They're too young. She'll pull it together."

"I can! But not without liquor! Then I can pull it together!"

Dampier, in disbelief, replies "Latham's too young to go it alone, but Torq is, uh, mature. Mostly grown is a better description."

"The baby will be born a drunk. We've already lost another. Could Billy advise her soon?"

"You want Billy and Shon together?"

"I want Shon to try acceptance."

"Accept what? The flat? Death and weather? Locals and murdering drifters? An unknown everything? We're here because we chose this."

"I understand, but it's our home. We have a town to ourselves. Today we have a town to ourselves."

"And there's ever' damn reason for that. Look, Billy is better at this and her secrets ain't elaborate. Basically, she hates people. But that ain't the freshest of secrets."

The twins sweep past the hips of Plil. Torq wants her face to face. He asks Shon "why're you fat? Do you got a lotta food?" Shon chinned at her husband and grimaced. Latham said "your drink is stinky." Shon raised the ell of her arm. It appeared as a sideways V. Ejaculating loudly with her finger on her temple she screamed, "it all fucking stinks! Get the fuck outside!"

"Don't speak to my children like that."

The rebuttal emitted with a responsory muffle from a window

in the rear of the room. A figure there, a rhomboid shape, through a piece of mislaid sod. She tapped twice on the window, the portal shuttered tight, Haw crossing the room to unlock it, reaching through for Billy's small hand.

"Hey Billy. Pleased to see you."

"Mama," the twins repeated. Copra and coir these boys. Copra, Latham. Coir, young Torq.

"My children ain't stayin with this woman."

Haw Plil is deflated, saying, "oh, okay." He gazes past Billy and to the expanse, these labyrinthine intricate flats, there shambling a line of horses, the riders slouched in sad vermillion, strobed by the wimpling sun. Without corners they cannot turn. Understanding their defeat is apparent. Haw wants a place called home. "Shon, we'll be okay?" Shon dramatically twists her head. "We'll do our utmost loving husband." She extends a hand to Haw. "Reach I to reach you and we are." She then giggled, burped and farted. "Pardon me, oh, very sorry. I should be ashamed."

Billy circled the house to meet Dampier, the Morgan craning its head on approach. Plil's horse she is riding neighs and snorts to counter the Morgan's advances. In the autumnal light that saulted the house Shon gets to her feet with assertiveness, to drag a chair to a pity soaked corner. While pouting in the foundling shade of the addition Latham silently walks to Shon. He runs his fingers across her stomach, petting and cooing the child within while Shon puts her hands on her face. Her sob is unfeminine and sauced with false pain and her husband clinches his teeth. Balls, then loosens his fists. Scansion this, you child, her crying; Latham is touched, Haw isn't. Such verse is wasted here.

Latham says, "I'm sorry Haw Plil's wife. The baby will love its mommy."

"You'd benefit by getting her citied."

"Reckingfort Soo is the best I can do. Billy, this is our home."

Billy's callused, says "shit" and "damn." Haw smiled as she spun her smoke.

"We weren't from a city back east. She wants to see water and trees."

"We're landlocked. Water is scarce. Has no idea we're here."

Haw muses on Dampier's words. "Yes we are, but this country will fill. It's grown on me and Billy. I can't speak for Shon."

Billy streams her smoke. The cigarette jetting horns to curl: "they's gravestones yet suchlike none seen. Mexican, Indian, white and black, you take your choice there gents, cause the folks that'll fill 'em ain't here now and it is they who invite the wrath. Not us, with our delicate numbers. We don't even dent the place. But there's gods that're sleepin ain't woke up. We gawp 'em enough, they'll stir. Stomp your feet and the bastards'll hear you. They count your steps comin and goin."

"Well said Billy. Well said."

"Thank you Haw, but if you please, I'm Mrs. in the presence of my husband."

Three laughs, chins up and the twins smile too, though that sense immense devours. Their elastic earth is a mother who is jealous and she wants her bizarreries acknowledged. They turn their eyes and as follows what they see is this: the steppes about the Soo sanitized but toothsome in a drab color scheme trailing its meaning with a nimbus about to attain it, to correct its unsalvagable indifference with an armament of olive-brown skin, with light as contour an unstoppable attributive, until the erosions of an unborn Nebraska, pieced there like the surface of the moon; fraudulent yes, to the plains that surround it, like a klieg-eyed angel who upon earth's inspection brayed to decree his blindness. Such beauty you cannot see. Billy says "empty, nothin," for something not being by unsaying existence births a thing that rises from sediment. If there is nothing on that plain around Reckingfort Soo then listen to its smallest vibration: the tymbal of cicada ataractic. Tersest of fly in buzz. The implorations of coyotes like precentors. They are separate from us with our counting of years and the portents we see, they don't. They are before our unsteady glimmer. An inculcate harmony hiding. Shon Plil knows something is there amongst the grasses, yet her interest in these limitrophe plains is to cross them to a saner location. Let Billy have her "empty, nothin." In her mind the surface of where they walk rejects their ever being. They are glaziers in a world of rock. When black ice fell in August, Shon called her husband "the displacer." Said it fell because "we are here." So for the moment she sits as her contemporaries marvel, Latham and Torq gamboling, colluding in vilest twinspeak. Shon Plil wants "the civil" but to Latham and Torq her "civil" lay around them like chessmen, on a board of undulate plain. The twins divine nothing from portent or omen; they eat, work, play and wonder. Disbelieving if arbitrary. Shon's detestable plains are their home.

"Take the time you need and want. They'll be fine with us." Haw spoke and raised his hand. Billy and Dampier led their horses away, Billy twisting in her saddle to speak. "We won't, they must," she said.

*

Threadbare won't be found where they're riding. He is north of the town and as Haw Plil fades he crosses the Canadian River, its eastwest flow like a mother braiding hair and in his joints he augures her near. He finds prints from other riders in the mud, the clayey bank hardstamped. Not Billy but he knows who they are. Dismounting he shucks his hides and boots and walks to his thighs in the river. There's a palmlined beach to his right in the sun and there stands Billy clapping. He splashes water on his face and submerges his body and looks at the beach again. Scrubstems, a Chinese elm, chined by lightning and dead. There's a vulture contriving to flap.

"The hag has planted her seed. And there her dark soul sits."

On cue the Percheron walks to the bird, the vulture deliquescing with the meandering hooves and like Billy, the bird is apparition.

"The crone has left me hollow."

With his hands on the bottom the storm implodes at the reach of his northeast vision. Alike the pitheads of a colliery abandoned, its eyeful clouds array, lapis and incharged lightning with thunder go-devil to the plain ricocheting. From the outgrowth of cloudbank the funnel is seen and it drops as if produced by a press, a perfect tornadic event, sweeping once, then twice, a third, a fourth pass, before detaching from its cloudbank body to be acquired by the prairies' torn surface. Its diminution, subsidence, funnels through earth and as the current of the river relents, the tepid water jars with a boil. Threadbare stands and closes his eyes. Back open and the twister is gone. With an accurate wind his back is then dried and on the bank a fawn drinks water. She is real and he allows her to drink, his hallucinations not being harmful, rarely seeing what isn't there. He then steps from the water and dresses, taxiing on an ait in the breeze, Threadbare asking his horse for assistance. It returns from trailing the fawn. He unsaddles the beast and it fords crossriver, the water rising wherever it stops. The flies on its back are green and highblack and when they bite his tail slaps wetly, water spraying to mane and they clear. When Threadbare snaps from the mud of the ait the Percheron quarterturns. The tenon is there above water, around his neck at his chest on the surface.

"Come here. Let me untie that."

Again the Percheron fords. The knot in the tenon is loosened and removed by lifting the string from the poll. The black and gray wig is wet on its tips and he'd seen the minnows nibbling. The vulture then lights again. He throws a pebble at the bird and it hops and clicks promenading with talons acocking. A nubby, aged, desolate head stares through Threadbare's presence. The vulture settles on a cottonwood stump, its cutting not killing the spread, other trees in a line closeriver. Again he enters the water.

"He is real and so is this."

Dunking the scalp he draws it upriver and a strip of skin peels off. Small life strikes and swirls. He lifts the hair and spins it, the excess water centrifugally shaping efferent to illusions themselves, and what is the shape they choose, if he be the center there spinning? The vulture whacked to fly as he gave this thought before pitching the scalp on the stump. The crone's hex has come with her body, though Threadbare claims his trifle. As her scalp drains water with the sun upon it, it's the hair of any old woman.

38

BILLY AND DAMPIER waded the prairie, walking their horses and neither in a rush beneath that gewgaw mica of stars, no lather on either mount, though they remove their saddles to water, drinking themselves before regaining the pace Billy has set when they started. Morning next they come upon Plimpton, spotted a mile to the west. Amongst columns of sotol he glowered, nibbling his rusk and waiting. He has goatsmilk stouped to soften his bread and to his back are lenticular rockforms, his musket siding his leg. He searched for his shirt as the couple approached and they can see he's a man of girth. Molded paunch moreso than Shon. He aims, foredooming, withdraws the threat, turtlenecking the pair at a distance.

"If he shows it again I'll kill 'em."

"Hot for a deathblow darlin?"

"No Billy. He's awful rambunctious."

"We're as come upon him as he is to us and we're the ones ridin in."

They penetrate his sotol redoubt, the yucca-like plant futilely grouped, more shade than self-defense. Neither party chooses to speak. As if speech were involuntary. Plimpton dips and chews and dips.

"Goatsmilk won't sour quick as cowteat. Find your shirt and dress. Will you please lower that shooter?"

Plimpton glares at Billy and scowls.

"I ain't listened to nothin a slit ever said. Now a woman is given me orders!"

"A courtesy. Not an order. And I ain't a goddamned slit. Backbore the plinker or I'll kill you."

"You ain't killin shit!"

"That's my wife fat fella."

Dampier reached and Plimpton fired, the barrel uptossing from the saltpeter grind, its firefly lead whizzing hotly, piercing a stack of sotol.

"Whoa a damn minute there mister!"

Billy does not fret. She's a-lilt on the ground with a razory slice of body from horse and saddle, the variations of movement a book in themselves, metastasizing with a clenchfisted stomp. Dampier fired a shot from his sidearm grip off a volcanized piece of debris, left side of Plimpton's head. From his sitting position Plimpton dawdled his ramrod and piddled with Billy's sleight charge, the toe of her boot landing mediad chin and like wind-raped thistle his powder found a breeze and Plimpton slid to his shoulders. Abed the plain he is wobbly and groggy, and there is no chance of standing. Five soft-rooted teeth he swallows. Regurgitating, the teeth fly outward.

"You're a goddamned slaver ain't you? A fuckin murderin pimp sweepin the plains for women to brothel as doxy! I'm gonna let you rove on your stomach after I remove your nuts! You alone? Naw, you ain't."

"I ain't talkin. Ain't done what you say."

Billy goes unchecked because unwonted is vital for the abundance of focus therein. She's crazily hypocentered, inside her guts an evenness polished, Plimpton rethreading a scarlet-glint pistol while he permits her to say what she will. If he dies Billy will kill him, or so fat Plimpton thinks.

"Stop loadin that goddamned pickle!"

"Awright missus," he says. Plimpton throws the gun behind him.

She finds vialets of Laudanum and smoke-tinged bottles with a cutlery set of bleeders that weaken the girls in cage. From the morticians trade are medicament liquids accompanied by pairs of syringes, for those who die in transit. There is fantasy and money in an indifferent New Orleans with its unnumbered ferine sins. Here market your imagination. He has a musette of ropes he uses to bind them with maps of the land he traverses, as detailed as slavery can purchase. There are thirty by count from a Mexican quill with the scratchings from Plimpton's translations. On the bottom right corner the maps are sealed in an arrogant calligrapher's cursive. Plimpton is his amanuensis, evilly surveying under the guidance of some warmad tetrarchs' pen. Billy sees the shells of their cells, those multi-tiered gaols for transporting, with their dustblonde sections of timber and lash with lapin to comfort the girls, as they trek to whoredom and death. How pleasant of this man Plimpton. How unlucky Billy should find him.

"Them pieces hold the girls? That's what the fuck you're buildin?"

"Might be for hides and such."

"Oh Lord Jesus," says Dampier. "Do you understand she'll kill you?"

"Take what you want and leave! Go prod another innocent!"

"You're shut on this plain as if in a room. Deal with Billy yourself."

Plimpton is sleuthing southeast, his headreach New Orleans by Christmas. He has seen the two mothers who hexerei loyal have discovered its malevolent servant. Plimpton watched the two women in their failed attempt at desouling Threadbare's body. He was patient with their track but they vanished. Plimpton wanted their capture.

Dampier attempts to discourse. Otherwise Billy will kill him.

"You scout for a pack? Are they near?"

"I ain't answerin shit."

Consider others downcountry to join this Plimpton or suppose Plimpton to them. Men with flat-bedded wagons and tortuous devices on a journey trussed problematic. Yet they revel in their task, the girls' loden faces, staring back through viselike pens. His accomplices have minor intuitions that cunning is sufficient safe passage. In and with abandon they cannot comprehend their annihilate closes on hoof. His citrine soul intact. They will die to the man en route.

The intensity is chinked, then muzzled, when she rolls her smoke to think. Billy flints the end to light it, ruminating on the dismal results of creation with the making of men like Plimpton, she drawing then handing the butt to her husband and with his own draw it is finished. He pitches the butt in the grass. Plimpton says, "that'll catch." She responds, "do not speak." She takes the horn for his powder from its place on the ground and christens his skull with a handful, reinserting the pourman's stopper. Plimpton doesn't react. The smoke that arises from the flicked cigarette was easy for Billy to find.

"That butt is as rare as a seagull out here, lest' that butt keeps smokin."

"Fuck you. You ain't shit."

Billy launches the fag and his head blueflashes before he slaps to extinguish his skull. In the midst of a stylized deepgourded glugging Dampier spat water on Plimpton. With worrying eyes he looked at his wife who would've permitted scarring. Billy drubs the grass for effect. Roots the ground for tinder.

"You're lucky he was drinkin you cocksuckin bastard cause I'd allowed you to burn!"

"I'ont want no more. What do you aim to know?"

Dampier takes Plimpton's musket, leniently prising its gears, thudsnapping stock on stone. Its clawshaft hammer rotates with the breaking, the three watching its irrelevant spin. Dampier says "pepper his groin," Plimpton mewingly whining, "listen! I ain't seen nothin! We got us a squaw to fuck! Ain't no more! Just her!"

With his words she draws her blade, downhacking a section of ear, the fatman abellow with urine stained trousers when Dampier touches her shoulder: "have you seen them burial platforms? Where all them bodies is raised?"

"Them moosehide warrior beds? Uh-huh, I come thu' there. Seen doublet squaws and follered their track, but I lost it in the dark bein cloudy. You halved my fuckin ear!"

"You see a white man shot around there? Big, whiteheaded, pocked up?"

"Billy, he missed all that."

"Naw, he ain't missed shit. He knows what happened after."

"It ain't no such thing as that. I know who the fuck he is." Plimpton speaks, looks between his knees. Here is finity, apprehension. Lopsidedly he searches the ground, no answer in the soil for Plimpton. A pismire crawls to a sunpoint. There's the scratch of a partridge by his foot. He says, "I know what you seek and he seeks you, cause who knows him knows that." The bespectacled lump looks to her. "Why the fuck did you bring him in? We ain't caught..."

"What'd you see?" Billy asks with a ruction suppressed. Docilely subsiding to interest.

"I ain't seen shit but I know what's there. The beds n' the pile n' the squaws. You can garner I ain't accompanied. That there is my fiacre remodeled to tote, cause I do what I do, there it is."

Billy whispers "don't you slouch. Don't you dare fuckin slump for sympathy."

"They ain't no squaws in this camp! Ever'body has done trekked south! We got enough to make a dollar! With a cherry intact they're a hunerd' a head! Ain't a goddamn thing to be done! Fuck the both of you!"

"You motherfuckin shit," says Billy. "You ain't got no pack of girls! The Comanche woulda slayed and skinned you!"

Plimpton, wide-eared, wide-eyed, is garbed in sweat and shame, his grubsteak waiting amidst pandemonium and he is lying because again he is eating, his deeds prosecuted subordinate to stomach, though Billy wants his head on a pike. He palms his stoup and dips.

"This here is God Dampier. Hatin you and me the same. We ain't humans on the prairie to him, we're three-hundred pounds of dung! How the fuck could he create this?"

"It's hard to give it reason when you speak like that. We got children together."

"Conjuration and reason be damned. It's like air holdin still for the weighin. Confused is my reason today."

*

Billy and Dampier press through it, this tale bearing Plimpton forevaluing intention for Plimpton knows where they're going. Towards his graven debauchees. Those consorted, merchants of flesh. They ride slowly, heading their mounts, Billy and Dampier looking for flits, that yawning snort or earflick, where beasts emotion others.

"Yonder," says Dampier.

"Three and another with the baggage. The fat fuck rode us to 'em."

"He hadn't a beam of integrity. An apellant contra evillest plight."

Billy laughs and brushes his shoulder. With borrowed books from Haw he has read to the twins, often quoting said verses at random. She loves him for this, their oncoming smiles, ideas and words their markers, on a path as wide as long and as deep as its height sometames the impregnable, which is superior to ignorance and fear. A disarticulating child in a jointed world is a child then unifying, learning to think for themselves, for no existence is the other or the same, no thing ever looming as it is. Even less so black and white. If you consider yourself a person alone, you're here now alone and with me. This is our world together. These pages, there being no other.

"They'll take you southeast for sellin. I'll be dead before that."

"Nope," says Billy giggling. "I was worth five-hundred till you split my fig with that whipcord coiled in your britches."

"I cannot deem that funny."

The three on horseback are staggered, trisecting, shifting to a spearheaded stance, the slavecart behind them between its dual flankers and they can see its construction was harried, boards from the floors of scuttered through mills buried in the marsh whence come. Their clothes are emblematic, from a place of moist heat, ragged from probling bayous, where the telltale greens are multitopped. These cages implemented they've seen with fat Plimpton, stacked three abreast in the rear of the wagon, rectangular and pattering with chainworks, tools used in the east to ship riotous slaves from Spanish Florida to the Chesapeake's hairline. Billy can discern in the cubical light the fingers of a girl agonizing. She sees the pair and calls in Salish, these men in business with others, for this girl is months from home. On the breeze is her scent, wastage of rot, a benefactress with nothing to offer. She is the only one they have.

"Billy, these men are armed."

"Fuck them with their slavin ways. That's a goddamned girl in a cage."

The man on the wagon speaks first.

"Un beau pays!"

Unanswered.

"Tout va bien?"

"Fuck you."

"C'est comme cela?"

She puts it together in her head, their bratticed wagon clinking onward, Billy Mox confoundedly adept, if the stress is at a level death appropriate: "that othern was unaccented. The fat man speaks their English."

"Billy don't," replied Dampier. "We're both dead if you do."

"I ain't gonna do shit. We got enough trouble where we're goin."

The wagoner whistles his frontman. "Qu'en pensez-vous?" The frontman answers in a tonsillized slang, lewd comments thenceforward like Babel, the driver of the wagon with his filthy red beard splitting the hair with his tongue. What the men want is to menace, though a night and day's ride and they're nearer to nothing except Reckingfort Soo and the Plil's. They've an inland Salish cross-country from home and New Orleans is rollingly foreign, its substancelessness overlain by their memories, these men gone now for months. Their employer thinks they are dead.

"Strange tactic," Billy says. "They're drunk."

"Let's ride on. Pommel your shooter. We're alive cause we're armed."

"I'm about to kill ol' redbeard. This .52 cal is awful damn heavy and when his mouth gets fucked by its lead, he'll wish that tongue stayed housed."

"Billy, please, let's go."

Slubbering, rankled, with baffling accusations their indictments fly at the Mox's. The slavers want enfeeblement from the pair of plainsdwellers, not pistols hidden by jackets, shooting irons that bend your wrist. When the ribald slavers fall silent, they cease circling and cower with the shielding of horses and the man with the reins then speaks. His prognathous jaw unshutting. "You cannot kill we four!"

They can see what Billy is carrying, the weapon the length of her ribs. Curving, they ease to the pair. Dampier's pistol comes up from its holster and is forced to his thigh with patience. "He's right," Dampier intones. "But I can surely mistreat him first." Their frontsman is then at the tip of his weapon, Dampier announcing with a general command, "ever'body back to the left of the wagon to fall in a desirable manner."

They do not ask for their pistols, knowing what will ensue, counterblows like mainsprings focusing death and either wife or husband will perish. They gather, hold them and wait. Billy says "no need to kill 'em. They won't last to the city." A ki-yiing pup with unpracticed yelp sounds from a pack of coyotes and the men realize they'll be eaten. Wounded or dead, they are food. They splice their hands on their heads in ritualized postponement and Billy says, "get the girl."

"Billy, she ain't alive. Poor girl is mostly dead."

Disagreement in perfumed Cajun. Redbeard responds in Parisian French as the four ogle young Billy.

"Don't eye me motherfuckers. I'll leave her. She won't be abandoned again."

They come from their horses to trust their own legs, backheeling, occultly reversing. Like thaumaturge ascending from the creation of suns they walk toe to heel backpeddling, ten minutes, then twenty, a completed half-hour, the horses grazing and following and grazing, the men around the wagon watching with care, the Mox's weapons never lowered, the muscles in their arms offended through degrees until the irons descend on their own. When they do they are dots on the plain, to the four who have not killed them.

The men and their hauler with its garmenture primeval then harken to employ her purpose. Redbeard tears the girl from the cage. She is raped in turns with a deflowering severity, Threadbare viewing her torture; embattled on a rise and yes, they can see him, but in a trice elsewhere he gallops. The four in their assault convince themselves he is another long trailing for the girl. No merchant rides forward to see. Threadbare's wrath is apace with their fibrillate heap, its interest exacted, compounding.

When finished the merchants prepare to seek Plimpton, the girl thrown back in her cage. Shrilly she screams in Salish, now atainted in additional ways.

39

PLIMPTON IS CONDUCTED by worry. He loads his cache by lugging its parts and heartens when he see his companions. They are stricken and amused by his sufferings, failing to mention their own. None of the four swopped words with Plimpton nor asked about Billy Mox. Rendezvousing on the plain was not their intention and they want Plimpton dead. Though they will not do it themselves. He, fat Plimpton, not afoul of their buyers as they themselves surely are.

"Lemme put her on a blanket and dick her. You fellas have a drink and a smoke."

"C'est ça. C'est une bonne idée."

"Speak fuckin English goddamn you."

"Fuck her Plimpton. Go to it."

Plimpton is invited to circle the wagon before its driver collects the others. Wagging his digit he exhorts the men, "faites bien attention," the groups' appetite whet for amusement. Plimpton's sandbarred and pulpyflesh is bared as he yells at the girl, grabbing her ankle to pull her from her lair to the ground and with knees apart, he finishes denuding his bulk. With the draggled hides of his buttocks exposed you can see the unlanced boils, the canyonland of his parted crack, the excrescent slaver rigid with erection as he flounders and twangs orgasmic, the eyes of the girl on a weazened rocket contrasting a plafond sky. What she's seeing is a floater in the fluid of her eye and though aggrieved it is something to see. He then dumps his seed inside her. "They's more, gimme a rest." The men laugh till they cry, rape her in pairs and in an hour the girl is unconscious. Fusilladed back to her cage. There's a seventh in observance, the man overattentive, screened by the brine of the shadows. Umbrageous shades at his back. Threadbare's parched from hate.

They drink their fifths and when each has imbibed the decision is made to drift. Beneath the boreal star they bivouac, apart on the North Fork Red. They should have belonged their fires. Therefrom comes what comes. Like armless rowsmen, larboarders at sea, they have cast themselves ephemerous. Past this, past judgment impaired, it becomes a matter of place. For on this tepid night, the year 1831, these slavers, men of the stars, field their camps and their saturnalia, south of the Canadian river. And he, Threadbare, is lotic, an implementer of waters perforce. He walks the Percheron through the herbage of the rivers and asserts from the Red their camps, by volubility and the smell of their flesh. In a jungle dark night underwashed by thick clouds, Threadbare streams from the river, smoldering their fires with the hiss of his urine he speaks to the men in their language. Obedient, they do as he says. Binding each other to one and the same they are bled with tiny cuts; draped and bedecked then weighted with a sennit of stones knotcinched and tied. Doddering to the shore, these four incommunicant, are instructed to submerge in the Red. From a pulpit of mud Threadbare says "turn" and resounding commands his horse. "Help them take their lives." The Percheron, homing, with his ears keyed pricking, eye-traces a streamlet to the men, but their wagoner falls and they flail. Limbtoed they sink, rockbounded and grouped and Threadbare apologizes. The Percheron, unstudied on whimsical humans, settles his muzzle in the flow, drinks from the river cool ebbing. Only Plimpton is left to awaken.

"Plimpton! Mr. Plimpton! I am here!"

There's a refuge of brush between them. Plimpton prophetic in sleep. His tulipped cheeks appear rather babyish, his palsy of lip with a snore ad nauseam, again and again chestdeep. A hand is placed on the face of the debauchee to exorcise his demons. Shrouded by the hand blood drips from his ears and his nose is a mush of snot. Plimpton's crypt is the dream he was having, in that place a sunland of vice wherein the desired is given as wished. Stay there in that world Mr. Plimpton. Enjoy the dotage of pox and sin with its tottering creeds that reel. Wake rested, slimmer and home.

While igniting the wagon and the wares of the merchants Threadbare hears her beckon. As the Percheron chews on a grampus the bountyman cuts their traces, the horses fanning to dark. He walks around to the rear of the cage, opens the catch, chains her pleading and she does not comprehend. What life holds she thereafter? He stares at the front of the wagon, listening to her begging moans. The trapfall is ripped and the woman unchained and she is pulled from the cage and freed. With pantomimic genteelness he directs her northwest after roping a horse she can ride, demonstrating the action of the Lucifer matches and how their heads make fire from a strike. He daubs her embrowned flesh with axle grease packed by the men he has drowned. Residual soot from a slush lamp tamps the shine of this. He says "do not ride by day." Use fire if fire means life. Besides that, keep your camp unattractive. There is more than himself between Reckingfort Soo and modern day Bickleton, Washington. She'll cross the lands of tribes in conflict. What can occur must not. *Not* being her consideration.

He says quietly "there you go." Watching like a patient parent. Walking northwest he reads her track until the sun with its farrow of clouds levers the eastern horizon. He sees no other print but hers. Threadbare stands in her ventricled wake. "My Salish is abominably weak. I need to get back in that direction."

40

WHEN HAW PLIL asked Shon her opinion the woman is too drunk to respond. They stood in their kitchen, she wind-vane shifting, with eyes of familiar hatred. Finally Shon admits: "do what you want. You make me fucking miserable. The Mox's are already gone."

Billy and Dampier are scouring the prairie for any sign of Threadbare's body, sprinting their mounts to equivocal limits of stopping and starting and stopping, Billy scoring the flank of her animal but the horse only widens its stance, the pair walking their mounts to a sandpit of water reeking with putrescible filth. The horses drink, the couple does not. There isn't enough for both. Haw and Shon Plil at that very instant are unable to feel his presence, his indwelling of immediate realms.

"I'll stay if the twins are a problem."

"Go on. They're self-sufficient." Shon places her hand on a chairback.

"Could you not drink while I'm gone?"

"Fuck no. Stay sober on a weekday, while you tear-ass about."

He hesitates. Shon lowers her rear. When seated she swills a dram.

"This shouldn't take the whole day. Verraco claims I sanded a hoof. I hope he hasn't shot it."

"You should plunk him with a headshot and steal his

belongings. Then we can fucking leave. I hate these goddamn greasy officers with their goddamn venerable prancing. I wouldn't fuck a one."

"Shoot, then rob a Mexican officer with the Texans claiming their lands?"

"Sell his fucking horse to that sunblackened bastard, Dipshit or whatever he goes by."

"Dipping Bird is a decent man. Your complaining doesn't help me. There's money to be made supplying both sides until Texas hangs me for it."

"Either the Mexicans or these pemmican chewers will kill you long before Texas."

"They've no reason to currently hang me. There's talk of some Germans settling."

"I'll pray to the god of those goddamn savages to bless your journey dear husband! Now get the fuck away from me!"

He soothes a thatch of her hair with its noodling oiliness and kisses the top of her head. Plil cannot recall creating the child that havocs her choleric womb. A piece of crockery, a cupful of sugar, then tips from the edge of the table, summoning a line of ants. Shon gets to her feet, walks to her bed and from under the covers she speaks. "Sweep that up if it's not too much. I'm not cleaning this fucking pigsty." Haw Plil does as commanded. Listens to Latham and Torq. Like fogwreaths they float past, Latham laughing and chortling in the street: "Haw! Haw! Haw! His name is Haw! Haw! Haw! Haw! Haw Plil!"

Plil steps from his house and into the street, next his gelding there stacked stolen furniture, the pile sufficient to saddle the animal, though their scaffold threatens to topple. Haw's saddle they hold to their chests.

"Together you gents are six?"

Torq slurs, "yes, we're six."

"Neither of you are three?"

Latham responds and laughs. "Together, we are six!"

Torq dumps his black eyes on Plil. Something to say but he won't. His world plagued cataractal with intervales blazing and hawseholes to view it through. His is a life disposed to bear torture and what injuries wait his maturing. Longanimity, indecipherable codes. A brumal incrusted soul. Headfirst from the cusp of this world he'll leap, though at present Torq is staring. Pityingly expecting his turn. A paragon of invaluable child. What names the gods chrysoprases. A verdant gem glowing black in its middle, Torq is that dark rough order. An applicable upborne measure. Come nigh like the suddenness of dark. Unknelled, there is no warning. He cannot cease being him.

"Torq, have you something to say?"

"I have nothin to say."

"You should've mounted his shoulders Latham. Handed the saddle upwards. But you shouldn't take others belongings. Even when they're gone for good."

"Torq done it," Latham said. "I ain't helped 'em none."

"Don't worry. They're not coming back."

Haw saddled the gelding after oating and watering and astride the animal watched them. Both children glazing him still. They skulked unconvinced but refused to hie houseward until Haw permits them to ride. He tries a tale to deflect their asking.

"In the woods in the winter where the wolf-lichen grows is the level of the snow after melting. It piles higher than this geldings' eartips. That's how deep it gets. Vermont is a land of snow. I've seen in the summer the wolf-lichen blooming at twenty and twenty-five feet."

They do not care to know. Sunnier climes the habit of the twins and they want to ride the gelding.

"Okay Latham. You're first."

Two laps apiece around Reckingfort Soo with the gelding comprehending, swishing his tail in the noontime heat and supposing by their weight they are small. He knows what sits his spine, the boys with their heels on the stirrups because their feet won't reach the footholds. On Torq's second round Haw Plil interjects, "Torq, I have to go. We've burned the morning to noon. Though our reasons were just I think."

While dismounting the child he sees the scummed-marked stain, the filth of the boy engrafted there and **LOST** is **LOST** as etched. Torq's prepared to explain. He says "that's from him, but they ain't gonna find 'em, till him gets fount when ready." Torq makes the face of *him*, what he knows Threadbare to be, as if the brand was necessary on the flesh tattooed, talismanic like a boarding sea, with its swash of ingled fire, and Haw Plil does not grin, for a soulless proportion of the evil he senses is there where he holds fast, upon Plil by metes and bounds, swirling and eddying like noisome hail, but there is no sound about them. The breathing of the twins he hears. And who knows Latham knows the fastness of child, while who knows Torq differentiates, between a child entertained by his ride on the gelding and another biding his time, because his instincts tell him a wraith has arisen, his mother and father searching for the evidence, when there is no thing left evident, for it unutterably stews to act. Threadbare is already there.

"Climb in the cellar if it storms. Shon isn't feeling well. Get what you'd like to eat. There's milk cold tubbing in the shade of the wellhouse. Lift the lid, dip your cup."

Torq and Latham affirm to the positive by saying "yessir" together, Latham withdrawing to find Shon resting and he is forced to play with his brother. From inside the house he propounds Haw Plil if his wife is dead or sleeping, her snores from the bed and aftermath groaning a precursor to bovine rigidity. That movelessness before they stink.

"No Latham. She's fine. Come outside. She's rather…"

"…drunk" laughs Torq. "Fuckin roved like a bowline and pregnant!"

"Torq, son, your language."

"My mama said it like that. I saw her and my daddy just a fuckin."

"I'll be back quicker than planned."

When saddled on the gelding he faced the horse west, pacing a rod then turning. There's action by the children, waving shoulder to shoulder, in the dust from the horse having fled. Haw sees the jewels of their teeth. A contravening Shoshonean with contrasted Athapascan is then published from the lips of Torq. When the gelding hears the tongues his gyrations increase, requiring Plil to lock his thighs. Numerable uprearings ensue, the twins counting to seven before Torq's command repeats half his first. Haw Plil returns rather flustered.

"Learn a touch from the locals Torq?" Plil conceals his disturbance and grins.

"Comanche and Apache," replies the child. "I won't do it no more."

Keen with their fun they watch Plil ride, walking after like finitude chased him. As if the plain were a gateway where ended what opened and shut an unnamable thing. The steppes safranine context were synthetically reddish, sheened postnoon as was common, the winds spinning to a westerly blow, pushing from the north with insistence, lifting the hat from the head of Haw Plil as he chased and out-manoeuvered its gusts, him thinking the hat like an aging wound toy, when wound it began on its signature path, the genius to surmise where it's going, to tack against tacking desire, to paraph on its side when finished. Plil caught the hat, suppressedly cursed, such unseasonableness not his custom. As if the weather cared for his comfort.

While resquaring his cap he leans downwind to gaze at Reckingfort Soo. Torq and Latham yell from its border. Pointillistic dotwork waving. Plil raises his hand before the twins are blanked by clouds of funereal gloom, the dust maiming the town and the pitiable children vanish when the dust is cleared. How shall they be delivered?

"Go back to the house little guys."

Beneath the quilt of filthy air he turns.

*

The boys shield their eyes and run to the house. Shon Plil has shut them out. Latched the windows and lined them with linens. Latham asked Torq if the woman called to them and the answer is "here we are. Look at them cracks where she stuffed 'em. Mama does that when it storms."

Latham knocks on the door to no answer. Torq stands for a minute then leaves him rapping before Latham curls on their stoop. Torq wants to torch their house. He watches his brother hindward, sees him go down like a dog, his arms crossed over his face, the child crying and "why"ing and Torq returns saying "fuck Shon Plil, you can wait." Seconds pass, Torq standing in the street, the wind refusing to calm. Another five go by and she won't let them in and Latham is slobbering and wailing, blubbering through a seam in the door. Shon Plil screams from her bed.

"Go play! Leave me be! I'm with child goddamn you!"

"Itsa blowin, we're scared Shon Plil!"

Torq corrects, saying, "Latham, you're scared! I hate you horrible bitch!"

"Go on! Stay out! I cannot nap with you bastards making noise!"

Latham crowds to the door as close as he can and retracts his hands and feet, like a gink in hell on a brimstone fender, no quailing of the wind around him, his brother Torq remaining stoic, his reclusion the offense he accepts, for the storm has marred their day.

Torq stands in the street until the blows' vim and snap fizzles to a chaste cold breeze. Hours corrode like acid. The sun sets in the west and he habitually anonymous considers his love, this aloneness. Torq's a temple in the dark of a jungle. A tiny crevice in a rink of ice. This attraction he should not have. Am I the only boy on earth? No you aren't and nothing can protect you. You're an unversed tracer of tracery's clues and do not understand who is watching. To the boy the plain is confusing, Torq wishing his father were there, to see his big boy walk out of Reckingfort Soo and march upon the plain solitary. Wringing his hands the boy toughens inward and hears his parents approaching, hobbling blown horses across ribband plains with their orangey flesh in diminish. Dampier and Billy are miles from Torq. Soon there is no light. He dusts his handmade pants and the dirt in his mouth makes syrup of the child's saliva. As Torq spits on the plain his mother says this: "that motherfucker is comin after Torq. His plan was to draw us back."

The evangelizing rodent warrants your attention with his head in and out of the burrow. You walk into the darkness for the prairie dog's challenge and when you reach his hole you are his. Reckingfort Soo is behind you. Whoso lights it isn't on task but sleeping, drunk and pregnant, Latham banging on her door and he'll knock past dawn before sleeping from the labor of fear.

You piss in the burrow saying "Torq must pee" and then your heels they feel the pounding, the plantigrade drag of hoof, rising dust where dust was not, the sound like walnuts cracking, this night their testa of a color unbroken and you go to your stomach like a dowser deepwelling, you and your behindhand position, as inferior in the open as a field of corn and you find with your eyes what comes, hopping to crouch and react. You are smarter on the plain than expected. Your age and size doesn't seem to deter you and what you lack are the years that will come.

"A horse with a rider speedin up."

You get to your feet, waddle three steps and the cawing of crows explodes, horse-hooves and the sound of the birds, your developing scream of blood-curling effect and the crows, they caw no more. They're like a handful of shadows being thrown. Torq is ripped from the plain and determinedly pommeled and invited to scream if he wants. But he doesn't, he begins to cry, asking his question sincerely. The pillarized dark onrushing.

"Can you caw like a crow or not?"

"I can make the sound of any..."

His response is left unfinished.

Run

Tomcat manning a window. Sunlight washes the reseda cell as it lifts its paw through a beam. A draught of its shape attends it. The outline cast is studied by the occupant for he is there admiring the cat. Behind the watcher is a mosberry plant sitting on a wooden desk. A thing from a wintery climate. Herein one hundred degrees. Our cat begrudges the scent of the plant, the occupant's eyes moseying to the calendar behind the lawman's desk. It's a two by two of cleanwhite dates as if nothing important will occur, before now or after this day. First of August, 1844, the majority of the year unusable to the sheriff and the occupant says "not a planner. Pussy, pussy, come here lil' fucker."

The youth speaks from an amity cell. Manboy, fourteen years old. Like some golem come tripping in from the desert, his years aren't the number he has suffered. Short fingers grip the bars, but the palms are rare wide, his right index healed bent. His hair is black, uncut in years, dark eyes that drowse when he speaks. No particular scar he's achieved by chance for grosser signs of gods he believes, superstitions requiring more seasons. A muscled back he disports like a heaveman. It's from kilnwork and piggering and lugsail mending on a shallop owned out of Cardiff. There are striations from the knout on his legs, his reeving of the halyards enraging an African, though that wasn't on the Cardiff shallop, on that vessel he the speaker of English. He is tall for his age, his appetite weak, weighing south of eleven stones. With another tube of light he makes shapes with his hands, a yellowhammer, a mockingbird, he envisioning birds in flight. The cat sees his quarreling covey. Somberly views their winging.

"Kitty, kitty, sss, get it. Fetch 'em aflutter baby."

He hefts the cat through the bars and strokes its yellow testicles and the cat sprouts a subsequent erection. The kid laughs at the unintended. Sitting in the back right corner of the cell he begins picking fleas from the tomcat. Mashing with his thumbs and a mad-eyed scorn he flicks the fleas to the wall and hears them click and with a bone remembered stiffness wants the cold. He recalls twenty below, that reified inversion of sky and flat plain when his inner voice shrieked death, saying *boy, you'll die at twelve*. By serrying with his dog he survived that night, by victualing with its meat he lived.

When the jailport sprung and a voice said "fuck," he shoved the cat through the iron-striped vent, aboutfacing to confront his jailer. His repast still uneaten. Nozzling the air he cracked his thick neck without giving the lawman his ear.

"Where's that goddamned cat? The woman wants her goddamned cat! Why ain't you eatin your food?"

The boy goes to the window outgripping the bars, his overseer noting his impatience. He relaxes his grip and exhales. The tomcat sallies forth to offend with his erection a missioness leafing through her Bible, the tom wrapping her leg precociously. Rolling to his back he reveals it.

"Hey lostness! Mama sent you money! I'll make a charitable contribution to your fellow abolitionists. Ain't that what you told his honor? After darkie stomped your ass, aboard that darkie vessel, you said you claimed no color and you all of tar black…"

"Twasn't an all black vessel you shit. There were nine other nations represented."

"I do not give a fuck! You're a cunt faced bastard as dark as they come and I cannot wait till they hang you!"

"Se rumorea que es una puta, por los toros excepcional."

"I know what the fuck you said! Speak American to me goddamn you!"

"I'd like to say nothin at all."

"Won't be long till you're quiet. Shootin for fun in the district, with us toutin fullbore Union. You casually sauntered into that drinkage and an innocent asks your business. I'd a gunned your ass to the floor!"

"They knew who I was and were waitin on me. You speak as if you can't read. You illiterate bumpkin fuck."

"I know my goddamned letters sufficient!"

"A,B,C,D,E,F,G…?"

"Where's that dick swingin tomcat?"

"Releasin his love on a stranger. You know I rather enjoy multiple shots. When initially killin I wielded a knife, the blade is ever so personal."

"What? When did you initially kill? Goddamn it's hot in here."

The sheriff is smitten with the flow of information. Withdrawing the pistol of the jailed from his holster he miserly inches to the bars. Won't touch the unreadable youth. His prisoner's like a floodtide comber, the sheriff weighing his options, replacing the gun on his desk. With pencil and paper in hand he breaches a louvered window. A cylindrical reflection somewhere in the room causes the sheriff to look, as if a hant has come through the bars. The manboy is staring direct. When seated at his desk he speaks.

"When again?"

"When what?"

"The murder?"

"You gonna hang me more than once? I knifed a Cree and a Chippewa curer, fishin on the Missouri river."

His parlance gives the task and a river. His inroads as stated completely unfollowable, his jailer opting for time.

"How long ago did you kill 'em?"

"Five years."

"What'd they do? Heavy penalty for killin a healer."

"They fished upriver from my corkhead markers. Mostly in the shoals, not deep."

"That's a feeble reason for a child to murder. The Missouri's wide enough for bargers."

"I was a tike. Impulsively harsh. My violence would not kneel. I'd kill you for a burnt tortilla."

"That opportunity ain't likely."

"Wanna go fishin and see?"

He pitches the letter through the bars. The youth glances at his mother's script, her legible, exquisite penning, the letters like stalactites forming, as if a writ of revolution were professed. When he lifts it from the floor he sees the money has been stolen and the top resealed with wax. Her perfunctory comments the usual: the selling of a hundred head. Settlers threatening Reckingfort Soo. Spring freshets giving them water, but no dominion or comfort will last. Haw Plil is rarely seen. They own every legal deed for twenty square miles and these contracts are Texas issued. The state's representative simply wanted them there, to which Billy replied, "we've been here."

After capture the letter has found him. If Billy Mox knew her son was to hang, his mother would be in the room, breaming the sheriff like a hull. Instead she's mailed the post to a port he'd quit in December of '43. From there Torq repaired to a whirlwind questing of the bottle and boarding with whores. He appears to be thirty years old, the lines on his face ingathered and branching to those lakelets of sleepy eyes. Claiming aeons spent in the bastardy of self and of innocence, what use is innocence, when your years have been negligible wagers. He's akin to his mirroring image. Torq's immoderately uncharacteristic. Unendurable to him isn't known.

"Latham would die before they arrived. Mother would have to come with him. Billy would kill this sheriff."

Torq folds the letter, taps it twiceover, stands to search for the tomcat, the river foreshortened by bend, the town of Infidente on the opposite bank, the politics of a state encroaching, the river unofficial where he's looking. About is dry desert with aspirant foliage, a shinnery here and there, the rest rockstrewn tenements of basaltic rocks with a multi-hued sundrenched inkiness, manylegged stripes there hatching, where the pliancy of waters have been and are not. Now the mavens of drought hold sway. Torq is jailed in a waypoint storing the condemned prior to their hanging downriver. He knows twenty different stories from twenty different men who knew twenty different others that stood where he stands and to the man they were hung and buried. No minister. Godless holes. Have your armload of dirt and some rocks. You jackals come and chew. These weren't inferior men, but they cannot remain amongst us in our world. Here the tigers of meek and plenty judge the damned as they damned well wish.

"Can I get to that river not dead?" Torq says it, the question then answered, the respondent standing in the room.

"Were you taught to ford to the neck? That's where their rope will go. I've had a word with your jailer. And yes, you would die."

The adverse voice slinking quietly through the door has twice bedded and rose the sun, though his baritone speech is impeccable. Vestal in appearance and rested in appearing though awake for forty-eight hours. The first night he lit candles for Torq, petitioned a grim-lipped saint. Now he is present with the cat in his arms, its neckskin twisted, the beast sedate, with a flutey nasally purring. The man's collar is slimy, sweatstained, his face dark as the son of morning, the priest salably and convincingly deadly and the tomcat senses his fix. Something in his clutch that besieges. The cat knows to purr and wait.

"Father Epigo. Fallen cleric. Billy sent you to deliver salvation, when salvation you can't recall?"

"Simple noes. I bring negations. Ashamed of the life you have chosen. I was a priest, a cleric before. You've shuffled the orders I taught you."

He gives the cat a trite blessing in Latin. Opens the door to freedom.

"Complector, plexus sum," says Torq. "To grab isn't to clasp. Therein an obvious difference."

"I see your looting, hoaxing and violence hasn't rotted you above the shoulders. Though soon that neck'll be noosed and your head have gone to waste. A malleable intellect vanquished."

"Did you come through the Soo? Does she know?"

"Saw them each sixty days gone. Billy said she sent a letter."

Torq spins the post on his bunk. When he sits the priest eyes back. Certain figures of speech in their stares. Coiled springs torrential and popping. Yellowy the dust binds its own heat as they exchange maudlin smiles.

"Trope is the word your mind can't find. Your lips are mumbling questions."

"I thank you kindly precious Father. Trope, a figure of speech."

"She's resorted to thinking you live your life in hidden desert solace. Planing mudbricks, thieving the dawn. Searching for springs eternal."

"She knows the fuckin deal. I ain't seen 'em…"

"Haven't seen them since then."

"They should've guarded their offspring better. I'll die without complaint. That sheriff took her money."

"He's recently had a crisis of faith, donating said sum to the church."

Epigo flicks the roll like an ace. It lands on Torq's left boot. Magnetically balancing there.

"I thank you sir. Now, where to put it? Must they rifle my longnecked corpse?"

"My God Torq, you're a boy. A bath and a feed and you're young."

"Please step closer Father. There is no youth left in me." He does, armed and unafraid, open holstered so Torq can reach it. There's a watchdog sense unmentioned, Father Epigo a goliard of innumerable worlds and their lines maintain attachment, he in and of himself a man disturbed by fate, horrendously bent; with a base for reaction that's immediate, as any thought of the actioning party. Torq speaks from his bunk, won't stand. "I've killed a man for every year I've lived on this earth and their money must go to Latham. His kind this world hacks first. I'm doomed, done, you see."

"If they were innocent, you will pay."

"Father Epigo, my chairborne judge, with the looseness of a collar you hastily remove to fornicate with whores in pairs. You're a man of reputation and a part-time priest with a footlong cock and his punches. Because of you whores retire, you hypocritical preachy bastard. Defrock and I'll listen to your sermons."

"My choices lock me in ice. I see out and you see in." Nothing else is said then Epigo admits, "I've oft been far from home and I don't like leaving my home. Without that safety I'm another."

"What a damndable perfect excuse."

*

Six months after Torq was abducted the Mox's made Epigo's acquaintance. They were tracking a painter accosting their cattle and while adrift and atop a meseta, the pair collided with the dark smocked priest, the man stretched on a meteope slab of stone, unquiet with his maker and begging, his impotent rage yet answered, no response to his "why, why, why?" He'd been a

Mexican citizen acquiring in Fredonia the tongues of the white and Comanche. Summarily Epigo was excommunicated from his order and diocese. Mexico City could not condone the writings of a vagabond priest, whose epithetic title for a coming dissertation would be read as follows: *THE ANIMALITY OF MAN AND APE or HOW THE TWO SOMEWHAT DIFFER*. Post debacle he kept his collar, hunting for hides and with the guerdon received buying whiskey, whores and books. His ambrosia the written word. An ignominious scumbled priest. He would squat on the plains by his fire for weeks, sketching his contraptions mnemonically. He architected a lewis constructed on the prairie between Reckingfort Soo and the homestead. Where geology disposed of its boulders. Guzzling through the summer the deadened priest shifted his satellite stones, to demonstrate how stones were moved, and he saw no God or mystery augment and so proved the point to himself, which was the goal of what he'd accomplished. A true eccentric seeks one opinion. Time constricting that genius to life. These lives are christened indissoluble. A fanatic bred from and towards truth doesn't need your available options. He can search for truth by himself.

*

"You and mother keep daddy in lies, or does he hear of a rumor now and then?"

"He believes you're abducted and murdered. They looked for eight months then relented. Billy says he writes you letters in heaven. Hides them from her in a sheepfold. She reads them and places them back."

"Your secrets? How do you keep them? Hold them in your breast and live?"

Torq wants to pick and harry. He claws at the lice in his hair. Looks at his bloody fingers.

"I'm an old stager to man. I think of myself less often. A veteran of shame I am."

"You serve yourself like a heart pumps blood."

"Dampier needs to know that you never lived for what you have become. He'll hear you hung, but the name he'll acquit, a mistake in print by an editor."

"Betwixt my takin and what you see, you'll never know what happened."

"Those years are yours. Your own. Stand closer to me if you will."

Epigo is embosomed by a chasuble, undercoat, tucked in and bunched, the vestment washed and clean. In the narthex of Epigo's eyes, where lay that violent shearer, a pellicle of the holy Torq sees. Without touching they meet at the bars.

"You gonna anoint me father?"

There's the sound of tinkling glass. He has pilgrimage water blessed by another for in his mind he can't and won't.

"Here we go," says Torq. "Go ahead. If you must I invite you to do so." He presses his head against the bars and a louse crosses his part. "Bless the livin shit outta me."

"I believe that good rests in you."

Resplendent oracular Latin. An incipit is searched and quoted. Here belief in a bettering world. A meliorists' audible dream. Torq receives it and refrains the verse. Epigo is pleased he remembers, pronunciation or otherwise. The black stare on conclusion is beplastered with anger. The moment of innocence fades.

"Father Epigo?"

"Yes, my son."

"My hands are free."

"As are mine."

42

"TORQ MOX! ON your goddamned feet! I gotta put this'un in with ya!"

"Put in whomever you want."

"This'n here don't talk nothin but Mexican so don't go makin no plans. You'll love 'em, he's fuckin intolerable. You're welcome to suck his dick."

"That priest has forgiven my sins."

"That motherfucker is cursed. He whooped Boney's ass and left."

"Boney of whorehouse fame?"

"Boney's respectable enough. His goddamned skull is fractured."

The inebriated man of eighteen years is led inside in chains. He's recently incurred the result of mescal when infused with wormwood bitters. He's seen embowering serpents, prismatic delusions and mono-chromatic terrapins, through goldflour rain their repand pulsing as they morphed into rock and a grizzly. He shot the Rio Grande full of holes and wounded a herdboy's leg. To him Torq appears a cryptomeria tree with its limbs empurpled and indolent. To Torq's rear, on the wall of the cell, scrawl ancient Chinese characters. They say *rain has no color until it is touched and then that color is the touching.* He does not read Chinese.

"La puerta... la ventana... están cerrada?"

The man asks the sheriff and the sheriff asks Torq who permits him to flounder and redden.

"You don't recognize a request?"

"Mox, shit, what'd he say?"

"Man wants to know about open doors and if the window behind you is closed."

"He ain't seein what is'n'ain't?" The sheriff grabs his chin, rotates it. "There's the door. Yonder, the window."

"No hay oso gris?" Torq shapeshifts to human, but the man needs reassuring. "Los miembros son miembros…"

"Soy humano," Torq says. "La especie más horrible. Y no hay oso gris."

The sheriff cuffs the man to his plain wooden desk. He discovers the mosberry plant. It animates, comes to life, he burying his head, shrinking to the floor and loosing a groan before sleeping, a fall flower hallucinogenically chilled. He dreams of glacial deposits, equinoctial nights, where ice is air, vice versa, and where not ice no breath. He mumbles in his sleep of a force that pursues, its procrustean station deep water. Torq listens to his Spanish sublimity, his tragic reportation, watching him sleep and whimper before he slips to his side and is voiceless.

"I'm leavin 'em where he's at. Ain't no charges bein filed."

After the sheriff's departure Torq leans against the back of his cell. To his left is a name distorted, the year rubbed by spitted thumb: **Herzen died in '37. Got dead after leavin this message**. With a tilt of his head, despatching, without a doubt he knows this man. Not Herzen, the one chained to the desk, as he borrows from remembered scenes. He says the name of the drunk and grins.

"Atajo, there you are."

Torq waits on death with no particular date. Atajo's nap he joins. They sleep for an hour and when both are awake, Atajo is staring at Torq. Oriented towards knowing himself. Like offset seasons overlapping.

"You remember me Atajo?"

"No."

Torq stands and launches a piece of plaster, Atajo dodging the flake.

"Torq. You're Torq Mox."

"We're all grown up Atajo. That's our rack and ruin."

"Huh? Epigo was in the street?"

Torq confirms and as Atajo stands the base of the desk is caught. Bolts reprimand his efforts. Torq grabs the bars to comfort the man without subduing his fear. Atajo's right wrist snaps. It jibs in the cuff like a sail despondent but the pain the man devalues. Torq Mox is standing there.

"Atajo, you gotta calm down. I'm in here. You're chained to a desk."

"Y la espalda, your back?"

"It's there."

Torq revolves, taps at the bars. Once irrotational he's naked to the waist with his ribwork and muscles enstriping like battens and the filth of his hair thrown forward, he hurtingly displaying his malice and brawn with its winglike jacket of bulk. Stiff for the lack of his years. Let's consider he was taught to kill. Endeared to death like worms.

"Can you see it Atajo? There."

Atajo sees the brand. Torq's attempt to officiously scar it. **LOST** is visible enough.

"Okay, Torq, it is you."

"I am me Atajo."

This Atajo, drifter, journeyman drunkard, has a brand of his own, that of woman. Young marriage, child wife, pearlescently stunning, typhoid citing her body, the fever refusing to peak. It took she and the child, maybe his, this of little to no importance, for Atajo has a sizzled **ES** on his rib and Atajo won't mention her name, the brand his own personal smithing. Torq concurs with a "puedes hacer eso" and Atajo is saddened but nodding.

"Cold, it is cold, sometimes in the desert? Hace frío... not now but a veces."

"Atajo, dear friend, it ain't never made sense for me to exist a'tall. I question the hairs on my arms." Torq ponders, spins and shirts. His words from a vomiting, dreading heart and who knows from whence it hove. Atajo comprehends.

"La muñeca... está quebrado?"

Atajo yanks against his wrist with its broken small bones. He doesn't want to relive it again. Atajo sweats for a drink, desk pounding his head before sitting as previously chained. Once while peddling snakeroot and juniper to the poorest aldeas thereabout, he saw Torq at a table with four rankling motleys quarteting and seated to kill him, the flip of a card meaning death. Torq glanced at the card and asked each of the men if their pistols were loaded and ready. They demanded he turn the card. Torq replied, "turn the card? Or put one of your pistols to my temple after spinning the chambers myself? Choose your finest weapon. Place it here on the table without peeking at the loads, for I'm sure your guns are prepared and my thoughts will soon be obvious. Splattered on the wall to my left." The acceptor was the grainsman Flambeaux. In his possession was the spear of his trade, boasting that his weapon was chocked and chambered and the shells packed by his hand. Torq said, "Flambeaux, if I survive, may I take your grain as payment?" Flambeaux agreed to the wager. Torq took up the pistol, thumbed back the hammer and pressed the bore to his temple. "Flambeaux," he said. "What of you Mox?" Torq replied, "flip my card? See what we need to know?" Flambeaux did as requested. Torq would've won for the number was even but they shouldn't have looked to see it, four holes with spray obtectingly erupting in the heavyboarded room around them, their heads leaning forward with their skulls together to view the card as flipped. With the blasts they redescended, sat back in their birchwood chairs. Torq's an honorable lad himself. With a chance out of five he would die Torq spun the whizzing chamber, placing the gun to his head. Four clicks, he put it down. With the grainsman's spear in hand, he walked past the slumping bodies. He took nothing from the men but the grainsman's pear, Atajo watching him go.

"You, Atajo, were in that room. Knew what I was planning to do."

"That, I did not know."

"We go back, what, eight or nine years? That card game two at least?"

"You are here. I cannot remember. You are very much alive."

Atajo digs a heel into the gorseplank floor as if to root a means of escape, his wrist swelling in cuff, his eyes and their rims charcoal black, he inhaling through his teeth at the pain.

"Yes Atajo, very alive, and you know how I came to be here."

"Solamente pedazos Torq. I don't want to hear no more."

"What is it you refuse to hear?"

*

Threadbare was inspirited with his abduction of Torq for the lineage of Billy was sacred, the blink of his eyes or the way he ate food the way Billy, his mother, would gesture, the means and chewing the same. He kept the boy on the range in the saddle to his front until Torq was five years old. Threadbare exposed him as hierarchate witness to atrocities unimagined, enacted by honing the habit, Torq attempting escape and evasion without Threadbare ever dissuading. For days at a stretch the bountyman tracked his disembogued signs of avoidance, until Torq would collapse from the chase. And on went the thorough destruction. They massacred a Crow on the Canadian border with a timbre of calls from a bank of black fog and frontshucked snow to the withers. Like an incensed ptarmigan mother they rebuffed and pealed from a glade. As the Crow made his hunt for the ptarmigan's predator there evinced a child before him, like a wooded afreet from the snow, his warclub slicing the air, the spray of gore across the face of the boy, Torq then cinched to a juvenile mustang from the string of the Crow lying dead, pissing its back and not permitted to walk till the stars incepted like flares. He was disallowed English, acquired swathings of others, and if Threadbare slept the boy never saw it and if a town was close it was suspect and into depths imbricating they loped, the isolation earsplitting from the silence between and not once did they cross themselves. Noncommittally oversmall on that endemic waste, they were premonitory beings unkempt, mere delegates of intellect, alike culpable beasts but what hooding dark shall close to take them exerting? Beyond the laws of men what sees? A thing pending from ocean or mountain? Might you shape it with a prayer then commence. Clang and toll if you find something other. We will listen from the safety of our valley.

 Winter of '34 and they were on the North Platte when the Arapaho collapsed their shelters. They chose a westernmost trek to find butte or mesa, anyplace to defend against wind, two hundred of their people lining like adyts through a white enmasking storms frigorific in a clime that heckled its sun, that butterfat orb in quondam vigil holding its warmth perversely, refusing to atone for its sleep. Through the drifts he came, the Percheron snaffled and he in search of game, Torq's mustang unled and following the pair, the spore of its being ignoring the weather for it traverses a generative plain, one prior to the spine of man.

 While Threadbare conversed with their leader a brave curiously stepped from the stragglers, having noticed a pack in twitch, its curses and grunts increasing. His comport was irregularly amusing with the suffering his people were bearing. Though warned he went to the mustang, untying its lappet headpiece, Torq sliding from the hip of the animal, neckdeep in accumulative white. Threadbare spun without finishing his sentence, threw the axe from fifteen feet, the base of the skull transuding its contents, the brave windbowing and bleeding. He fell as if simply exhausted, as surprised to be dying as the man bringing death before Torq in polite and fluent Algonkian said, "I'm him. The lost. The boy." They had no idea who he was, their elder rather easy with Threadbare. He asked the killer to collect his hatchet. Said the brave should not have been curious, his dead unadornedness facedown in the snow surrounded by forty others. Men and boys with heads inclined. Terrible viridian stares. Those faces painted green to attract some attention, but there is nothing out there to attract, these beings acquainted with profanation and that fervor resulting in death, this child come with Threadbare dislodging his weapon from the skull of the man he has murdered, the braves' comments unindicative, not a snide word is said, when Torq extends the ax to his keeper. "There it is," announced the satrap. "A child as evil as you." This elder, squalid from hunger, was direct and Threadbare conceded. Instead of dying where he stood while he listened to the man the elder spoke plain and harsh: "the boy will come with us. You can leave as you came or die." The concatenate continues without a lacuna as what man wills or doesn't. Exchange your life for the disembodied, for soon the boy is theirs. Threadbare replies "your choice." He surmises when the snow has melted he'll abduct an available Torq. He says, "take the boy and his horse, but the brave will remain where he lies. Perhaps he needed excising." The elder replied, "what did you say?" for Threadbare has jumbled his meanings. Speaking slower, this elder, rather openheartedly, said the following as patient as Job: "your kill was my son, the youngest of eight, that have heard you speak on his death." Threadbare scaled an acclivity and vanished like a caitiff swimming from an ominous plague.

Southern pushes after that for the west became colder, their zigzagging path unintended, herded buffalo likely ahead, if they could manage a day of sun without snow and plod faster to catch the herd. When sun did come the Arapaho trailed them and they spake of larger forces, their workings amongst their people, lunisolar but tenebrous occurrences. They said the animals were visions and their hegira polluted because Torq is amongst their numbers, he a child of phantasm and curse. And the herd did escape their scouts, Torq ridiculed and blamed for their fleetness, the boy changing hands from the Arapaho's suspicioning to the Apache and the Hopi and the Pima; then back east with a swageman, a maintainer of demiculverin. About the roll of the die and a plate of black beans with a barrel of agave brew, Torq was dealt to a camp of labor, its creation for the veering and the wayward, the boys sold like cinderblocks northwest of El Paso where a merchant some called Tanna, claimed hydrophane in underground vaults. If one couldn't dig, rocks had to be painted, for a Mexican trail heading north, used by Tanna's accomplices, for the vice of an eclipsing frontier. With no specified allegiance nor country supported Tanna sought his opal in wells, sold certified stocks to Mexicans and Americans and especially to a district judge, gifting shares for the writ of attainder the judge locked in his vault for Tanna.

Torq met Atajo and ten other boys for excavation broke them to pieces. The burgoo they were fed wasn't innutritious, but portions were doled by size, the smaller boys painters of rocks as guides; Torq and Atajo, then six and ten, both weighing under eighty pounds. Neither were afraid of the others hemmed there but Atajo kept to himself, whereas Torq refused to be tamed, spewing interleaved blasphemous and hellbrothing comments in the language of the boys and their masters. Unprovoked he challenged those twice his size while bedecked with heterodox arms. They were chiseled by hand while the weary camp slumbered, working beneath his blanket. Like his forebear he would not rest, or wasn't caught sleeping if he did. He was allowed to roam without threat of escape, no delict if you ventured outward, for where would that searching take you? Into the arms of a group of recalcitrant Apache buying wholesale Tanna's dream. After six months of grueling child labor Torq began straying from the camp. The boy gathered his food and slept where he fell, returning to his rocks by dawn, skylighted by miliary Apache. What would happen had to happen and it did. Amongst these no status quo.

The camp guards were ordinands, pedophiles mostly, who abandoned their folds for Tanna. They carried pockets of sweets and catkin whips with hardbitten demeanors abased. Torq invited their flogging to protest weakness but would never submit to their touches. Swaying in huaraches and puddles of blood he was determined to withstand his assailants, recoiling with their chants of "lost little boy," but the incident Atajo recalled. After that their words were hardly corrosive for jeering had a relevant price. And then came the older boy Victor. Victor was the son of a devout whoremistress who tended to wallow with opium. She traded Victor for the cash to inhabit its dazement with its raining of rags and bones. Unifiedly his mother endowed her skin with its rhythmically biting serpents and for opium Victor was sold. He was white, English speaking, and from charity to charity and jail to jail had been passed until Victor was dealt, to his final resolution with Tanna. Here at the commencement of his fifteenth year he stood before a mound of unpainted rocks partnered with a child of six, who refused to comment on the rashness of their work and would not raise his chin. They were paired because a language was shared and Victor collapsed in the mine. Atajo and his companion were behind them, another pair a mile behind them. They'd a small cask of water, brush and whitewash and a pound of burgoo apiece, spearheading the crews in the desert, Torq having demanded the front. Tanna hoped the Apache would slaughter young Torq, killing Victor because Victor was present.

On the third day he spoke. Walking to their work Torq informed Victor their tongue meant death if used. The pair at this time were miles from camp, north in that connective of aenigmate, their rocks an irrelevant artery, draining what heart deadrisen, alike incubates from sand and intolerable heat, when Victor chose his retort: "Torq Mox, fuck you, you pigstuck cunt. You're a cocksucking motherless shoat. You best stay alert in the evening. Your goddamned sleep may be troubled." Torq walked away with his brush and his bucket, a hundred rocks thusly aligned, packed bleak in the sand, in demission, resigned weights unpainted in the desert.

Bunched around a mainfire a fortnight later they protected themselves from the ordinands, two lighter than Torq being maimed. The sky was intershot with a gallery of stars, Vega, Arcturus and Altair meddling with an impress of others tumescent, less swell with the morning that threatens, the smell of opobalsam and lit burning moxa for a guard has been knifed by Torq, followed by Victor's awakening. He, the child, stole in from the desert, an eldritch infrasonic clothed wretched; smeared with the blood of a sacrificial boar, a spirituelle sunbaked to revenge. His blade, as fashioned, is stunted from a tortoise, its handle pyroclastic rock.

"Victor, wake up, it's Torq."

"Motherfucker! Get the fuck off me!"

"Shhh… you'll wake the others."

Four hours later Victor squats by the fire with Atajo staring at his whiteness. His eyes are cast down and he's sobbing. Tanna is summoned to question the boy and he asks him to lift his chin, wet bib of stale blood on his shirt and neck and fresh drainage on the corners of his mouth. He shakes his head when asked who has done this, though Tanna will do nothing but seethe.

Atajo then stands, throws the tongue at his feet and Tanna cannot move. "Los indios cortan la lengua, y se fue… se fue… se fue…"

Tanna listens to the words of the child and then asks as safely as possible: "y Torq? Torq Mox, Atajo?"

"A desierto, pero Tanna, los indios no mata Torq. Tampoco el diablo también."

Tanna stares at Atajo and his words are mulled over and all is disregarded. A detachment is sent to pose. Four men ride out and quickly come back for his tracks are olding there. What they find is meant to confuse them. Could be Torq. Could be any.

43

LATHAM'S KEPT HIS collar pulled above a blister from the burn of the sun on his neck. If Billy reminds him he's usually kerchiefed, but her gift has been lost in a downpour intercutting their contemptible herd, made measly from his father selling down, Dampier wanting to think he's smartly invested and that the railroad will soon cross Texas. Latham's driven the remains of the cattle due north to escape the control of his mother. He's thirty miles from his parents realizing the Kiowa camp east around Darrouzett, Texas, on a creek later named after them. The fresno of their gametrails appear as paved roads for the men who hunt the bison. Here before, not here thereafter. Latham stands his horse on a trail with his herdlet as they low, weakly graze and stare. He's brought them to range, sleeping in his saddle, jerking alarmed and awake, no one but the devil and his wind, the part-toned jetties of plainscape asserting their right to do as they wish. Latham says "hello" and "fire" and "cow" and "dog" and "meat" in Caddoan. He guesses that his brother can converse. Billy keeps his living from Latham, but Latham prods Billy and he knows. Torq is jetsam floating at sea to his brother, an infallible being himself.

Before he left these culled twenty, the undesirable cattle, grazed close to their trebled ranch. They now have a backbone of barns and corrals with tanks that fill and recede. The herd was skiddish, uncertain and bestirred, a summer paradisaic having fattened their barrels with forage and feed fresh ground. Unbranded they move like fragments of space with their distention of gut and fourfold stomachs scissling invitiate cuds, their janizary bells exclusive to the mothers Dampier didn't drive to the railhead. But they refuse to lie down for the abundance of pasture has made the bovine homely, leery of elsewhere drifting, Billy looking through the window, yodeling his meals, as she watches him watch them safely, the boy mumbling "goddamn, stop dotin." It is Billy who has told him the pastures to avoid though for Latham their ranch is that place. He has to get away from his mother.

"Them grasslands north of the river are loaded with roamin Comanche."

"I know mama. They's Kiowa too."

"You don't know nothin child! Don't stray more'n five or six miles!"

"I'm gonna ride Mourly and he ain't sensitive, how will I know how far?"

"Five miles, no more, Latham Mox! They's things that'll bully your dreams! They nest in this fuckin prairie!"

"He stoled Torq! Not me goddammit!" Latham murmurs "Threadbare is dead." He is without reason to think this. Denial his central plateau. Billy Mox has no response.

*

Latham herded the twenty through the Coldwater onto the flats of the Rita Blanca. He's told his mother he'd be gone for a week. There as foretold in the words of the woman was a thing to bully his dreams. The octet adjusted like oscillating nautch, feminine and tousled in a portrait of dance until Latham drove his cattle right to them. Eight vaquero standing at attention watching his approach as he made it. To their backs are lahars incommutably waiting, coterminous and spatial as humans themselves, what home their demesne volcanic. The flows like snaking hair. A humeral veil of encrusted sanguinity, enshrined in unfadable red.

"Hazme un favor?" says Latham. "Ustedes tienen una lima para pezuña?"

"Por que'?" Three say it, but one is in charge, and he doesn't have to speak.

Latham wants and needs to file Mourly's hoof though the why that comes from their consult tells the youth no file is amongst them, for they depend on boneshod Indian ponies as wild as depredate viking. Each man is engarbed as the southerly gaucho with escopetas a hundred years' old, their accents unhymned from the Mexican tongue riding niellated saddles of dons, though these men are impoverished and starving, the sash at their waists at twenty-four inches and there's a pair on the ground speaking Caddoan. Latham says his memorized words. The vaquero that turns to the mounted boy has a blue spotted face with elevated cheekbones and contrastively squints his eyes, the lids almost touching as he looks at the speaker and begins in his hybrid language, saying "you, there you are. You unerringly appear as your mother, and if not she then your father, and if not he then your brother, and this man to my front, he will kill you. Do you understand what I'm saying? It's important you comprehend."

"De que' estas hablando?" Latham hasn't comprehended. "I just needed a goddamned file." No looks from one to the other. He nervously coughs and Mourly is trembling as Latham farewells the horde. They refuse to return the gesture, inviting his amending by showing their backs as if protecting a punitive secret, a tale lost like thurible smoke, its wisps aloft above pipes and cigarillos as the blue spotted man checks his wound. Anewing their discretion they vet Latham's departure, his intercourse with plain and sky, the youth riding painfully slow, as they wait and watch and wait. Affrightedly his cattle come after. They follow Mourly and a mothercow belling. He's a mile from the group when the pop stops the cattle with an eruction of throatymoan belches before they wean to a marauding silence. There's another report from their stand. Latham halts Mourly to muse.

He roams a day and a night, chewing through his jerky and he isn't alone or unseen. Next day dictated by hunger, he shoots an obese hare with a fortunate shot that nicks his bull's pinbone. Latham doesn't know what he thought or was thinking until he fired above its rump, the hare exploding from the gold of the grass in a light appreciable enough for Latham, the boy shooting from his scabbard with the eight gauge, its borehole both of his thumbs. He cleaned the hare, impaled it, and as the rain came down he'd sufficient fire to cook. In the eiderdown softness of the grasses thereabout some creature snapped the reeds for the entrails, a tear, a rip and a growl; the sound peculiarity soon married with lightning and without any draw or shelter for protection he is made to mount Mourly and ride, wandering the cows where they wish, the shot bull contumacious and bleeding in droplets, he leading the cattle around the toothfelt strikes as if opposing God's antecedent to portray his world as desired, the bull without Mourly condensing the herd, supervening their numbers as targets, a bolt stopping his herding with a deglutitized burst entering his openmouthed bawling, the bull dead where struck as his heartgirth floods and from his eyes come epibolized blood, the beast stiffening in stance as a mortalized being immingled with immortalized things, within that whirl or a purge in between, where embitterment no longer assails you.

"Holy fuckin shit."

Latham considers the bull sacrificial. *I had to offer something to the storm.* Already the distress of the cows and the death has been lessened by bovine tranquility and the wilt-quick passage of threat. Mourly, without Latham commanding, attempts damming the flow of the nineteen head but they spread like puttering chicks.

Mourly unexpectedly bucks. Latham launches headfirst with a flip. Lands on his feet then his hands.

"Shit Mourly! What the hell was that?"

The horse intuits the question but trails the loose reins to a candied-colored hole of rainwater. Oily liquid. Oily reflection. Mourly touches his tongue to decide if it's sugary before lapping the pool to mud. Latham sits and watches him slurp, apologizing for cursing the beast. On his girthstrap is a four-in-hand knot creaking with Mourly's hydration. The horse drinks then pursues the cattle, shaping them by proportions. Where uncenteredness offends him he snaps them in line before driving again columnarially. Latham Mox fights warm sleep. Lies down in the grass and yells.

"Mourly, keep 'em close! I'm gonna nap for a minute!"

Latham's visitor is not from the seven vaqueros but his impetus is thwarted as he watched them. Finding Latham changes that energy. The man discovers the escarpment, its rise a slim totem, as he backcuts his mount to the rise. He's dueled over threats on a scabblestoned beach in the year of Hamilton and Buhr. The spyglass obtained has been in safekeeping in the cenotaph erected post duel. His foe was buried with family, but he's taken the prize from the corpse. The spyglass was a gift from a birding enthusiast and is inscribed in the language where made: *votre tout devoue*. *Ton ami, Miraboix Isabelle*. From the head of the escarpment he reverses its locks and the debarred lens protracts. It has a garish assortment of inguinal guards and he releases them as they're presented. The blooming gold phallus extends. There is Latham double x'd on the prairie. Asleep in the grass unprotected. His face sweating in the oculate disk. Past Latham stands Mourly and the herd, he surmising a mile and a quarter. He's educated himself on distance and measure but is thwackingly loud while preparing descent and Mourly realizes he is there, plodding towards Latham with the cattle. Their faulting of security, mooing and drawling, startles Latham and he stands upright. He has slept soundly and within that slumber has been floating in interwomb fluid, next his twin in the dark and the heat. Latham touches his brother and asks "are you Torq?" saying "brother, if we speak she will know us." Now Latham is awake and remembers.

Latham stirrups into saddle to count them. In two minutes time he dozes again and the man has fled the escarpment. He loads a .44 caliber in a swain-hide holster with a fosse on the inside grip. He's worn the iron by vicariously thumbing the grip without wanting to stroke the piece. Taking three long years to do it. Greyly he stands his horse on the plain stroking the fosse as is habit. Shy of seven pounds with its millstone grips the .44 has been storied from cannon, seized by British irregulars, from a barkentine filled with contraband items, including coffee and hardtack for Washington's troops and an armoire for Franklin's study. He is proud to carry the weapon. Even knows its smell.

Prior to his killing of Latham he waits for the evening to cool. The boy sleeps on as the sun casts anemic, a miasmal fog blowing south. He ties his horse to a decurved extension of slate at the base of the escarpments' tower. Here the comet stove lies hidden. He's entrusted its creation to his very own hands by crafting the stove from a chalice. The cup was heated, its lip domed-in, what remained a goblet enclosed, the man snaking the top with a three-foot wire, ventilating the sides with holes. Its base is removed with a thurl, chopped and hacked and freed. The wire is run through the bottom, wrapped around the handle and a crackersized doorway cut. Here what you burned in the comet is inserted to idly smoke. When one wanted fire they swirled the heavy chalice and the air through the holes kept it burning. Smoking moss, bark, twigs or grass, any cinder aired would light. You placed them in the door, lit the stove once and your job was to keep it dry. This particular comet has burned for a year, sputtering and at times growing cold, but his swings are concentrically vicious, tramping the night with light.

He spins it twice and the glow increases. While mounting his imperturbable beast, the stove singes hide and skin, a fetor releasing but the animal, angered, makes no sound as heard. He thinks *not like this, but the other.* Dismounting, the bridle, bit and oiled reins are agitatedly removed from the horse. The aplite blanket and saddle are dumped with all their finery intact, a dragonfly of blue landing on the beasts' back with a heatherlike rumble of wings. The horse slashes with its tail, the man tipping his hat, his serpentine locks of white-matted hair untilled like a field of wet cotton. He stands, waiting for dark. Wants night with its avowing insistence. On the eaves of silvertan clouds ingratiate wrens are cheeping. The man strips his sweated shirt. From his packs he removes a mirror. Hop-poled, cut and beaded; upon its glass sit capitulum paints, daubed and shaped like bone protuberants from ceremonial Pawnee sages. He spits on the pads of his parchmentlike palms and hustles those hands together. His naked body he adorns with black, red and yellow, and a fern leaf shade that is greasy, all pressing like cambium layers, between wood and bark and bark and wood on the body of his horse and his own. Like-like dements and paranoiacs assembled the pair is a head amorphous, a gagglement of raps from impassable lairs with nocturnal mists seeming bluish, where moted dust blocks out the sun. They twinge and sweat in the blackboard night, lastly blackening their eyes. Like sentries of a Christianized hell. It's dibranchiate tunnels surround from its core, within its middle the burning envisioned. Latham sleeps on as if frozen.

Once he is ready he bends back his body and though aged the drive hasn't left him. He mounts the steed bare and it's there. The horse bristles with his heels in its ribs, he inservilely and brutally bludgeoned by the comet between his trembling legs, his gaskin suddenly alight, the horse quaveringly rearing with a torrential bugling, that in that emptiness is an unknowability congealed as enumerative delusion, maliced by its hate of silence, though

Latham hears nothing to alarm him. When the .44's barrel strikes his wide croup an unbeseeming whinny vaults from the warhorse and Mourly unitedly crouches, as the man and his mount gallop forward. Latham remains asleep. In his right the comet is spinning. To his left the pistol held tight. He's a ministrant bound for the un-understandable and an oughtness that ought not be, stoled in paint with a musculatured nisus and an ungual grip of his weapon, thirty paces out and if Latham is asleep he will stay there sleeping till death, the comet soaring past his slumbering head, scattering the cattle and any and all from their annexed space of plain; Latham yet unbucked, tethered with his fist soldered to pommel as the man slows the pace of his horse, the .44's muzzle then pressed to his heart and *motherfucker you mind your mother...* Latham blurring and falling from his saddle, with the jolt of the dream and his words.

Mourly's cathexis while the boy was sleeping has taken the herd due south. Eight miles in six hours with a frightened heifer leading the cattle in haste. It is 12:01 in the morning, Latham sleeping through half the night. With eyes like a troll the young man is alert and will not sleep till he's home. The habitual is the end of thought. Latham's habits won't change again.

*

Latham didn't know his knife was missing until his mother asked for the blade. Latham immediately lied: "I sewed you a jerkin from rabbit. Musta left the knife on the plain."

"Where is that particular jerkin?"

"Left it and the knife I reckon."

"You took 'em north of the Coldwater didn't you? After I told you no."

"No mam. Five miles north. Let 'em graze as they wished."

"So the jerkin and the knife and one less bull are together yonder on the prairie?"

Billy looked at her son. He's now a head taller than she, standing owlish for the beating to come. Welts she does not make.

"No response from nary a Kiowa? There's good grass north of the Coldwater."

"Mama, I went, I lied. Rode straight to where you told me not to."

"But you didn't check your dead now did you?"

Billy stared north at a lectern of cloud, a storm trudging behind it in black.

"Latham, always check your dead."

44

TORQ SUPERINTENDS THE building of the gallows from the window of his incarceration. Tragacanth drips from the wood and white block, an effort at waterproofing, suggested and brought from afar. He tastes it and smacks his lips. The sheriff has convinced their district attorney to hang Torq Mox posthaste. Saving the trip downriver. Torq prattles at the work of the donated carpenters and corrects them where strength will be crucial. Brittle twigs will not suffice. From his innerward cell he heckles the men without purpose or sense to be made. With dialects and inaneness he repeatedly yells and they've no idea what he's saying: "a white crow means rain in the desert! After that gallnuts will grow! If I remain in jail I am bucksawed timber crawling from the ass of your wife! Pick it up! Pick it up! You're to kill me!"

While driving nails in crossbeams and cognizing shape the carpenters listen and laugh. In six hours their berater will hang. He has scant timidity towards death itself, irrationality its own utter comfort, his instincts blowing like a prophesied wind and Torq Mox will not relent.

"Sirs! You men of the scaffold! These are holy-broke times though I have it on authority Satan quotes the Bible like an angel, though his company gives a warmer reception!"

"Torq Mox! Shut your goddamned mouth!"

"Ah, words from the shrieval tubby! Why're you hidin from me?"

"I'm droppin my load in the jakes! Shut your mouth or I'll do it for you! I cannot shit with you hollerin!"

From his cell Torq can see the corner of his jake and the top of the sheriff's head.

"You in there masturbatin? Thinkin of a goat or a horse? Perhaps a cousin or a sister or an aunt?"

"Torq! Some folks speak English!"

"And through the cracks in those jakes women wash their pots with their skirts hiked up to their waists! You can see 'em in the river just a scrubbin! This I know cause I see 'em myself!"

"These here are public toilets!"

"Public enough for you! The whole town can peek down in 'em!"

They won't get it finished because they can't square it level so the foreman of the crew, a sotted Kilmarnockian, speaks to the sheriff off site, telling the lawman it won't be completed unless the base and the joists are flush and plumb and the sheriff orders it done. The Scot reminds the sheriff that bargaining with mystics will entice an unmystical death. They'll gladly hang the Scot as a heathen. When the sheriff asks why they can't hang Torq until the base is flush and plumb, the burghman shakes his head: "ah sheriff, he was spewed from damnation and that pit is imperfect you see, though it perfectly shapes God's fallen. And that's a Catholic God I remind you. If you're to be doing an archangel's work, for they're given the worst of the tasks, then your angeling, though sicklied with the puniness of human and the cumbrous steps of man, had bett'r be level at least; for every handmaiden of the great divider, Satan in doom and plea, is irreliable for good but reliable as spirit to return as will and wished, and return Torq Mox he shall, to follow these men with hammers hereabouts to their graves and else thereafter. I am rather unbiased myself, but ably drunk and tired of continuing my work on this scaffold dearest friend. Tis' a calculus is it not, this annoying fucking world, with its vain undiscoverabilities?"

"I'll pay another bastard to do it! What you've earned is now forfeited!"

Midnight comes the day before the hanging, a Freemason declaring it finished, after the brief delay. From his rickety bunk Torq whittles a duster with the serenity of a Yaqui shaman. He slides in his four fingers, taps at the bars, seeing the torches extinguish, burning their wicks like crayfish wounded, total darkness, its particulate stars, then stippling to activation. They are changelings which brighten as earth wields dark gravitating to a world of illusion, with its sublate and unified wider dimensions and not an inch is unascertainable. Torq can see as if night were day. But who dares walk refutable night with its slow-vast chunks of unvoiced beings downing from their hemisphericality to opportunely hang for your scent? Up or down from percept abysses. Where you go they impend.

"Ever-one in this world is pursued."

Atajo is roaming the street by night and whorehousing his days in ecstasy. He doesn't notice Torq staring from his cell as he rises on his toes to gaze in. The wrist pains him daily but a bout with sobriety disinterests this heartrent man. When his chin clears the frame Torq fingers his nostrils curling his friend to the bars. Torq snorts "Atajo, no," dropping Atajo to earth. The man sleeves the blood from his nose. Netting a reaction and vising his fists he looks at Torq in the window, there his simian shape window present.

"Go fetch that fuckin Scot. I'll give you these dimpled knuckles."

Atajo retreats amain in a stumble crashing down the crumbling bluff, a pokesack of wagtails expecting liberation long cooing when his body strikes them. With their choker sack open baby wagtails emerge from the poke to circle his head. Atajo brushes them past as their mother limits their spread. A man who is there to watch Torq hang asks Atajo if he can swim. He says "into the water. I want to see your stroke. Swim downriver a bit." He then stands in the brambles and waits. Atajo knows the voice.

"You-are-not-here."

"Why am I not here Atajo?"

"You, you'll bus' Torq out."

"Torq Mox can escape when he wants. He doesn't need me to do it."

The man gazes at the queue of water and river with the shelterbelt pruner in hand. As he dismembers Atajo the pieces are floated, eventuates to gulf and sea. The pruner is left on the bank. The whetter for its edge he keeps. His horse he has hobbled on some scraggly illuvium, the mount stamping his approach intimidatingly. Wellnigh complete with Atajo's blood the man before the horse lethalizingly swells, thinghooded by darkest impulse. His beast approves. He doesn't.

"I loathe that messy shit."

He feeds his horse a pocketed apple. Of this pair enough for now.

*

The torches are relit two hours later because a child finds the shelterbelt pruner. Torq has begun his assault. Avowedly desiring attention, he commences questioning heaven. An alderman exits to inform the sheriff and within several windows lights burn. Early morning wagglers, heads covered superstitiously, listen to his drastic asserting, his hiatus from acceptable curses, none believing the boy right-minded.

"I've marked you ever' one for killin! After that I'll sully your virgins!"

Stepping back from the porthole to a corner he awaits the sheriff's arrival. Torq slides to his rear, extends his small feet, switching the knuckler to his left. He slams the back of his head against the cell wall, a puzzle of plaster landing in his lap before he breaks his own nose with the duster, simultaneously loosening teeth. He drools on his shirt, his chin touching chest, then blackens an eye with his toy. From the door you discern parts of his legs, the remainder inferable shadow. The door opens and through it he comes.

"Sonofabitch Torq Mox! Shitassin ingrate fucker! Where the fuck is Josiah Corn?"

The night deputy is nowhere in sight. The sheriff lights a lantern and has not seen and will not for a while. He illuminates the empty calendar, speaks to waste more time.

"Goddamn Blane I reckon! Mox, has Blane been in here? I outta just give you the keys!"

When there is no opinion shuffling or standing or a scathing remark from the cell, the sheriff with an impoverished and weakened resolve has a flutter of emotion and pity. He believes Torq Mox to be quietly frightened by a death realized as pending. In the silence the sheriff thumbs through his papers, perusing the schedule again, as if the men should suddenly appear. Augmenting the wick of the emptying lantern he licks his lips and sees. Torq's legs haven't moved and don't. His denial is otherworldly.

"Torq Mox, scritchascratch them feet. Did Atajo bring you more chicha? I thought I bought the rest of that swill."

No movement of limbs or air. In a stepwise manner, inasmuch recomposed, he wants to delete his fear without going into the cell. His lantern won't repudiate dark.

"Torq, say somethin goddamn you!"

Torq Mox is a sculpture that has dried. Watch his toe, its abbreviate twitch. Confirmed by sight, but was there seeing, and does he want to know?

"If you're kilt, be dead, but if I come in, I ain't comin in for lovin."

The sheriff sits. Knows better. Don't do this. Not alone, not with him. Threaten the boy manifold times with your voice and with your weapons. Sixteen, three-inch bars, filter his alleged criminality, without you daring to draw that lock. The sheriff stands and steps to the bushing. It's an old figure eight, a bank-vault stripe, with a frontspiece plating and quadrature boltments enlaid at ninety degrees. It has since been through a fire. While Atajo lay in his stupor, Torq turned the locks with the tine from his fork then caged himself again. He told the sheriff the guts were coated and that soot made the lock susceptible. The sheriff replied, "fuck you Torq. Come out here if it does." Nestling on his bunk he had grinned.

"Aw hell. Aw shit. Aw no."

He hesitates, draws the bundle, Torq to the left of the entry. The sheriff sits the lamp by his feet. Sees his face and the blood, smells the urine. The analyzable clues with their translatability comprehensibly ignored by the sheriff. The scene is cozily familiar, other suicides, other places, the jailed here and just downriver.

"Caved in his own fuckin melon."

The sheriff goes to the window because the sheriff hears voices. No person is there as perceived, which has brought him to Torq in the cell, the sheriff intruding when the boy was silent, his knowledge increasing as it wildly adapts nearer a thing absolute. The sheriff sits on the bunk with the impotent lamp, the back-left leg dipping floorward. He scoots to his right to adjust. Nothing amiss for the sheriff. Torq's feet have been crossed and recrossed again while the sheriff gazed out the porthole.

"Damn, I wanted to hang you."

The front door of the jailhouse is partially ajar. It comes inward with a patient hand. The sheriff speaks to Blane. Words about a cart and a burial. A phrase about an untoward holing. A rabbited suicide. Blane tries to relate that a gospel realizer would've never chosen Torq's life. "Oughtn't be a Christian burial." The sheriff replies, "Blane, fuckin leave. What the fuck did I just say? Do what the hell I said." Blane is also the probate minister for the six who won't become Catholics. He piously backs and closes the door and the sheriff is alone with his lion, Torq's unseemable parity of pulse commissioning his blood to flow.

"Are you in hell you fuck?"

"Fuck no, we're in Texas."

Torq says it with eyes and carnassially chipped teeth popping open to twist their gleam.

"Aw hell. Aw shit. Aw no."

He gathers his heels and body akimbo, committing to an unmade rising, giving the sheriff a chance to run, the lawman unaccepting. There's a stinging finality, an invariable countenance, as the sheriff reviews his life. Torq peeks between his knees in the oil lamps' thusness deciding how to proceed. He giggles and bugs his eyes, opening a lid, closing another, hiding behind his knees. He says "peek-a-boo you" and the sheriff has to say it for he remains unharmed and seated. "Why ain't I dead Torq Mox?"

"You're the fella holsterin a shooter. I ain't armed except for the duster. You're currently still in charge."

"They's a fuckin-mess wrongness that goes thu' the heart and another that ladders the spine. Yours meets in between."

"Pull the rod sheriff, leave the cell and lock it, you're free to roam as usual."

The sheriff does as instructed. Torq pinches his calves as he crosses.

When the deputies march in to wait for the dawn the sheriff mumbles instructions. Doesn't mention what has occurred. "I'll be right back. Wait here." They light four lanterns after brimming the oil and the unsparing shadows depart. Death by heat implores. No one will open a window. Torq says "gentlemen, remain awake," but the deputies are asleep in minutes. When the sheriff returns his men are missing, Torq Mox having placed them elsewhere. Torq's sitting at his desk, the jail barren and warm, the floor drenched in a fetid liquid. Torq is toothing a match.

"Aw hell. Aw shit. Aw no. What'd'j do with the others?"

"You walked right past 'em yonder. Their parts are in this tote."

The sheriff glances out the door at the doubly hung youths. By their feet they swing from the beam of the scaffold with their ears partially docked. They are conscious and wining for the sheriff's attention, the spectacle unjarring to the citizens present, for goggle-eyed they've locked their doors, dousing their candles to wait. As if with tributary the sheriff reenters to speak to the youth at his desk. Torq repeats his offer. The sheriff still hasn't drawn his pistol.

"You for them. That's what I said."

"Me what?"

Torq flips the desk and draglights the match on the sleeve of his coarse shirt. He blows it out into dueless space, the flame then reemergent, a lampwick in his fingers sorcerously lit with a balefire flame at its top.

"At your feet. Look down. You smell it? Two inches of your own lamp oil. You must've ordered a whale squeezed dry. It runs to the side where you're standin. I've hardly a spot around me."

"Aw hell. Aw shit. Aw no."

"You're gonna hold this wick standin right where you are. Reach across here and get it. It's liable to drip anytime."

"Why ain't the smell blow'd us up?"

"I won't be answerin that question."

The sheriff is handed the wick. With a pomegranate tongue licking his lips he races through a carom of thoughts, foremost amongst them is "do wicks drip?" and "what the fuck is a wick really made of?"

"Sheriff?"

"What? I can't move. I'm decidin what to do."

Torq leaves and returns with the door wide open, passing through its threshold twice. He overrules past deeds in the throes of his decision then surmounts the gallows to release them. Alive they join their sheriff. In gravelspeech Torq asks for the wick. He throws it at their feet in the tragacanth sealer where it hisses, sizzles and floats, redressed by the semidivine, Blane begging it not to explode. Torq locks the three men in the cell. When the passkey is extended to Josiah Corn the boy says, "sir, I thank ye. Life is all to me."

"I am sorry about your ears."

The pistol of the sheriff when it clicks six times onslaughts like a willowswitched child. It is hawkish and aggressive with the residuary filth of a man given his chances. "Aw hell. Aw shit. Aw no." His arm is through the bars with the bore three inches from the back of Torq's spun skull. He turns in disbelief, the rod of the sheriff now flat to his forehead and again he clicks the weapon. Torq's words are a world of awareness.

"Sheriff, what I've read I've generally stolen from homes I robbed and looted. I once read a vague author when I was eleven, made the Latin from a bought dictionary, cause no person is completely a rogue. He said conquerin generals in Rome kept a slave in their ear to remind 'em that the present was transitory. Means it won't last forever. FLUXUS was the way it was said. I am heavy and enraged with you. Josiah Corn wanted his life."

The jail was then burnt to the embers. Torq stole their horses and left.

45

LIKE A GROUND for a world from unbridgeable source they are watched with determinateness, observed daily as they traipse their pasturage. Dampier must deliver his cash-rended monies to the railroad consortium's bank. This is their time together before their time apart. She appears young and sturdy, Dampier beside Billy with his ailing incompetence, an untouchable blob of a newly conned man who does not deserve this woman. He is infectious inferiority and shouldn't share a family with Billy. In a time come and gone Threadbare recalls that the woman was forced to join him, he causing the death of her family, when Dampier should've turned himself in. This bound his irrelevance to her. What choice did Billy then have?

As he peers through his birding glasses he sees them holding hands.

"What a will-o'-the-wisp he plans. She should take his money and kill him."

On this stroll they're in search of a citadel of rock Latham has recently mentioned. They wonder if they own it outright. To its side there obtrudes an apse in the structure leafened with a shakelike, neolithic pattern scratched to recount known shapes: wild thyme, blue bottles, majoram and squirrel corn are etched with burdock pricking. There are seaside murex and a flaxen-haired child west gazing for originative causes that come from the deepest of blues, as if to master a world revealed. This designata, this veridical perception, has been repainted by Threadbare for years. He lay in the grass fifty feet from the pair to observe their initial reactions on what he considers creation. Threadbare listened from the spike-dwarfed foliage to the truth for the sake of her husband. Billy knows the bountyman's work.

"This ain't ours Dampier. The stake is inside this. We can get it, but it ain't ours."

"We're a mile and a quarter northeast of the house. Latham said he knew the rock, but he ain't mentioned this."

"This is that crazy Yurok. What come from California. He tongues in Algonkian with an Arapaho wife and I seen 'em smeared with this shit. They make it outta wattle and daub. It's colored and grease is added."

"That there is scratched to stay."

"He eats them mescal buttons. This was brought from another world. He wasn't in this'un when he done it."

"I am unfamiliar with him."

As they continue northeast they walk through him, his composition spiritistic, comminutive stardust at best. Like seeing ivy in an ivied wall. With the attributes of Latham on their routinary lips Dampier maneuvers to Torq.

"Torq would contrast Latham I bet."

"Neither'd be runts I tell you. None of my bunch was runty."

"Naw, they'd be fine." Dampier embraced his wife. "Reckon we got enough happy?"

"I ain't in the practice of contentment. Bein soft for when it gets hard is a habit best left to the idle."

The reports of Torq by rumor or paper came to the Soo eventually, Dampier an efficient denier, the brutality of the killer named Torq Mox another cretin claiming his name, disesteeming the Mox's of Reckingfort Soo, the encore its printing in papers. When he heard that a crime or a murder was committed he assisted his wife in keeping him shielded from the horror of a truth actuated. When Torq's sketch and name and repetition of exploits spread from the east to San Jac, Billy began taking in scraps, pieces of news from a clew of authorities on the nature of the crime and the criminal, the how and the why of its happening. She storiographed notes in a chantey-thumbed songbook and compared them to Threadbare's own, wondering uncertainly if the bountyman's way was the path of her very own son. Eighteen years prior on those chthonian saltflats Threadbare had transpired to the ontic, his mediate existence ascending. His reasons for pursuit were unalterable, numinous, of a tensor hidden stretching Billy's own will with a particular emended unlimitedness... *Billy... your skin winnows taught... o'er a shell of silence evasive... when falls your tresses the hair that you gather is the scent in his nostrils alone... you both inside you buffeted by winds and the moldering smell of time... without him you're inconceivable... as with him you are unseemed.* He has an angary right to you being you, or so Threadbare now thinks. You cannot sluice him away. He's a vein inside a vein.

"What has come has left Dampier. It ain't interested any longer, whether Torq or *him* or God. I refuse to make sense of shit. Even quiet is limited by what it can say and it won't say a thing."

"Bad don't sit for appeasin."

"The bad get fucked like the rest of us shits, they're just tryin to get through the day."

"I reckon," he says. "Awright. These are earthly concerns."

"Your tillage is the fit of the plow. Ain't nothin realer than dirt."

*

Three days without sleep and a sunstruck weariedness and Threadbare leaves them alone. He stands like a pluton flanking, but the couple walk right past. He remembers a whore with a handsanded voice whose softclenching mouth gave him pleasure. She pursued her concupiscent undulate careering on a mat of tatami and yew. She said Plato, her favorite philosopher "fucked on a bed of yew" and "that every orgasm by man or by woman was a threshing by death itself. A piece of your clay removed."

He walked six hours north on a whiteskinned plain singly his own without pack. Threadbare the disenfranchised, a dweller where nothingness reigns. Southern rains hadn't fallen where he trod and the anthills were swollen plump. He counted a thousand and ceased, the horse hearing his steps to come from his ribs, the mount yawning with a skeptical tranquility. Threadbare has attempted to replace his old horse with another he bought from an Iowa. The Percheron, instead of retiring, out-thrust his snout, clipped the other draft's throat, drenching it's owner in blood. Threadbare paid for the death. He then settled on a Morgan to carry their gear, the horse waiting in the heat for its master, voluntary in keeping his distance, a half-furlong north and waiting. Not accustomed to being assaulted he makes a by-path wherever they go. He only comes when Threadbare calls him, the Percheron watching them both.

"Don't fuck with that Morgan please. I have the caraway oil for your ears."

He loaded them both to move. When saddled the Percheron hung its back hoof, launching an incensed kick, missing the animal's head.

"Stop! We have to have him! I can't load you as if you were three!"

The Percheron twisted his neck. His blinking eyes blameable of others. With his percipient pragmata of stare and indomitable jealousy and pride, he asked Threadbare to say it again.

The Morgan was returned to the Iowa. Threadbare insisted he retain the money.

46

TORQ RODE WEST in a battle of attrition. An inapt posse of seven he towed before three were disposed with deceit. He sent a horse man-weighted with rocks due north into a pale and untenable wilderness of tephra with its bloodless multivalence, a jaggedness of avid fragments, dispersed like pieces of a segmented body volcanically showered to earth, spewed from a centerworld cosmos, globed about as if earth were his own. Terrenely it was spread to hide Torq Mox but the boy isn't there. An indeceivable lot man shines himself, this master come north from the ape. The four remaining are tasked with his capture.

*

"You Hamblin, Jimenez and Foretok. That's his track right yonder. Follow it north through them fuckin sharp rocks and watch you don't snag a hoof. If you see 'em, shoot his ass dead. Them lawmen was burnt to ash."

Torq listened to Uriel give them their orders, that extrusive waste before them, an inaccessible undivvying copse. North they rode observing, Torq backing himself into a slew of large boulders like-rolled by senile giants with the Rio Grande to his rear. He removed his boots, head sacking his horses and tying their hooves together. Closed tight amongst the boulders with the sun's synoptic stare they slept without bending a knee. Torq scrambled and found what he sought. Watersmell and their sound of warning. He threw a pebble agitating their nubile instructress and she coiled to proclaim his presence. The female was sunning on a carinate rock, her adytum of children behind her, athwarting river stone that has tumbled. They move like waves, slivers of death, ceaselessly awake and writhing. He says, "there you are, you mean motherfuckers. I cannot let you be." Torq plans to attain some goal esoteric, its rarefaction becoming material. He looks at the pictograph above their den, its tattooing in red and yellow. Threadbare has seen it, its copy for Billy chiseled on the citadel rock. It's of a mammoth with fangs touching the ground, a watermark dissolving its legs. Before it knelling in a sacred grove is a group of seven men. Grasping lances they have gathered for worship. They've every intention of hunting their idol, or a thing dissolvent by rumor, what seeks to disgrace their god. These men face east for the rise of the sun untrammeled with ideations, reverencing the ideolatrous beast, the sun warming the back of the mammoth, the head of the instructress then slithering upboulder blotting the pictograph's message. He throws a dissident stone to arouse the den and the rattling brings a shout from Uriel.

"Stay the fuck away from them boulders! Them on the right has snakes!"

The other three remain where they are. Will not shuffle an inch. Won't imbreach the withering sound.

*

Two days later Torq is still there and the three he sent north don't return. Deviltry has dealt with them. The other four make camp, two men at each entrance to the corridor of boulders thus held. Torq watches as they slide and stumble, refusing to remove their boots. They shoot through their loge of ample ammunition and slide from the boulders like scree. Uriel asks the three to please stop firing at the feeling of the killer in their midst. To them he is "there" and "over there" and "up there" and "down there" and "I just seen 'em." They're reduced to twenty rounds per man as the third day comes to a finish.

That night Uriel makes a fatal mistake, bonfiring the gap between the rowed boulders where rests an isoclined stage, a wharf of rock inviting assault, illuminating the means to do it. From dislimited night Torq summons the group hoping sense can be made from his action.

"Uriel! Don't target these boys! That's a helluva vantage you're givin!"

They empty their rods at the voice. Their rounds are reduced by six.

"Steady men! He's fuckin with us! Keep your heads about you!"

Foretok's brother screamed, "you keep yours! Imma watchin you loadin your shooter!" Another said "goddamn right!" The fourth won't speak for he isn't an adorer of the dark and the incorporeal. He thinks Torq is more than one, though in that onement deadly.

"I'm gonna start killin if ya'll don't scatter! I did the sheriff and those two a favor!"

"A fuckin favor?" Uriel doesn't scream this.

"Time ain't on 'em like you and me! Hear it tickin you ornery fucker?"

Uriel suggests they sleep in shifts then falls asleep immediately. Foretok's brother stands perimeter guard, slowly exhausting their kindling. With whiskey his timidity morphs, pacing Foretok's brother forty steps west of where he's supposed to be, boulders on either side, he leaning to smoke while armed. His hammer is back and the pistol is raised and with thoughts of whores and a bacchanal he recalls a past congress with a woman, the bleating of "don't" in his ears. Torq clings to a boulder on his back-left side, creeping north from the river drawing water for his horses and he as silent as that forsook. When he slides from its face to land in soft sand the watchman spins and fires, inveighing with curses and ricocheting cylinders until the others empty their own. The shots dampen the coven of serpents, the seizurous rattles unheard. Shots whine and their surfeit bravery melts as night impounds them surely. Uriel announces "men calm down" but inside their leader is sick. These men are anathema to unpatterned realms, Torq whispering "don't calm down. Calm is the rim of the bucket, before it tumps and spills."

Torq recovers the instructress and five other snakes. Seventy pounds of venom. Foretok's brother remains alone and unaccompanied because he's drunk enough to be brave. The other three circle their fire, reloading their cylinders like whirligigging moths grouping for death by flame. Foretok's brother hears the tote being shaken, the man climbing to the top of a boulder to conceivably capture Torq, his pistol then stripped from behind. Torq Mox is a star of indeliberate fame, the youth brimming with comedic acid.

"Go on, leap on top, they're in a tight space and waitin." Torq grabs his rope belt, leans him forward: "they're not crawlin unless we move 'em, and I ain't goin down there."

"I'd prefer not to pounce on them rattlers! The fuck if I'm gonna jump!"

"Yes, you are you idiot. Someone has to move 'em."

He leaps with a push, manages to slide, catching his boot on an eyetooth projection sufficient to hold his heel. Below him no rattling cacophony. Elsewhere their ventriloquy echoes. Into the closeted fit he eases. Torq looms above his head.

"Hey you. Look up here. I'm now inclined to help you."

Foretok's brother then grubs and scratches, trying to foot an escape, pleading with a God never questioned. Torq doesn't need to speak for the present situation is supplemented by unspeakable suggestion. Foretok's brother says, "you ain't shit! You're dead when I scale this fucker!" Torq replies, "I'll help you then." He reaches down a hand and the man looks up, screaming, "fuck your help!

You'll shoot me!" Torq pauses for the man to gain questionable footing before the tote is dumped on his face, their rain of a venomous bearing, for his enclosure is the width of his shoulders and reversing he tumbles back in. He tries to fend from his feet where he can, Foretok's brother their stopper, the serpents striking and holding and striking and they've ample flesh to pierce.

"I hate a goddamned fuckin rapist."

*

The night is shorn and the sun is welling when the others discover his body. They searched as a group and in that pack find him wound with a cultus of snakes, chin tilted in a frostworked scream, eyes fixed in quietude. His coloration is pale and his face ploughed through by nicked and winding serpents, their quarrelsomeness shimmed to an evenness of rattle, the instructress begging the sun. Foretok's brother remains.

Torq waits for Uriel to lead the men down. Catenas of snakes by tail and snout helicopter into camp by the minute. Not a shot is fired. Impatiently they shift and huddle. He snaps dry chaparral later in the day, dropping it afire on any individual attempting to break from the trio. They cannot dethrone Torq. The belligerent works the boulders, he himself at home like an infant in a kingdom of conic breasts, barking and baying with the pleasure of his throws until Uriel exposes himself. He strolls from his stonemired hiding, boulders to his left and right. Out of confidence, tact or futility, he speaks to challenge young Torq.

"Boy, the rocks is yours! But we ain't gonna leave till you come out or your body gets drug due east!"

"Best discuss that with your posse! They ain't eager to charge!"

"I ain't brought 'em with me to die! Now they hate you so much they can't!"

Uriel empties a dreg filled cup. Manna or physic therein. His pistol is belted, his bravado increasing, nothing left to debate. No siege, no otherwise. He's like an opera performer trapped on stage by an untranslatable verse, his left hand in the air grasping the cup when he announces, "damn you boy!" Uriel takes the steps he is given, subpoenaed by something pulling him along by a string or a tie less durable. The heart of the world beats beneath its thin crust, instilling its thumps through his soles, an undertowing being procreant, a moralic tender of rules. It lies arid, immaterial and vacant. We all return to that.

"Be smart Uriel! Improve your position! They're two other boys to consider!"

His words change Uriel's perspective. He doesn't pretend to respect him.

"I'll have you know motherfucker! You ain't cuspidor spit!" Torq's pistol then snugs against Uriel's temple. Appears like a tidal fin. Uriel smells his sweat. "Don't scarab your body like that Mr. Uriel. Turn your eyes. Look here. I cut a forked hazel branch to look for water. We can build us a barn with a hayrick. Get a deep ol' rug and stretch out."

"I ain't diggin no well for you."

"Then your body'll rot above ground."

Torq's shadow is enormous and moving, environing the boy with dark, his black hair like an entailed carpet attached to neck and shoulders. His shadow is squeezed through the rocks whence he came, succumbing the shadow there holds, waiting for Torq to come after.

"How'd you get through that crack? Them boulders is inches apart?"

Torq bumps Uriel's temple. "I fuckin flowed, then I formed."

"I ain't yankin this iron to give you a reason. Yours'll hafta kill me."

"Then Uriel I'll treat you as company." Torq lowered his pistol to holster. Wound his hands in his greasy black hair, the fingers jailed by filthy black locks. "Uriel, you have the jump, the initiative yours to take."

Torq backed down the schema of boulders, forefooting and imprinting myriad shapes with a toe-heel drag inexplicable. He made white starflowers, a mandrake strata, while Uriel watched his feet. It was an epochal sketch Torq Mox created, his style and the means all a matter of balance and he appreciative of lonlier times, when he sketched as he wanted and wished.

"Don't watch me walk," Torq said. "Keep your mind on your present duty."

Torq split the boulder's alley, a trail on either side, Uriel akin to the wharf of flat rock, the man ignoring the advantage. Do not face this one off. Torq halted to his front at twenty-five feet with a choice of four escapes. Uriel is limberlost. A husbandman of indecision. He thinks his thoughts before they congeal. Flinches and tries to retrieve them. Uriel's never faced a gun.

"Uriel my man, you're jumpy. Better to brandish and fire. My hands are haired securely."

Torq allows the first shot to whiz past his head, slamming the blackschorl rock. A flurry of bats echolocating emerge and return circularly, their motility like chips of superelevate lightning as they aerially wheel in a cluster. The last of their skirling falls dead on the wing without any explanation, as if their lair would not receive him. In the sand the nocturne expired. He alone died where he fell.

"Uriel! You're aimin! Don't aim!"

Again he fires at the intrusive grin, the sand denting well behind Torq, from his trembling hand Torq shoots the cup, the metal spinning and chroming in the air. Torq is five steps closer and waiting, his palms by his side and free of his hair with his pistol reholstered, expecting. There's a powderblue rise of smoke. Torq Mox blows a hole through its middle.

"My hands slid outta my hair. They were left to hang or shoot."

Uriel gazed at the cup to his rear. Hole through its center and the sand is wet as if the cup has sustained a wound, an apostasy to shoot that straight, when you come from your head to your hip. Uriel then turns back. Torq Mox isn't grinning.

"Uncanny? Fuck if I know. I try to aim, I do. Bring 'em out of the rocks my friend."

"Deal with me. They're fine where they are."

"You, sweet sugar, are dealt. I'm willin to call it a draw."

In bas-relief something flies overhead. A nebulae opaque, symbolic? Both study with their eyes for touchstones are few and the test is not in Torq, but in these others who have come for his taking.

"Owl," Torq says. "See it?"

"That weren't no fuckin owl."

"Then Uriel, name that thing."

There is shuffling to his left, someone shinning a boulder, curses quavered, then climbing again. The other two boys reconnoiter obliquely without removing their boots, their heels scratching with hips like engines. Torq cannot see them but knows what they're doing from the habits that bind their threats. Both are inhabile and can't stand conflict and the youngest won't stand for stinking, he carrying a hickory and sassafras poultice, the former still sweating in his pocket, the smell wafting to where Torq waits. The other is consumptive, a disease broadly signing and he's tracked the boulders with blood. Torq notes the crows, their roistered interest, knowing as seeing is attention that the crows will group where they sneak. He doesn't want these boys to die. They have come for the price of their meals.

"Uriel, request that they close a touch quieter. Maybe use a path in the sand. Their cocksureness might get you dead."

The youth with the poultice, his neck stiff from crawling, slides from the boulders behind him. There's a bulge encircled in his front left pocket and though astern of Torq with his weapon unsteady Torq insists he care for the hickory by keeping the packing from heat, including the warmth of his testicles: "they're made for drawin pain, not for killin your stench. We all stink like shit hereabouts. Hey, is your mama Lo-rena?"

The youth behind Torq is vexed. Uriel simply amazed.

"Leave that kid and his mother alone or I'll allow 'em to shoot you in the back."

"He'll do it without your help. Hey kid, don't fire that shooter! Your mama is a reputable whore!"

The kid screams "my mother!" with his keen face clouding, the perceptible becoming its opposite. Torq with the euphony of a click in his ear spinning to take the bullet, but the primer fails as he turns. In mid-collapse another shot rings, the kid examining the pinnule of his meek old pistol while standing in the corridors' center, someone having fired before the boy posts shot and he doesn't realize he is hit. The wound roseates above the pocketed poultice, his hand quickly covering the spot as if to hide what's happened, as if to gain it back. Inditing sorrow through eyes like his mother, he says "you didn't hafta kill me dead. I ain't no more than a saplin."

Torq replies, "my weapon is holstered." Uriel repeats the same.

The consumptive boy concurs from the boulders then quietly asks "who're you?" There's a purgative wheeze, the scrape of a blade and only Uriel and Torq are the living, besides another who has come to kill. The gutshot boy has the poultice in his hand breathing its scent in gulps, saying "mama, Lo-rena, she made this." He looks to his left ascertaining his distance asking, "please, may I come to you? Stay there, it'll be but a second." He totters into cover and is gone. There's a septate counter from the screech of the owl sheeted by the neigh of a horse. Not a mount of the five who were present, Torq and Uriel left to discern.

When the exoteric hoofstrikes baffle the men, the two listening have nothing to say. What horse takes its leave, takes its lone rider, alack what's befallen the dead. Pontificating their positions they each decide dogged will only do.

"Uriel, we've experienced another."

"You brought that other I guess?"

"Even I wouldn't do that."

Torq Mox unwinds from his seat as Uriel calls to the boys, a vast schism and odic on his thin lips separating the youths from death. He promises vengeance, salvation by deeds with decretals of why they have come there to suffer their very own murders. To be devoured by a source unrelentingly present, and why and then if by serving this Uriel, were they sent to a world without him, and how isn't their demise his fault? The three he sent north are dead to the man, Hamblin, Jimenez and Foretok lying awry in septentrion desert. Torq listens to Uriel sobbing. As he cries he does so in prayer. Torq looks at the clouds himself. Why not grieve young man?

"Uriel," Torq says. "Look here."

"What of you?" The man is spent. Upon his knees paralytic and stony. Without qualm and wanting to die.

"Go to sleep Uriel. You stay here. There are things only I can do."

"I beg you, put me with them. Six promised mothers and not but a body and I know them others is dead."

"I may yet find another body. You can take him home."

Torq takes the steps, pistolwhips his head, the man concussing but life is left in him. He then curls Uriel within the pendants of his fists. Beds him safely on the wharf of rock. His distaste for violence increases. Torq doesn't want to be what he is.

"Stay here Uriel. We've company." Torq speaks, adjusts him, his head then pillowed with a jacket and a tuft of debris. He's as comfortable as guilt will permit. The man moans, "boys" is repeated.

Torq is until dawn in search of the two, Foretok's brother where he left him in the rocks, the other boys scrubbed from existence. With attunement Torq doubly, triply runs tracks, climbing moonlit boulders for signs. "Nothin, not a fuckin thing." There's a physicalism, something unforeseen, in the way the boys were taken. Like a corduroy road through a wilderness, the tracks are obvious, so obvious they aren't.

In the twilight the print is seen. Lost souls tend to moniker the hinter.

"I got you motherfucker," Torq says. "You've takin to shoein the bastard."

Torq is six clicks north on foot from the boulders scalestone tracking for breaks. Sees where the dowel broke through. Where the abutting horseshoe and nail are impacting in a pattern to throw the shoe. He finds it in a thicket of senna where the clue was pitched for the finding. The tracks after that can be seen without searching as his ellipse commences curving. The four-pound shoe is its apex. Its width as thick as twin-stacked hands. Torq holds it and huskily whispers.

"The motherfucker has circled for days."

To his east the many-sided terracing rays of the sun are his humming reality. Drylands lifting by intergrown light. A detumescent solitariness is the dark that releases its hold for the prolix of day. View me, my hot orb rising. In my stomach see that relic of dust? Is that a horseman invading my center? There is copious matter and sunbeam about him and Torq is becalmed by knowing, if he truly comprehends what is seen.

"Ahead. He's always ahead."

When Torq returns to the boulders Foretok's brother has vanished and Uriel's slab is empty.

47

BILLY NEEDS TO find water, invites Adivina, the hydromantic the work of this woman. She's planned a line of shade trees she'll water from a well, their tanks warred by drought and cattle. Adivina arrives to consult.

"Billy, oaks require a biblical flood. That or a viaduct."

"Not those kinda oaks Adivina. The smaller, shorter brand."

"Oaks won't take in these parts. Not the kind you got in your head. Pick any other tree but that. These plains used to be stone."

Four hundred miles southeast Dampier leaves his railmen for home. He's told Billy he won't travel alone, whether Epigo is coming northwest or not Dampier will find a party, Germans or Dutch or city born easterners who have heard of Reckingfort Soo. Billy thinks, stares at Adivina, reconsiders her thoughts rather blankly. Dampier, he'll find the accurst. Epigo will come with the man. Like two mites in uniate on that otiose scape they'll traverse the desolate prairie, crossing their gamut of microtomed plain, sensorily picking their trails, the ecclesiastical millinery of the rider that leads stained with whorehouse whiskey and the snotslick tracings of cunt; Dampier following the heretical priest, listening to his ribald stories, their mesmeric flow like a medium droning as he draws and inserts his pistol with every tale of fuck.

"It'll take them two a month at least." Adivina repeats "a

month." She then thinks about Latham and says: "keep 'em close. Near to see. I ain't givin fuckin advice."

"You're a direct waterwitch now ain't cha?"

"Your torments are hereinafter. Longsuffered, not what you reckon. Make your play but study my words, fear birthed the god of the whites, besettin sin left god and man separated and no two humans together know what god they fear. We are each and ever' one secluded you see, back before we come outta trees. You're as lonely in a room with a roof, as stranded beneath the sky."

"Good God! Thank you Adivina! May I slit my throat?"

Adivina replies "but there's love. Love afore' fear came God-ding."

She is an aged Blackfoot rover, caustic with what speaks. Her father was shamanic, a diviner of sorts, walking southeast with his ten year old daughter when the Goliad post was Spanish, the garrison hunting bear with recurved bows and lances with yataghan tips. In those years San Antonio's mission was a place to vend your wares. Though Adivina's father seemed indefinitely beclouded as he lulled by their January fire. He peeled cactus figs, clipping blood-red camellias, devoutly making her bed, on a night petticoated with mist. When she awoke her father was gone. Left was a bundle of eagletail rectrix periscoping from identical stones. A flexible cane from her grandfather's shelter was allotted with catgut lashing. With the three brought together undereearth waters were findable and portably moving, as if Adivina could place the wells, wherever she wanted them to be. The "bough" as she called it would always heel over, having found the first water at Reckingfort Soo and a seep of aboveground oil two miles from the Mox's ranch, where something other than water was felt. Adivina was instructed by an organon vision that the oil was of an interest forthcoming, the crude summoned for Baal were athirst. She was drunk when she ignited this seepage. It burned high and black and tunneled and pierced and unstinted continued to burn. Billy watched the black smoke for a month. Its taffrail of soot with vibrato of flame seemed a place where hell was gored. On the homestead daily you could smell it.

"Do as you will Adivina. I'll be around here with Latham."

"No. Go get the boy. He needs to witness the bough. Needs to quit starin at that goddamned fire, that oil won't burn thisaway."

"He's nervous like his daddy I reckon. Says he's got a fluttery heart."

"Fluttery heart? That's bullshit. He's got his fluttery hand on his pickle and it's an inch or two at best."

"Adivina! That's our son!"

"Son or not, they yank it for change and not a goddamn penny drops out."

Latham's mending a rabbit's hutch while listening to the termagant offend, the fertile soil in the brain between Adivina's ears a prefigured discomfort to him, for the look in her eyes are pictorials becoming before his future is set. Adivina knows what he is. She stares and listens to his verbigeration, ridiculing his lack of speech, saying, "Latham, life ain't supposin. You suppose, it's already there." He wants sense, regular lines, a path that is linearly known.

Adivina hears the boy thinking. Knows he wishes to avoid her. She throws a chunk of soil, the brick clearing the house, scattering a venire of chickens.

"Stop fuckin with that hutch and come here!"

Latham attentively straightens. Billy is there and she gazes at Latham and "go to her, she knows why you're dodgin." Latham tittles with the wire then snips it, asking Billy to "let me be." She takes his burse of nails, handmade cutters, his mother then regressing to quiet. "Son, I'll not ask you again." Latham loops around the hutches as if househidden seconds will centuple her age and kill her. To his annoyance she inrushes a grin, there with her smile and her head cocked sideways contemplatively aggrieving her face, her smell of attar the same as good bourbon making Latham contract like a plant, her proximity caulking him in, standing with her bough like a penis, Adivina is proud of her cock. She twitches the bough and innumerably spits on his shoes and pants and thighs, throwing back her head orgasmically. She's a twisted, profane woman, a joy to have on the place.

"Adivina, how're you? Don't start. Mama made me talk."

"There are too many wrinkles both here and here." She points into each of her eyes. "But since I ain't blind I have to ask what roars in that chest of yours?"

Latham glances at her deerskin boots. She repeats it in Algonkian. He timorously answers by disarming the woman with a brittle silent return; thinking *silence, like under the sea. A hoveto nothin of lil' importance racks about inside my chest. That's how I answer your question. That's what roars within.*"

"Ah, I see, no answer. You ain't got a thing to offer?"

His mother loops the house to assist him. Knows what the woman will do. Billy turns her palm up, sweeps it to Adivina and gives her the answer in Algonkian, asking Latham to do the same. The boy says, "nothin roars. And this is the language I'm choosin."

"Then the roar is with that twin I reckon?"

"Torq is dead," Billy replies.

"Ah yes, of course, long-dead Torq and some-dead Latham to follow."

"Fuck you old woman," he sneers.

Billy grabs at his hair to yank back his head. Adivina asks her to stop. "That's what I wanted to hear. We busted a wen and drained it. I got work to do. Go fuck with your rabbits junior."

She elevates the bough to a crosscurrent wind, the rectrix blowing north singularily. Her panatella slips from her head, she says "Billy, roll me a smoke. Latham, put it to my lips. Don't touch my hands or face." Billy takes the panatella and throws it on their porch and can see that the woman is disgusted. "Nevermind, Latham has a bad disposition and needs to stand back from my bough. We got half a million years on these motherfuckin plains and a dickhard…"

"Adivina please! Latham ain't nearly grown!"

"Alright, roll it then."

The woman takes the cigarette, thricely draws, lawabidingly blowing on the rectrix, notching the smoke where the spar nicely gathers and "time to beg the spirits. You whites fucked it up and what gods'll want smoke will need drink and food and coaxin. What inhabits the depths around here also covers the water with darkness, flouncin and dancin to block it. This confuses my bough and upsets me. A younger Adivina would right 'em, but not with a century on me."

"Horseshit! You ain't a hundred!"

"Horseshit indeed shortdick. What exactly do you know of my years?"

Billy is afraid Adivina might slap him. She crumps and flops a question: "Adivina, where did you go when everyone abandoned the Soo? The last time, not the others before that?"

"I ain't gonna touch your boy. What do you mean, everyone?"

"Most, I reckon, have left."

"I went to talk to daddy." She points at the oilslick smoke. Her apartness resonates as the bough does its reading and when she lifts she's a sozzled old woman, her demeanor stressing Latham, externalizing his unasked questions. Billy asks "your dead father?"

"Uh-huh." She tips the bough, lights the grass and stomps it, watching Latham watch her back. "Makin your study there shortdick?"

When the cigarette ashes she says "they're sated, but hungry and wantin to lead." She tapped the bough six times in front of their house then walked through the open door, asking, "why've you got steps?" Out the back she leans on a hutch, Billy following with Latham behind her.

"Adivina, what's wrong, where is it?"

"There's water in the center of your house. I told you that before."

"You did," Billy replies. Latham shook his head. "I recall you did," she says.

"There is water where you want but deep. They's tinstone and ore right beneath your house. Piss and tinny water taste similar. Though a tree gives a fuck about such. Let's shoot for a well above that, cause there's another source I think. Water the trees with that. It's out away from the house."

"You're completely nuts," says Latham.

Adivina laughs at the counter. She dismisses the two as the day begins heating, removing her worsted cover, its dark bock an adherend to sun. She finds shade in the alcove of plank and rock where Dampier has partitioned more house, where the original sod lay cool. To her back she hears Latham discussing his plans to move in the cool downstate, swineherding with a friend or two, to be agile where life is slow, to succeed at anything else, to readmix some set thing as if it called for his hand alone. His approach this thing awaits. Sulking for he does not hurry. There it sits like a wooden shoe. Adivina knows the talk of youth.

"He thinks yonder could never be here. Comfortin for him I suppose. A fuckin pig is a pig on flat fuckin plains as much as a pig amongst trees."

Water fonts and their sources are obscured by fatigue, Adivina nodding to sleep, a steady rain accumulating to wet her legs, but Billy and Latham don't wake her. Animal-like and unaltered she sleeps against the suncracked sod of the dwelling, Billy mentioning to Latham that Adivina's method included a nap when finished. He says "I seen her once out there." Latham found her plainstanding, irradiated by heat, mid-summer on the prairie and there she was chanting dictums with repeated vows, without a square of clothing for cover. Drooping breasts. Gray pubic mound. He walked his horse right past, counted five hundred steps and turned to see her praying, suppliantly clothed on the ground. He rode back to his herd and a camp had been set and there was fire where fire was required. The space about the flames was never his camp, though a camp he had in mind. The first summer snow in the brevity of his life came that evening with she. She bedded late, was gone before Latham, and he did not see her leave. The shape of womankind was left in the snow with a sandalwood scent in the air. A line of steps circled in black, incurvate to him without exit, as if to examine his sleep. Perhaps to crawl inside him. Perhaps to fill some space.

*

Adivina stirred after midnight. Shat in the Mox's yard. Dry dead leaves from her guts. Iron pyrite needing its flint. She looked at her waste and laughed.

"Imma damndable shriveled mess."

Counting frames of starwork she made her own trail. The moon shone bright, palatial to touch, séancing cloudy from the west. She asked it to clear and it did. "I forgot to mark their water. I'll wait on the plain and return." Another thing untethered was near her. Adivina felt it prolapse, thrilled the woman approached.

"Bright moon, bright day tomorrow. The moonshine knows what comes."

She found it's scent a mile from their home. With the wetness the smells behaved. Fainter yes, but separated, like eggs in a paper carton. You got glands and fur and droppings, what was fed, its deeper tracks. Even the weight of the feeding, if the eye had tracked for years. When something was injured the effect was constant, if not its stealth deceived it, the wet map of the plain washing obsessions into hints of traceable scent. Adivina knew how to read them. They leapt to her nose like an allergy. She thinks of the man she is tracking: *and here is where you stood and your eyes are still good for you saw us talking water in their yard. You know Billy wants shading trees. Wants the branches of her past northwest. You could've had the boy but you didn't. Something drew you to the setting of the sun.*

The week old bones he left to be found for his tracks come and go. From where Adivina stands above the slain doe she can see his tactic clearly, the morning mist concealing his movements, a slight rise to cover his work, his building of a fire and drying of venison in smoke as thick as fog. He knew the winds by watching the weather. By asking his gods for unlimited favor requests became demands, Adivina then hearing a voice in the wind and Latham is checking his hutches. Night boy. Lone guard. Night fears. She realizes how the doe was taken. Adivina talks to the bones: "you took his arrow in the dark because he wouldn't let you smell him. Two had been fired when you did. A shaft for your heart, another for lungs, his tips the same as my bough, his requirement a breakable head, the bow that he carries of plated worn bone and his strength allows him this arrogance. He collected the shafts and dressed you. Your meat was full of shards."

Adivina flips the skeleton. The shortbow's trauma is there. A third arrow breaking a hip. There was no entry wound. Brownskinned scat from several coyotes lay arrayed on the ground still soft. "You're a cruel uncaring bastard. You left nothing for them to eat. These bones are barely gnawed."

From the doe his trail is blatant, a path of repetition, coincidental with Billy and Latham, looping their home longstriding like a footman felled from his fleeing carriage, trying to chase it down. He's been to the back door and then to the front, watching her sleep through the window. Adivina follows his steps, waiting for Latham to abandon his hutches before she stands by the window herself, an acolyte organized for her service.

"Big, so big with your tracks. You knew I would know it was you."

"Adivina, what're you doin? Why're you standin in my window?"

Billy stands in the dark with a shawl about her shoulders holding a pieplant root. Maenadic soul herself. Liable to kill provocated. She and Adivina are as isthmus to strait but never to isthmus again. Cross them and wait for the flood.

"How long've you been there Billy?"
"I walked to the barrel for water." She displays the potted root.
"Yonder comes the sun," she says. "It's slowin in its comin you know. Before it stops we'll all be done. I marked your water with the bough just now. Bring it to the Soo before Christmas. If you miss me you can keep it."
"I can pay you Adivina. Take it."
"No, not yet, let the bough draw the water. When the boys begin to dig, it'll be a shallower well."
"Boy. Only Latham. Adivina."
"I meant Dampier," she replied.
"Sorry. Alright. Stay with us?"
She goes without responding to Billy's affectionateness, statuetting in the yard for an instant, wanting, not needing to tell. She hears the words she would say immemorably clinking and sees Billy nodding her head, offering something from a knitted remembrance, words avulsing the point and purpose, something akin to her being careful as if Adivina hadn't mentioned he was there. The hydromantic leaves it alone.
"Adivina!"
The dowser turns. There's a moment and the Blackfoot waits. Neither will act as intender. Neither will say, "he is here." This is what Billy offers: "Adivina! Take some water! You'll be the entire day gettin back!"
Adivina's rebuttal is a hundred foot stare. She then lurches and finds her pace. She's a profile on the path to Reckingfort Soo until the sun makes its morning and the impost of dark pauses for projecting its night. Dark is hidden, as night should be.
"I can smell you, you sonofabitch."
She throws her nose in the air like a primate. Wards a thing off with her hand. Billy watches. Allows her to go. What will keep her from it? Adivina, in going, has left.

48

HIS PROMONTORY FOR fire is a barrow of the dead, where the seed of samara brought maples and elms and a set of ash trees men have cut. It is west of the path to Reckingfort Soo and those who know where it lies are the driftage seeking its seclusion. Bindlestiffed walkers mostly, he though a horseman unique. Here others, ancients, have come to be buried and the man by the fire knows their history.

Adivina cuts for the sign of the horse he is riding. The firelight delivers her slowly. There he sits on a stump of ash. To the best of his memory it's been fifty years since he permitted himself to be found, not realizing the person was present. In the saw of the blaze he stands for the woman, a spark catching and singeing his hair. He allows it to burn for a count, pinching it obsolete. Adivina is tersely blunt.

"You're too close to the Soo."

"Ten miles. Three from the road. You know how far it is."

"I see you're stripped of baubles and scalps. You do not look like yourself."

"You appear as Adivina. Speak your own tongue if you'd like."

He speaks it better than she. Cataloging familiars and kin. Threadbare's Algonkian as equally Blackfoot as any of the sixteen tribes discoursing to ferry the language. She listened with prowess to her own genealogy and he does not miss a link, nor mispronounce a word. As he finished his recitation, the Percheron incoursed from her back, his flanks hair roughed with symbols of sleep from the ungauged rolling prairie. His pupils themselves show orange blackpalms intermixed with Threadbare's face. In the hematite flames he's announced, the light in his eyes demising, the horse rearing to hoof but the lifting of a hand stayed the beasts' momentum. Adivina shunned his efforts.

"He understands commands, comprehends death, the commands and deaths you deliver."

"That horse does what it wants."

"Did you mean to be careless with that Mongol bow? You could've killed that doe with your hands."

"That bow is too loud for hunting. No arch for the longer shots. It crushes the heads I make. I'm waiting for the boy to return."

"He's there with her. You know that." Adivina takes her own stump. Does not move her age. Thinking clearly she returns to her place. Threadbare sits back down.

"I know Billy and Latham are there. The other one comes from the south. He's changing, wants to be his daddy."

"He must've not taken to ruination. Suffice your fuckin example."

"I could never…"

"Indeed you could. You're a fearful, deadly man. What'll halt you sits before me."

"Things change. Thought is fluid. Sameness is never constant."

"Still stealing and reading your books?"

"I read what I buy. Scratch my notes. What other worlds lay before me? I study the one I know."

"And the present cuts you in twain?"

"I've rehearsed enough not to answer that. Even Christ had his violent reactions."

"Threadbare, Christ was peace."

He smiles, knows she has heard it, her path a learned traipse: "pulchrum est paucorum hominum."

Adivina laughs, translates, counting forth its rhythm by rote: "beauty is for the few? The Catholic mission still wants you cleansed? How can they stand to be near you?"

"Gold, protection and drink, for books, a pallet and meals. They know what I do and forgive me. The sisters have a lending library. Aptly, a quiet abode."

He makes his response without any pretension, she across the fire with her usual contentment, as intertwined with these plains as he. He'd seen Adivina a thousand miles north, multiple times in fact, searching afoot for witch hazel or rebus enhavened in a hearsaid cave, some pre-man scrawl there storied, a cislunar reading having sent her. She was not to be touched and this was obeyed, though no warlord made her unhurtable. Adivina is a product of magic, of profuse and ambiguous journeying, to the extent that the fiercest of Apache and Comanche were restored upon seeing her present, considering her death a definitive sign of extremer natural changes. Threadbare was informed that with the last of her breaths the oceans would send their waters to cleanse where Adivina died. Her name was an ambulant mystery made more than it was by her years. Threadbare shared this belief in slices, its realization staring right at him.

"The Kiowa, Apache and Comanche consider you somewhat immortal."

"I'm the mother of the empty Threadbare. The Kiowa have seen me with cycad ferns and a sealant, the glue of bitumen, what held the bulrush ark of Moses together in a solid floating piece. When they ask I tell 'em the truth, what I'm searching for. In the Chisos, does scoured rush grow? The Comanche and Apache know this. I respectfully ask them questions. Curiosity ain't generally rejected."

She made as if to go but the Percheron blocked her with an

unexampled check of her frame. Threadbare ignored these proceedings, checking the skies asininely, his rebuttal casually silly.

"He decides for himself, really. You and that horse are similar."

"Your horse doesn't like change. No person should find another, if the one being searched refuses. He expects you to do the finding."

When he grunts the Percheron steps aside and Adivina is led by the dark, the barrow with its stumps to her square shouldered back while the man at his fire sits the same. The Percheron returns to his bed. Enough lighted so Threadbare can see. He isn't given the order he wants. The horse whinnies, clawhoofing from assimilable black, dabbing down grass and guttering light, one spin, then another and he settles.

*

The west-east rivers are cresting due north and will submerge her seasonal herbs. Seven days later she walks from the Soo to witness the reckoned destruction. She takes no bundle, isn't burdened with possibles and has left her bough with Billy, Latham waiting for his mother to tell him to dig and wondering where the grass has gone. Where she placed the bough it is dead. A centrum of compromised space. Billy tells Latham to leave it alone, "that stick can do as it pleases."

Adivina's discovered sixty miles north by a Blackfoot male of eighty. Knows her face and name and mission. He was headed southeast when he found her, eight yeanling buzzards carping, waiting for the eldest to finish. They retreat and organize with a sortie of passes, hopping and rantingly bitching. He turns her over for an estimation, the woman broken, trampled, from face to foot, but her scalp and eyes are intact. What struggle she offered was minimal. Her permissiveness makes him go numb. In the pocket of her dark bock worsted cover he finds the untransplanted, a Jerusalem artichoke. There are strange tiny seeds the Blackfoot doesn't notice and he refuses to take them from her, Adivina being who she was. In that leathern desolation she hadn't chosen a path and what has come hasn't left its track. The Blackfoot chaffers with the god of his people to requisition a solution for burial. This is Adivina. While the geomancer waters his horse from his hat he ranges a mile from her death. The old man is absent at the drip of the spring for an hour and a half with this chore. When he returns, Adivina is gone. He shrugs and thinks that such are his years, but there is no press of grass, no buzzards about being fed. His anguish settles to chest. The Coldwater Creek then floods.

Six months pass and our nomadic elder is camped on the Arkansas River. He's with a Creek and a slave, this Creek's brother, and they've hacked his owner to death. Montgomery sends no posse. Such men would die pursuing. Best leave these two to fate. The Creek speaks Muskhogean, the half-black slave translating their exchange as he's done for thirty years.

"My brother knows this woman Adivina. She was amongst the Creek for a season."

"I could not find her body. The story I'm telling is true. My heart is heavily pieced."

They go about their drinking from a passed calabash, the gourd nigh drained as they speak. It's no fault of the Blackfoot who could not find her, the guilt in his chest like blasphemy held though in his dreams Adivina forgives him. The Creek voices worry with what he delivers, candidly offered through his brother. Slowgoing to start, some of this, some of that, for they say what we say when common solutions bode some other matter. When what we think is obviously false. When the sense of the thing is indestructible.

"My brother says without her wells the earth will drain itself and the water pull us under. He says the maker of the sun has hidden her soul and her body wasn't yours to find, it returning from whence it came, another soon to follow suit. He is sorry if this isn't clear. This idea lacks from its legs. He thanks you for listening to us, this swopping of tongues being difficult."

They go about their drinking and do not speak and the finder of Adivina sheds tears, the Creek tapping his brother on the shoulder, saying "tell him this war isn't ours. It is fought without our intervention. Carried forth since the stars nailed through the black, since black was opened by light. Since came the boiling of suns, and the we that is us came existing, for we're a shred of all that is light." He then smiled at the elder, he an elder himself, and the Blackfoot man was soothed.

49

TORQ'S MOUNT IS unaccustomed to the punishment given. Three days north of the boulders his back left cannon creases. Its coronet is endways twisted and sliced, the hoof festered and cracked like a dam, the animal carrying him so. Torq's mistaken his wince as terrain. He lands the blame entirely on himself.

It palls on Torq that the journey before him is a thing disinclined to his favor. His horse cumbers its head to his chest, as if the life that it lived was a time short remembered that could not come to this; but it does when he twists its neck, Torq clutching a jaw and turning its head to see what his negligence wrought. Ruination and shame he reaps. He kisses the forelock, scratches his chin and triggers the shell through his forehead with a wrenching sober compunction. Torq rests the horse on its side. Not a vein in his body or that of the animal betraying the effort it takes. The Colt has delivered with depth. There's a perfect round hole through which the shell entered and not a swatch of hair lay varied.

"I'm goin to hell for this."

Beneath the carbolic broil of the noonday sun he considers the trip before him. An arras of storm northwest of his trek threatens to cool the desert. Piddock rocks, cairned by the Kiowa, he stacks about the corpse of the horse. He seeks mortification, self abuse, but this penance might charge his life. For the rain he entrusts to find him, is in a storm of wind and sand, the water it affords wet with grit, like a husk is sweeping the land. Torq admires the track on the trail. Same size, same width as his. He imprints his own foot upon the unblown wedge of the heel of the boot of the walker. Steps with the man he will follow. He walks a mile then two before Torq looks south at the trumpery of his catafalque built, horse and rock as a nodal in rotogravure before a copy of a branch of a path mistook leading to unslaked regions. But he cannot reverse his course. He has no string of horses; the beasts freed in the boulders and if Torq turns back what waits to be conquered enmingles, like a brawl of the worst imagined, if not that ahead.

*

The northbanked cabin on the South Llano sits on a silt pitted river. Torq kneels and slurps at the mud. Rising, his face wears a slime caped mask adhering cool and rooty. Torq draws in the clay with a finger, outwaiting the weary sun. In the cakehunched mire he makes syllabary into missives hideously runic to read. The man watching from the opposite bank can't decide if they share a language.

"Is that a grainsman's spear? You ain't gotta drink that, pools are thataway." East is pointed and east is observed. "Did you come a far piece to get here?"

"That I have done," Torq answered. He wipes his face with his sleeve while pulling the Colt. "That's a grainsman's spear and this is a pistol and kindly pitch your weapons."

The man shakes his head, relinquishing laughter and "you ain't gotta threaten me, cause you ain't in a state to command. Who're you and why ain't you mounted?"

"I rode my horse to the deck comin north from the border. Fucked its hoof and didn't notice."

"You was in them rocks with that posse. Torq Mox is here with me."

A parallelogram of shadow works the South Llano. They recover from hostilities rendered. Their hands are to their fronts and like amethystine mirrors both men are brown with mud, the owner of the cabin scoundrelly filthy, as muck is his usual wear. When he smiles his cheeks tense with their wrinkles, the filth cracking a face to existence. White teeth ingratiate Torq. Not a tooth in his head has been lost.

"I mud my skin cause the goddamn skeets will drive a fella insane."

Torq's reply is blunt, discursive: "Reckon so," he answers. "Especially with rain. This spear won't do any good."

"They're rewardin on you and you know that. Suppose I could collect. They'd send a goddamned Ranger they would. I'm peculiar about law and arrests."

"Who'd send those bastards here?"

"Fuckers in the settlements would."

"You got food?"

"Come to the cabin."

"I smelled your bakin bread. Why're you this far west?"

"Nobody can see to spite me. What other reason is required?"

He refused to give his name and his manner was pawky, too rural as if modesty required it, his filth streaked face a sympathetic addition, addended to the tracks he had made, his heelprints fostered before Torq lost his horse, his stern of a scow in the ulster of weeds beside a river not running, not trickling. Where did this man float from? Where to go, why come here? Torq is suspicious as the men wash their faces and then he sees his own face at fifty. He draws a kneedrag nearer, both kneeling at the trough, like dissentients from a cult of outcasts, twins yarded for slaughter by pairing. They are father and son without, Torq marveling with a stare and the look is returned, both men simply revelated.

"This is as odd as has happened to me. You're me when my features were delicate."

Torq replies "my mother is Billy. Dampier was my dad till now."

"Son, I don't know neither. Let's shirt ourselves, have a seat inside, what I got to eat we can halve." He pauses and says, "please ask it."

"Not a lot of floatin this time of year. Why're you hidin that boat?"

"There was water when I first come down it. It's hid cause Comanche'll burn it."

"That's a goddamn lie and you know it. That scow weighs half a ton."

"And the result for the truth is what? Same as a fuckin lie. Go inside, please sit down."

Torq walks into the cabin with its basic desideratum and the build is the same as his families. Their original hovel erected. There's a handbuilt table sitting in the center with a heated cataplasm rimming smoke. Freshbaked bread beside that. No flies. No bugs. No filth. His older self then places a Colt like Torq's on the crest of a six-tier shelf. The texts are conventicled by subject and year, back and forth to the edge in the shelving. Torq takes a chair and sits. He leans to sniff the boil of poultice, casually inquiring its purpose.

"Shot myself through the neck. Suicide attempt. When I first come down the Llano. The scow would float, then I'd pull it. Ain't nearly as heavy as you think. I lost a child to the fever and that child wouldn't go, so I did what requires the poultice. Been sore for fifteen years. Ain't hopin for fifteen more. The shell's hung and the metal is stayin. The wife didn't want me around."

"Where'd you do that?"

"Right where you're sittin. Put the bore to the pulse and fired. The throb moved outta the way. I seen you lookin at the book on Charon."

Torq found the thin volume on the second shelf down. "Charon was a boatman like you. Roman slaves wore his mask to drag dead gladiators from the ring of the coliseum."

"You've cornered a thought or two. Might yet pay dividends."

"Maybe I'll float through the desert."

"Perhaps Yahveh will deliver unto you, another of Moses' precepts, number…"

"…614," Torq adds. "You're that stagecoach robber or the man that's behind it. You expect me to believe the other? Floatin west on a river of dust?"

"Both're true. The first and last."

"You write letters and tell 'em where to go to be robbed. Which leaves nowhere to go. New Orleans had a story in the paper. They'll come in droves and then you're fucked. You're gonna get tricked and shot."

The man takes the seat opposing. Offers Torq a rip of bread. He chews while the coffee is poured. It's cold. He apologizes. "My dutch oven is hid up river." His day is an aching illusion where he talks to the child that has passed. Her clothes are stacked in a corner and pressed, arranged by color and season. He misremembers what wasn't so. Anything to quell not dying. You get accustomed to pain and invite it, it's like licorice stuffed with tar.

"I don't see the stages myself. It ain't done how they reported. People pay tribute to avoid the Apache. The money I split with Aodh. That ain't his name, that's what I call 'em, while we got us a decent arrangement. What they pay, it ain't unreasonable. Besides, a bullet, an arrow or hatchet, costs more than a few percent. It ain't their land and they're gonna get raided. This way, nobody dies. As for me, I keep a coin or two, to lock me away from the world. Can't see any children…" and Torq says "enough, I understand what you're sayin." He takes his pistol and spear and in the front right portal the weapons are placed without threat, other loads hidden in boot, sharp obsidian knives aligned on his leg, a capeskin inseam not allowing them movement unless Torq gently pushes them down. He asks his older self if there is firewood stacked and the man admits his lie: "my oven is some fire heated kiln. It ain't nothin fancy. But there's a cottonwood cut rotting in sections a quarter-mile west in a draw." Torq Mox has it back in an hour. The bread is sliced on the table with butter fresh-churned, fried white meat and gravy. His older self has divested the poultice, but the ring on his throat shows its use, Torq watching himself in years to come standing in the door of the cabin; a brainstemmed shell, a caudal damnation, wagging whenever he walks, underhumming at the base of his thoughts, telling him with its pain that the innocent world is as pleasing as the next dead child… while he himself builds himself a fire, he in the door seeing you in those years when a fire and a meal did matter, you helping young you by doing his splitting and telling young you "you can eat," he looking at you which is he then himself, saying "sir, with luck and my finger on the shell I can prob'ly get that loose, because by cuttin on my very own body, I've acquired the sawbones' trade." He replies, "it's best that I keep it." Like a flatiron or fieldstone under his skin the reminiscing bullet will stay, the child lost and recollected again, with every poultice and twinge of pain.

"Misery can't be killed. Then God can't use it to defeat us. Wanna eat before it gets dark?"

"Yes I do, but I want hot coffee."

Your younger you then boils your pot, the sun licking at the wounds of the waste before you, its setting actinic and ermined by mountains perceptible a hundred miles west, as if they claim the sun that is foregathered there a nova made weak by its setting. Perhaps the rim of your world has consumed it. Probable dark now reigns?

"Shall we sit down at the table?"

"We shall. Let me get the coffee." Torq reaches for the pot, like boiling means cold, placing his hands in the midst of the flames to cradle the pot with his flesh. His other nods in affirmation, for there are pains the rare can't feel.

"I got it on the table. Bring your coffee on in. Thank you for the help with the wood."

"You're welcome. I hate cold coffee."

"What else is there to hate?"

"Sumbitches that ride down horses. Cause I'm the sumbitch that did it."

"Onct is enough and it's done. I should hate I shot my neck."

"Makes it tough to gnaw wild pussy."

"Loads of that shit out here."

They laugh, then they stop, then they laugh. Torq says what they said and they can't quit cackling so they run from the laughing therein. They return to the table and again they laugh, Torq saying "we must not talk." His older self then replies "gnawin wild pussy" and the laughing commences anew. Their transitory shift is aided without by the cymbal-like beating of hooves. Torq's older self explains.

"There's intersects eighty miles east. The northern trail is taken by others."

"Taken cause you knew I was comin?"

"Nary a man knows you're here. If suspicious, I understand. You are at my table."

"There's no other table to be at."

Their hands are on the sides of their pot-tin plates. Torq can see where he's shaped the dinery, malletting the disks, impulsing their edges, Torq asking, "why have two?" Life springs individually from the thought in his eyes as his older self responds: "I got two plates cause I set her a place, but she ain't comin in to supper, cause the dirt's too weighty atop her. Now allow me to fuckin listen. I'll tell you what them travelers is doin."

Hooves then strike the novaculite bank with a sedimental crunching noise. When they low their origin is revealed, English Herefords leading their rustlers, dry throated and smelling the water. Fifty head slurp in the dark from the quay of the bank due east as mentioned. With their series of lows there are men in retort. These are rustlers with settlers behind them.

"They bring Herefords through Matamoros. Drive 'em north into San Anton'. Ever' one bawlin is stolt. They're good as beef cattle but there ain't no forage, not where they're drivin there ain't. Some derelict swiped 'em fifty or sixty and got lost followin draws. He never thought to look at the land. To consider what it becomes."

"There ain't a goddamned Hereford west of East London. What the fuck're you sayin to me?" Torq slams his hand on the table. He's earned a lecture and advice forthcoming.

"Son, let me tell you somethin, then you're welcome to leave as you will. The last of my memory ain't gonna be you and your temper takin my life."

"You don't want that life to begin with."

A patient hand then lifts to stop him: "you're near a place to get dead. You're wonderin if we look any closer, what'll be there to await you. You can hold your own but there are packs of you for ever' dusk souled creature of evil. Fierce men that require mayhem and sadness in a world resolved without pity. You think horror don't claim its own maker? Don't worship what's hewn from the black? These men are accustomed to killin, cause their world can't remain as it should. They don't do it to prove a point. Nay build a reputation. They consider themselves deliverers, like prophets cast from kind. They want us to forget they're here. That way they cease to exist. That, Torq Mox, is evil. That's what walks amongst us."

"Some more of your biblical shit."

His older self produces a ripe red tomato. Whole in his hand as he holds it. Right palm flat on the table. His left beneath the succulent fruit. Torq sees no blade, hears no cut, the red dominoing anon in slices before sheeting with a thunk on his plate. Eight pieces in ordered asunder.

"What we figure don't hold shape. You've heard such talk

before? Lotta years wasted if you haven't. There's too much life for death."

"Like you? You've all but quit."

"I never looked for an out. I left one."

"You don't make an inklin of sense."

"What does? What're you expectin? A kingdom and throne to await you?"

"I don't reckon it waits for me."

"But it don't really matter when them eyes get shut. Do what you can while here."

"All I can do I've done."

"You ain't even been dropped to your knees."

Torq pushes away from the table, its contents jerk to the floor. He steps right and up and his weapons are there and he dresses himself for death. Going, not knowing where. Froward to the pang of longing he has felt resorts Torq Mox to violence. He sees his older self in the light of a candle salting a slice of tomato. He does not look at Torq. He's a thing moth raddled in that artificial glow, salt precipitating from his shaker, the slice a bloody red pulp.

"Does it look like a heart with the candle?"

"Enough of your crazy shit."

"If we could but hold our hearts," he says. "Could but see their beating."

Torq evicted himself, barged through his fire, while his older self sat still. With the grainsman's spear aloft in his left he walked east in the bed of the Llano. Ten minutes later an arboreal spread blocked the moon and stars, Torq sinking to his waist in an inland sea as his sheetanchored feet held firm. How blind can one man be? Here beneath the trees stood a series of pools, the largest broad enough for swimming. This bend of the river is puckerbrush lined with oaks, mesquites and dogwoods, in epiphenomenal rows, not voluntaristic but placed here as such eidetic to one man's woe. The child's grave you can see in a cannula of shearlight where the scow has delivered her body. Flooded times of some years past. *Hold little girl for your mother hasn't come and I flee to place you here. I am just down the slue in my misery. Though alone, await my return.*

To his right in the congested growth of the bank a drought exposed root will hide him. If it comes he is there concealed. What it is he does not know. Torq Mox, the boy, is frightened. Hereford's prints allow the bank ploughed under where the cattle have watered and rested. Torq crawls through the mud beneath the root, though the divot in the sand isn't beast. The sleeper here is the man he has left at his table, from under root her grave at a level, for he can sense himself long buried, she entombed in the bank across the Llano. This place he's prepared for her rest.

*

Rain in the night with unmerciful gusts and Torq, ensnared, awakens. He was faintly disturbed by stutters of flash and the deluge of water that pinned him, the hand yanking him westward until he could float, dragging himself up the bank. Torq squeegees his eyes, searches his arms, the spear by his side in the soil, tip down and trembling aslight, the remainder of his arms in holster and pocket but his savior isn't in view. The river is a fathom deep. As it steepens it licks at her grave. What still water varve that held the embankment begins its crumbling before him, the rain malingering, pushing across it, the South Llano seeming to slow. Torq's pleased her grave will be spared.

"Sweetheart, if your daddy would've cheated you closer you would've been washed away."

His eyes graze her grave from across the water with its headstone shape there dimmed, underhanded by the limbs of the trees. He understands that the Llano has taken her body to the Devils and the Rio Grande, there dispersing the child in the Mexican gulf for whatever recurred thereafter, perhaps a thing beyond our scope, with our wishes of discorporate breadth.

"Child, you aren't even there."

Light of day returns him to the cabin. The river's run is to his knees, minusing force and by night the flow would be minimal. He has no reason to hide his tracks and that's precisely why he wades. "Sir! It's me! Torq Mox!" No answer, the other isn't there. Torq unholsters his weapon, clicks the probative charges, the sound like a knife being whetted. "No, that will not do." With the tail of his shirt he removes the grit, dismantles and mantles again. He reviews the shells without stunning their caps, the barrel implemented as an eyepiece. When he swivels the three are there. Torq watches from a mile of plain. Two wait in the roadstead heading ten wagons and the expanse consumes their train. The man in the cabin rides cautiously to them for they will not approach his home, who or what having chosen these steppes a man most surely unnerved. A being you permit to converge.

When the three meet they gesticulate as if they've met before. People leap from the wagons to join the group, the one in all black waving them back, his partner a shifting emotionalist. Torq cannot see their faces. He knows his older self knows the man in black, though perhaps not so this other. And he shouldn't for that man is Dampier, the black clad Epigo leading.

Torq finds the horse tied next to the cabin whickering and equinely aware his brand new owner is before him. A Palomino with a combed blonde mane. It wears a cavalry saddle with olive-yard reins and the brand of the Texas militia, scarred waxy on a back right hip; its breastbone ratite to the left of the shoulder, an injury from ramming in battle. Torq fingers the mend, tracing the bone, simultaneity to spear or pike, the scar a blow from an axe-man perhaps.

"You've been in the thick my friend. You're too beautiful to fight."

He gets a lick to his face. His head submissively lowers. Torq kisses his poll and rubs him. The note is triangular, saddlebow fastened, written in sharpened coal: **back to what is you.** It is scratched on a page from Genesis.

Torq leaves his own note in the book on Charon. Flattening the work in his chair. His older self has left their silage tied in a cloth and sitting. Torq takes the food, unhitches the horse, having lined the table with obsidian knives and gifting the grainsman's spear. His response reads as follows. Same page, right below his:

A lot of good this trade will do you. Thank you for the time as given. TM

Torq smiles and leads himself out. He mounts the Palomino and rides the South Llano to what will be Junction, Texas. Torq makes a northward feint. To present day Menard, Eden, Pearl Valley, Doole, Millersville, Glen Cove, where for a day he scans the prairie. When no one closes he makes Buffalo Gap through Cross Cut, Lawn and Tuscola. Here the Clear Fork Brazos with a frothing indifference debouches onto the prairie and for a week he cuts for sign. No thing pursues young Torq. Northwest the two ride steady. Scanty even life. When finally seen by another the dawn is a thermalized gray. It is easier to quarry stone with hope than to know their progress watched.

50

BILLY COLLECTS HER bough and money. Latham's left with the work of digging. Thundersqualls make Billy impatient, an hour before dawn when the first falling drop prinks the cistern out back. Soon the water is an off roof curtain inundating the unguttered rear. It lathers the dust into a chocolatized cream as a hen joins Billy at her table, the air electrified by a vittate bolt with a groundflaming bundle of blue. Its faradic crawl ignites a grassfire but the homicidal rain destroys it and there is no fire as set, the acetone smell like the breath of the waking as it wafts through the window to Billy.

"Mama, that hit close. Still wanna go in this?"

Latham speaks from his hollowed extension. Her son is peculiar, requiring the open, building a depot of sorts, an unsightly appendage connected to their house, for privacy where privacy abounds. This breezeway he's filled with a dosshouse mattress and he always sleeps in his clothes. When Billy asks Latham to bathe, Latham responds "for whom?" He prefers his time unwasted.

"Latham, son, are you communicatin from the seclusion of your shanty shed, which as of yet, has only a roof?"

"I feel independent in here. My mattress is wet clean through."

"You need walls and a door before winter. We'll finish it when daddy gets back."

"A cow's chewin the shucks in the mattress. Storm musta scared it inside."

"If a goat were in your bed you could common-law marry. At least in Alabama I think."

Latham gets embarrassed when his mother is raunchy. He strains to evict the milker. There's a rattle like dice in an earthenware cup followed by a vetchling aroma; burning grass, chuted bolts, the smell of struck lightning, before the storm moves on as it must.

"You leavin me somethin to eat?"

"Wrapped in the cloth on the table. I want you diggin on the well after daylight."

She appears in the hole to his room. A four by six agape. They'd amused themselves tearing at the wall for what seemed to give him pleasure. The frame and roof he'd already built and he begged her to allow him an entry. "I need a door into here, not a wallowed out hole. Can I have a doorway?" Their matronly milkcow swings to see Billy then walks to a rabbit's hutch. Pink eyes recoil in terror, their fur sopping wet from the rain. Billy blows at the wick of her candle. Uninterruptedly blows it again. I need you more yon sun.

"Colder ever' night. He needs to get home."

"He's travelin with that fuckin priest."

"Latham Mox! I'll slap your face!"

Billy sniffed at the trailing smoke, inspecting the hole they'd made, the capacious plains without, their lay inert with emmer wheat growing but nothing jostles within this. Things tend themselves by stillness. Billy goes to her room and from beneath the bed retrieves a pair of workpants, sniffing and smelling her mate. She inadvertently begins to get wet. When they're fastened she cuffs the legs, her skirts dropped over the layer.

"Why're you wearin his britches?"

Latham's come to her door to watch her. Looking down when

her thighs showed white. Something twinges, something discomfiting, the facula of the sun on his mother.

"I ain't hitchin that silly hansom. Your father bought it stolen."

"Take the flatbed mama."

"Too slow. Is your saddle still on Roger?"

"It is," Latham replied.

"Well, I'm positive it ought not be."

"I ain't been asleep but an hour."

"An hour from doin what?"

"Rode Roger to the pit to watch the hole burn."

"What did Roger think?"

"There's a stinky fire I reckon."

"There's more in that hole than oil."

"Roger's done been fed and watered."

Warm tortillas are left on the table with three eggs he can fry when he pleases. Billy points at his coffee in the greasy black pot, telling Latham to lift with caution: "it's boiled itself to the grounds. Add water, drink away." When Billy shuts the door Latham walks to a window to watch his mother mount, the panes clear from their cleaning with vinegar. Billy throws him a kiss. "I'm too fuckin old for that." When he looks back Billy Mox is staring, mouthing "son, dig the well." She cranks Roger's head to the east, chasing the juddering sound, the revitalized storm patiently rolling, its periphery maimed by rain. Billy sprints Roger to a noisome pace, tacking pinion like mechanized gears, larger and longer distances, Roger sensing what Billy cannot. With his sudsy-rimed coat of unwashed salt the horse knows what has already happened. The force halts the beast with a stall tectonic, Billy feeling his apprehension, leg locking on his flanks for the headlong dive threatening to remove her from the saddle.

"Roger, sweetheart, what is it?"

She walks the horse for an hour through a bent southeast with the vulture riding the drafts, addled that Billy approaches, the dark waterwall of the storm she was chasing southeasting, pacing benignly, antithetic for its back is unambiguously blue and there is no discord present. She is in that blue herself, Billy's holster crowding her breast, the woman drawing the weapon to cock it, the screwed together piece of iron as efficient as the female grasping its handle.

"Son of a goddamn bitch."

He's Comanche. Impaled while he lived. The conflagration three days old. His face is bemired with an infusoria of black and his flesh is flaking. What remains is submerged in ash, the rubble of his body having slid from its impalement as his bellower watched him roast, fire attending this sager man of his clan as he screamed through a mouth pried open. Part skull, some soilside skin, sticks to the ground like paper. Beads lie scattered near the scene. A red, a turquoise, a white anemone, but his trinkets are teeming with ants. Her anterior view through the hole in his skull displays his precut penis, scissored balls in his open mouth, each positioned after the burning. His readable tracks are the width of his body for the man was drug by his hair. Immolated with articulate precision.

"Who to tell? Who'll want this?"

The rub in the grass is fifty feet north. Roger goes to its scent as he's called. The horse is dwarfed in the vassaldom space. He then trots in circles before Billy goes to him, Roger's hackamore braced and twisted. He nudges Billy, she holds his head, but the horse won't look at his owner, some entelechy scoring the beast, the form that was presence now present in form and there is no soothing his fear. Billy rubs down his trembles, his heart hyper-rhythmic, sensately tickling her fingers. Her own skull is savagely throbbing. Billy pushes her finger in past her tragus to the pulse of her inner ear. The heart she has felt is her own. It is twice what normal should be.

"The Comanche needs a grave Roger. He was…" about quietly innocent on a daily chore, an insoluble coincidence causing contact with a bivouacked horse and rider. In his drumbeat Shoshonean he asked to share fire, its maker responding in kind with an equivocal patter of tongue. He said, "come into the light of what shall be yours, for you'll share it indeed grandfather." The elder turned to run. Ran into an equine barrier. Reorienting, he could not shed it. Submitting, the elder went back.

"Grandfather, back to your fire. I've a notion presently awaiting."

51

ADIVINA KEPT A hovel in Reckingfort Soo, Billy calling to her friend from the entry, no doorway to impinge. Afternoon voices, the ones Billy hears, shout greetings, curses and oaths, Billy breaching the hovel onto the dirt floor, an interruptive burst of beam lugged light penetrating the west cracked brick, those passing between the light and squat casting reddish, uncut and illiquid figures smote when they turn the corner. The single pot in the room Billy then hefts but the ash is cold to the touch, the pot blacked on its bottom and strigil scraped clean and she wonders why this has been done. Billy walks upstreet to ask the man Hoskins if Adivina has been through town, the bootlegger offering to respond to the question for a dime or a pint or "that honyocker pussy, betwixt them short, hard legs." Billy smoldered while purchasing the bootlegger's product as he stared at her chest and crotch. "That ol' bitch is gone. She went to fuck wit' her plants or some other bullshit north where them rivers is a floodin."

"Did she say when she might be back?"

"That there is another question."

After unsaddling Roger and bucketing his water Billy takes her pint to the hovel. Her apishamore is wet but is spread for her napping as Roger looks inside. Billy asks the horse if Adivina's bough could be felt in the girth on his back. "Or does it feel like a goddamned stick?" Roger returned to his bucket. When empty he flipped it over.

52

THREADBARE SCINTILLANT AGAINST the blueblack sky with his body mobbing light from the dark. The Percheron remains on the lumpen plains while his keeper walks the streets of the town. Reckingfort Soo at night. Coughs and wheezes and whines. Hoskin's cabin is the first in a row of seven dwellings, the scent of sour mash pervasive. Inside a child has fallen from its breast, seems an imp in the lap of its mother. A curled, decisive fig. There sliding from the gloom, behind a drip filled tun, is a battledressed child of six, reeking of stench and covered in a tunic of pried-back, incurved stave. He's adorned to be a barrel himself. Outside in the moonlit darkness Threadbare stands like an autarchic symbol, the boy unaffected by this being in the street, its height and breadth irrelevant. He says, "mister, I gotta pee."

"Pee ahead."

"Not with you starin."

Threadbare turns, the stream hitting his boot, nothing said to harm the boy. The child's forehead perspires, glistens with sweat and he's nervous for he knows who is there. He has had the moment he needed.

"I'm sorry mister. I peed on your boot. By any likely chance are you him?"

The boy gazes back and then he looks forward but Threadbare

redirects. Backing nonpareil as done before he is lost in the empty street. The child asks, "friend, where are you?" Then his malnourished brain says *don't*. This voice the child obeys. Reversing inside he strokes his mother's gaunt wrist and the infant she was feeding wails forth. There's the mummery swipe of a dramatized hand and the staveclad child is floored, the susurrous peal of "out, goddamn you, and take that shit off your chest!" is followed by the boy clanking, he into the street to remove his stave tunic and again he speaks to the idol. "Mister? Sir? Hey you?" Nothing in response, he is safe. Then comes that respirable fear, the sudden fright of what he's avoided. It's like the edge of the world at the length of a toe without a speck of light to receive you. Often we know soon after. Or we never feel fear in the least.

*

Threadbare walks to Adivina's squat. Stands in its threshold portal. There are shadows cattailing, issued and crammed, striping the hovel's interior. They seem the pikes of since dead soldiers. He says "anybody home in there?" Billy is in the floor in the sleep of the drunkard being pummeled by dreams forthwith. He goes to his torment, smells she's been drinking, but when he squats there is no sound. The man is silk being thrown from a building. With his palm on her back he intrudes on her breathing with the spidered mass of a hand. Billy coughs but does not stir. He flips her over, arousing himself, the woman's clothing bunched and cramped. Threadbare skirts a breast, the V between her legs brushed by the heel of his palm. He curses beneath his breath, Billy Mox recumbent before him, his hands sliding to squeeze her throat. He touches the tips of his index fingers at the nape of Billy's neck, her vertebrae gently creaking.

"The boy can't fend by himself. You can't leave Latham alone."

"Fend," she replies. "My Latham."

When his hands unclench he stands. Threadbare's head skullpierces the wattle, light fascicles of reedwork falling, Billy covered with the holepunched weave. If she opened her eyes she could see the sky; but she can't, does not, and will not awaken, for in the dream she is having she will not rise from her place in the cold of the floor, and in the dark of a winter yet lived, the plains unthawing from their vast swept icing unalterably dense and black, the humiliating cold transcending, its largesse running south and Billy in her vision is a blonde of rarest beauty, their sodworked cabin exclusive on the prairie, like the touch of a mother speaking softly. Billy watches the man upon the cornhusk mattress and his bites are on her back and thighs. She claims her wounds as a bail disbonded, her legs and body torquingly bruised and her chores can wait themselves. Billy leans to wake him, the big man groaning and "I meant to leave it in." And Billy, "it was best you did. Your weighty fuckin has wrenched my guts. That pain my want of you. My sickenin want of you." She then moves about the cabin, a degree above zero, their unmended fire rifling her breath into columns of particulate ice. They tinkle on the floor like diamonds. Billy shivers and returns to their blankets. His smell is of hide and horse and sex, a mouth soon sweet with blaspheme, his breath the scent of sunburned flesh and if this is love he hates it, for they will never be one in the same, she inside him and he inside her, though what he does will have to suffice. She has a husband to go back to. "You bit me," she says. He looks to her. "I'm apt to bite you again." She replies, "I like bein bit." And he, "like it you say? It's a tolerable need I guess. I'll bite you again and again." She kisses his bottom lip. He thumbs a bruise on her back and presses. Enveloped by his arms she exhales. What is then imperfect isn't. The man blankets dream Billy to pierce her. She moans, "shit, no deeper. Deeper." One solitary aching gasp. "Woman, be still till I'm through."

*

Billy opens her eyes to the light. There's a gust of sharp wind and snotty nosed Roger is stamping and kicking his pail. Her skull is grated, vision in fits, a boon of pain in a chest congested. People are passing the hovel, what people there are to pass, the conversation gravitating to the whiskey merchant Hoskins forfeiting by taking his life.

"Without a mark on the bloat of his sincursed body. I think a demon done took his soul. That child of his, with that wooden vest, said a mare come and done it in the night. But it was likely intemperance what caused it."

Billy stumbles into the street. The two ruddy-faced protestant settlers await her interference. The thick birthers cherish demanding and cannot wait to judge her.

"Billy, Billy Mox," the left one said.

"What of the bootlegger Hoskins?"

The woman on the right said, "ain't you done listened?"

"Yes, I heard you Tilly."

"Why're you hidin in her hovel?"

"Hopin cunts like you will pass by."

She lifts Roger's pail, Tilly following to speak, trailing Billy to the Soo's lone well. Chivvying, she teases, but Billy ignores her, clasping the tentacled handle, its copulatory shape cranked smooth.

"You've yanked a few of them I reckon."

"Your husband and father bein two."

"That neck of yours. Them bruises." Tilly points aghast like a snow-flanked beast is charging through a chancel of rock. "That's a damndable whorish mess. Bruises a ringin your neck. You allow Dampier to lift his hand and they'll be a funeral for you."

Billy grabs her own throat as if to instruct another how to strangle a human. Her neck is tender, thickly ringed, the bruises shaped like vials of black. She replies, "he's southeast." Tilly knew where he was when she spoke. Her value of piety is exceptional. She turned her back on Billy and searched for her partner to expound on the handling of males.

"I put a knife in mine when he hit me. Left thigh, deep ol' wound."

Her partner replies, "I'd cotton to that. A sumbitch ain't a highknucklin me."

Billy splits the two to speak: "Dampier ain't home right now. Was that not clear when I said it?" Tilly is prepared. Has measured.

"Then you'll do even worse by makin 'em a cuckold with a man that wrings your neck! It's enough with a husband dick stickin like a chigger, but I'll be damned if I want two goobers a jobbin the hell out of me!"

Billy rides from the Soo by noon, whiskey claving to the roof of her mouth, Roger's double body horsecast as shadow, the sun faultlessly mining the day. While potshotting at a rookery of tan scattered birds the bough slips its hitch and falls. What magic she exports in the leaving of the bough is magic the woman has lost. An enchantment lax in returning.

53

WITH HIS MOTHER in the Soo Latham awls the round circle for the well Adivina has proffered. There are callable beasts in awatch. They swat their tails and chew with bovine chillness as the boy awlspikes his mark, the caliche hardbursting and Latham's spade dropping echoingly singing thunk, bouncing off what and when; an inch, then two, running to a foot and he is sweating and an hour has lapsed. He hasn't eaten because hunger, its chewing, has nothing to do with his thoughts.

Come evening, no mother, no worry. Latham goes to her stash to twist a short smoke. From a candle on the table it is lit. The sun in its hunker comes through the shade as the penny book sketches are spread. With a raspy pull of his brain croggling smoke he views his scandalous purchase. Hand sketches of whores in a Parisian bordello that are commonplace sirens enough, if secluded on a plain with your mother. A former turner, a Welshman, discorded from herding, sold the sketches to Latham for a copper. He asked Latham "have you ever been fucked?"

"Never had a woman," he responded.

The Welshman was soaking in Coldwater Creek, immured from the cold of the pool, tugging on his stiffening sex. "Oft times a hole is a hole. Tell you what, I'll switch you one, allow you to bugger me too. And I'll throw in the sketch of the sapphist. She's a mighty tough giver of face."

"Mister, I'm ridin due south. I reckon you'll reach for that shooter."

"Wait a minute boy," the Welshman said. "Take both them scrits for that copper. Reach into that plowhead satchel."

Latham dismounted, gunpinned the turner, taking the sketches as asked. He lobbed his money into the pool. "What is this word, sapphist?"

"A slit licker my boy! A filler of rooms! She inhabited the dark where I drew her! Go watch her muss her mouth!"

Latham kept his gun on the waterborne turner. The man stood in the pool, his body slate blue, jerking and stroking his penis. "A hole is a hole as I said!" He took an arable stretch southwest. Latham circled to see if the man would pursue, his track terminating in a weld of grassed snow, without a scratch as if pieced in a maelstrom. As if borrowed from his lecherous self.

*

Latham opened the windows and doors of the house for if sin be within, so without. Three candles were enough for the viewing, the sketches enjoined for their masturbatory quality and it won't take much to fulfill that, as it will in becoming a man. The two husksheet sketches had to be mated to divulge their retrospective, the artist giving details, a plumpness as matter, of a human carnation being torn. The minutiae of the piece are confusing. The artist is seated in a chair like Latham's in the sketch the Welshman has rendered. From the back a voyeur or any young man admiring the prostitute's work. Yet the artist is also the body of the man in the picture framed in debauch, his duplexity filling the room.

"You're a sharp motherfucker now ain't cha?"

There's a mattress on the floor with the sapphist on her knees and her face between the legs of another. This other, half woman, papercut mid breast, has her nipples on the edge of the sketch. Sodomizing the sapphist is a headless invader so the seer might place himself there. Latham recognizes the build of the Welshman from seeing him naked in the pool. His fist looks to fall on the spine of the sapphist, to distribute his revenge on her trade. There are vanillas and blues and lunacy blackings that rhymester these beings in fuck. Mother of pearl like abalone cunts with the chyle of a thousand men. Fantasist limbs lay strewn on the floor in and about copulation. Are these blowndown trees Latham is seeing beneath the clutch and the tongue of the sapphist, or in themselves tiny nacelles of fuck, candidature cells of whores being reamed by men with the heads of goats, one particular inhabitant sporting a cock with its shaft tattooed in blood. I TROD WATER, it says. Swimmer here, where do you tread? In an ocean of semen encased on a limb beneath a sapphist ensketched in her trade? You're a bentworld excrescence in fuck yourself and Latham wants to be you, resonating in death an emptyspoke promise to fuck a sordid world unconscious. Latham says to himself "I wish I was there" and semen explodes from his penis, without Latham even touching his member. Sighing, he treasures his sketches.

Late night Latham on his dosshouse mattress and he cannot come again. The doors and windows left open set knocking, the kitchen receiving what starts as a breeze before becoming the wind that it is, its lilt and blow like a hand being formed and what cannot hold itself in place is stirred and given wings. His candleheld sketches remain on the table, their peripheral borders clapping, slowly working themselves to abandon, the liberate sketches catching a breeze to fly through their southern doorway. With husksheeting implacate, heavy for duty, they wing muzzy towards Reckingfort Soo. Latham's sapped the pieces together and they hold to a dizzying height, sometimes flapping, a crease here and there, before bowling over plain to a halt. Some muniment weed, having grown by the road, catches and holds the sapphist. The sketch tears on a breeze, is cut in two, a boot stomping the sapphist's head, her torso snatched from the air. Threadbare takes the dissever, this critic at large, knowing better, but the artist is commended, is accoladed for his use of the limbs, those miniscular blowdown nacelles of fuck, which he lifts to his eyes to inspect, maculating with the flame of a knot. He then smudges a tiny correction.

"This is worthy. Captured well."

The Percheron, heavily exhausted, watches the critic at work. He drawls and insculps twin streams of hot breath refined by the night to smoke. As the vapor wanes empty, its ibidem, emitter, screeches with a howl like the burning, the Percheron begging acknowledgment, the horse deep pawing revetments of dirt, light stone and grass flying thither. The sketches are tossed to the wind.

*

Threadbare combs through his saddlery, the plowhead satchel, there bagged with the scalp of the Welshman. There was an overawed look in the eyes of the sadist when Threadbare rose from the plain, the neck of the horse with the Welshman atop snapping like a bobstay in gale. Like a trousered ape he leaped from his mount to land and skid on his knees. "You've broken his neck," he said. "How the fuck have you broken his neck? You wrenched at his snout and…" Threadbare replied, "why're you trailing the boy?"

"Sketches. I sold 'em pictures. For twisting pizzle, he's lonely you see."

"Why're you following the boy?"

"You're Threadbare. Admired you are."

The Welshman wouldn't answer. Seemed to be drunk. Hazarded a sexual glance. "I can take you in my mouth if you want. Empty your set for my life."

"Take me in your mouth?" he replied. Buttonholed in the depths, the vastitude boxing, the Welshman devised his escape.

He saw his aggressor look past his shoulder and when he did the Percheron neighed, the Welshman trapped between the two.

"Take the horse in your mouth Caligula."

"I'm not sucking the cock of a horse."

"But you'd rape the tail of a youth?"

"A man gets his fun where he finds it."

Threadbare considered the sadist. Looked at the horse he'd killed. Its body to his right, the snout broken backwards, a horse-painting of a draft in an erumpent of color with the oil drying there on the plain, dead horse and sadist and the Percheron waiting for Threadbare's decision coming late.

"You've the copper that Latham gave you?"

"Yes," said the Welshman, rooting for the coin in the plowhead satchel worked loose. "I've paten too, a goddamned stack, stolen from the church in Las Norias."

"You robbed the church in Las Norias?"

"I did. Those beggarly fucking fools!"

"Their God or not is their own decision. They're simple people enough."

"Fuck them. Shall we barter?"

"You'll take me in your mouth, correct?"

"You can tear loose my scalp. Grab at my hair. Not a drop will fall on the ground."

"Tear loose your scalp?"

"As you wish."

"You sir, have a deal."

54

LATHAM ISN'T THERE when Billy returns, his mother sliding from her saddle and onto the porch and "Latham! Latham Mox! Where are you?" The well in its depth is a five-foot maw in a circle easily blocked, the fresh thrown soil like the tell or the grave of some miniscule buried idolater, his musk in the dew on the mound, no work being done as of late.

"Latham!" Again, "Latham!"

Billy goes to the well, kicks at the ruff, her swipes breakbending the newdead tendrils, the grass splitending like hair. "Grass," she says. "Grass. Fuckin grass and rocks and sun. Miles of the shit and my child is upon it." *A thread in completest carpets. And if that thread has been plucked from the weave the life I've lived is voided. I will wait then I'll leave and he'll follow.*

Billy leans against their split rail fence. There's an ululant howl from some venery beast, the animal sounding his kill. Billy stares that direction while searching her pockets for a secreted pouch of tobacco. In the distance the oil pit burns, snaking smoke to cobalt blue. Its corpus piles, cracks, coughs dark breaths, a black-bodied being in rise.

"Mama?"

"Latham," she answers.

He rides to his mother in silence. She embraces a mounted leg, reasserting her lean on the fence.

"We gonna start back on this? The fence, diggin the well? That's what I come to do."

Billy puffs once on her rolled cigarette, sees the world through its ash and embers. "I'm awfully young for all that has passed. Reckon I'm just bein silly. Ain't done a damn thing but respire."

"I'll do what you ask mama. You're safe with me wherever."

"But you ain't safe with me."

Her custard scarf is inundated with sweat. When it droops Latham sees. Has my mother been with another? There are bruises betraying his father. Dampier has instructed that the feminine wile is factually and permanently that, an ensnaring of desire separate from man with the intention of fording him misery, though his father has yet to complain. Billy watches her son, the twist of his wristlets, his adjustment of a collar near perfect. Picking at the scarf, she chins it, bringing round its back and the bruises aren't there and with her neck beturbaned she is chaste.

"It's gonna rain," says Latham.

"Rain comes and it goes and is gone. Comes and it goes and is gone."

"Mmm hmm, mama. Mmm, hmm."

"Adivina wasn't in. Did I tell you?"

"No mam. She wanders. Perhaps through the winter. Lowbry said she walked to Canada."

Billy purses her lips. A pollination of rain on her face. She's done what she's done to invite him. He is there as there is her son. She can feel the man in her teeth.

"She ain't comin back from this one Latham. Adivina is no more."

"Gone to her people you think?"

"Yes, gone to her people."

Billy's legs fall asleep for an unknown reason as the clouds of the front block the light. Drizzle with a clatter of thunder. Latham does not shift from his place in the saddle when the droplets touch

Billy's hair. Gelid woman transfixed by her thoughts. No words are exchanged as they drown. They await an abduction giving no sign from a source whose signal is absence. How to prepare for that?

"Let's unsaddle and water these horses."

When Latham and Billy are safely inside nothing is said of the order. Latham's thoroughly cleaned their home. Her nose sniffs the acidulous; lupine, cyclamen, and why must she think he is present?

"Latham Mox, who came in?"

"Me. Nobody else."

She looks at their fire. The breastwork of chimney. Back to ordinary life.

"Did you rattle the damp before buildin that fire? If you didn't I'll do it myself."

"Mama, that fire is hot. You'll be adjustin a handful of iron."

"Why not do it firstly?"

"I don't…"

"Fuck it. Forget it."

Both watch from their stances without want of a chair as the flue accepts the rain, the water spitting and smoking and the logs in refusing bear the mark where its quenching assails them.

"Latham."

"Mama, what?"

Billy places her arm on his shoulder. Between the two is what she can't say, so she says what spills from her mind.

"You're both too big to sit on my lap. But I remember when you could."

"Not sure what you want mama."

"Nothin. Not a damn thing." Billy goes to their history. Waits on the words. Rehearses inside her head: *son, I'm your mother and Dampier is your father and here, I've brought you here. This is where he wants us to be. And you look at me queerly with the heaviest of brows and that look in your eye is your brother's, though that heart in your chest isn't mine. For mine is near broken from impact. Look there, you've the same hands, the structure of Torq, an identical model, grown from the center of me. If only from that middle I recall being decent before my collision with him.*

"Mama!" Billy comes back. "What have I not been told?"

Long pause as it builds and it's tall as is thick and its density increases in seconds. Latham wants to know. Billy says, "Latham I'll tell you."

Her story takes an hour continuously streaming and is brutally delivered without intrigue. Like a hole in a roof the water has found, widening and curing to shape at the edges, dripping and falling to the floor. She relates the days she recalls, warning Latham what wandering wrought, how the weather or another, what you do not know, supplants the course of the traveler. She says, "when I met your father this is what he was doin," but omits what Dampier did. Latham asks, "why was the devil after you and daddy for that?" It is then she castors the lie, rolls it about as she wishes: "Mims Nickel was the name of the place. Me and your father was in it. There the ire of the meanest come to be heard, surfaced for seein as proper, if all men be evil and butcherous. We'd done nothin illegal but were held as a draw for the man who is after us now. We were guilty as vagabonds tend to be, committed for wanderin earth. Why should man have such bald freedom, when another decides he shouldn't?"

Latham wrinkled his brow when the gaps were blatant, accepting the fissures as is, his mothers' exclusions so obviously glaring he had no idea where to start. Billy crafted a history, where evil, by chance, lay in your path like a mountain or maze where inobvious sides were expected, but were gone in the instant appearing; like a plan to illuminate dark, if dark be the world as it is.

"And then we came to this patch where we built. The first settlers wantin to stay. I'm guessin we'll stick if you want. Your daddy and me will die here."

In that silence past personal history both are seated for mulling.

Shoulder to shoulder in chairs. Sitting, they stare at the fire. The rain has passed east to exclude them. Latham rises to become the man that he isn't by turning his back to the heat. His clothes are smoking in seconds. If sorrow could certain a thing unreplenished could certainty be more bleak, or some lightless bleaker still? When convinced of his thoughts Latham speaks.

"Threadbare, I know of his doins."

"He is that thing that I feel. He took your brother off."

"You feel 'em? I don't understand."

"Like that fire at your back he is here. As here as the smoke comin off it. As actual as what makes it burn."

"You and daddy ran from him?"

"There is no runnin from him. We've paid a biblical score for such."

"But him chasin you ain't right?" He corners his mother with the question. The details he needs she keeps. Particular grotesqueries, their barrenness uttered, seem exclusive to Billy's fables. Latham, her telling, the gaps in the story, elude you as matter of fact. You cannot stave him off. You'll not be alone for long.

"No. His pursuit ain't warranted. It is false, that's what it is."

"False?"

"He needs me because I am. I thought…" no Billy, you will not think, his gallop like a hammer on an anvil at dawn and from a minute due south he is closing, rain and thunder at the back of the rider like emunctory organs in filter; he of, on, and about no path, Billy sliding the bolt on the front and back doors and obsequiously slamming their windows, as if he won't choose to invade. She's beside herself with fear.

"Latham! Stay where you are!"

She comes back to her son and they both watch a leak run a timber to clang in a pot on the stove and it drips and is soon unable to create the noise of the drip, the bottom of the pot a diapason voice with the sound of the rain on the roof, the boy scooting closer to his cowering mother to grasp her wrists like a jailer.

"It is he, him," she says.

The rain stops but the leak flowers on the ceiling and it breeds and promotes its own. One leak becomes seven and seven then ten, but when the blanket outside yardfalls from the line they come to their feet to listen, hear the hoofs with their sucking intention, his survey of the pair within, through walls as thin as want.

"It's Apache mama, Apache."

"Apache," says Billy. "Apache? We, my precious, are through."

They wait an hour then two and the house becomes hot and the sun through the leaks and the mis-set angles of the house project its rays. Multitudinous cracks abound. As if the home is being wrenched by the shift of the plains and the structure must follow or else. Protestations do no good. Their temple is tearing apart.

"Latham, I done what I could."

"I know you did mama. He'll go."

"What you know ain't all that I done. But the now of what's done is here."

"Don't matter mama. I love you."

His adoration lifts above a whisper and when it does the Percheron snorts, the blast through a seam in the backhouse portal, the flare and the snot and what screech he makes followed by the door flying inward, its bottom half halving to top, the bolt she has slid bulleting the room, jacking like a knife in the farside wall, Billy and Latham entwining, the room filling with smoke for he's capped the flue, though there's been no sound on their roof.

"Pray to God. Pray now Latham."

He responds "how're you calm?"

Billy steps her son patient to her room and bed and he bellies underneath to hide. She squats to observe in a corner. In that time taken an enigma: the logs in their fire are removed by hand, and though a paling fence of smoke is present, the fireplace is vacant and empty. Their time in the bedroom becoming incidental and they have not heard him work. They are stunned by unreality. Lost in a whorl of time.

"How long have you been in this room?" Latham taps his mother from beneath the bed, hissing "mama, what did you say?"

Billy pauses, "be ever so quiet."

Threadbare circles, details their house, to the cadence of the Percheron's whinny. He loops it twice, leading the horse, Billy joining her son in hiding. His third and fourth laps are the quietest, the silence broken by his slewing warning.

"My pursuit is finished. Final."

The voice is at their feet. Reacting they kick and gasp. It is there and not there and it hastens to naught as if no voice had worded. As if a mouth without body had spoken. It takes its piece, as every word does, and is gone as gone is cipher, like the dust that quiet creates. For words between humans slough when in silence, as if speech could shed the unseen.

55

THEY REMAIN IN the house for the next seven days. Therein they have what is needed. When their homestead stock and ponies are rustled they're numb to the sound created, lying mother and son in the bed of wired Billy when the men who have robbed them call forth, without daring to enter the house, the men screaming through the broken door, as if the one before who has splintered the passage held sway over those that didn't. His voice isn't familiar.

"Billy! Hey you, Billy Mox! Come to me and I'll fuck you proper!"

Billy and Latham climb under the bed not expecting he knows where they are. "Latham," she says. "Let the man talk. He ain't gonna come in this house."

"Who're they?"

"Heathens come north, to escape some deed or other. It don't make a shit if we know 'em."

Latham rolls from under bed and with a shambling stoop opens a window and fires, the musket leaning in a corner presumptively waiting for the week they've squatted in terror. The shot careens and whines in the night. When it hits the rustler dehorses, the beast curvetting and running to dark. It's a middle back strike with a weakened inertia that is fortune and no thing else; unkilling but scouring, the rustler's face wincing, hitting lintel stones akin a macadamed road and the pain is ahold in an instant, his teeth rife with breaks like needles.

When Latham's breathing slowly evens to a syncopative rhythm he announces, "I hope you're dead!" He reloads but Billy is there. She throws the musket on the bed like a pillow.

"Latham, don't invite wrath." She calmly adds "okay? We ain't gonna thwart what's due. Do you understand what I'm sayin?" She is bleary-eyed adamant with a lost child's seriousness as Latham backs away. He speaks from the dark then the light of the moon with its sackclothed ruse of palement. He himself of a soulsick tone. "It's been a whole damn week mama. He ain't comin back."

"Are we alive?"

"We are."

"Then he's here."

*

They dry river run the herd rustled from the Mox's with their lows orgiastically bawling. When the cattle smell water it is somesuch branch and they throatily drink and grumble. The man Latham has shot near spinewears the ball and in arriving announces he's spent. "I ain't ridin no more and I mean it." His face is a surface of blood and torn tissue and he's speaking to a surly pairing. All three are eastern born settlers, come west from the lands of the Choctaw; where, without complot, they've murdered a village of women and children for hides disused, which they burnt.

Vestry Dor is the man with the lead in his back Latham has blindly shot. He is the esteemed grandson of a Lieutenant Dor General Washington wedged under Gates, and whom Gates recycled to death, rearactioning Dor against a Hessian skirmish alone with four other privates, Gates fleeing from the British in retreat. Vestry Dor exchanged a life of privilege and position for a drift on the Mississippi River. The Choctaw were razed in transit, Dor sending his people west to the Brazos and he will never see his family again. He cannot and will not confide in the pair but he does not survive unassisted. Releasing his reins he collapses. Falls in the branch face first. With a gangly plop and a forearm rise he curses the watching men.

"You two are lucky this horse circled back. Which of you can harvest this wad?"

Dor inquires man to man. Minzo and Top won't answer. They watch the herd in its drinking from branch and mud before winging their cattle southeast. Dor can do nothing but plead.

"Come on fellas! I was just kiddin! Take my share and sell 'em as wished!"

Top replies "we done have!"

In a while Dor is lucid and aching. Wonders if the shot went through. Rolling to his stomach from his hip onto his chin brings a yelp another can hear. There is no camaraderie present, between insulter and insulted the same, the rules we apply quite suspect, for the irrational waits in den. Whether gods of futility, abandonment or longing, each of these gods are the same. Answers from each Dor needs. As he begs them in turn do they hear?

"I can yank that wad," says the voice.

"I knew you could Minzo. Come forward."

Vestry Dor thinks Minzo returned. That Top guards the herd on a crest. He reaches for a smoke but the pouch isn't there and he cannot flip to ask.

"Got tobacco on your person there Minzo?"

The boot steps between the knees of the miscreant Dor and by scent Dor knows he's another. The rolled cigarette drops over his shoulder. Lands in his palm like a twig. A stoppered canteen is lowered on a pry, blunted from its work in a colliery, angled from the wedging of rock. Dor asks if fire is available.

"Put it in your mouth. I'll light it."

"Come around front so I can see you."

The other does as asked with his long stringy hair and the dissonance of a being corroded. He then squats in Vestry Dor's face. See you there my unfamiliar. The canteen is unstoppered, water is poured, Dor lapping like a dog and it's wasted on his cheeks and he will not look at the man. By decipherment fear is sufficient. You don't need a face for that.

"Who the fuck're you?"

"Don't say that."

"I'm sorry. Can you hep' me out?"

He wears the wrap of a bruin though there is no cold. Face smudged to kill down white. He's ridden through rains and hailstorm winds, late summer, earliest fall; where predicting a front by dint of appearance is surmising a dying proportioned. Who knows what arbitrator nature will bring, who expects that outside knock? Man hopes he rules this world. Unsettlingly prays he doesn't.

"That your horse I hear nickerin?"

"It is. Vestry Dor, you're considerably feeble."

"Think you can find that shot?"

"I've done worse to a body that lived. In a time of need that is."

"My time of need is here."

"Isn't it funny when such as that comes? When now and need embrace?"

"Carve as you will. Tis' assembled."

"If the puss and rot get in it, won't matter if I was deft."

"Sonofabitch! Cut the thing out! Enough with the goddamn musin!"

"As you wish. As I shall."

He hefts a long and curved blade with a tip that is bent from hard packing shells on the border. Without permission he lowers onto Dor. Rips open what is left of his shirt. The lateral muscle has slowed it. If not for the distance he'd be dead. The shot has curved to the right and though the spine is secure, our rancid physician palpates him. As the tip penetrates to search for the ball a cigarette is stubbed on his neck, Dor screaming through the seconds required for the probing and extraction of the bedded shot. With the squeezing of the wound and its serum, the procedure comes to an end. Vestry Dor is rinsed in blood, his mouth like a chow chow blackening.

The moon obscures, its light in fade, come the maul of the fresh day sun. A necropolis of stone is revealed, a red bird in fantod fitting close to them and "Vestry, your blood is her color. A sign from God perhaps?"

Dor breathes and in breathing doesn't speak.

"You want it burned over?"

"Fuck no," says Dor. Weakened, his voice struggles. Dor's still an obstinate man.

"Where did you and those men gather that herd? Those brands are familiar to me."

"A homesteader cunt and her boy. Most come from there, not every."

"A homesteader cunt and her boy?"

"Minzo started talkin with the Lord. If not for that the woman was fucked. Last bitch I topped was my wife."

He continues to hold Dor down. Whether compromised network of vein or lone artery is punctured he does not know. The wound's extravasation slathers hotslick and Vestry has told his truth.

"I don't feel so good," Dor says.

"You're bleeding to death. Feel poorly?"

"Can't you do nothin about it?"

"Can't or can, what's the difference?"

"My back is real warm. The rest ice cold. Like snow. The frozen kind."

The surgeon worms his finger into the wound, pressing when

he feels the spurt. The pressure stops the bleeding. With the heel of his hand formed over the hole there is blood and then there isn't.

"Hey," Dor says.

"Yes?"

"Think I feel," Vestry Dor repeats.

"Think you feel your life in leaks?"

The blade is swiped on his pants, placed behind an ear, gently tracing the coast of his hairline. He does not use the edge. Vestry Dor watches with eyes half circling, his surgeon returning the blade sub-lobe and not a scratch did the surgeon render, as if measuring Dor's scalp for another.

"Who're you?" Dor adds, "you're him?"

"My brother is a terrible shot. My mother your homesteader cunt."

All is muffled by the coat from the bruin. Vestry Dor relaxes. His knife is withdrawn and when the blade is in scabbard he remembers the blade is filthy. Torq Mox then says "I'm slippin." He rinses the knife in a sink.

56

BILLY WANTS THE door mended but to rehang another they will have to craft their own. To cut and plane the merchant's oak, the man vending sections of "sixty board foot that'll door your house for the winter. With twenty four board foot a door can be fashioned, eight foot in height by thirty-six inches" and he sold them for his lumber was minimal, the merchant headed west to the village of Bueyeros for a load to return him east. This was before the twins. The wood lay covered where the timber was unloaded and where exposed the sun has molested, Dampier never staking the tarp, barely using the wood for expansion. The bottom most boards are rotten from their wait, the ones in the middle being spared.

"Latham, can you hang a door?"

"My main skillset is sittin on a horse watchin cows eat and shit, but I reckon I can trim it and true it. Mama, where is my brother?"

Billy shudders, dazedly fields it, responding with adeptness and candor.

"As relates to your brother he is elsewhere. I believe this feelin is mutual."

"Alright then, okay."

Latham's standing in the frame, a seamy ragged figure, where a door should be, but isn't. This boy is an angel tumbled downward. The angelic in the boy tightly bound. Billy watches her son from a chair in the corner, sobbing and coughing and slouching. *I love you that much that he comes. You'll forever be in danger with me.*

"I shouldn't have said it like that." Billy speaks as if righting disorder. As if command realigns said purpose. "Rule it the best you can. Sixty-board foot will make maybe three. Try not to fail more than twice."

Latham hunts for a saw and the rule that he finds is branded with his father's initials. Like some thing or some what might violate his tools to consult on a build far away.

"Why the hell does he brand his initials? Who the fuck wants a rule out here?"

He recollects two years prior, when the gray heat of sky and the fog lay hot on the Llano Estacado early morning. Thunderheads increased with the break of day as they searched for a calf in a draw, the found driftwood amorphous there on the plain with his horse wreathing angrily around it, he and Dampier roping the log, but their tugs and pulls became static, the wood anchored by something beneath. When their lariats snapped the twenty-foot log remained as remains a torso, its charred and careworn marrow within deign to go with any. His father looked to him, said "it ain't gonna budge" and "how it come to be ain't knowable. Such cottonin to bafflery vexes. What's brought it here's long dried by the sun and this wood has been left to awe us. As do the ways of a workin God."

Latham finishes his thought, gazes at the house, Billy watching him think from their portal, disappointment grounding the woman. The youth lofts a feeble gesture, her scream without sound, she unable to lure him towards her, for he's the validest son at a task.

"Stay where you are Latham! You look like your father standin there!"

A windriven cloud ordains him. His shape changes, then mutates. From her vantage it reechoes as another. For a second

Latham is Torq. The wanton blizzard then debouches fiery snowing. Yell boy, he is here.

"Mama! In the house! That there!"

Jarringly, the home, it shudders, Latham pointing at his mother in confusion. He sprints around a hutch but she doesn't react, Billy shawled spectatorially with light, the yank inward claiming her body. The hoofsplit door folds out in a pincer, rebounding to sever, but hang. When he makes it to their clothesline paces from death the lash picks at his toes and trips him, a second strike encircling his feet. Latham's drug like a streamer, back around the hutches, to squirm behind their shed indirectly, his weight meagerly concerning the puller, even less when he flips him facing. Torq Mox looks down at his brother. Covers his mouth with his hand.

"Shhh, little man, hush hush. You bray like a fuckin calf."

Latham straightens his digits, proclaims a shamed silence, with a flathanded show of his palms. It says *this I do not want*. Torq gives back his words by loosening his grip and Latham can speak if he'll whisper.

"Torq?"

"I am. We are."

Torq frisks his body in search of an injury, pawing at his brother for a subsequent denseness to consider this flesh as twin. Latham's eyesockets, the shape of his skull, are all he's willing to see. Torq's features are precise like enamel, hermetically sealed in ice. His eyes are of a ratcheting beam, the darkest of thoughts there positing worlds other than the world of their maker. Latham Mox is none of this.

"Yes Latham. It's me. Stop pantin."

"Why're you here?"

"For the reckonin. He wants us grouped together. That interest not extendin to daddy. Are you hurt, outside or in?"

"I can handle my on. You stayed run off…"

"I was fuckin taken Latham. No matter, we've plenty to do."

Torq came to his feet with his boot on his brother, his double-jointed fingers drumming thigh. Restrained in the dirt Latham looked at his twin, pushed against his leg but was held. Torq plotted. Peeked around the shed. No movement inhouse was apparent. Threadbare had their mother confined and relegated to a position inherently chosen.

"Torq, I want to get up."

Torq's gristled bullneck with its shoulderlength hair twisted right, left and back. He said "what did you say?" and his brother repeats it, Torq then appearing as older. His pallor changed color with the bright sun's center, his wan face cordovan dark, like the walls of a dyeing plant. "The light casts violet over yonder. I should've cornered the house back there. Yes, get on your feet."

Torq verbally challenges Threadbare. Decides on another approach. During contemplation Latham offers the history of what has abducted their mother. Torq gazes, looks through his brother, patient in voice and manner.

"I know the man well Latham Mox."

"What I'm sayin is the fucker is hard. A reputable son of a bitch."

Latham seems even softer with his curse-laden statement. He pats his brother's shoulder and smiles. "Here you are Torq, my own."

"Don't," replies Torq. "She allowed him to scoop me. Stay the fuck out of my way."

"I will."

"He wants heads. Needs three, yours bein third."

Torq stepped into the open, to the sprawl of yard and plain, withdrawing his weapon to cycle it, dropping in his shells with a variance of grains because these are the loads he has. Threadbare watched his protégé from the backside wall where the hardware of the door had penetrated. Billy dangled on his left held in moribundia in the retreat his grip imposes. What will come when my throat is collapsed? She considers her life, its tock, her discriminating tick in arrears. There's a stilted Billy murmur, then Threadbare speaks. It is clear, foreseen and apocryphal: "he'll take my horse because he hates it. He doesn't hate me because he thinks himself equal. That, your son, is not. Will you call forth to warn him?"

"You're the fucker holdin his mother. The coward hidin inside."

"Defiant I see. Nothing held back. I'm going to let them watch me."

When Torq whistles the Percheron, the horse he was gifted, appear as movement is sound, trotting fetlocks dragging and disproportionately insouciant impearling palling dust. Torq's mount has a wound on his shoulder, blown with his head cast down, the Percheron spinning to snap at his haunch, the Palomino showing white teeth, its plethora of emotion beneath the mass of the other and he but a toy under hoof. As he bleeds it is leaded black poison. He submits only when called.

"Come on, give me a run."

The Percheron acknowledges, eagerly accepts, leaping forward from a backhaunch spring. He's a hundred feet distant and coming. When he sees Torq waiting he skids and trenches, the bulbs of his hooves digging deep. His chuffing power decreases. The dust covers Torq, but the Percheron pivots, an alternate plan being made.

"Come to me, you heavyboned fuck. Give your boy a run through tramp."

Where mythic flame would bloom in camphine bursts snot jets from the Percheron's snout, the beast luciferous in calculating options as scenarios bleed from his mind. Threadbare's taught their pruning. Begin here, then the brother, crush both, his keeper can deal with the woman.

He sprints towards Torq until thirty feet nearer before he corners and charges at Latham, the boy crumpling in the dust to the left of a hutch in an alley where the Percheron is funneled. Torq's shot is at the croup or thigh, the horse sprinting away, not to him, Latham down on the ground amongst the roughcast hutches awaiting the Percheron's hooves. When he squeezes the initial the withers spray blood, his second hitting poll through the forehead, the brainy red matter volcanic. He does not fire a third. In careen the Percheron vaults from the living, balancing his steps as granted, his gaskins and thighs then collapse. He lands on his rump, thuds to the right and there are breaths though they're guarded and collected; his last flash a perpended blood red haze with a straining sunlight filtered, his propine snout nearest Latham's left hand, there extended to receive his touch. Latham looks to his brother with a cheek in the dirt and at the topskull resting near. When he reaches to check the Percheron's pulse the beast ignites, snaps, and is dead.

Threadbare sees it unfold. A hand clutches Billy's dark mane. Elvish in his grip her elevated heels whump on the floor as she dangles, his eye pressed between the slats of the shutter.

Torq reloads, the jackets penetrating, clockwisely clicking home.

"Latham. Move. Get clear."

Like recycling from a ruck Latham rolls back to breast. Stands away with his hands in his pockets. Torq's shot disattaches the remainder of the poll and the Percheron's face is removed.

"Goddamn Torq! Why do that?"

"Damn God at your own risk Latham. I've a feelin I'm about to meet him."

Threadbare looks to Billy. So many years gone and the finger he excised is scarred, but straight, innominate. She grabs the top of his arm, begs for their lives, but just such lives Billy Mox did stake by evincing on that great salt flat.

"You picked me and then us for no other reason but his bounty and that was his."

"Possessing you and yours was my constant. Tormenting has no reason."

She's released, lands and is stiff, Threadbare posing as if fitting for something. His hair is long white, complicatingly matted, with a humanness of feature psychotic, like a man behind a window enbarred and enclosed, the lines about his face caused from the weather with others inflicted by thought. As if thought should supplant delusion. As if he believes in no one thing, but in things of no one source. She inspects his throat, the leavings of a garrote, with a slice inflicted by his hand. He knew misery when he saw what it was. What it is. What it came to be.

"No man done that," she says.

"Twice I attempted to take my own life but the horse brought the Bannock, then the Pueblos. He did not wish me dead. Can you fathom the depth of my sorrow, with your children awaiting their deaths?"

Billy hawks and spits. Blood flies. "Go on then, if you can't do it, Torq will do it for you."

"He's the son we could not have?"

Billy refuses to answer. His words ring darker truths.

"I do not, can't…" and he exits. Revolves at the door to question. Not a word can or does he utter; his punch upper-cutting and the strike is meant to kill her as her head hits an oblong brace, nailed where the roof is patched. Threadbare lifts her by the chin, scraping up the wall, throws her body on a pallet of quilts. Her figure slumps in a sunwashed pile. "Dead, Billy Mox is naught." Through this rage his thoughts have been cordoned, and by his violence their summation comes due. He lights a palmful of tinder but snuffs it. What he must do is beyond elemental and cannot be blamed on fire.

Threadbare steps through the door, doublefists the frame, its plosion, the chinking above it, raining to the floor behind him, what hatch of a door that is left, spinning like debris through space. It recollects their clothesline inward, the cotton rope balling in amongst itself like a seriocomic intestine. Threadbare squares and searches for Torq. Battering his flanks, dust rises. Torq is there in the tumult waiting.

"As stated, a willing pupil. All grown up and wanting?"

He's twenty paces from Torq and see them: perfect similar stances. Loosened hands at their hips with elbows in bend, fingers searching highsewn seams. Foul sensing the two are corralled and confined; cratered and resentful with coaldark faces weirdly empathetic. These men require risk by existing. Their culmination has to be this, for there is not enough world to hold them if apart, each deepening black as is.

"Did you kill her?"

"My apostle, young Torq."

"Is she dead?"

"Your mother's been thrown."

Since becoming themselves separate from others these men have assumed their own presence. What they are is what they've become. Framed for what they are doing. Herein the end of what they have done. Threadbare quietly subsumes the direction he'll take from the myriad paths before him. Twitting then raising his clublike arm he reaches to tug at his ear. He comes back parallel with the yard at his feet and Torq sees the shot in the barrel, the snap of fire from the oil of the muzzle, his left quadriceps thrown back with the burst as the great extensor muscle is split, the cap of the shot settling in. A dull ache permeates with a wild rapid heart and *it's my death. My death. My death.* Threadbare thumbs back the trigger, smiles before speaking, advising as if to live.

"It pays to know where you are. Next time, do what I taught you."

His next shot takes the top of Torq's right thumb and the flange disintegrates. With his compromised leg Torq Mox hops sideways attempting to level and fire, sacrificing what steadiness his mind can collect by moving to his left and having to skip to force his foot to obey him, Torq asking himself where the pistol came from without an answer to this obsolescence, Threadbare watching him hop with the drawndown bead bouncing as he skips in extremis, going on and reaching for an unseen cover bringing Torq to the edge of the house. Threadbare grins with his pistol conducting, his wrist casually directing Torq's dance.

"You could deem this unorthodox punishment. And you would be correct."

Torq marvels at Threadbare's indictment. He blatting and moaning deep beneath pain, dollops of his blood running in his boot, Torq soldered to the sight of a bluebird in flight, her demonstrative run from a silvery predator whose traitorous assault found her chicks. She can neither escape nor attack. Torq thinks *go to sky mother bird*. As if safety was never alighting. You will come down to something.

"Don't make it a game motherfucker. Latham's watchin us both."

"I know. And the boy will suffer. Same as your mother and you."

Torq waits for the sally's release, the sole of his boot now blooded, the meat of his thigh effusing dark sweat like a red rubber sheet has sealed it, the left side of his body unable to bolster what his right is presently demanding. Torq grasps the corner of the house, Threadbare's shoulder drawing even the same, the bountyman grinning right before firing when a blast erupts from inside, from where a new door does not hang; its light is supraliminal, illuminating the interior, the triphammer slug hitting Threadbare's chest, his body levitating philippic; his breast floods with numbness, legs in refusal, before he settles lying prone in the yard. Billy steps forward to speak.

"That'll be sufficient goddamn you."

She crosses their threshold, descends to the yard, knowing the damage she's wrought, Threadbare's heart with its skips beats faster, slower, the man calm as if never being, as if his past demanded this.

Billy's torment shades his face, Threadbare's eyes upon her from a place irrefutable where maps refuse to plot. Where the zig of a trickle bequeaths a scruffy red line of red that runs to his cheek. For her his look is galvanic. An expression of detailed woe. Torq says "mother" and Billy says "Torq" but it goes no further than that.

"Put another in the cause, his brain."

"No Torq. Find your brother."

Torq limps and calls and Threadbare listens to the boy pulling his leg. He then grabs Billy's ankle, no words then exchanged as the creep of the numbness takes the grit from Threadbare's teeth. Bars though they are to chew with. It's a whisper and she bends to hear it.

"You'll never be done with me. That tear will never fall."

When it does it lands on his cheek.

"Enough," she says. "Enough."

The spent shell is dispensed from her handbuilt model. In the barrel another inserted. Click of breech. The hammer goes back. Her eight-gauge bore is rooted in his mouth and the barring of his teeth wrap around it. He shuts his eyes and Billy says "no, keep 'em open and that grip on my ankle. Look at me, see it all."

There is a singular charge from a mind in wander found by oblivion's snow, it to him, not he to it. Threadbare walks in the open. He is lithe, but youthless, scarred as is, whole and without path. What he was is there to greet him, not the thing he came to be. This mulches his soul. Assumes it. He is then disseated from being.

Billy Mox says "you" from above him.

57

LATHAM HEARS THE shots from the darkith of hiding, the commands his mother gives. The sun has begun its westering roll for an earth it brackets in warmth. Torq lumbers, trips, arrests his own fall, his brother detachedly catching, stepping in and supporting his weight. He says "Torq, put your arm around me." Billy appears behind them. Through insectile buzzings recommencing post fire he is wincingly delivered inside. Torq is lowered to sit on the bed of his parents while Latham tugs at his boots, the thigh open, clotted, its realwood muscle the shade of a tree stump rotting. From his back Torq asks for their help.

"It's settled in the meat, but I think it worked out. Dress it, do what you want. The thumb is of little concern."

Torq Mox is then unconscious. Jell of mindfull sleep. With cleaning the tissue is bared, the wound obedient when flushed with the bourbon Billy maintains in abundance. The wad is found and the shrapnel removed. She feels no fracture, saying, "breaks swell more." Latham shrugs, then smiles and speaks.

"I'm glad he's alive and here. His thumb ain't even bleedin."

Billy tugs from the bottle and he asks with his eyes and his mother says "Latham, drink."

To the evening they sit in their settlement home as vespers and twilight diffuse. Inadept at comfort their chairs are enough as they sleep, start and sleep. Torq's wounded horse laps and whinnies for there are too many dead lying round.

With the rise of the sun Billy shakes Latham. He knows, is prepared and will help.

"I can get it hitched mama. Will you come for the buryin after?"

"His goddamned horse can be burned in the cleave where that sandwash runs from the draw. Light it with a gallon of lamp oil. If it happens to catch and burn this world clean, your mother does not care. Get it goin, I wanna sit here. I need an hour with your brother bein quiet."

"I..."

"First feed and water his horse. Grease his galls if he'll allow it."

Latham pauses. Cannot ask.

"We'll tend to that bastard later. We ain't wastin supplies on him."

Two mules by reputation hating anything living are hitched and prepared to pull. Torq's horse is amenable to what Latham does but he will not relinquish his saddle. When Latham returns to his mother, his brother is nodding in dream, his pulse strong with a chest in heave and Billy is prepared to go.

"Meanass and Satan are hitched. Torq's mount is gonna be fine."

"What'd you dress 'em with?"

"The new un's. Ones I cut out. That bar-bit, it ain't rusted."

"Converted. Not cut out." She winked at her son in the doorway. Latham replied "converted, from that dandy hauler he traded. The man knows a bargain when he sees it."

"Your father swops like he's blind and deaf."

The Percheron is drug by the neck. Their pull is two hours and the track that is left seems an umbra of a dissolute people, beings having pendulumned from a void chaotic and unto theirself nomadic, this horde is going nowhere. They are extant souls negated by their signings and we wonder if they've ever been. Arriving, she instructs on the burning.

"Ride the draw till they falter in the sand. Pull your outfit and pile it atop. Heap what wood there is. Use ever' last drop to douse it. Burn the lot to a fuckin crisp."

"That whole conversion's new worked. Daddy'll bust me for burnin it."

"And I'll bust you if you don't burn it all! If it touched horse or man, or was remotely close to the pair, I want it risin in fuckin smoke!"

Billy walked back unassisted by the mules agonizing over Threadbare's body. It hasn't gone elsewhere. In the late afternoon she sees the sungleam broken by the plica of the Percheron burning, impending a sky blueblack, fleck of flame resonating on a garnitured horizon, a paralimnion of plain like lake. Billy thinks she sees him dancing. Her child without partner or tune. Latham's three miles north on a bitterweed glacis and he, like she, is unsure. They consider themselves alone; the savage god of fatigue taking its toll, their minds anxious to buckle under; they, themselves, now without his threat in a world that is all too vast.

Latham arrives with the dark. When he comes in they stand above Torq and the boy is alive and breathing. A cowbird foots on the gantry-framed window. They observe, knowing portent. Her cataractal idea then emerges.

"That's a good omen mama."

"Adivina would consider it so."

"And him?"

"I'll deal with it shortly. I know what we're gonna do."

"I put his body on Meanass. Satan wouldn't have him. I yanked 'em on his back with her. He's stiff but I wrenched 'em down good. His ends are touchin the ground. Meanass'll stand until you're ready with whatever you want to do."

Adivina's pit is a two-mile trek. Billy and Latham walk. The mule Meanass shimmied around till his body was positioned for travel. The weight of Threadbare is easily accorded, the seep now groined by a channel of fire, the percipient mule avoiding it, clipp-clopping past the rill of flame, the fire beneath running to quench.

"His body won't fit in that. Let's just bury him mama."

Billy looks across the mule at his disliking face, a prodigy affrighted by youth.

"Latham, oil-tar is hot as hell and this bastard is goin in."

The rictus is smoking, the maw belching heat, but he won't go to ash on the surface. Latham unties his lashings, the mule throwing Threadbare off, the stiffened corpse thudding soundly on the brindle.

"It's wide enough. Don't trip and follow."

Latham replies, "let's do it. I want this done with now."

There's an atonal bubbling from depths unseen and they cannot look inside. Black smoke in their faces and lungs, someone lipping the hole with random triturations as if damnation might need better footing. Billy takes an arm, Latham a leg, while the mule returns to the night, to a dark where symmetry fails. Over macadam crushing Threadbare is drug until they hack in the belching smoke. Before he is launched to an irrelative depth Billy asks Latham to leave her. Alizarin glow on their cheeks. Latham Mox then disappears. Billy gets to her knees at the small of his back and presses her palms to his flesh. He is warm from the heat superjacent. With her history ricked she stands. Billy Mox then walks away.

When they arrive at their home Torq isn't there and his horse is gone from their stable. She grinds her teeth. Rebreathes her breaths.

"Latham, fill the washtub."

"For what?"

"Strip his bloody linens. I'll strain 'em tomorrow first chance."

Latham taps the bedroom door, watches her touch the stains. The borne afterimage of the blood within, but there is no life upheld. No shape of son or brother.

"Mama, he'll be back."
"Why? To help you and me?"
Latham doesn't respond.
"Latham Mox, there are things of which we won't speak…"
"I ain't got shit to include."

58

HENCEFORTH THEY DO not speak. Hours later the men arrive. Epigo removes the saddles. Dampier inspects the yard. They think Billy's asleep, but she isn't. When he comes to their bed she pretends to be resting with her right hip up, turned over. He doesn't disturb her and they cannot sleep so the men take their seats by the fire. She drops her feet to the floor when she wishes. Meets her husband at their bedroom door. Epigo does not move.

Billy enters the arms of Dampier. Tiptoeing, she speaks to the priest.

"Father. Good day. Good trip?"

"Hello Billy. Sorry to wake you. We broke off from a bunch and came on. I told your husband to wait for the light. Said he could smell your soap. Almost galloped his mount to death."

"I said no such thing," he countered. "Billy, we seen us a rider. Goin east. Was somebody through?"

"No souls have passed through here." Epigo looks estranged. Attempts to read her face. She stares back in condescension. "Want coffee? Food? A drink?"

"We've eaten," Epigo answers. He continues to stare at the woman. In the firelight Billy is lying. It was mist when first she spake it. "No souls have passed through here?"

"Not a single floatin haunt."

Dampier's curious about the sheets. Billy Mox, she hangs her head. What cannot clasp its silence, shall boast of the world as it is.
"Billy, where's our son?"
"Which son do you mean Dampier?"

THE END

EPILOGUE

November 9th, 1850. California is two months old. There are those streaming west who come through here to abandon non-essentials. We find a man abandoned thus. A misanthrope he is not and futurity tells him the ruins he inhabits are safe. Mims Nickel has remained somewhat. Early frost glazes the loutish heap of the fort with its since burned timbers. There are stories, rumors, he does not know and other things he never will. When the convicted served here he hadn't been born to an earth he'd soon be leaving. Amongst the ruins he builds and with enmity watches a fire he will stare into coals.

Another sockets in the boulders that night. The man by his embers describes it as shadow before his mind senses the danger. He calls to it. Nothing returned. There's the charge of a light to its smoke. Dimpling fire, a tip that is lit.

"Hey you! Come to the fire! Why smoke by your lonesome out yonder!"

Amongst the boulders the watcher is home. In the rocks he's become fear, a creation the other does ponder, for he is that thing created.

"Well, damn you to hell then neighbor! I ain't sittin to be shot from the rocks!"

When the other moves west he does not watch, the whinny of his horse and the stench of his body conspiring to reveal his stealth.

He has no mount himself. Afoot from imponderable reaches. Shaking loose a dry fagot it is thrown on the coals and the sticks they crack and burn. As for his shape, I won't describe him. He is nothing for you to see.

In the course of the night he hands through the flames to withdraw a log in its fury. Choking the blaze, this man from the plains, blows on the axiom heat, the impotent fire disengaging, the fingertips of flak with the beck of his wind taken to smoking indifference.

"I procreate you. I made you."

He blows again and the log reignites; trick remnant, dark blight, though he's done this before without audience or human to witness, the man pitching the log back on the fire before trouncing the blaze to ash, the smoky tendrils then booted past smell to emergence and never a fire there burned. How once to emerge from that?

Dragging his feet through the lie of what was he begins to follow the other, the eastern light coating heavy behind him. Look back saint, for though you are horsed, the odious expands incarnate. You've only a tatter with which to defend and this being is indefensible. Find another of your make and creed. A solitary man is insufficient.

Made in the USA
Lexington, KY
04 November 2016